East Winds, West Winds

Mahdi Issa al-Saqr

Translated by
Paul Starkey

ARABIA BOOKS
LONDON

First published in Great Britain in 2010 by

Arabia Books
70 Cadogan Place
London SW1X 9AH

www.arabia-books.com

This edition published in agreement with the
American University in Cairo Press

A full CIP record for this book is available from the British Library

Printed and bound by CPI Mackays, Chatham

ISBN: 978 1 906697 22 8

Face One
Fox's Paradise

1
The Desert

Every day that goes by while you are here, you will discover new things. For the first few days, perhaps the first few weeks, you will float over the surface of events, seeing nothing except the appearances of things, seeing them through the eyes of a tourist in a hurry. You will hear what others say, but most of the time you will only see and hear echoes of your views and your ideas of the new world in which circumstances, or chance, have willed that you should live. But the passing, dazzled gaze of the tourist cannot last long, for the strange and the new quickly lose their brilliance and become familiar or commonplace. Then, gradually, what is hidden beneath the surface (the essence of things, as they say) will be revealed to your eyes and conscience, and reality will strike you; true reality, not the reality you have imagined, will strike you with a hideousness that will rock your being.

To live in a tent in the company of others, for a day, two days, even for a week, might be an amusing thing, like an excursion (despite the small annoyances), but for your refuge to be a tent on the edge of the desert, for a stay whose length you, as the son of a secure and stable city, do not know, you will then become like a gypsy, wandering God's wide earth with no roots anywhere in particular. Your companions in the tent are strangers like yourself, every one of them living his obscure life, hiding his secrets under a veil of friendship and familiarity. You will later discover that with some of them friendship is no more than a cover, usually a feeble one, to hide some lapses and mistakes. But at that moment you can know nothing about them, for you are watching the things and people around you innocently, and innocence and blindness of the heart are usually the same thing, so I have heard—and so man's experiences over the centuries have confirmed. Istifan Yuhanna—you do not know him yet—will always remain innocent and pure of heart until the day of his death in the al-Akhraq incident, a moment of recklessness in which his sense of valor got the better of his natural fear of death. This young man will die without any of us feeling gratitude toward him, for the two men he will try to save will perish before him—without his knowing it, of course. The self-sacrifice that he will make to save others will therefore be futile and meaningless. You could say, if it weren't for your fear of scandal, that it will be laughable! But you are anticipating events, anticipating events because Istifan's death will happen the following summer, a few months before the big strike. Everything is recorded in your black diary . . . everything. You will start recording the events of your new life when you have the idea of writing about people's lives here, in this place in the far south, this place that is almost cut off from the world, shut in between the long wall of date plantations that stretch along the banks of the Shatt al-Arab and the vast desert whose face is covered by salt throughout the year. You will write about a time that has escaped memory. That was the means you chose to combat boredom.

When I reached the camp on a cold winter's night I had with me Istifan Yuhanna, a young carpenter who had migrated from the north of Iraq to the south looking for work. I did not know what shape my coming days would take in this lonely place (though tell me, who can know the shape of his coming days?). It was the first time I had lived in a camp. The tents appeared, in the blackness of the night, like black lumps spread about in a big compound. Pale patches of light illuminated the sides of a number of the tents, but they all appeared quiet, as if there was no one in them. When we went in—Istifan and myself—to the tent that they led us to, I wasn't surprised to see a drinks table set up in front of two strangers, for drinking is sometimes the only consolation for those sent away to distant places. The two men greeted us with smiles. One of them was extremely obese, with a bloated face. I thought he might be about fifty years old, but perhaps older, for you cannot accurately guess the age of a man that well built. The effects of aging are hidden under folds of heaped-up fat. The other was a younger man of about thirty, muscular and good looking. We were both about to put our cases under our beds when the fat man shouted to us not to: "No, don't put your cases on the ground!"

I looked at him in bewilderment.

"When it rains, the water sometimes gets into the tents," he explained. Then he turned to his companion, "Muzhir, my lad . . . some stones!"

Muzhir and I went to look for stones near the barbed wire fence that separated the camp hollow from the public road. There was a pool of light on the other side of the road, some distance from the camp, inside which a number of men could be seen, like small, indistinct skeletons.

"Is that the work area?" I asked Muzhir.

"That's the tanks area. They are laying the foundations now. The offices and laboratories are a bit further away."

"Do you work at night?"

"Only the shift workers work at night."

"And those lights in the distance over there? In the palm groves?"

"That's where the foreign managers and engineers live . . . with their wives," replied Muzhir, gathering up some stones that he had found on the ground and handing me some.

"In another camp?"

His sarcastic laughter rang out in the silence of the night.

"The managers' quarter isn't a camp," he said, snickering.

I followed him back to the camp in silence, weighed down by my load. You can't learn everything that happens in this place on the first night. Only if you've lived here a long time will the days reveal everything to you . . . or nearly everything.

In the center of the camp Istifan sat on the edge of his bed listening to the fat man.

5

"Relax on that account," he was saying as we came in. "Muzhir, what's the name of that boy in the camp behind us? Udishu, Ishu?"

"His name's Dankha," said Muzhir, correcting him.

"Yes, a good man, always singing. Mud up to the knees and this Dankha is still singing!"

"Which village is he from?" asked Istifan. But the fat man didn't know the name of the village in the north where Dankha had come from.

"Anyway, you'll see him in the mess tent in the morning," he said, putting an end to the discussion. "Him and the others."

We put the stones under the cases, slightly relieved that the water wouldn't come over them in the event of a downpour. Then we started eating the tinned food that Daniel, the camp supervisor, had given us, for we had arrived a long time after suppertime.

"We know the name of our friend here; what's yours?" the fat man asked me.

I told him my name.

He gave me a friendly smile as his hand slowly came down, putting his glass on the box that he and his friend had turned into a table for their drinks.

"Welcome! Have a very nice evening, and afterward come and join your uncle Abu Jabbar and brother Muzhir Said in their drinking session."

I should have refused this request, even though other people's kindness sometimes leads you to make too many concessions at the expense of your health, if you are shy. I knew from previous experience that I would sleep afterward like a log and wake up in the morning with a dreadful headache.

Abu Jabbar carried on for the whole session, eating and drinking, smoking and singing, talking, eating, and singing again. His friend Muzhir sometimes sang with him, or listened to him with a smile as he heard him relating dirty stories about his passionate sexual relationship with his wife, most of which were probably made up or exaggerated. Meanwhile, an evening breeze had begun to shake the walls of the tent as stray dogs barked or ran between the tents on a seemingly endless chase. Istifan seemed happy (how it pains me now to recall his face—his ruddy face now attacked by worms).

I quickly felt dizzy (this dreadful sweat!) and emptied the contents of my stomach in the gloom of the night outside the tent, then changed my clothes in front of them without feeling embarrassed. I was drunk. Then, as I lay on the bed, I heard what sounded like pebbles falling on the walls of the tent. What was this? What madman was this, throwing pebbles at our tent at this hour of the night? After a little, however, I discovered that it had started to rain. Large, sporadic drops of rain started falling for some time on the roof of the tent, under a gloomy sky in which the winds had dropped and the dogs stopped barking. Everything seemed strange, as if it was outside of time, while I fell . . . fell into a sleep like a well full of mud. No, drink would not be a comfort in this faraway place. I would take refuge in my books, pen, and papers. I would try to observe what went on around me here and write. I naturally couldn't have known when I took that decision that what I wrote would eventually be a document that incriminated me . . . I couldn't have known!

2
The Foxhole

It wasn't sensible to wake up like this on your first working day in this place. In the morning the camp looked like a large lake on the edge of the desert, surrounded on three sides by an earth dam, while the fourth rib of the dam was formed by the road that ran above ground level and led down to the city of Basra. The rainwater had flooded the ground inside the camp during the night, and some of it had come into the tent, though the water had not touched our bags. The tents seemed in the sunlight like small, isolated islands. Each tent stood by itself. I could hear the men shouting in annoyance as they walked swaying over pathways that they had made from crooked rows of stones. I saw some of them—those that were in a particular hurry—stumbling barefoot in the water and mud, carrying their boots with their socks stuffed inside them. I saw crowds, crowds everywhere, at the wash places or, to be more precise, at the cold water taps and other facilities. The toilets consisted of a long row of holes dug into the ground with pieces of damp wood over them, surrounded by a curtain of sackcloth, with no roof and no doors. As you passed a number of men squatting over those holes, smoking or staring sullenly in front of them, you recalled another scene that you used to see when you worked in Shuayba, during the years of the Second World War, with some difference of detail: the British soldiers would sit there relaxed on what looked like a long coffin, with their trousers hanging down over their legs and their plump red bottoms exposed for anyone to see, smoking and chattering and reading the newspapers to find out the latest news of the war, while their foul smells dispersed through the air around them.

The mess tent, which looked like a large marquee, had been erected on a raised bit of ground. It was full of men, some eating standing up, while others were taking their food with them as they hurried along the path to the work areas. You were hurrying along the path (you, Istifan, and Muzhir, with Abu Jabbar trying to catch up with you as he dragged his heavy body along), when the air was shaken and you were taken by surprise by the long-drawn-out screeching lament of the work siren that would henceforth rule your life (so long as you stayed in that place). The work siren continued to emit a shrill, insistent screech that made the men move even faster, as if the impatient noise was a whip inflaming their backs. Then the screeching was silent. At that point, you quite clearly began to hear, as you hurried with the stragglers on the path, the sound of footsteps—dozens of hurried, irregular footsteps striking the paved, still-damp road. You saw most of the men walking with fixed expressions, frowning. You wouldn't hear any of them speaking. Some of them were chewing the remains of their breakfast and panting. Sometimes there was nothing in the morning air except for the sound of hurried footsteps and the echo of the insistent metallic call that echoed inside your head for a long time as its reverberations outside you gradually faded away, to vanish in the distance of that open space. Meanwhile, the men were hurrying indoors, to disperse, swallowed up by the laboratory buildings, the big warehouses, and the various work areas and sections.

In the administrative office, they took Istifan's papers that he had brought from the project base in Basra, then gave him a letter and sent him on to the maintenance division. Thus, his preordained fate was decided without the knowledge or intention of anyone. He took his letter and went off happily to meet the destiny that he would fulfill the following August. The elderly chief clerk asked you to wait until the manager, Mr. Fox, was free to meet you. You could see the shoulder and part of the face of the manager, with his blond beard, through a small square opening covered with a pane of glass in the wall that divided him from where the chief clerk sat (an opening that allowed him to see what was going on inside the big rectangular room where the employees sat). There was a man of about sixty who looked like an Indian, who was overcome from time to time by a coughing fit as he bent over his papers trying to write something; a youth of about twenty who was typing; and the office assistant, who sat sullenly by the door with a cigarette in his hand.

The manager moved the pane of glass away from the opening and said something to the chief clerk, who got up immediately, buttoned his jacket, then went in to him and shut the door. Then the office assistant left his place, came up to you, and said in a voice that was almost a whisper, "Are you going to work here? Welcome, sir!"

A thin man who had lost his left eye stood in front of you. His head was wrapped in a kafiyyeh, and he was wearing a loose-fitting uniform that was not his size. "I am . . . Mazlum," he muttered hesitantly.

You looked at him in bewilderment. What could you do for this man when you hadn't even started working in this office yet? He noticed your confusion. "I mean, my name is Mazlum," he said, "not mazlum in the sense of maltreated."

"I thought . . . ."

"I know. No, I am well, praise be to God! I just wanted to say that I live in the village, and if you need anything . . ."

You had the feeling that this man perhaps enjoyed seeing the reaction on the faces of strangers when he said that he was "mazlum"—the bewilderment and confusion, the feeling of embarrassment, the disappearance of the smile, and the preparation of some excuse for being unable to help him.

"Thank you, Mazlum," you said, trying not to look at his blind eye. "An aspirin and a glass of tea, please."

He hurried out of the office to carry out the order, while the chief clerk came out of the manager's room. "Mr. Muhammad, the boss wants to see you!"

You were hit by a powerful smell of tobacco, which filled the air (what a wicked tobacco this was!). Mr. Fox took his pipe out of his mouth. The pipe's moist edge glistened under the rays of the sun that slipped at an angle through the window in the wall just behind his back. The air in the room was warm and comfortable, apart from that cursed tobacco. The manager sat surrounded by several telephones that crouched around him like a group of crows. Some of them had been placed on a small table beside him, while others had been put on the edge of his spacious desk that was covered by a thick pane of glass. He looked at you with his gray eyes, then looked at the letter that was open on the desk in front of him.

"Your name is Mohamet Ahmet?"

He had a rough, deep voice and pronounced your name in a curious way. Although there were several armchairs in his room, he didn't invite you to sit down. You stayed standing, looking at him. He asked you if you knew Arabic, while your eyes were fixed on a double-barreled hunting rifle leaning against an iron safe that rested on a strong wooden base. Perhaps he kept his secret documents in this safe and shot wild pigeons in the palm groves in the afternoons and holidays.

"And what about English?"

Questions you found unnecessary because they had tested you at the project base and written everything down for him. Perhaps he wanted to make you understand that your fate was in his hands. You told him you could translate for him anything he wanted.

"There's something else," he said, rubbing his beard.

He had a pointed beard and twisted mustache that resembled the mustache of an old-style Ottoman officer. He put his pipe, which had apparently gone out, on top of his desk. The image of the pipe was reflected in the pane of glass beside the image of his inverted face. His hair appeared bright and transparent in the sunlight. But what was this other thing he mentioned?

"I don't want you to form friendly relations with anyone," he said firmly.

What a strange request! The man wanted to take away your freedom to choose your friends. You looked at him in astonishment.

"But I live in a tent . . . with three others . . . in a camp full of people. And I have to speak to them."

"I know that," he interrupted coldly. "That's why I'm warning you. Friends outside this office will try to find out the office secrets."

So this was the reason! You told him that you understood what he meant.

"I hope so, because I won't be easy on you if you don't!"

He said these words in a threatening tone, looking you straight in the eye. You promised him to be discreet. He lifted his pipe from the surface of the desk and said, "We will see!" Then he turned his body toward the gap in the wall and shifted the pane of glass.

"Mr. Jirjis."

The chief clerk started up and turned his lined face toward him.

"Explain to Mr. Mohamet his duties, and give him what he needs."

"Yes, sir."

Jirjis pointed to an empty table beside him. "Sit down here, I'll take care of you."

Then he turned to the Indian clerk, "Mr. Fadlallah, be careful!" and left the office. Mr. Fox was busy talking on the telephone when the Indian clerk got up, seizing the opportunity, and approached you.

"I am Fadlallah Bahadir."

You stood up and pressed his outstretched hand, which you found limp and cold, as if it had no blood.

"Sit down, lad."

He spoke quietly, throwing cautious glances—the glances of an oriental bird—at the square opening in the wall.

"Mr. Muhammad, anything you want in the English language, you ask me."

The skin on his face was dark and yellowish. The skin under his palate hung down like a black rag, but his amber-colored eyes shone strangely (it could be the sign of a serious illness). You thanked him and said that you would come to him when necessary. As if to apologize for a mistake, he added, "I know a little Arabic. I just know how to read the Qur'an."

He said that leaning with one hand against the edge of the table. The skin over his finger bones seemed very yellow. The man had burned around half his cigarette, and a finger of ash remained hanging at the end of it, about to fall but never falling. Meanwhile, Mr. Fox finished his telephone conversation and hurried back to his place. Fadlallah was shaken by a fit of coughing and the finger of ash at the tip of his cigarette was finally broken and fell onto the surface of the table. When the coughing subsided, he took a large, crumpled handkerchief from his pocket, opened it and spat into it, then looked at his spit for a considerable time without speaking. Then he folded his handkerchief and stuffed it back in his pocket. He opened the middle drawer in his desk just a little, and with the edge of his hand swept the ash that had fallen on top of the table toward the open drawer and left it to fall into it. Then he shut it again. (When Fadlallah departed the following year, he left behind him a drawer full of ash.) Mr. Fox got up from where he was sitting and left the room. "Come here, Abdul," he said to the youth behind the typewriter. (You later found out that the young clerk's name was Abdullah, not Abdul.)

"And you too," ordered Mr. Fox, looking at you.

Abdullah picked up a large register and followed the director. You went out behind them. The director left the balcony and walked, with almost military steps, across a barren garden surrounded by willow trees whose yellowish leaves were scattered on the ground. Unemployed men crowded behind a fence waiting for the chance of work. When they saw him they watched closely, but he didn't go very near them. He went just far enough to see the expressions on their faces clearly—then stopped. You saw a large crowd of men of different ages, most of them dark and skinny. They were wearing dishdashas, or shirts and trousers covered in dirt and spots of paint and grease. They got excited, pushing and shoving each other, all trying to be first in the queue, while some of their hands grabbed at the bars of the gate eagerly. The guard himself stood inside by the locked gate. He seemed to be watching the faces of the shoving men carefully and alertly, preparing himself for any eventuality. Everyone was silent when the manager stopped and faced them with his broad chest and beard. He didn't look at them at first, but raised his head and looked at the sky. The dark clouds that had settled over everything during the night had released their load of water and dispersed, and the sky appeared clear blue overhead. The rain, though, had soaked the ground and gathered in the depressions, and the air was full of the noise of the pumps brought in to drain the water from the ground in the camp. Finally, the director turned his face toward the men, and an imploring sound rose up: "God bless you . . . I've had a month!"

Then, all of a sudden the voices exploded. But Mr. Fox raised his hand in their faces and they were silent; only a few scattered voices could still be heard, then they were silent as well. The manager ordered his clerk to begin. The clerk approached the door, opened his register and shouted into the eager faces, "Sirhan Muhawdir!"

The guard repeated the shout, only louder. There was no need, however, for immediately there was a scuffle between the men, as the man of that name tried to force his way between the packed bodies, then came to a stop, squeezed between the pressure of the men jostling behind him and the bars of the iron gate in front of him. He gave a smile of delight as he waited expectantly for the guard to finally open the gate for him. He stepped inside through the gate that the guard had opened to allow him and no one else to enter, then stood to one side to adjust his headdress that had slipped from his head and was hanging down over his shoulder. He avoided looking his out-of-work companions in the eye. A piece of dark flesh from the knob of his shoulder was visible through a tear at the top of his dishdasha, but he didn't seem to be feeling the cold. He seemed happy enough as his comrades continued their shouting from behind the fence. But Mr. Fox silenced them with a second wave of his hand, and Abdullah was able to raise his voice to call out the second name. Soon a group of twelve men was standing inside with a satisfied expression on each of their faces, while those waiting outside continued to hope for more names. The manager, however, said to Abdullah, the clerk, "Abdul, that's enough for today. Send eight to Daniel to help clean the camp and four to the stores." When the men without work saw the clerk shut his register they began shouting even louder, but Mr. Fox turned back to the office and you followed him, while Abdullah started to allocate the men who had been chosen for that day. Then the voices behind you began to break up and die away. Just one voice, a single, powerful voice, with clear tones, continued to pursue the back of the director as he moved away, pleading, "Sir, they need me in the stores, ask them, sir, ask them . . . ."

Mr. Fox ignored the solitary voice and continued on his way, with his pipe in the corner of his mouth.

The voice cried again, "Sir, God prolong your life, and that of your wife's dog Podgy . . . and save the king of Great Britain!"

The manager went up to the balcony and was about to go into the office when the same voice cried again, in an angry tone this time, "Sir, God take your soul . . . and the soul of Podgy . . . and the soul of King George VI!"

The manager stopped when he heard the name of George VI and turned to look at the men without work behind the fence, trying to make out which one the voice belonged to. Meanwhile, Abdullah returned carrying his register, while the outlines of four men disappeared behind the building on their way to the stores. Another group went off on the other side of the road in the direction of the camp, accompanied by their long shadows that trembled on the ground.

The angry man was silent, perhaps because he was afraid when he saw the manager stop and try to identify him. But no, here was his voice rising up again as he shouted angrily, "Sir! Down with Great Britain!"

Looking at Abdullah, Mr. Fox asked, "Who's the one shouting that?"

"It's Farhan al-Abd, sir," said Abdullah, trying not to smile.

"And what did he say?"

He directed his question to you this time. You wished he hadn't asked. Abdullah could have translated Farhan al-Abd's words for him, so was he wanting to put you to the test?

"He's expressing his anger at not getting work," you told him hesitantly.

"Don't tell me what I know already. I want to know exactly what he said."

I felt a little impatient. "He's saying, down with Great Britain," I said.

He put his pipe back in his mouth and began to smoke, while his gray eyes stared at the tall, dark man who stood out like a mast among the men behind the fence. The rays of the morning sun fell on his back and part of his face, illuminating his short, wavy hair; his head was more than a foot higher than those of his fellow unemployed who stood behind and on both sides of him, listening silently to his curses against Britain and the king (or so you thought, as you watched them from a distance. Anyway, when one of them whispered something or let out a sympathetic laugh, it was only the guard who was standing in his place who could hear him).

"And what did he say before that?"

Mr. Fox didn't take the pipe out of his mouth as he spoke.

"He wished you were dead," you told him, "as well as your wife's dog, and the king."

If Mr. Fox felt at all angry, it was not apparent on his face. "This man is mad," he said coldly. Then he looked at Abdullah and said in the same tone, devoid of emotion, "Abdul, don't give this black man any work for a month."

He went back up to the balcony toward his office. As he followed Mr. Fox's movements from a distance, Farhan al-Abd, as he was called, reckoned that something not in his interest had been decided at that moment, and shouted angrily as he shook the locked gate, "Bastards . . . sons of a whore!"

When he saw Mr. Fox's form disappearing inside the building, he kicked the steel gate with his foot, then set out on his way back to the village followed by a large number of men without work, while four or five stayed waiting expectantly, in the hope that the project administration might need them to undertake some work at a later stage—or perhaps they stayed sitting in the sun by the edge of the paved road because they had nowhere to go at that time of day.

"This Farhan is ridiculous," said Abdullah, laughing. "He works like a donkey but can't control his tongue!"

"Why did you pass him over, then?" you asked as you went up to the balcony.

"It's the director's policy."

"Toward Farhan?"

"No, no, for any hourly-paid employee."

He turned around cautiously, then added, "We don't employ any of these people for more than five days at a time, and Farhan has been working. . . ."

"But why?" you enquired cautiously.

"Because if we employed them for more than five days without a break," he replied quietly, "they would be entitled under the law to demand payment for a day off."

"And so. . . ," you said in disbelief.

But he hurried into the office, not wanting to prolong the conversation. You went in after him, harboring a suspicion that Mr. Fox was a man who made the rules up himself and that he therefore had a lot of secrets that he didn't want to be exposed by any means whatsoever.

3

Barking in the Face
of the Setting Sun

stifan looked at the desert, in which there was nothing to attract the attention. "I don't understand," he said at last. "What do you see here?"

An endless land stretched out in front of him, a wide land covered by salt (salt that he thought was ice the first time he had set eyes on it). The cloak of salt in which the earth was clothed, which had become thicker and whiter after the rainwater had evaporated, was taking on colors under the rays of the sun as it began to set. The one thing that appeared out of place in the desert was the enormous oil rig that had sprung up at a distance from the dam. Its engine was thundering in the silence of the desert while its iron jaw descended with a dancing motion, to bite into the body of the earth, then throw what it ate on the back of a truck that stood submissively at the front of a line of identical trucks. The tedious movement and the clattering and screeching that accompanied it were all Istifan could discern amid the silence and emptiness.

"You could write better in the tent."

Writing inside the tent was an impossible experience. Abu Jabbar stuck his face into everything.

"If you like, we can go down to the village . . . to enjoy ourselves."

He thinks I need something to occupy me, by distracting me. We had gone down to the village on the first rest day after the rainwater had dried a bit. We walked for about five or six kilometers along the edge of the road leading there from the city. You found it in the bright morning sunlight, tucked away, worn out and neglected, on the banks of the Shatt al-Arab—like a servant girl raped by her master who then turned his back on her. The streets were muddy and the air was filled with the smell of rotten fish. We saw the workers' houses in the Port Authority built of brick, and then the local people's houses built of mud. We saw the fishermen's boats moored on the shore and the Port Authority's abandoned ships. We wandered around in the narrow streets and markets of the village. We looked at the shops selling henna and salt (is salt here as well?).

We saw women selling bread and vegetables sitting on the ground. We stood in front of the cafés crammed full of workers. I saw Farhan al-Abd there, sitting in a café chatting and laughing, his white teeth shining in the middle of his dark face. Then you could see him clearly. He looked like a stoutly built man of about forty, but perhaps he was older than he looked, for it's well known that people with dark skin usually seem younger than they really are, until gray hair suddenly catches up with them and time makes its final destructive assault. You had often heard that dark rebel shouting angrily as he stood upright and threatening among the crowd of unemployed men behind the fence, but now, as he sat in the café among his friends and followers, the vigor of his youth was apparent to you, and it was the most beautiful thing you saw in the village that day. After that, we stood watching a man and his son sitting on the ground by the wall of a house, making beds, armchairs, cradles, and cages for nightingales from green date-palm fronds. This out-of-the-way little village had often attracted the attention of strangers who came to it by chance and wandered about its streets, taking photographs of its women wrapped in black wool abayas, and other pretty scenes from a country that the sun never left. They would later show them, after returning home to their family and friends for relaxation, as they sat comfortably near the fireplaces in which the flames danced, drinking whisky or some other drink to hand, while the sky's face outside glowered ever more strongly and the rain teemed down again in their miserable world. But you are not a foreign tourist wandering around the streets with a camera dangling on his chest staring in amazement at the thin dark faces, the minarets of the mosques, and the mud houses, pursued by a crowd of barefoot boys shouting a language that he doesn't understand and looking at him just as curiously (perhaps even more so), as if he were a strange animal that had invaded their quiet world unnoticed by time. So one visit to the village would be enough.

Then Istifan made another suggestion, "I think it would be better to go back to the tent. Until evening, that is."

"You go," I said to him, angrily. But he remained standing where he was, trying to discover in the emptiness something that would make you come here every day, if the weather was fine, carrying your books and papers, and sit on your own on the dam until it got cold and the sun gathered together its rays and departed.

(You heard the sound of his footsteps and the soil crunching under his feet as they climbed the dam, then his voice asking, "Brother Muhammad . . . Will you let me share your silence with you?")

You knew him by his voice. It was Hussein Tu'ma, the assistant surveyor, who had come in the spring to share our accommodation in the tent about three months after Istifan's confused stop on the dam. You looked at him and smiled. Who was this who could share his silence, his pain, and grief with another man? He took his handkerchief out of his trouser pocket, spread it on the ground and sat down. He threw a glance at the papers scattered on the ground and at my diary but didn't say a word. He had already broken the silence, though, just by sitting down beside me. He made me think about him; the desert stopped repeating its sweet whispers, and the state of purity that I was living in was shattered.

"What are you looking for in this emptiness?" he asked after two or three minutes.

"Who told you that I . . . ?"

"All of us are looking for something. But you are looking in the wrong direction."

I had arranged my life, since coming here, far away from other people's interference. I had cocooned myself, and derived a certain amount of spiritual satisfaction from transforming the annoyances of my daily life into purely philosophical worries, trying to forget everything else. I would watch what was happening and try to write, without involving myself personally in the events. I was sitting on the hill, as they say, that is, sitting on the dam.

"If you want to discover something meaningful, look in this direction," said Hussein, swinging his body around and making a sweeping gesture with his hand that took in the managers' quarter nestling among the orchards near the banks of the Shatt al-Arab, the work areas on the other side of the road, the camp, and the small faraway village that was hidden behind the wall of date palms. As I followed the movements of his outstretched arm I saw a number of men leaving their tents and hurrying to the mess tent.

"I can see some men running to the mess tent desperate to eat," I said to him laughing.

"Brother Muhammad," he said, unexpectedly, "Have you ever experienced life in prison?"

I looked at him in astonishment. "And why should I have been imprisoned?"

"It's not always necessary for there to be a reason. Anyway, this isn't what we are about. What I want to say is that when food becomes our only concern in life, that means . . . . But you are not listening to what I am saying. We'll continue our conversation some other time."

Then he got up, took his handkerchief from the ground, shook it, and slipped it into his pocket. He brushed the earth from the back of his trousers and went back inside the camp.

Istifan had stayed in his place beside me on the dam. He lifted the collar of his jacket, having completely failed to find anything worth bothering about in that white emptiness that had become deep red. "It's turned cold," he said.

The sun retrieved the remnants of its rays from the face of the earth to travel and spread them in some other place, while the shadows piled up in the big holes that the drill had made in places scattered around the edge of the desert, growing blacker and blacker by the minute. At this point the air bore on it a wild barking. Whenever the evening shift fell to the rig operator Fawzi Abu Shama, who brought his dog with him, the air would be filled with a wild barking during the last vestiges of sunset . . . a barking that only lasted a few moments before the dog fell silent. When the rig stopped to wait for the trucks to come back, a deep silence like a thick fog would settle over the desert, inspiring grief. Every time you would wonder, as you listened to that complaining voice coming from the drilling rig, then spreading through the open space at the end of the day, what was it, do you suppose, that made that dumb animal raise its voice and break out in that whining bark in the face of every setting sun? (When they—he and his friend Fawzi—were surrounded by the floodwaters that swept over the desert the following spring, the dog barked again from inside the rig, but it was a bark with a different tone. It continued for several hours, barking insistently in the face of the murky water and darkness of the night. Of course, he could have thrown himself into the water and swum as far as the dam and saved himself, but he didn't leave his place. He carried on asking for help for his friend until the last moment). It was a stray dog, one of the dogs that wandered the lanes of the camp, skulking among the tents night and day looking for leftovers. One time when he felt lonely and lost, Fawzi the rig worker had come across it and they had chosen each other as companions and remained inseparable ever since. They had been inseparable for more than a year and a half, each enjoying the friendship of the other, until the day came when a fatal bullet separated them.

"Let's go to supper before . . . ."

But you didn't write anything. You gathered together your papers and your diary, stuffed them into the pockets of your overcoat, and went down with him.

The stray dogs were wandering around the entrance to the mess tent. Inside, the men were making a great clamor, and the smells of the food mingled with the cigarette smoke that collected under the roof, turning the air gray. Abu Jabbar, who usually went to eat early for fear that the best bits of meat would be gone, had finished his supper and left. He took his fat body between the tables crammed with men and headed toward the door carrying his portion of that night's fruit in one hand. A yellow apple appeared tiny in his enormous fist. He walked slowly and heavily until he saw us. He burped in a deliberately loud, drawn-out manner as if it pleased him to announce to the whole company that his stomach was full, then looked at us and said, "You're late!"

Then he looked toward me and said, "Muhammad, my boy, you've been communing with the desert!"

I ignored his sarcasm and we walked inside. Each of us carried a wooden tray on which we set empty plates and a spoon and fork, then we took our place in the line of men who stood waiting their turn to receive their food. Daniel, the camp superintendent, stood behind the cooks as usual, with his gray hair, swollen eyelids, and red eyes (an addict's eyes). He stood watching the distribution of the food, afraid that one of the cooks might be in league with the men and give them more than their share. Istifan led me to a table where his friend Dankha and someone else were sitting. You could hear them talking in Assyrian, but Istifan switched into Arabic so as not to make you feel out of place among them. They were talking about a well-known soccer player who had become impotent after suffering a serious injury in an extremely sensitive place, but I carried on eating without taking any notice of their emotional conversation, which had become just part of the clamor going all around the big tent. The food wasn't bad (though it didn't please Hussein Tu'ma when he came to us some months later on transfer from the project base in Basra, for he started complaining about everything—the food, the tents, the toilets, the arrogant behavior of the managers, and the transport that the project management provided to take the men to town every Saturday afternoon to visit their relatives during the weekend break. The trip to town in open trucks was a real punishment, and for that reason Hussein quickly found people ready to listen intently to his angry words).

When we emerged from the mess tent we found a collection of black and green flags leaning up against the wall of the tent near the entrance and a number of flares on the ground. Some of the workmen were trying to light them. Istifan said that the men were getting ready to go to the village in a big procession for Ashura and that he and Dankha were going with them. I smiled and left him to go back to the tent. I saw Abu Jabbar standing under the lamp looking annoyed, thinking how to spend the long-drawn-out minutes of the night without a drink. "Ha, my boy, I see you've come back alone," he said in a wondering way.

"Istifan wants to go with the procession, him and Dankha," I told him.

"You're joking, of course!" he said in disbelief.

I told him that I wasn't joking. He started to laugh, and his belly shook like a big full waterskin that had collided with something.

"But what's it got to do with Istifan and Dankha?" he asked.

I was busy changing my clothes. I no longer felt any embarrassment about changing my clothes in front of others. When you are living in a tent with a number of people, you begin to regard a lot of things as quite normal after a while.

"Perhaps they wanted to enjoy being among the men," I said to him.

He shook his head in confusion, not satisfied with that reply, then went over to his bed. His broad shadow spread over the floor of the tent. When he put his large bottom on the edge of the bed, there was a crack from some planks of wood that he had put under his bed to support his heavy body, so that the taut wires would not snap and throw his body to the ground when he turned over in bed during the night in his dreams.

"Exactly!" he shouted in surprise.

I took out a book and stretched out on my bed. But he wouldn't let me read. He had nothing to occupy him. Almost every night he would set up a table for his drinks in the tent or else go to drink with Daniel in his tent, but with the start of the month of Muharram he had stopped drinking alcohol. He said that he was always anxious to stop drinking during the first ten days of this month, however great the temptations.

I heard the planks of wood groaning under his bed and I saw him getting up. After a little I saw his fat face dropping down over me.

"What are you reading?" said the face.

"A story," I replied in a neutral tone.

"A nice one?" he asked like a child.

"It's okay," I replied in a noncommittal way.

"Tell it to me," he said imploringly.

"Abu Jabbar, why don't you stop your alcohol denial and relax?"

He took his face away and withdrew, apologizing. "I'm sorry. Read in peace," he said and went back to his bed. The boards would break and the wires come out if this man carried on lifting up and putting down all this mass of flesh on the bed one minute after the other. Meanwhile, shouting and calling could be heard in the camp alleys, people coming and going, activity that seemed to convey a sense of urgency. Then Muzhir came in.

"Hello, dark one!" said Abu Jabbar in a welcoming tone. "I didn't see you in the mess."

"I was busy," said Muzhir, taking his coat from the edge of the bed. "The boss's car needed repairing."

Abu Jabbar winked at him. "You're certain that it was the boss's car?"

Muzhir ignored him and mumbled to no one in particular, "I'm going with them to the village."

He left the tent quickly. Abu Jabbar stayed glued to his bed like a pile of rocks. Outside, the men's voices had begun to ring out in chants that spoke of the bloody martyrdom of the Prophet's grandson Hussein, commemorated at this time of the year, year after year. The voices that seemed closest were more angry than sad. Abu Jabbar left his bed again, attracted by those men's voices in harmony that had, as well as words that spoke of pain and grief, the rhythm of a sad song repeated by a large choir in the camp's deserted night. He stood in the entrance to the tent, the light of the tent lamp falling on his legs and part of his back. Then I heard his voice, quick and insistent, "Muhammad, my son, come here quickly, for God's sake!"

I stood beside him, shivering from the cold. I noticed Istifan and his friend Dankha walking at the front of a procession, each of them carrying a lantern high above his head to light up the road. The procession had finished its "review parade" along the paths of the camp, then begun to move up to the public road heading toward the village, cutting its way through the darkness and silence of the dark night with its lights and clamor.

I hurried in, fleeing from the cold of the night, then Abu Jabbar came in behind me. "Do you think they intend to change their religion?" he asked me anxiously, as the wooden planks groaned beneath him. (His mind was still preoccupied with Istifan and Dankha's participation.)

"No, Abu Jabbar, they're just bored."

The voices were moving further away like a thin thread in the quiet of the night. The camp began to recover its eerie silence. "Perhaps you're right," said Abu Jabbar. "Boredom kills the soul. I would have liked to have gone with them but I can't walk all that way."

He sat silently for some time, then asked in a voice that seemed sad, "Tell me, my lad. What does a man do when he is bored and fed up with everything?"

"He reads," I said.

His face relaxed and he smiled. He seemed like a good man when he smiled. A fat, peaceable, good-hearted man with problems that could be defined and whose solution was at hand. Food, drink, sex, and sleep.

"I thought you had a solution," he said, disappointed, then got up from his bed. I'm going to visit Daniel."

"To drink with him," I said, joking.

"Heaven forbid! Do you think I'd do such a thing during this time of year?"

His voice and heavy presence left the tent, so I took advantage of my being alone and took out my pen and papers.

4
Sounds

The sides of the tent are flimsy. The winds batter them and voices penetrate them easily. The hum of night insects, the barking of stray dogs, their panting and the patter of their feet on the ground as they wander around the alleys, the muttering and footsteps of the men as they move from one place to another. Their laughter, their coughing, sometimes their singing, the buzz of the machinery in the workshops on the other side of the lane, the squeaking and creaking of the rig in the desert as it eats into the ground, the hum of the trucks that carry the earth to the various work areas — then that shouting sound that we heard in the spring. When it came to our tent for the first time, I thought that a machine gun was firing bullets insistently from nearby. I stopped reading and sat on my bed confused.

"Don't be afraid! They're not bullets! They're soldering iron onto the tank walls," said Hussein Tu'ma, looking at Istifan's surprised face. The hammering escalated sharply and insistently, shattering the silence of the night, stopping only for a few moments before resuming its assault on our tent again. Annoyed, Abu Jabbar mumbled some words that no one understood, but they looked at him. He repeated his words to them in a louder voice.

"I said, they will fly when they've drunk!"

They sat around the empty wooden box on which they had set up their evening drinking table.

"I suggest that you should speak frankly to your friend, Mr. Fox," Muzhir shouted. "Tell him we can't drink in peace!"

Hussein Tu'ma laughed and Istifan smiled, but Abu Jabbar seemed cross. "Please, Mr. Fox isn't my friend!" he shouted, his face glowering. "Don't press me to reveal what is hidden!"

They were about to shout in each other's faces. In fact, all of us started talking in raised voices, trying to struggle against that dominating sound that swept in its path all the more usual sounds that we no longer paid any attention to. It was a long, sleepless night, that first night. Muzhir, Istifan, and Hussein could sleep a little, numbed by drink, but I remained unable to sleep until morning. I spent the whole night hearing the wooden slats creaking under Abu Jabbar's bed. Alcohol didn't affect him much. In the morning, when he got out of bed, he seemed worn out, as if he had been walking the whole night.

"Hey, folks," he complained. "I couldn't sleep a wink yesterday. I was thrashing like a fish out of water."

Hussein laughed as he took his soap and washcloth to go to the washroom. "Abu Jabbar's fish!"

But we soon got used to hearing the noise of those electric drills beating the nails into the plates of iron. At night, as we walked along the paths in the camp or stood at the tent doors, we would see the blue glow spreading from the iron welding equipment. The halos of blue and yellow sparks flew like great flowers of fire, opening in the middle of the pool of light made by the searchlights. We would hear the whine of the oxygen equipment. The men working in turn on the other side of the road would fill the night around them with voices and colored lights. The sight of them working there no longer inspired amazement, and neither did the sound of the beating on the iron keep us awake. It had become part of the ritual of our daily life in this place, so that if it stopped for any reason, we would start from sleep bemused during the night as if a hand had woken us. Even the dogs, which had been startled and lapsed into a frightened silence when they first heard that strange barking that savagely appropriated the night, quickly got used to it and resumed their chases among the tents. Then another noise hit us—a heavy, stifled sound that came to us from the distance, from behind the palm groves, from the banks of the Shatt al-Arab, where an enormous hammer had begun to drive large posts into the riverbed by the bank, to build a pier where tankers could moor. The noise came to us during the night. We didn't so much hear it as feel it in the shaking of the ground under our beds, with every blow that struck the head of the post to drive it further into the solid clay. There were other men working to extend the pipe into the desert, but they were a long way away from us. Like us, they were living in tents, but they would move their tents from place to place like the Bedouin nomads, and we heard no sound from them. The noise of their machines dissipated in the desert. We could see them when we were in the backs of the trucks on our way to the city for the weekend holiday. The nearby noises continued to fill our nights and days until finally the day came when everything was finished and the clamor died down. Only the production machines shook the air with their continual droning day and night. But now, the noise was at its peak, for in the tank area, on the other side of the public road, men were scattered all over the vast square . . . you could see them everywhere, standing on the ground, perched on scaffolding, sitting on the crane towers, moving beside the oxygen machinery, passing by in the trucks that carried the earth, or seesawing above the earth-leveling machine. A perpetual movement, like that of ants, and a mixture of sounds dominated by the continuous hammering that seemed quieter during daylight hours. The blue sparks flying from the welding machines, which looked bright in the darkness of the night, seemed fainter by day. Sometimes during the noon break, after finishing lunch, I would stand behind the fence, watching them building the steel walls. I would see the big plates dangling from the crane cables, while men waited for them on the ground or on the scaffolding with taut nerves, their heads thrown back, staring nervously at a steel plate swinging in the air above their heads as it descended like an enormous guillotine over their fragile skeletons. Then they would stretch their arms out toward it and clutch the edge of it with hands covered in heavy gloves. They would cling to it hard and calm its frightening shuddering, before guiding it gently, like men guiding a wild animal, to put it in place in the wall. In this way, the walls, with their wide circular forms, gradually took shape; one tank after another would be completed, until eventually the space was filled with several of these round, flat-topped tanks. Then I would see the men painting them silver to reflect the rays and heat of the sun. When the line of pipes into the desert was completed and the oil finally flowed, I saw them one day fighting a fire that had flared up in some oil that had flowed onto the surface of one of these tank covers. Eventually they got the better of the fire, before collapsing to the ground coughing and spluttering, their faces grimy with smoke and flushed from exertion and the heat of the blazing fire. These same men were afraid of consulting authority—in particular, administration HQ. This was an obscure world that hid itself behind walls and locked doors, where rules and regulations and instructions were formulated; from where orders, reprimands, and sometimes dismissal notices were issued; and where personal identity cards and files were stored in cupboard drawers, together with reports on them written by faceless men. A frightening world of riddles, plots, and plans, where a man had to be on his guard, and extremely careful. For this reason they were afraid of the administration HQ, and entered it—when they absolutely had to—timidly, to put their cases with a politeness that was more like subservience, and generally in confused or ambiguous words. In fact, only a few people went in with steady steps and a straight back, especially if they knew that Mr. Fox, the director, was lurking in his office. They knew that the red-faced man with the fair, trimmed beard and the handlebar mustache pulled all the strings in this place and knew everything about them, or almost everything. He had spies who brought him all the news—their colleagues at work, or friends, perhaps, who would sit with them at mealtimes in the mess tent, smoking and gossiping, joking and laughing with them, living in the same place, perhaps in the same tent, who knows?

I myself saw two of these informers visiting Mr. Fox repeatedly. At first, I thought that they were coming, like other people, because of some problems concerning themselves, but their visits became more and more frequent, and when one of them came to the office he would ask to see the manager at once and not tell anyone else what he was up to. Then Mr. Fox would shut the door and stay alone with the man for some time. There was something that united these two informants as if they were twins. It wasn't anything about their features, as they had different faces. Rather, it was a resemblance in certain aspects of their behavior: that suspicious but flattering look with which they stared at other people, and the strange smile that they gave you if you looked at them for too long, as if they were apologizing for the damage they were going to do you. There was also their swagger, which you were hardly aware of until one of them was upon you. While they were waiting for permission to go in to the manager, one of them would turn toward the Indian clerk and ask him effusively, "How are you, Mr. Fadlallah?"

Perhaps he thought that he would be able to form some sort of friendship with this man who, with his scorched countenance and yellow eyes, seemed a complete stranger, with no connection to the local people. Mr. Fadlallah, though, would stare at the speaker as if he was looking straight through him with his eyes to stare at something else behind him. Then he would sputter his dry, disturbing cough or use the edge of his hand to sweep away the ash and shreds of tobacco that had collected on the surface of the table in front of him and stuff them inside the drawer, before replying in his slow and gloomy drawl, "I'm fine. Are you okay?"

After either of these informers had left, Mr. Fox would open the door of his office carrying a small scrap of paper between his thick fingers, head toward the cupboards containing the personal files of the workers and slip out one or more files, then take them back to his room and close the door.

Hussein told me that these two men did not pose any great risk because the workers knew them.

"The danger, Brother Muhammad, always comes from the people that it doesn't occur to you to suspect."

"You mean that there . . . ?" I asked in astonishment.

"Do you think that Mr. Fox would be satisfied . . . ?"

"I thought . . . ."

"I know, and that's why I'm advising you not to talk too much in the presence of others."

I laughed. "But I haven't got anything to worry about being exposed."

"That's not important," he said with a serious expression. "In times of doubt, one word can have a thousand meanings."

But this Hussein, like most people who give advice to others, didn't act on this advice himself.

5

Oleander Flowers

During the long days of summer, life becomes less of a burden. After coming back from work in the afternoon, you can rest for a long time on the dam, looking at the desert or writing before the sun goes down and night slowly comes. Sometimes, you can hear Fawzi's dog barking fiercely in the oil rig in the last moments before sunset. But the air in the tents becomes heavy and oppressive in the summer and it is difficult to sleep. The men carry their beds and set them up in the open spaces of the ground outside the tents, leaving their things scattered here and there so that their tents seem almost deserted when you go inside them. If the air is clear during the night, you can enjoy a peaceful sleep under the glow of the stars, then open your eyes at the first light of dawn, as it touches the palm fronds and the silver walls of the tanks on the other side of the road, and washes the remains of the black night from the salt in the desert. But if the winds decide to blow from the east, bringing the humidity of the sea with them, they will make you uncomfortable all through the night, and keep you awake, not knowing what to do with yourself. You will hear the groans of men as they mumble curses all around you; you will hear their intermittent snoring, occasionally interrupted when they are worn out by sleeplessness, and the grating of the wooden planks under Abu Jabbar's bed, driven almost delirious by the hot air during the hours of the night. But the east winds here have no fixed hour. They may blow at any time. When the breeze is moderate, then after supper (which you have here at sunset like prisoners or hospital inmates) you can walk a little in the direction of the town or the managers' quarter (without daring to enter it, of course) and afterward sit on your bed listening to Abu Jabbar's chatter; he never tires of talking about his sexual adventures with his wife night after night, while the others laugh and interrupt him sarcastically or encouragingly, as they drink or smoke or eat something. While Abu Jabbar talks excitedly, recalling the tiniest details, your own mind, like any other man's mind listening to a description of something or someone, is working at breakneck speed of its own accord to create its private imagery, changing the words into lewd scenes which you parade before your eyes like a forbidden pornographic film, the shooting and screening of which are happening inside your head at the same moment. You can see them, Abu Jabbar and his wife (whom you visualize as just as fat as him, although maybe she is slim, or maybe indeed doesn't exist at all), panting passionately in the positions he so shamelessly depicts, their corpulent bodies bathed in sweat.

One evening that summer, however, Abu Jabbar interrupted his usual conversation and announced in that booming voice of his, "Listen, everyone, I've got news for you!"

The picture show stopped inside your head. There was nothing for the imagination to seize on. "Listen, everyone, I've got news for you!" he shouted in his booming voice, as if delivering a speech to an assembled audience. The hammering on iron on the opposite side of the road had stopped some time ago, when the construction of the tanks had been completed, and there was no longer any need for him to raise his voice when he spoke, but it seemed that this habit had stuck with him. He sat alone on his bed, and no one joined him, for fear that the planks under his bed might break. He was dressed only in his underclothes. His private parts, his stock-in-trade in his present life, formed a ball like a small sleeping cat under the fabric between his thighs. The other three, Muzhir Said, Hussein Tu'ma, and Istifan Yuhanna, were sitting on a bed opposite, with the drinks table (or rather Abu Jabbar's empty wooden box, with the mezze plates, glasses, and arrack bottle lined on top of it) set up between the two beds. We looked at him intently, but he remained silent, staring at us. He liked to see the signs of eagerness on others' faces when he was the bearer of what he thought was important news that touched the destinies of others. Then, looking at us from over the top of his glass raised in his hand, he said, "Say goodbye to the tents!"

No one understood what he meant. "Goodbye to the tents, and then what?" said Muzhir, urging him on.

"We are going to leave this camp soon," he said, in the tone of someone who knows everything. "We shall be living in new rooms. We shall have baths and toilets as we deserve, not holes in the ground."

"Is this right, what Abu Jabbar is saying?" asked Istifan, delighted at the announcement. Istifan, who is dead now, had a quite ridiculous faith in other people and used to believe everything he heard.

"Yes, my son. It's true. We shall be living in a new camp."

"And where is this new camp?" asked Hussein Tu'ma, lighting a cigarette. "Did you see it in a dream?"

"No, Hussein, it really exists. I mean, it will exist!"

"Where?"

"There!"

He stretched out his arm, with its dark, flabby flesh, into the darkness, toward the road extension going down to the town. Unintentionally, his arm also indicated the outlines of a number of men sitting or lying down on their beds between the tents. They were smoking and talking quietly, while stray dogs roamed among the beds.

"There, half a mile away, opposite this camp, on the edge of the desert."

"On the edge of the desert again," said Hussein grumpily.

"How do *you* know?" Muzhir asked Abu Jabbar.

"I've been given responsibility for supervising the construction of the camp."

"I'll believe something's changed when I see it!" replied Hussein sarcastically.

"Hussein, my son, why do you doubt everything?" Abu Jabbar interrupted angrily.

"I don't believe anything exists, unless I've seen it with my own eyes!"

"Even God Almighty?"

The atmosphere immediately became electric. For a short moment, there was complete silence, until Hussein spoke, looking at him sharply. "Are you trying to rile me?"

"Come on, everyone, please, we want to get away...," interrupted Muzhir quickly.

Meanwhile, Istifan started to fidget where he was sitting, not knowing what to say. But Abu Jabbar gave an unexpected laugh. "By God, you are a strange fellow!" he said, his belly quivering as he looked at Hussein's flushed face.

"Okay, everyone, let's drink to the construction of the new camp!" said Muzhir, raising his glass cheerily.

Istifan quickly accepted the proposal. Abu Jabbar raised his glass, and Hussein eventually joined them. When they had put their glasses back on the table, Abu Jabbar turned to Istifan, "Go to Daniel, my son... tell him that Abu Jabbar sent you to ask for two cans of meat. Come on, lad, quickly!"

Istifan got up without any hesitation and disappeared behind the tents. You wished he hadn't followed Abu Jabbar's instructions. You didn't know at the time that it was his immediate compliance with other people's requests that would eventually lead to him lose his life . . . for nothing.

"Is it certain, this news?" asked Muzhir, when everyone had calmed down.

"Yes, certain, though people don't seem to like it!"

"Take it easy," said Hussein, trying to calm everyone down. "Who doesn't want to get out of the tents? But the question is, when?"

"A few months, God willing," said Abu Jabbar, confidently. The administration has commissioned Husam Hilmi, a new engineer who arrived a few days ago, to supervise the construction of the camp."

"It's certain, then," said Muzhir, happily.

"Of course, I've seen the plans myself and this morning I was at a meeting between this engineer and the contractor, Hajj Sabih. At first, I thought he was British!"

"Who? Hajj Sabih?" asked Muzhir, looking at him.

Abu Jabbar shook his head. "No, my son, I meant the engineer Husam Hilmi. He's a fair-skinned young man. His hair is almost blond. He's just like a foreigner!"

"The important thing, Abu Jabbar, the important thing is, when do we move?"

"A few months, perhaps before the end of the year. The engineer seems keen to finish the camp quickly."

The young engineer whom Abu Jabbar spoke about enthusiastically that evening, and then later started to speak about with hostility in the days and months that followed, Muhammad got to know a few months later, at the beginning of winter. He was standing in a daze on the road near the exit gate from the work area one Saturday afternoon, watching the trucks loaded with men as they rolled away on the road to town. He had no choice but to go back to the camp and spend the night there, and then to travel from the village the following morning. Then a black Humber car had emerged from the work area, stopped a short distance away, and began to reverse until it was in front of him. From the car's rear window the face of a man looked over at him, whom he supposed to be European until he heard him speak.

The man directed at him a question that seemed like an order at the same time. "Do you want to go to Basra? Get in."

He hesitated for a moment as the car's engine continued to turn with a sound that could hardly be heard. The driver, however, whose face he had seen in the camp before, quickly got out, opened the car trunk, then took the case from him, put it in the trunk and closed it.

"Please, Mr. Muhammad!"

He was not surprised that the driver knew his name, for the workers who worked for Mr. Fox were known in the camp, like insects that had been put under the microscope. Meanwhile, the man opened the car door for him and moved away to sit at the other end of the seat. The car carried them off. Muhammad's face was still flushed and he was shaking.

"Are you ill?" the man asked him with some concern.

He saw a small tuft of his almost-blond hair fall onto his brow. He found him almost exactly as Abu Jabbar had described him, when he had spoken about the administration's determination to build a new camp.

"No, I'm not ill," he replied.

But the man stretched out a long arm and closed the window. He was really shaking with anger, not knowing how he had had the idea of going to the transport manager and asking him for permission to ride in the cab of a truck beside the driver, as Muzhir and a number of other men did. Muzhir was vague when he asked him how he had come to have that privilege, but Abu Jabbar encouraged him. He told him to submit a request to the transport manager ("It's a piece of paper, you won't lose anything if it's refused"). Abu Jabbar wanted to amuse himself, and Muhammad didn't notice the shifty look in his eyes when he made the suggestion, but the transport manager, who was sitting behind the wheel of his truck when he went to him, didn't say a word. He gave him a single glance, and a single glance at the request, then screwed the piece of paper up between his fingers, threw it to the ground, and drove off. Everything happened very quickly, in less than a moment, perhaps . . . a few movements, executed without a word, like when a man's head is cut off with a single blow from a sword. You bring it down skillfully on his neck, without your hand wavering, and the head rolls away, the face still looking stunned and surprised, not believing what has happened. That's roughly what he felt at that moment, as he watched the truck move off into the distance. Then he looked at his crumpled piece of paper, thrown to the ground.

The car carried them off along the public road and swung onto the side road leading to the managers' quarter. "One moment," said the man, "I'm getting some things from home."

In the distance, scattered between the palm trees, some small white houses appeared, with dark arched roofs, like those he had seen in foreign color films. After a few minutes the car stopped in front of one of these houses and the man got out. He opened the door and went inside. The chauffeur got out and opened the trunk, while he remained seated in his corner of the car, staring through the glass of the window at the neat houses with their carefully laid-out yards. He calmed down a little at the sight of the houses and the greenery and began to relax. How could they make the shrubs grow and flower in this salty earth? The Shatt al-Arab waterway wasn't far away, for it flowed just behind the palm groves. Since his arrival here a year or so ago, his eye had never before fallen on such a rich mixture of colors as this, for entry to the managers' quarter was forbidden to those living in the camp by order of Mr. Fox. Only the servants were allowed to enter this place (as well as the maintenance workers, truck drivers, and refuse collectors, of course, and other people who just did their jobs and left). At the time of the day that the car had stopped to wait—with him inside it, gazing awestruck—the place had seemed quiet and completely calm. He wound down the window beside him and was immersed in the air coming from the direction of the Shatt al-Arab, carrying with it the fragrance of palm trees, the earth of the plantations, and the stagnant water of the small streams. In the distance behind the houses he could see people playing tennis. Through the dark trunks of the palm trees, their clothes appeared bright white as they moved lightly over the ground of the courts. The afternoon breeze, a little on the cool side, carried to him the sound of the ball hitting the strings of the racket, gently puncturing the silence that had settled over the whole place and making the silence seem even deeper. He started to listen to the noise, which gently vibrated in his eardrum: tap, tap, tap, tap . . . as if the little ball bouncing between the two players was leaving some light marks on a surface of soft earth. Then an almost complete silence took its place. But it did not last long. In a few moments, the ball that he could not see came back, bouncing between the two players, and again he heard the sound, tap, tap . . . .

"They're playing tennis," said the driver, who'd come back and was standing beside the open window. He wanted to strike up a conversation with him somehow. "The club's there." He pointed to it with his hand. Muhammad could also see a petite woman, with straw-colored hair that had been scorched by the sun as she walked from one house to another. In front of her a black dog the size of a large cat was rolling on the ground. He saw the woman walking slowly in time with her dog, walking when the dog walked and stopping when it fancied stopping to smell something or other, or to raise a leg and leave some moisture beside the trunk of a palm tree.

"That's the wife of your manager. She walks her dog every day."

The driver was behaving like a tour guide, explaining to a visitor from abroad the sights of the foreign city and the quirks of the locals.

"That's Mr. Fox's wife?" he asked with interest.

"Yes."

This was the dog Podgy then, who Farhan al-Abd mentioned in his curses. But Fox's wife seemed like an aged dwarf. His attention was caught by a boy of about four riding a tricycle near one of the houses. In the garden of the house on the opposite side of the road he spotted a man tending his bushes. The man was wearing just a pair of khaki shorts, leaving the rest of his naked body to the cool air. He was a little plump, with a broad back and red, sunburned skin. He couldn't see his face well. The driver had moved away from the window to pick up a bag that a thin servant with a pale face had brought out. He saw the servant go back inside the house while the driver proceeded to put the bag in the trunk and stood behind the car waiting for the rest of the luggage. The rays of the sun were falling on the windows of the houses at an almost vertical angle, making a pool of light on some of the panes of glass that dazzled the eye. Most of the windows were covered with curtains of white tulle. His attention was caught by a small movement at the edge of a curtain in one of the windows whose occupant was busy in his garden. There was a hand that moved the curtain a fraction, and a face appeared from behind the glass. He couldn't distinguish it (was it the face of a woman?), but the face soon disappeared and the

40

white tulle covered the windowpane completely. The man who was giving him a lift left the house, followed by the same servant carrying a number of small bags; then the driver hurried up to him and took the bags to put them in the trunk. He heard the man say to the servant, "If Mr. Fox enquires after me, tell him I've left."

The servant murmured something then went into the house, while the driver closed the trunk of the car and came to sit behind the wheel. But the man didn't get into the car. He went off to meet a woman wearing tennis clothes who had come out of the house opposite. He saw her cross the road toward him quickly with a tennis racket in her hand. She had a small blue bag hanging from her shoulder, of the sort that airlines give to their passengers. The woman was wearing a white sleeveless blouse and a short white skirt that showed the bottom part of her underwear and the roundness of her thighs. Her hair, some of which could be seen under the edge of the white cap on her head, was a shiny brown. She was an attractive woman of around thirty from the appearance of her face, but she had the body of a young girl. They stood chatting. The woman, who often got close to the man as she spoke to him, was constantly moving, as if she was standing on tiptoe on a hot piece of ground, and her hand that was holding the racket was never still. Sometimes she would swing the racket to return imaginary balls, sometimes she was striking the taut strings of the racket against her leg muscles, and sometimes she would put the edge of the racket on the ground and make it spin with a quick movement of her fingers.

"That's the wife of John Sullivan, the transport manager," said the driver, glancing in the small mirror in front of him.

He started up as if someone had woken him from a state of mental torpor. He quickly turned his head in the direction of the man who was busy watering the bushes in his garden. Yes, it was him! How could he have failed to recognize him? It was him, the man who had treated him as though he was dirt. But look at him now. How nice he looked, busy with his roses. So this was his wife. A sort of satisfaction came over him, as if this tall man, with his frantic whispered conversation with the wife of the transport manager, was somehow taking revenge on his behalf. He watched him carefully, but Mr. Sullivan carried on watering his garden for a few minutes, then carefully turned off the hose tap, put it to one side, and walked toward the house; he disappeared inside without once turning around to see what his wife was doing. He felt frustrated as Mr. Sullivan's wife continued her passionate conversation with the man, as she fiddled with the racket and moved around, meanwhile throwing hurried glances at the car from time to time. Perhaps the man had told her that there was someone waiting. He saw her finally looking at her watch, then she lifted the racket and brought it down gently on his shoulder. He squeezed her bare arm gently to say goodbye, then went back to the car. "Let's go, Abbas! Let's go, we're late!" he said curtly as he got into the vehicle.

He waved to the woman from behind the window as the car moved off. It turned a half-circle around the woman, then straightened up on the road, while she remained standing between the houses, smiling, in her short white tennis outfit, her blue bag dangling from her shoulder. Her bare arm was raised, as she waved the racket, bathed in the afternoon sun. She faded into the distance, along with the little houses with paths and trees and fenced gardens. The man waved to her for another brief moment from behind the rear window of the car, then sat up straight and took out a pack of cigarettes. The woman would be lowering her arm now, if she hadn't lowered it already, then turning to go back to the tennis courts to play with her friends. The man offered him the pack. "No, thank you, I don't smoke."

The man lit two cigarettes and held out his hand with one of them over the driver's shoulder. "Abbas! Take it!"

After a few minutes the car moved out onto the public road. It was nearly five o'clock and the pale disk of the sun was quickly slipping down toward the city with them, as it drew closer and closer to the earth. To their left they could see the desert covered in a thick coating of salt, glowing a deep red with the remnants of shadows in the hollows. In the orchards to the right of the road the empty spaces between the palm trees had turned black, and the leaves at the top of the trees glowed, as if some fire had taken hold of them. But the sun soon plunged into the earth, and the palm groves became a long black wall, while on the other side of the desert there was something like an enormous black carpet whose end was lost in the pitch-black horizon. The lengthy pipe, which the workmen had finished laying a short time before, was like a long black rope, appearing and disappearing, appearing and disappearing, with the undulations of the ground.

Meanwhile, the man carried on smoking, lost in thought. The way that he smoked made Muhammad think. He saw him let the smoke emerge slowly between his lips and rise up to his nostrils, where it disappeared, or most of it disappeared, then let it emerge from his mouth again, before taking another breath and leaving the smoke to take its strange circular course.

"Which department do you work in?" the man asked him, after a long silence between them.

"In the management department."

"In the police?" the man asked, with a smile.

He didn't know what he meant. "With Mr. Fox."

"And what do you do there?"

"Translator."

"And what does he need a translator for? Sorry, I don't mean you personally, I mean, he knows Arabic!"

This piece of information surprised him. "He knows Arabic?"

"As well as you or I do. Didn't you know?" said the man, looking at him slightly surprised.

"No, really, I've never heard him speak it. I didn't imagine that he could." Meanwhile, he was trying to recall everything he had said in Arabic in Mr. Fox's presence. An impossible task, for it was such a long period.

"And what do you translate for him?"

"His interviews with the workmen. Books that come to us sometimes from the local manager in the town. Extracts from local newspapers."

"Like what?"

"Workers' strikes in Iraq, market prices, tribal disputes."

"Strange. And why should he be interested in any of this?"

"I don't know."

The man lit a second cigarette from the stub of his first one before putting it out in the ashtray that was fixed to the ledge in front of him.

"And do you know what he does with this information?"

"I saw him once storing it in a steel cabinet in his office."

"And then?"

"I don't know what he does with it."

"Haven't you tried to find out?"

"No."

It had never occurred to him to try to investigate the matter. The man carried on smoking in silence. He didn't ask him anything else. It was better that way, for he didn't know him, and Mr. Fox had warned him from day one not to strike up friendships with anyone so as not to be tempted to reveal any of the administration's secrets. But how could he reveal secrets anyway, when he himself didn't know any details? It hadn't even occurred to him that Mr. Fox might know Arabic. Once again, he tried to remember anything he might have said during the period that had elapsed. When he was translating what the workmen said while they were with the manager, he usually ignored any degrading words of flattery or groveling that somebody might have let out in an effort to secure a job, or clear himself of accusations brought against him; he also ignored any harsh or aggressive words that someone might have spoken in a moment of desperation. He had thought that by doing this he might have protected himself against any damage. He had never noticed that Mr. Fox had been aware of any deficiencies in what he had said. All the while, then, he had known what was going on but kept silent! Had he been setting a trap for him all this time while he was unaware of it?

The forests of palm trees stretching out to his right seemed like a long black cloud sleeping on the face of the earth. The car lights illuminated about fifty meters of road in front of them, after which the light was dispersed like a pale yellow dust whose tiny particles dissolved in the blackness of the night. The car, though, went on through

44

the darkness as the driver guided it carefully over the worn-out sections of the road, while the man sat smoking incessantly, swallowing most of the smoke in that curious way of his. After some time had elapsed, however, enough smoke had gathered to fill the inside of the car—at which point, the man put out his cigarette and rolled down the window beside him, leaving the cold night air to stream into the car. Then he closed the window again. Meanwhile, the darkness had surrounded them, so that they were unable to see the things slipping by outside, which increased the sense they both had of another person sitting close by. He heard the sound of the man speaking in the darkness.

"Do you live in the camp or in town?"

"In the camp."

"Happy there?"

"No one is happy in the camp."

"You'll all be happy when you move to the camp we're building for you now," said the man, consolingly.

"We're waiting. They say it will be completed in a month."

"Who told you that?" the man asked, a little surprised and annoyed.

"A man with us in the camp. He is a work supervisor."

"What's the name of this man?"

"Abd al-Khaliq al-Mawla, but they call him Abu Jabbar."

The man grunted angrily. "The camp will be finished," he said after a little while, "but not that quickly. And how do you spend your free time in the camp?" he said, changing the subject.

"I read."

He didn't tell him that he was also trying to write. Writing is like a love affair: a man only talks about it to a friend, and he was just meeting the man for the first time.

"What do you read?"

"Novels, mainly."

"By Jurji Zaydan?" he asked, laughing.

Why had he thought of Jurji Zaydan rather than anyone else?

"No, other writers, Arabs and foreigners."

45

The car slowed down a bit and he heard the driver say with a hint of boasting, "Sir, here are the project trucks. We've caught up with them even though they set off about an hour before us." In front of them, in the murky distance, he could see some red lights shining as they teetered along the road.

"These foreign writers, do you read them in Arabic?" asked the man.

"No, in English if the books are available. The translation is usually taken from another translation."

Meanwhile, the lights had caught the backs of some trucks ahead of them on the road. Four black shapes creeping along the ground in one convoy. The first time he had been forced to ride on the back of one of these trucks, he had stood hesitantly with his little bag in his hand, watching the men escaping through the big gate after being searched by the guards, rushing toward the caravan waiting at the edge of the road, carrying purses and bags holding their dirty clothes. Besides that, he had also noticed almost every one of them carrying an empty cement bag, whose purpose he had not grasped at the time. He had almost decided not to go to the town that day and return to the camp to spend the night there, then set out from the village the following morning. But the men's voices rang out, urging him to get in before the convoy set out. Hands stretched out in his direction to take his bag, then grabbed him by his arms and shoulders to help him up. They almost picked him up off the ground. He found himself sitting among them on cold steel, with his bag between his legs. When the convoy set off, the sky over their heads was lowering, and the men looked at it uneasily.

"I wonder if I could borrow some books from you?" said the man beside him in the darkness of the car.

"Of course, I've got some in the bag," he replied at once.

He was happy to be able to perform a simple service for the man, who had arranged a comfortable journey for him to town after he had been standing lost by the roadside. The outlines of the men in the rear of the convoy began to form themselves in front of his eyes. He saw them sitting crumpled up next to one another to protect themselves from the cold air. When the lights of the car shone in their faces, they turned their heads to avoid the glaring light, or perhaps they turned them out of embarrassment. The truck drivers began to turn off the road one after the other, clearing the way for the small car that was coming behind them. The sight of men crammed together on the back of the trucks was repeated time and time again, almost without variation, until they had passed the whole convoy and the road opened up in front of them again, empty and deserted. Finally they left behind that pitch-black emptiness that joined the earth and the sky—the desert that had accompanied them—and the car slipped along between two walls of palm trees. They were swallowed up in the groves of the village of Abu al-Fulus. The car lights cast a scattering of their quivering rays on the mud walls on both sides of the road, on the trunks of the palm trees in the open groves, and lit up the bushes and dry grass on the shoulders of the road. "It's really nice here," the driver said, suddenly slowing the car.

He could see the asphalt of the road glistening in the car lights in front of them, and the wheels gave off a continuous screech as they slipped over the wet surface. He turned his head and looked at the sky through the rear window, and was surprised to see a black space with not a single star shining in it. The man was sitting silently in his corner. After a little, the car began to take them slowly along a road lined with closed shops and small cafés. Some empty taxis were stopped beside them, their newly washed roofs gleaming in the light, while the café seats arranged on the sidewalks, their wood damp from the rain, were deserted and naked. He noticed a few heads moving inside the cafés, but the cigarette smoke, the steam from people's breath collected on the windowpanes, and the movement of the car made the faces appear fuzzy and featureless. The car was at this point making its way greedily through the village of Abu al-Khasib. The city of Basra was still a long way off: they would reach it in about half an hour. When the car left the village, it started its journey along the twisting road. The turns began to follow one another at short intervals. Sometimes the car would leave

47

one turn to go straight into another, but the road was well surfaced. Drops of rain began to fall gently from the sky and strike the roof of the car.

"Great, we've left that road behind," said the driver with satisfaction, as he turned the windshield wipers on.

Safe from the rain in his warm comfortable corner, he stared at the moving expanse of road lit up in front of them by the car lights He gazed at the oleander bushes at the edges of the palm groves, with their big white and crimson flowers bowing down to the earth under the weight of the rain. The rain was getting heavier by the minute, and something like steam or smoke had started to rise from the surface of the ground as the rain fell on it. The streams of water falling in front of the car—thousands of them—gleamed in the headlights. Once again he thought of the men on the backs of the trucks on the road. When the rain came down, they would slip out the empty cement bags from under their bottoms and cover their heads and the heads of their neighbors with them. The air around them would then be filled with the smells of cement dust, mud from the wet road, and salt from the desert, while the water ran over the cold steel underneath them. Despite the rain, he thought they would be happy when the convoy started along this twisting road, for that meant that they were now near Basra. If the rain stopped while they were on the road, the young men would start singing. It astonished him that they were singing—perhaps they were intoxicated with the smell of the earth from the orchards, the oleander flowers, and the palm leaves bathed by the rain, as well as the happiness of approaching the city and seeing the faces of their loved ones. The breeze carried their voices as they sang in the face of the cold moist wind, leaning against the driver's cab, for the whole length of the road between the palm groves. The convoy was now moving quickly, despite the dangers on the winding road. The sides of the trucks struck the tree branches that extended over the road, leaving behind them a smell of damp leaves, some of which fell on them as the singers continued their chorus with thundering voices that shook the night of the villages nestling in the depths of the

palm groves. They would chant the name of each village they passed
through as if the name was one of the words of their songs—beautiful,
but a little sad. Al-Mahalliya, al-Hamza, Hamdan, Balad Salama, and
so on. Of course, they couldn't actually see the villages: they only knew
they were there by a little bridge, a mud wall around a palm grove, or
a light twinkling in the darkness. Signs that Basra was no longer a long
way off.

The rain fell on the men on the backs of the trucks and pelted down
on the roof of the little car that was hurrying along the twisting road.

"Sir! Some truck drivers call this turn 'the turn of death,'" said the
driver as he negotiated his way around a sharp bend in the road.

"Watch out, then!" replied the man, then turned to Muhammad and
added, "Actually, fatal accidents are more common on straight roads!"

He couldn't see his face well, but his voice seemed kind enough.
It wasn't the arrogant man that Abu Jabbar was continually cursing.
"On straight roads, you get a false sense of security," the man continued, a little absentmindedly as if he was talking about something completely different from the bends in the road. "You relax and drop your
guard." As another car approached them from the opposite direction,
the streams of rain shone brighter where the light fell between the two
cars, then faded as they drew apart. After that, the rain quickly eased
and then stopped. Then he noticed the screeching of the wheels on the
ground and the sound of the wind striking the top of the car, making
the leaves on the soaking trees bend wearily. They were approaching
the city. Here and there along the road, houses could be seen, then the
palm groves started to move farther away from them. Lights appeared.
The car took them over a bridge that crossed the al-Khura River and
the city swallowed them up. He saw the cars with their shiny surfaces
washed by the rain, swept up by the broad street that opened up in
front of them. Here was Basra at last! He looked at the people moving
on the pavements. He looked at the houses. He looked at the trees, at
the lights and the traffic, as he sat comfortably inside the car. He felt
no embarrassment. The men traveling on the backs of the trucks had
stopped singing before they entered the city. The singers sat down and

the men soaked by the rain snatched anxious glances at Basra, saying nothing so as not to attract looks.

"Where do you live?" the man asked him.

"Not far from here."

"Okay, we'll take you home."

He thanked the man but asked them to put him down on the road, in front of the boys' preparatory school in al-Ashar. The car stopped for him where he had asked.

"One moment, I'll get the books out."

"No, not now," the man said to him. "I don't want to hold you up in the cold. Take them with you when you come back. I'll send Abbas to you."

"Sorry, we haven't been introduced," he added, suddenly remembering. "I am Engineer Husam Hilmi."

He told him his name. "Okay, Brother Muhammad," the man said as he bade him farewell. "I'll see you again!"

Meanwhile the driver had taken out his bag and left it for him on the pavement. He saw the car cross the bridge then disappear between the other vehicles. He stopped to wait for a taxi to take him home. The city around him was throbbing with life. It had been a relaxing journey and the man had been kind, if it is possible to judge people at a first meeting. But what was it that he had said and that had kept niggling him all the way, like a fly buzzing around you in the darkness? He had said that Mr. Fox knew Arabic. Yes, this was the fly that had continued flapping its wings inside his head the whole way. For days he had been translating the words as he thought appropriate, wrapping his Arabic around him like a thick cloak. Then he discovered that the other man also knew Arabic. He was overcome by a feeling like that of one who suddenly discovers that he is walking naked in a public place. You only get a feeling like this in dreams, in nightmares. Was Mr. Fox setting a trap for him?

When he returned from his weekend break he asked the Indian secretary, "Mr. Fadlallah, is it true that the manager knows Arabic?"

He wanted to be sure. He stood with him in the office garden at midday, during the break after finishing lunch. Mr. Fadlallah looked at

50

him curiously, then asked him quietly, while looking at Jirjis, who was standing in another corner of the garden, baring his chest to the sun, "Didn't you know Mr. Fox knows Arabic?"

"No, I didn't know," he said.

"But I thought you knew," said Fadlallah, panting slightly.

"But how would I know, if he never speaks it?" he asked.

"From his eyes, my son, from his eyes!"

That night Abu Jabbar and his colleagues collected their bottles, cups, and empty plates and moved the box away; they were swaying about, especially Istifan, who got drunk quickly. Abu Jabbar seemed the steadiest in his movements. He saw them get ready for bed. The camp residents had been asleep and quiet for a long time, and as he looked at the darkness between the tents, he could see nothing but stretched-out bodies on the beds, and dark heads thrown onto the pillows. He couldn't see a single man upright on his feet or sitting on his bed, the length and breadth of the camp. Everyone was sleeping, preparing themselves for another day's work. So Mr. Fox knew Arabic like an Arab. And he had been speaking in front of him with no precautions, depending on his ignorance.

6

One Big Happy Family

Mazlum the caretaker came into the office, agitated and out of breath. The morning siren had sounded more than an hour ago, urging the men to hurry to their workplaces. Jirjis looked at his watch and shouted in his face, "What's this? You're late. And Mr. Fadlallah hasn't come yet! You know the time?"

"Sorry, sir," mumbled the caretaker. "I didn't sleep yesterday because Mr. Fadlallah, who lives with me in the house, as you know, sir . . . he spent the whole night coughing and spitting blood. The whole night!"

Jirjis's stern look softened a little. "And where is he now?"

"I took him to the clinic this morning, and waited and waited until Dr. Sami came. He examined him and then . . . ."

"Okay, okay, I understand!"

The chief clerk got up, buttoned his jacket, and went in to the director.

"Mazlum, come here!" I said.

The caretaker came up to me. "What did the doctor say?" I asked him in alarm.

"He told me to go to work. But I heard him ask the nurse to send Mr. Fadlallah to Basra, by ambulance!"

"He's in a bad way, then."

"Very!"

Mazlum's one eye looked moist and swollen. Was he crying for that foreigner? Fadlallah's life was quite obscure. Mazlum says that the man had been a soldier in the Indian military units that entered Iraq with the British army in the First World War. Then he got left behind by his unit and settled in Iraq. He married, acquired Iraqi citizenship and was driven by the necessities of life to move from job to job and from city to city. After that, his wife died. No one knew whether or not he had any children. When he came to work on the project, he couldn't live in the camp for long. He wasn't the sort of person to socialize with other people much, so he rented a room in the caretaker Mazlum's house, who had started to look after him as if he were his own father. Jirjis came out of the director's office and we were expecting that he would tell us what Mr. Fox had said when he heard what had happened to his Indian clerk. Instead, Jirjis directed his words at me.

"Muhammad, the boss asked me to go to the camp. To see what Daniel has done about the preparations for tonight's party."

"And Mr. Fadlallah?"

"The boss will be getting in touch with Dr. Sami," he added. "To refer him to him."

"I can go to the clinic, I have to catch up with him!"

"No, my boy," he said firmly. "You know, the boss is extremely concerned about tonight's party!" And he left the office.

That day, January 19, 1952, was a day never to be forgotten. It was the day on which the project management arranged a celebration to mark the loading of the first tanker from the new quay. It was also the beginning of the end of Fadlallah's life. A life of exile and loss. After Jirjis had left, Mazlum said firmly, "I'm going back to the clinic. I'll see. . . ."

"And if the manager wants you?" asked Abdullah.

"Tell him I've gone back to the clinic," he said angrily, and left the office.

Mr. Fox stretched out his hand and drew back the glass from the square partition in the wall. Then his voice came, "Mohamet, please ask Basra to send us a photographer. I want him in the workers' canteen before six this evening!"

Mr. Fox, as Jirjis had said, was worried about the success of this evening's party—meanwhile Hussein Tu'ma and three or four other men were making a corresponding effort, if not an even greater one, to ensure the celebration's failure. Hussein had been saying to men he trusted—he would meet them in the corner of the work area, on the road, or behind the camp walls—that anyone joining that celebration would be like someone sharing the happiness of thieves who were robbing his own house. They supported him as he happily told them that. I told him that I also supported him unreservedly but that I had to go because of my job, because Mr. Fox was determined to give a speech to the men and I had to be there to translate it for them. In fact, there was also another reason that prompted me to go. I wanted to see the celebration for myself, so that when I talked about it in the novel later my words would be derived from experience, not just photographs. But he didn't know yet that I was trying to write something. I recall that he'd said to me at the time, "Okay, your presence won't change anything, go, so you can describe for me the signs of defeat on his face"—meaning Mr. Fox's face—"when he enters the celebration venue and finds it almost deserted."

In the evening I saw Hussein sitting on his bed in the tent, still wearing his mud-spattered jacket. His hair was a bit untidy, and his hands held a newspaper that he was flipping through disinterestedly. He seemed tired from his rounds of the men, to check for the last time that they were keeping their promise not to attend Fox's party (as he called it). He had done all he could—him and the three or four others—and sat awaiting the results. He was happy, even if he appeared, despite the nonchalant way in which he was turning over the pages of the newspaper, slightly uneasy. Perhaps he was feeling at that moment like a student who has finished the exam but is still asking himself afterward whether he has missed a question, or half a question, or if he has made a mistake somewhere.

I left him alone in the tent, his happiness still incomplete, and went out. As I approached the mess tent I was hit by the noise resounding from within. I saw four or five men, including Istifan, standing hesitantly near the entrance, but my going inside put an end to their hesitation and they quickly entered behind me (they were all using the others' entrance in front of them as an excuse, to keep their consciences clear). I found the large tent crammed full of men standing in two long lines around tables set about a meter and a half apart. They were chattering and laughing where they stood, for Daniel had emptied the canteen of chairs to make the place seem larger. The air inside the tent felt warm and soothing even though you could smell, along with the cigarette smoke, a faint smell of oil wafting from the oil heaters that had been placed there. When they brought supper, the canteen workers brought it to the tables. For the first time, you were not forced to stand in a queue waiting for your helping of food. It was special food that night: scores of trays full of rice covered with a layer of nuts and raisins with great pieces of roast meat, carafes of milk, trays full of sweetmeats (they had brought them from Basra), and baskets of apples, oranges, and other fruits arranged everywhere on the tables. You could eat as much as you liked, and some people filled their pockets without anyone stopping them. While the men were busy eating, the photographer, who had come from the city, was busy taking pictures, while his assistant carried his flash apparatus. They moved about from place to place. The photographer put his finger on the shutter, and the camera gave out that familiar sound as it snapped pictures of hands stretched out toward the food; another picture of fingers dripping fat as they grasped a piece of meat; a picture of a line of faces bloated with food (but what did Mr. Fox want to do with all these pictures?). Some of the men, when they saw the photographer pointing his apparatus toward them as his assistant let the brilliant light loose on their faces, would suddenly stop chewing to smile merrily at the camera lens. They would smile for a brief moment with the food stationary in their mouths or motionless in their hands, while the camera clicked, then go on eating again. When they had finished eating, the canteen workers quickly cleared the two long tables, followed by Daniel with his never-ending orders, moving behind them with his slight frame and his swollen eyelids. Here now are the servants, coming in with crates of beer that they put down on the ground, then handing around the bottles. One in front of every man. The din becomes louder as the hands stretch out toward the full, unopened bottles (meanwhile the photographer is taking more pictures). But Daniel shouts a warning to the men: "Wait, wait! The boss has to arrive first!"

Disappointment crossed their faces. Jirjis and Abu Jabbar were now standing in the cold outside the tent waiting for the manager to arrive. After a little they stuck their heads out and shouted quickly in a single shaky intertwined voice, "The manager's car! The boss has arrived!"

Daniel hurried out and the hubbub inside subsided. The photographer and his assistant got ready. Meanwhile the sound of a car coming to a halt could be heard. The men's faces were now turned toward the entrance. A few moments of anticipation passed, then Mr. Fox came into the tent crammed full of men. He entered cheerfully, with his black pipe in the corner of his mouth, accompanied by the transport manager, Mr. John Sullivan, and the fire service chief, Mr. Durham, both walking beside him, but a little behind because the space between the men was so narrow. He was followed by a retinue consisting of Daniel, Jirjis, and Abu Jabbar, walking politely along, while the photographer moved backward in front of the entering procession, and his assistant walked backward beside him, careful not to collide with the men, or to hit an oil heater placed in an unsuitable position or the crates of beer, some of which were still on the ground. The lights and the lens of the camera were trained on the approaching faces: successive snaps of Mr. Fox coming into the mess tent with his colleagues and the procession. Meanwhile, nothing could be heard amid the men's silence except for the footsteps of those coming in and the click of the camera. Then the photographer and his assistant got out of the way. More quick shots of Mr. Fox walking between the rows of men, who turned round with slightly puzzled faces to look at him passing in front of them with confident steps, as if he were a king or head of state reviewing the guard. The manager and his two colleagues stood in the middle of a row of tables. Silence reigned, unbroken by anything but the scraping of some tense feet on the ground, and a dogfight over some scraps of food that had been thrown in the rubbish bins behind the tent. Mr. Fox turned his gray eyes on the dark, hardened faces, which all turned in his direction to stare. Faces burned by the sun, and eyes—what eyes!—that began to look at him suspiciously, as his face became downcast. He took his pipe from his mouth, put it on the surface of the table, and muttered quietly to his colleagues, "I don't think that these men like me!"

The transport manager smiled in satisfaction and the fire department chief whispered jokingly, "They know what a bastard you are!"

Mr. Fox continued to stare at the faces for a moment or two, then, rubbing his palms together said, "Okay, let's get it over with!"

He turned around. "Where is Mohamet?"

I felt a hand on my back propelling me forward. Jirjis was pushing me. Mr. Fox cleared a space between him and the transport manager, so I pushed myself in between the two men. John Sullivan gave me a kindly smile, which reminded me of his unconcerned face when I had seen him washing the soil from the shrubs in the garden of his house in the managers' quarter while his wife stood flirting with her neighbor a few feet away. "Look here, Mohamet," said Mr. Fox in explanation. "I shall speak a few sentences, then you translate them, and so on. I won't talk for long."

At that moment, however, Daniel arrived, followed by a servant carrying a silver tray with three bottles of chilled beer and three large mugs. He put the bottles and glasses in front of the director and his two friends, and they both went away again. Another set of servants started to go round the tables opening the bottles for the men. When the men's muttering had subsided and there was a pause in the clinking of bottle caps falling on the floor and the noise of the bottles hitting the surface of the tables, the director raised his head and started to speak.

"Gentlemen! I am happy to see you here, to share with us in the celebration of this great event!"

My voice seemed foreign to my own ears in the heavy silence of the tent. I saw the men turning their gaze to my face, but they looked at me impassively, while their looks directed at Mr. Fox were full of confusion and amazement. It was the first time they had heard him talking to them in a calm and friendly tone.

"I am very happy to see that you have all come, although, as you know, some people tried to persuade you not to attend this celebration as a sign of protest, but a protest against what or against whom? I really have no clear idea."

A quiet murmuring began to be heard . . . a whisper here and there, as the men exchanged quick baffled looks. They suddenly felt that they were standing before him exposed, with nothing to protect them. But he changed the direction of his words: "The fact that you are here in such large numbers is an indication of a feeling of belonging. And that is an important factor in the success of the project."

Some of the men started to stroke their beer glasses with their hands and draw lines on the cold glass with their fingers. When a sound escaped from one of the glasses, the man concerned would lift his fingers and turn round in some embarrassment.

"You have no idea, of course, of the sheer amount of money we have spent to achieve this result. Millions of pounds and all sorts of expertise!" The photographer and his assistant brought two chairs, which they stood on, as the photographer, who could now command a view of the whole place including every corner, started to take more pictures.

"Of course, we should not forget your efforts, and the efforts of your colleagues in Project HQ in Basra, or those who are working in the al-Zubayr fields, but . . . ."

Mr. Fox raised his hand in the faces of the men to indicate the importance of what he was going to say next. "But capital comes before everything—money!" (as he uttered the last word he rubbed the side of his thumb with the side of his index finger) "—and then, expertise! These two factors . . . ."

But the faces had begun to seem annoyed. People's eyes were wandering and they were no longer looking at his face as he spoke. I saw people looking questioningly at their colleagues' faces, or gazing up at the roof of the big tent, which hung over everyone like a dark cloud, or staring into the beer glasses in front of them, which had begun to warm up the longer Mr. Fox's speech went on. Or else, they would look at the photographer and his assistant moving from place to place, carrying the two chairs with them wherever they went, careful at the same time not to make the slightest noise.

The men were moving like thieves in a house full of people as the photographer took pictures, unheeded by anyone present, except for the quiet, clipped sound like that of a night insect, which announced to those whose thoughts were roaming far away that he had just taken a snap. While Fox was delivering his speech, heedless of the men in front of him, the photographer was standing above him, capturing the gathering in his lens in a group photograph that included everyone—a panorama of faces, glasses, and tables, with Mr. Fox and the men around him at the center. Then the photographer and his assistant moved: a mid-range snap of silent faces. From another angle, a shot of Jirjis standing behind the back of the manager, his head bowed as he listened almost deferentially to his words. Then a wide shot of dozens of hands, coming together or parting in the unexpectedly loud and merry applause that broke out when Mr. Fox had finished his short address. He started to laugh amid the noise of the handclaps, "Scoundrels! Addicted to drink!"

Fox and his colleagues filled their glasses, then Fox raised his glass into the air. "And now . . . ." He waited until the voices had completely subsided. "And now, let us drink together, to the success of the project . . . for the benefit of all . . . and for the success of your country, Iraq!"

It was a unique picture that the photographer succeeded in taking at that moment of Mr. Fox and his two colleagues gulping beer from their large glasses, and of the men with their lips covering the mouths of their bottles in an almost coordinated movement. Dozens of raised hands, and tipped-up bottles, heads lolling backward, and faces intent on drink.

This picture appeared later in a magazine published by the project management in London, which reached Iraq about two months later, with these words underneath it: "One big happy family!"

Mr. Fox stayed for a few more minutes, during which he asked Jirjis about his son, who was studying in Britain, and enquired of Abu Jabbar whether he was happy working with Engineer Husam. Abu Jabbar tried to take this opportunity to lay out his concerns, but the manager wasn't ready to listen to complaints of this sort at this kind of event, and interrupted him sharply.

"Later, Abdul, later!"

He turned to Daniel and told him not to stint on the beer that evening, provided that things did not get out of hand. Then he and the two other managers drank what was left in their glasses. He took his cold pipe from the surface of the table, slipped it into his breast pocket, and left the party rather hurriedly with his colleagues. They were escorted to their waiting car at the entrance to the mess tent by Daniel, Jirjis, and Abu Jabbar. When the men heard the sound of the car driving off they raised their voices demanding more drink from Daniel, who had come back into the tent. The servants brought more crates. The air was filled with noise and smoke and the smell of beer. I left, for I could imagine what would happen after that.

I found Hussein in his place, his newspaper unread beside him on the bed. I was surprised to see him sitting in the same place all this time. He hadn't changed his clothes yet.

"So, is the party over?"

"No," I replied, "but Mr. Fox left so I left too."

"How was it?"

The tone of his voice worried me. He wasn't keen to know what had happened.

"You mean Mr. Fox?"

"No, the party."

"I can say that everyone came, more or less," I said, sitting down on my bed exhausted.

I looked at his face. What a disappointment he must be feeling! But instead, standing up to change his clothes, he said quietly, "I saw them."

"You saw them?" I asked in astonishment.

"Yes."

"But I didn't see you there!"

"I didn't go in. I saw what was happening through a crack in the door. I was standing in the darkness."

"You were standing in the cold, all that time?"

He smiled, slightly sadly.

"No, I stayed a few minutes, while he was talking about the millions of pounds, and the expertise."

"And you saw them drinking with him, to the success of the project?"

"No, I didn't see that," he said, folding his trousers carefully. "That must have happened later."

I started to change my clothes as well. I saw him put his trousers under the pillow. He sat on the bed, putting on his dishdasha and putting his jacket over his shoulders. After a few moments he said, "I know what is going through your head. You want to say that these people can't . . . ."

But where had that idea come from?

"I never imagined anything like that. All it is, is that . . . ."

"All it is, Muhammad, is that their lives are empty of anything to be happy about."

Was he trying to convince himself? He took his newspaper and immersed himself in reading it. Perhaps he needed to think about the men's behavior and reassess his calculations. I took out my papers to record my quick observations about the party before Abu Jabbar interrupted us, for he had been trying to find out what I was doing for a long time.

At midnight we heard a commotion—shouting and noisy laughter.

"It seems that the party has finished at last!" said Hussein absentmindedly.

"Yes, and the drunks are coming!" I replied.

Their voices spread through the night air and filled the paths between the tents. They were returning to their deserted tents. We could hear the words of people who kept stumbling as they walked over the nearby paths, walking on for a few heavy steps, then stopping while they chattered nonstop. "Quietly! Quietly, my friends!

Mr. Alwan Mushari, from Tuwairij, will give you a speech, on this happy occasion. Where is the translator? Never mind. Mr. Alwan will speak in Arabic. Please, Mr. Alwan! No, wait, Mr. Alwan, please! Ha, ha, ha, please, silence! Gentlemen! Yes, speak, gentlemen! I am happy . . . . and I am Abbas. Ha, ha, ha, please! Please, please, silence! Please, sir. I am happy . . . . I know, so what? I am happy because you . . . Where's Jasim gone? He's gone to pee. Your presence . . . is an indication of your feelings of longing (a wave of guffaws and whistling), of belonging, you feeble bastard! Belonging . . . you lot . . . honestly I didn't understand what the boss was getting at. We feel as though we are part of the family. What family is this? Hoppy's House? Ho, ho, ho! We must . . . Enough, Mr. Alwan. Applause for Mr. Alwan Mushari. (Some people clap feebly.) You know, my friends . . . Fawzi today . . . he can drink more than ten people! Really! He saw people not drinking so he took their share. Every quarter of an hour he went off to pee. He drank from here, and drained it out there. The tap stayed open, long live the tap! Symbol of manhood. I see you're erect! And when his belly was full, he shouted in English, 'Enough, enough!' Fawzi, is that right, what I'm saying? Of course, I'm a miserable so-and-so! Down with Mr. Fox! Long live Farhan al-Abd and Araq al-Zahlawi! Down with the atom bomb! No, God curse you! Okay, okay, don't be angry, long live the atom bomb! God curse you, Fawzi, you've confused me, you don't want 'down with it,' and you don't want 'long live the bomb' either! Alwan, help me! This has ruined us! He can't walk on his own. Come here, Fawzi. Put your arm on my shoulder. Where's my dog gone? Awwad! This is him. He's walking behind you. Imagine! All the time. And the dog's waiting. In the dark. Outside the mess tent. A boy or a man, this dog? Slowly, slowly."

Their steps faltered, and their voices moved away. They started to grow softer and disappear, as they dispersed and withdrew inside the tents, one after the other, to sleep at last.

"Did you hear them?" He seemed almost contented.

"Drunken prattle," I said to him.

"True, but it somehow gives the game away . . . ."

Dankha and his fiends were approaching, singing an Assyrian song in a merry tone. Then we heard Istifan's voice bidding them farewell. He came into the tent looking happy, but his expression changed and he looked embarrassed. When his eyes fell on Hussein, he mumbled in apology, "Brother Hussein, I saw . . . ."

"Don't worry, you weren't the only one!"

Istifan was sound asleep by the time Abu Jabbar came back. The breeze wafted to us the sound of his voice, a voice that changed strangely and became like a young man's voice when he sang. Before he had reached the tent, he was singing a well-known folk song: "Above the palm trees, above, above; my eye's above the palms, above."

Hussein folded his jacket and put it on his case under the bed. "I don't want to see this man tonight," he said hurriedly. Then he lay down on the bed and covered his body completely. I hid my papers under the pillow and took out a book, while Abu Jabbar sang drunkenly as he approached the entrance to the tent, "All the girls are stars in my eyes, and you are their moon!"

But he stopped singing when he came in. He was carrying a bottle of beer in each hand. He looked at me slightly surprised, "You left the party . . . to come and read?"

I laughed. "You know, Abu Jabbar, I don't like . . . ."

"You didn't have to, son, you didn't have to stay watch them!"

"And where is Muzhir?" I asked, changing the subject.

"I don't know. He vanished suddenly. Perhaps he went to repair the boss's car," he added, laughing. "John Sullivan's, that is."

"At this time of night?" I asked him innocently.

He laughed cheerfully and his belly started to shake, and the two bottles of beer in his hands shook with the movement of his body. "Yes, son, yes! This is the best time to fix broken machinery," he said with a strange look in his eyes.

Then he looked around him. He stared at Istifan's body stretched out asleep, snoring softly, then looked carefully at Hussein, of whom nothing could be seen under the blanket. "Is he asleep?" he asked in a whisper.

"I think so."

He went inside the tent, put two bottles of beer under his bed, then opened his metal chest, took out his dishdasha and sat down on the bed. The wooden slats groaned under him. He took off his shoes and put on a pair of sandals. The air in the tent was filled with the smell wafting from inside his shoes, which was stronger even than the smell of the beer wafting from his mouth. Then he got up and spoke softly as he busied himself changing his clothes, nodding and gesturing with his eyes toward the body of Hussein, who was completely still under the cover.

"He imagines . . . no one knows!"

His belly, with its dark, flabby flesh, was completely bare, and his belly button looked like a black hole, with what looked like a few small wisps of dirty cotton inside it. Then he took off his trousers and put his head into his dishdasha, continuing to speak in a whisper from behind the material.

"He doesn't know that the boss doesn't miss anything."

As he waved his arms around and continued with his clipped, rattling words inside his white, flowing dishdasha, Abu Jabbar seemed like a headless ghost. Then his head popped out of the neck opening. "Mr. Fox," he said, sighing contentedly, "the bastard knows who his father is!"

The slats creaked under him as he sat down on the bed again. "You've seen yourself, with your own eyes . . . all the men . . . ."

He gave a searching glance toward the hidden body.

"You mean . . . ."

He looked me carefully in the face. "You know very well what I mean."

I could detect no influence of drink in his eyes or his voice.

"Give him some advice, my lad, give him some advice. Don't let him ruin himself. You're his friend, perhaps he will listen to what you say."

"And you?" I replied. "Aren't you his friend? Don't you drink together almost every night?"

He looked at Hussein's bed, and a trace of doubt appeared in his eyes. Perhaps he was saying to himself that when a man is asleep, his body doesn't usually stay this still for that long. There was no sensation of breathing, no sigh, not the smallest movement. I saw him turn toward me and speak regretfully, in a voice that had suddenly become cautious, "Of course I'm his friend. More than his friend. But he, may God preserve him, believes that I am Mr. Fox's ally. A spy, that is . . . imagine!"

"No, it's ridiculous for him to think that."

"Anyway," he replied, in the tone of someone who doesn't hold a grudge against anyone, "for my part, I don't want anything but the best for him. May God be my witness!"

He walked past me with his dishdasha flapping around him and went out of the tent. I heard him peeing in the darkness nearby. The silence of the night was broken by the sound of his urine pouring out in a long, fine stream. The quiet, continuous sound penetrated the silence for some time, as if there had been a horse urinating behind the wall of the tent. Then he came in. He pulled down the covering over the opening and muttered as he walked toward his bed, "Goodnight, lad!" He lay down on the bed and covered himself up, hiding his face from the light. I took out my papers from under my pillow and hid them and my book in my bag, then put out the tent light and stretched out on the bed as well. (Of the family of five, only Muzhir's bed remained empty.) Outside, almost complete silence reigned. The drunken voices in the alleys between the tents had subsided some time ago, and only a few scattered voices could still be heard from time to time, carried on the breeze from place to place. The barking of dogs in scattered places between the tents, the noise of an engine in the storage area on the other side, and sometimes the groan of a man vomiting up the contents of his belly—the food and drink from the party—in the darkness of the night. I was aware of Hussein's body stirring at last. He pulled the blanket from his face and turned over on the bed so as to face me. I saw his eyes glowing in the darkness. Our silent glances met through the cover of the darkness. Then he made a slight gesture toward me with his hand, as if to say "goodnight" and turned his face away from me. I have no doubt that he spent that night awake, after all he had seen and heard. So Mr. Fox knows everything, says Abu Jabbar with confidence.

From that day, I began to fear for what would happen to Hussein.

7

The Dam

Just before sunset one spring day, I noticed a pool in the desert in which the rays of the sun had carved out a river of blood. I looked at the pool carefully, thinking it must be a mirage. But I hadn't changed the place where I sat every day, and the sun hadn't changed the place where it set. Where could the mirage have come from, then? Then I saw the pool getting wider minute by minute, and I realized that what I thought had been a mirage was really a raging torrent sweeping over the ground, heading for the camp. Hadn't the rig operator noticed it coming? Or was he taking a nap in his room, waiting for the trucks to return? (His dog had barked ferociously at the setting sun a few minutes ago, then fallen silent.) No time to think of the rig operator! The camp first! Who knows what might happen if the water reached the dam? I gathered up my papers and left quickly.

In the camp, the men were blithely following the monotonous routines of their daily lives. Most of them made quickly for the mess tent, drawn by the smell of food that filled the air, while the flood, which they knew nothing about, crept up on them like a snake.

I noticed Daniel coming out of the supply tent on his way to the canteen. I called out to him from some way away as I ran toward him. He turned round in an agitated way.

"Mr. Daniel, the flood, the flood is getting nearer!" I said in alarm.

"What are you talking about?" he asked, in a voice slurred by wine.

I pointed to the desert behind the dam. "The water . . . the water's advancing on the camp!"

He looked at the desert but could see nothing from where he was and looked at me doubtfully. "Come and see," I said insistently.

I took him by the arm and he came with me hesitantly. I helped him up the dam. He looked at the desert, which had turned into a lake with astonishing speed. "Holy Mother of God!" he exclaimed.

I heard Fawzi's dog barking in the drilling rig, which looked like a floating oil platform (the surface of water that extended between the rig structure and the dam gave the dog's barking an extra clarity). I heard another sound: a terrified human voice coming across the water, obliterating the insistent barking. It was Fawzi Abu Shama shouting for help. But what was holding him suspended up there until the flood-waters had surrounded him? He could wade through the water or swim to the camp. What was keeping him there? Daniel only stood there for a short moment before getting down, muttering in alarm, "I'm going to tell the boss . . . he ought to know!"

He turned around to warn me: "You don't tell anyone. I don't want any messing around!"

What was the point of this useless ranting? The important thing was to stem the tide of the flood. Daniel left quickly and I went back to the tent. I put the papers in the bag then put the bag on the bed, prepared for any eventuality. (Books and papers before other possessions!) In the mess tent the men were bent over their plates eating their food voraciously, gossiping, exchanging jokes, and guffawing, while the dark waters surrounded them and ate into the earth of the dam. I finished my food quickly and went out.

There were some shapes moving in the darkness of the evening over the back of the dam. Perhaps someone on his way to the toilets had heard that continuous barking, like no other barking, and the faint cries for help, and discovered the floodwaters that were surrounding the camp and raised the alarm. But those I had left behind in the mess were still ignorant of what was happening a short distance away from them. Meanwhile a large truck arrived. A number of men got out and set up three or four searchlights on the side of the dam facing the desert, about thirty meters apart from each other, making a sort of chain of small pools of light, in the midst of which could be seen, floating on the surface of the water, various rubbish that the flood had carried along in its path. Broken huts, papyrus reeds, small dead birds, and branches.

The number of men on the dam started to increase. Daniel continued to shout loudly, having completely regained his composure.

"Get down. This is the last thing we need."

Fawzi's dog let out a hoarse bark.

"That's Fawzi, he's in trouble!"

"Why doesn't he swim?" asked someone standing there, baffled.

"He doesn't know how to swim," said someone else.

"He's sinking in the water . . . he's not. . . ."

"He's afraid of falling into one of those holes they've filled the desert with. He and his friends—can't you hear what they're saying?"

"They're leaving him hanging like that until the morning?"

"No, of course not. Look over there!"

"Look at what?"

"There are fish in the water!"

"Christ," shouted Daniel above the noise. "If you don't come down, I'll complain to the boss!"

"May the boss's soul burn in hellfire!"

"Who said that?"

But the fire engine was filling the air with the noisy ring of its bell as it made its way into the camp, preceded by a small black truck. "What are the firemen going to do?" asked one of the people standing on the dam. "Put out the water!" Their laughter rang out, as the fire chief, Mr. Durham, got down from his fire engine near the dam. Meanwhile, a number of men in blue uniforms with shiny red helmets jumped down from the sides of the fire engine. They lined up, waiting for orders from the chief, who had climbed the dam. The men dispersed in front of him, revealing Daniel's slight frame that had been lost among them. The outline of Jirjis, who seemed preoccupied, also appeared.

Abu Jabbar stood there as well. The three men (the most prominent personalities in the camp, from the point of view of the management) followed Mr. Durham, then stood silently behind him, while he
proceeded to survey the sea that had sprung up in the desert. The breeze
still carried the sound of persistent barking from the rig. "Is there a dog
on the rig?" the man asked in astonishment, turning toward Daniel.

"Yes, sir."

"And the rig operator?"

"Him as well, sir!"

Daniel didn't reply. Abu Jabbar and Jirjis were also at a loss. No one
knew what had made Fawzi not notice the approaching flood. Perhaps
he had been asleep, waiting for the trucks to come back. Perhaps he had
been daydreaming or overcome by worry. Perhaps he had been caught
up playing with his dog and had not noticed as the flood of water covered the parched earth in minutes. Fawzi was calling out the names of
his colleagues who took shifts with him on the rig, and the names of his
other friends, including Muzhir, who took his clothes off and went forward in his underclothes to go down to the water, but with a wave of his
hand the fire chief told him to stop. Muzhir wrapped his arms around
his naked chest and stayed there, waiting. Mr. Durham asked his chief
of staff to bring two firemen and ordered one of them to go down to
the water. The men in the camp watched the water making its way up
the body of the fireman who had rested his arms on the side of the
dam and cautiously gone down to the water, crawling on all fours. Then
they saw him release his hands from the dam and swim. He wasn't sure
how high the water level had risen. When his feet touched the ground
he stood up straight. At this point the fire chief and the people in the
camp realized the extent of the flood that was surrounding them. They
saw the water wetting the yellow buttons of the top pockets of the fireman's suit. Mr. Durham left the man where he was and asked his most
senior man, with the help of the electricians who were standing beside
their lorry, to gather together the searchlights in one place. He was trying to make a path of light across the water. But what they produced
seemed more like a short finger of bright water, pointing toward the

far-off shape of the rig. Mr. Durham turned to the other fireman and ordered him to go down with his colleague and fetch the dog and its owner. Muzhir came forward as a volunteer.

"Let me go with them, sir, Fawzi is my friend!"

"All right!"

As they waded into the water, the three figures left long scars behind them on the gleaming surface that quickly healed. The men slowly made their way from the dam. Then they disappeared from view between the dark water and the brooding sky. The quivering silver threads remained behind them in the patch of light, then they too disappeared. It was as if the men—who had walked into the water a short time ago under the gaze of the entire camp—were just an apparition.

The people standing on the dam didn't pay any attention to the truck that had stopped a short distance away, but Mr. Jirjis noticed it and called out in relief, "The boss has come—Mr. Fox!"

Daniel called out to the people standing on the dam, "No one is to stay. Everyone get down quickly!"

This time his voice seemed to have authority. It derived its power from the presence of Mr. Fox, who got out of the truck and nimbly climbed the dam. The men quickly got down and gathered at the bottom, while Mr. Fox started talking to the fire chief. From time to time he would turn round and look at the public road, over the tops of the tents that nestled obediently inside the camp perimeter. A small dark vehicle then appeared on the road from the direction of the managers' quarter, stretching a long yellow tongue over the ground in front of it. When it entered the camp enclosure and stopped beside the other vehicles, three men got out: Senior Engineer Macaulay, Engineer Husam Hilmi, and a neat, dark-skinned young man with a pipe in his mouth. The five men stood on the dam consulting among themselves. The senior fireman brought them hand lamps, and they went off, walking slowly, each one with a yellow disk of light dancing in front of him on the ground (they were inspecting the earth of the dam, on which I had spent several hours writing and gazing at the desert, like a group of doctors examining a sick body, without any of them being able, or

70

perhaps not wanting, to express a decisive view about the treatment). As I looked at them, I asked myself: do you suppose that all this time I had been supporting my weight on a flimsy dam that could collapse at any moment, under any pressure? The workmen used to speak openly about the possibilities; some of them would place bets on the dam's solid structure, while others would raise doubts about its holding up in the event of a flood. It was a continual debate, though usually in hushed voices. The water surrounded the camp on three sides, then came up against the edge of the public road, which was itself like a long dam. If it hadn't been for that road, which ran over a raised piece of land, the flood waters would have submerged everything on the other side—offices, workshops, stores, warehouses, the managers' quarter, palm groves, and the far-off village—then continued its broad sweep before mingling with the waters of the Shatt al-Arab. The dam—which extended beside the desert for around five hundred meters, and whose sides were around half this length—seemed on the surface to be sound, but the repeated stops of the group of managers and engineers, and the long discussions taking place between them while they were there above it, suggested that there was a flaw. The men watched them moving away, then climbing again onto the back of the dam. The dog was still barking hoarsely from time to time, though it soon quietened down. The men saw the lights on the rig go out. A long time elapsed after that, as the men in the camp fastened their eyes on the darkness of the water, beyond the finger of light cast by the searchlights. Then, from the heart of the total darkness, one could hear the lapping of water accompanied by vague voices of men calling out to each other.

Meanwhile, the five men who had been absorbed in looking for signs of weakness on the face of the dam returned hurriedly, and the men in the camp came down to clear a path for them. When the five men reached the place they had started from, they began to walk more slowly, examining the other half of the dam. The people in the camp wanted to see the rig operator and his dog when they returned, so they came down again. The voices of the men who had waded into the water began to reach them more clearly. Then four heads appeared, as they

71

arrived at the edge of the illuminated area. One of those standing there called out, "They're back, everyone!"

"And Fawzi?"

"He's with them! Can't you see him? Carrying his brother in his arms!"

It was easy to recognize the two firemen from the shine of their metal boots. One of them was acting as a guide for the rig operator, so that he wouldn't fall into a hole, while the second was bringing up the rear, ready to hurry to help if necessary. Then two dark heads appeared, moving in the middle. When the picture became clearer, Fawzi appeared, carrying his dog, while Muzhir, with his bare chest, was walking through the water beside him.

"He's killing himself for that ungrateful dog!" said one of those standing there in confusion.

"Dearer to him than his son . . . if he had a son!" said another.

Fawzi carried his dog in his arms. One side of the animal's body flopped down into the water but the dog seemed relaxed in its master's arms, turning its head to look at the faces moving above the dam with moist eyes, as if he had been crying a short time before.

"Thank God you're safe! We were saying . . . ." some voices said.

"But what were you doing when . . . ?"

"Asleep."

"Come up, come up, give us your hand!"

They greeted him jokingly, laughing among themselves. They were not much bothered by the problem of the flood at that moment, for they didn't have anything precious to fear for, just their clothes and some other small things. Fawzi did not bother with them. Muzhir and the two firemen helped him to climb the muddy side of the dam. When he finally put his feet on dry ground, the water dripped from his soaked clothes and the mud covered his feet. He put the dog down gently. He seemed cross that they had left it hanging there for a long time in the drilling rig. When one of the men tried to apologize, the dog shook its soaking body and sprayed the bystanders with a spurt of flying water, and they leaped away, half angry, half laughing. Fawzi left

72

them and moved down from the dam followed by his dog with its head bowed. Muzhir found his clothes, which he had left behind him on the ground, picked them up, and followed him. The material of his short, sodden underclothes was clinging to the swarthy skin of his body, highlighting his thighs and the details of his private parts.

At that moment, Daniel hurried up in alarm, gesturing to the men with his stubby arms. "We must evacuate the camp at once! The boss says at once!"

"Where are we to go? Where?"

Daniel left that question in the air. "Truck drivers!" he shouted, looking at their faces. "I want all the truck drivers!"

"Where to?"

Despite their predictions, and despite the floodwaters that were throwing all their weight against the dam, the order to evacuate came as a surprise to the people in the camp. (Only a few moments before, they had been amusing themselves looking at Fawzi and his dog, and now they were ordering them to leave their tents at once.) As voices were raised and merged with one another, chaos reigned. The men split up, shouting and racing each other, as they dispersed along the paths. They were swallowed up by the tents that were no longer silent, filled with their voices and agitated movements as they gathered up their clothes and meager possessions, getting ready to travel to another safe refuge, out of reach of the flood waters . . . perhaps.

8

Searching the Foxhole

This is a comfortable place!

We spread our bedding on the ground, side by side, in the gap between the tables and steel cupboards in the office. "And we'll be on our own, you and I," said Jirjis happily.

The Indian clerk Fadlallah was lying sick in the project hospital in Basra. Abdallah and the caretaker Mazlum were living in the village. So we would be alone, he and I. What would my life be like with him . . . this man who usually glowered when working?

He tapped on his pillow with his veined hand. "We'll be free, with no one to disturb us!"

He spoke as if our stay in the management building would be lasting a long time. I heard our neighbors in the other rooms (they worked in accounts and auditing) arranging their things that they had brought with them from the camp, getting ready to stay for the night like us. I could hear the sound of footsteps and chatter on the balcony. Those confused questions with which people usually greet any sudden upset in the course of the life to which they have become accustomed; then the rush to express the feelings that come in the wake of some trial, when things settle down and people realize that their losses were not really so great, and that they are still alive.

Jirjis contemplated his bedding calmly, then opened his case. He first took out three or four boxes of medicine, which he arranged along the edge of the table next to his bed, then busied himself taking out the clothes he needed. I left him with his bag and stood at the window, trying to make out the main features of the camp we had just left, but I couldn't make out anything in the darkness of the night. The camp had been abandoned in a short space of time by the people staying there, then everyone had gone away, leaving the camp to its anticipated fate. The lights had gone out, everything had become dark, and that place— which only a short time previously had been a home and a refuge— became just part of the dark night. But how did things move so fast: how did those still waters that from a distance looked like a deceptive mirage, colored by the rays of the setting sun, turn into a flood sweeping over everything in its path?

"Aren't you changing your clothes?" asked Jirjis, standing on his bed as he undressed. His ribs could be seen clearly under his pale, wrinkled skin, and the thinness of his legs was apparent. I turned my face away, took out my dishdasha and my sandals and washing things and left the room. When I came back, I found him on the balcony on his way to the bathroom as well, carrying his soap and his small yellow towel slung over his shoulder—"Hey, son, is there any hot water?"

His eagerness for hot water that spring evening puzzled me. I told him that there was hot water, then went into the office carrying my shoes, the clothes I had taken off, and my bath things. I left my shoes on the floor, hung the clothes I had taken off on a peg in the corner, and put my soap, tube of toothpaste, and toothbrush on the edge of Abdallah the clerk's table. (It made a strange sight in the midst of the files and typewriter.) I sat down on my bed contemplating our new residence, how it looked at night and how it might turn into something like a hotel. I saw the door to Mr. Fox's room, opening onto a dark empty space. What secrets do you suppose lurked in that darkness that I could feel enticing me, holding my hand, and drawing me on to penetrate it and explore Mr. Fox's hidden world? What if I tried to discover something to expose the doings of this devious man? I jumped up. What if Jirjis surprised you inside the manager's room? But Jirjis wouldn't come back now! And if he did come back? said the hesitant

75

voice, with a hint of warning. Go in, don't waste time! I was spurred on by the other voice, which wanted me to expose what went on, in spite of the dangers. I went up to the door of the room and stepped into the dark interior. I touched the cold wall with my fingers. I discovered the light switches, and the place lit up. I started back, as if the light switch I had pressed with my finger had not simply spread light through the room space, but had caused an explosion for everyone to hear and come running, to stare into my startled face. The blinds were down, and in the still air of the room were the remnants of the smell of that foul tobacco that Mr. Fox always filled his pipe with, the smell that gave him away wherever he went, and indicated that he had sat down in this place, or passed this way. The steel safe was secure on its firm wooden base, closed on the secrets inside it. The man was not so stupid as to leave an important document thrown down carelessly on his desk. Nonetheless, even intelligent people sometimes make mistakes, and sometimes forget. I went closer to the desk. He was there, sitting in front of me behind his desk, in his full splendor, with his gray eyes, his blond, pointed beard, and his clipped mustache, looking at me with surprise and disapproval. His desk was clean. The large glass pane that covered the surface of the desk glistened under the light (Mazlum the caretaker had wiped all traces of dust from it before going back to his house in the village). There was nothing on the pane of glass except for a penholder on a base of white marble, with two or three pens standing up from it like long black fingers. There was also—sleeping calmly on the glass pane—the knife made in the shape of a dagger, with which he opened the envelopes of his private mail, or the official letters stamped with the word 'Secret,' which Jirjis would not dare to open. The intercom and black telephones all stared at me in silent curiosity. Everything in the room was staring at me doubtfully as if I were a thief or a spy. I could hear a voice inside my head advising me to leave quickly, but the room was also pulling me toward it, and silently shackling me. I saw just a single sheet of paper left in the in-tray, a paper that aroused no interest. It contained the translation of a small news item about a strike by Iraqi workers in the Habbaniya camp, published in one of

76

the local newspapers. Jirjis had ordered me that morning to translate it for the manager to read. I was about to leave the room after an unsuccessful mission—before Jirjis could see the light peeping through the material of the curtains and come running—when I noticed on the underside of the single sheet of paper some words written in a different hand. This was the manager's handwriting and the color of the ink that he always used! I snatched the piece of paper and read the words in English: "Dangerous sign! More care to be taken here. Enquire from B.C.B. for more details."

What did Mr. Fox mean by these words? I left the paper in its place. I switched off the light so that the darkness returned and settled in its place. I went out. But who was B.C.B.? A person or an organization? Could it be . . . ? I heard Jirjis's footsteps approaching on the balcony, and left the room at the critical moment. Jirjis came in, small drops of water still clinging to his gray hair. He seemed happy.

"Hot water is a blessing from God!"

He put his washing things under the table beside his bed, and hung his towel on the peg. I sat on my bed so as not to arouse his suspicions by standing up for no apparent reason in the middle of the room.

"In the camp, we were deprived. Hot water, when you wash your face and arms. Before going to bed . . . ." He did not finish, however, but walked between the edge of the bed and the tables toward the manager's room, shut the door, and locked it.

"Muhammed, the boss's room is not our business. We're . . ."

Had he noticed something, do you suppose? He pulled the key out of the door, stumbling against the sides of his bed, walked over to the peg in the corner, took his bunch of keys out of his jacket which was hanging among the other clothes, then walked over to his desk. Then he opened one of the drawers, put the key to the door of the manager's room inside and shut it. He did all this with a determined motion, his face suddenly covered with an "official" look—a mask devoid of affection, which his subordinates could not easily penetrate. When he was satisfied that the manager's room could not be violated, he breathed a sigh of relief and threw his "work mask" from his face. He spoke to me, holding one glass in each hand, and holding his arms out in front of him as if they were full, "All our things would have been lost if the boss hadn't ordered the camp to be evacuated at once!"

His thin fingers around the two glasses seemed pale and dry, as if they were made of wax. I don't think he had noticed anything, or he would not have spoken to me so openly. . Just to be on the safe side I decided to play along.

"That's right," I agreed. He looked at me without speaking from behind his glasses.

"Don't you drink water while you're sleeping . . . I mean, during the night?"

I told him that I didn't drink water after my head had hit the pillow.

"You're lucky, you're still too young for these nuisances. My blood pressure turns my mouth into a piece of wood—not to mention this wretched prostate!"

With his shattered posture and his complaining tone, he seemed like a crippled old woman. Was this the chief clerk who imposed his rule on us during the day, the next in line to Mr. Fox? This wretched creature, surrounded by illnesses and oppressed by life? The man paid a lot of attention to his health and always tried to walk with an upright bearing. During the day—in winter especially—if the weather was fine, I would see him during the afternoon rest period, after coming back from lunch in the camp, standing in the headquarters garden, exposing his body to the rays of the sun. Every few minutes he would turn one side of his body toward the sun—sometimes his back, some- times his left side and sometimes his right. He would give his chest an extra allowance of sunlight, saying that that would strengthen his heart and lungs and invigorate his circulation. But his aging cells let him down and hindered his attempts to keep his body fit. He had lost his youth a long time ago, and time continued to press heavily on him day after day.

Jirjis picked up his two glasses and left the room. I looked at the locked door of the manager's room. B.C.B.—was it an organization or a person? If I found out, then perhaps I would have discovered the identity of the party to which Mr. Fox was sending all the information he was gathering about events in this town. I would ask Engineer Husam Hilmi, if I met him again. He might know. He lived in Britain for a long time, and he is now living among them in the managers' quarter, and must know this sort of riddle. I sank onto my bed and rested my head on the pillow. How restful it would be to sleep on solid ground that did not shake underneath you. The slats of my bed in the camp dangled more day by day, so that I would only enjoy a comfortable sleep once a week or fortnight when I went home and threw my exhausted body down on our wooden bed beside my wife.

Jirjis came back from the washhouse carrying his two glasses carefully. The water in the big glass reached a little over halfway, while the smaller cup was full. I sat on my bed as he came in, in deference to his age and seniority. I saw him put the big cup on the table next to the medicine boxes, and the other (the full one) on the ground near to his pillow, so that he could stretch out his hand and take a sip from it whenever he felt thirsty during the night. After he was satisfied that he had put each glass in its place, he turned toward me, "At first, they were different . . . ."

I didn't understand what he was talking about. I saw him take his boots off and sit on his bed. He leaned against a table leg behind him and gave a sigh of contentment. "I mean, the engineers."

He seemed happy, sitting on his bed, having washed his face with warm water and gotten ready for sleep. He seemed happy, like an exhausted traveler who had found a place to rest at the end of a long journey, before night took him by surprise. Stretching his hand out to one of the medicine bottles, he went on, "Mr. Macaulay believed that the dam would withstand the pressure. It's true that there were some small cracks in the wall, but there weren't . . . ."

His fingers were meanwhile unscrewing the cap of the bottle.

"Engineer Sultan al-Imari supported Mr. Fox, but Engineer Husam . . . ."

His fingers took a tablet from the bottle and put it on his tongue, while his other hand brought him the glass of water.

79

"He said that the dam might . . . ." He washed the tablet down with a gulp of water, then, as his hand put the glass back in its place, said, ". . . have collapsed before dawn!"

"You mean, it was Engineer Husam who decided to evacuate the camp?"

He laughed quietly, took off his glasses and put them on the table. He looked up with a new face, a slightly strange face, with small and duller eyes. The skin in the part of his face hidden by his glasses was duller as well. The glasses were a part of the features we had got used to seeing in his face, and when he took them off, his face seemed naked or even stripped. He rubbed his eyes, then opened them as far as they would go, and took hold of his kafiyyeh that he had left on his pillow.

"Muhammad, my son. Decisions like these are only taken by the boss."

He put his kafiyyeh on his head and wrapped the edges around his neck. He looked like an old man from the country.

"So Mr. Fox relied on Engineer Husam's opinion?"

"Yes, although he hates him."

"Why does he hate him?"

"An inexperienced youth. And they say that he messes around with the English managers' wives. Just rumors!"

Jirjis looked at me a little doubtfully. "Muhammad, please do not say things like this in front of anyone. They might think that I . . . ."

I told him that he could rest assured on that count. "The British, my son, don't hesitate to take decisions when their interests are threatened. Do you know how much the materials stored in the camp were worth?"

I told him that I didn't know. "Thousands of dinars! Thousands! My son, I'm afraid you're half asleep, and I . . . ."

"No, I'm not half asleep," I said to him. He looked at me for a bit without saying anything. He seemed hesitant. Finally he spoke. "There was another disagreement. This time between the boss, our manager, and this engineer. I mean, Husam Hilmi."

I could hear the sound of footsteps on the balcony, and said nothing until the sound had disappeared.

"This man, when he saw that the boss relied on his opinion, tried to interfere in matters that did not concern him. He proposed that the workers should move from the camp to . . . to . . . ."

"Where, Abu Basil?"

He looked at me with incomprehension. He would have liked to have taken back the words he had uttered, but they just came out and went around the place. Perhaps he then said to himself that mentioning part of the truth and leaving it to others to guess the rest as they fancied was more dangerous than telling the whole truth, so he decided to come out with everything he knew.

"Mr. Muhammad, what I am going to say to you now is known to no one except for myself and Daniel and Abu Jabbar. We were walking behind them on the dam. I don't want it repeated. If it is repeated, it will become like, 'Who said this? Who said that?'"

"Don't worry, Abu Basil!"

"This engineer is not just naïve, he is also mad. Imagine, he proposed that the administration should move all the people in the camp to the managers' quarter!"

"But how? Are there vacant spaces for more housing?"

"No. But he suggested they stay in the new managers' club building. He said the building was big enough and still needed decoration and so, until the camp building was complete, we could stay there."

"A really bold idea!" I said smiling.

"A mad idea! Imagine, all that number of men with their temperaments that you know well! Amid those honorable English families!"

"And Engineer Husam suggested that ?"

"I wouldn't have believed it of him. Even this new Iraqi engineer, Sultan al-Imari, didn't like the idea."

"And what did Mr. Fox say?"

"He rejected it, of course. 'Impossible, Mr. Hilmi,' he said in front of the others. 'That is a mad idea!' Then he closed the matter and issued his decision to move us to the work areas. Aren't you happy here?"

"Very happy. But . . . ."

We were like two ghosts, sitting face to face, speaking alone in the silence of the steel tables and the cupboards full of the workers' files, stuffed with reports and warning notes, and things passed on by spying eyes.

"These British, my son, they don't like people who stand up to them. As for those who serve them . . . ."

I looked at him slightly puzzled, without saying anything. In all the months I had spent with him in the HQ, he had never spoken to me this frankly; he had never spoken to me at length in this way, and never entrusted me with a secret. Then we came to live in the same place and everything changed.

"I haven't spoken to you about what they did for the sake of my son, who studies with them, over there."

The tone of his voice changed as if someone else had taken his place and was speaking on his behalf. His voice brimmed with tenderness and affection.

"Basil is my oldest son. You know, imagine, it was they who got him accepted at the University of Cardiff, and arranged his travel."

I saw him stand up. "If you want, we could leave one of the lamps alight during the night. Some people prefer it."

"There's no need for that," I said. "I'm used to sleeping in the dark. And there's a bit of light that comes from. . . ." He went over to the light switches and turned off all the lights in the room. A little light from the lamps on the balcony came in to us through an opening in the door and the windows, touching some parts of the surface of the tables, the cupboards, and the ground, but most things in the room were clothed in gray. As he went back to his bed I heard him say, "You wouldn't believe me if I told you . . . that Mr. Reynolds, the director general of management and personnel in Project HQ, found him the lodgings he is living in now himself. With a nice old English lady! I mean, from all this talk . . . ."

He sat down on his bed again and got ready to sleep. I waited for him to lie down before I could lie down on my bed too. I was tired.

"You haven't seen Mr. Reynolds. A humble man, who jokes with young and old alike. You'll see him one day, he sometimes visits us."

The name Reynolds begins with "R," so it can't be him that was meant by those three letters that Mr. Fox wrote on the sheet of paper.

"Muhammad, my lad, you're dizzy. It's better for us to sleep. Goodnight!"

He turned his back on me, still sitting where he was. He didn't lie down. I noticed his hand stretch out to his face. He seemed to be scratching the skin on his face, or perhaps wiping his mouth. Then I saw his hand move away from his face, rise a little over his head in the air, and touch the big cup on the table. I heard the plop of something in the water in the cup, and was surprised by the cup laughing in my face! Up until then, I had always believed that the small white teeth, carefully arranged inside his mouth were his natural teeth that he had been able to look after carefully, just like everything else that belonged to him. He had turned his face away from me and did not venture to talk to me again. I lay down too. In my imagination, there was the face of an aged woman bent down on the pillow, with a toothless mouth and two sunken cheeks. In the following days it became hard for me to look at the face with which he greeted me during daylight hours without seeing the other face, his aged face that he laid down on the pillow at the end of every day.

Tiredness was creeping over me like a mirage of glistening water. Before I became submerged in its magical depths, I was aware of Jirjis getting out of bed and leaving the room to go to the toilet. He continued moving back and forth between his bed and the lavatory all night. Every time he got out of bed or returned to it, I would start up from sleep, despite the fact that he was moving extremely carefully. I could see his set of false teeth soaking in the water inside the cup that smiled in the darkness on the table, the cold, stupid laugh that we see on the face of a skeleton.

When I woke up in the morning, after a patchy sleep, I found the floor beside me bare and the room deserted. Jirjis's bed had disappeared from its place. Our neighbors in the other headquarters rooms were getting ready for another day's work. The morning breeze that poured through the windows with the first rays of the new day's sun bore with it the smell of tea, bread, and fried eggs. I was busy folding up my bed when Jirjis came in wearing his day face, his official face.

"Muhammad," he said in an imperious tone. "Put your bed on the balcony. It's not right . . . ."

What had happened to his friendly words in the night?

"Good morning!"

"Sorry, good morning! The place needs to be tidied in case someone comes."

I picked up my bed and put it on the balcony. I saw several folded up beds resting here and there beside the walls along three sides of the building. They looked odd in the middle of headquarters. In the barren garden the willow trees stood almost still, their small yellow leaves shining in the sunlight. Those without work were standing behind the fence. I was struck by the fact that there were not many of them, just the tall man, Farhan al-Abd, and four or five others. When I went back to the room to collect my washing things, I found Jirjis sitting behind his desk, flipping through his papers early in the morning. He seemed to have been affected by the HQ atmosphere that reveals all its details to the eye in the morning light (papers, files, telephone, typewriter, steel tables, and cupboards) and was bent over his papers even before the work siren told him he had to be there. I asked him where we should eat.

"In the stores courtyard," he said. "Behind the building. But don't be late."

I washed, changed my clothes, and went behind the building. The canteens and tables for food had been hastily set up under one of the long roofs of the storehouses. Men were eating breakfast standing up, or sitting on the ground with their trays of food in front of them. I stood in the queue. Istifan spotted me as he carried his breakfast back from the cooks. He stopped, and I asked him where he had spent the night. He told me that he had spent the night in the workshop with Muzhir, that Abu Jabbar had been in the stores with

Daniel, and that Hussein had spent the night in the engineering department. So after being together in one tent, we had all spent the night in different places.

Hussein was eating his food standing among the men who had gathered around the tables, while Muzhir was sitting on the ground. There was no trace of Abu Jabbar, who ate before everyone else. Istifan took his food and moved away from me, disappearing among the men who were busy with their food, laughing and gossiping in the space that opened up to the clear sky. Their faces were brushed by an invigorating spring breeze. I felt happy. The atmosphere that enveloped the place was a sort of holiday atmosphere in which everyone could be happy. As I took my food from the hand of the cook, though, I was disturbed by eyes that I found staring from behind the fence, where a group of unemployed men were standing, with some old men and vagrants. As if the birds of the night had brought them the news, so they had drifted in from the town and the neighboring villages at dawn, to brush their bodies against the wires of the fence, or dig into the ground with their feet, trying to carve out a path to the paradise of food. Meanwhile, the men stood silently, looking at us, at the food and at the cooks, looking and waiting silently. My appetite subsided at once. But that was on the first day when their looks initially surprised me . After I had seen some of the cooks hand them leftovers over the fence, I persuaded myself that no one in this world would be dying of hunger (so after that I could take my food without feeling guilty). Nonetheless, I still occupied myself by talking to Istifan or listening to the workmen chattering, and avoided looking at those men. At the same time I avoided approaching Hussein, who tried, when I met him at midday, to make them the subject of a political discussion.

He said that the future for them was in the afterlife, and he spoke of their present misery with passion as he laid into his food with gusto. I told him that the important thing was today, this hour, now. He told me that I was thinking in a simple, emotional way. While he was talking and expounding the evidence for his views, I was gazing far away to the lake in the desert, on the other side of the road. The tents, which Daniel had not found time to take down before the dam burst, looked like a herd of buffaloes floating on the water. The remaining parts of the dam, the parts that had resisted the pressure of the flood, stood here and there, abandoned, surrounded by water on every side. I turned my gaze to the new camp, half a mile away from the submerged camp. The wide dam that the project management had built around the camp seemed secure and solid. Inside could be seen rows of rooms in neat lines. But when would we be moving there? The men said that the management was very concerned, because it wanted to evacuate us from the work area quickly. So perhaps we would be moving to our new quarters in a couple of weeks.

How I wished that were true, to get away from those eyes staring from behind the fence, stripping us and raking our faces without mercy!

9
Dancing to the Tune
of the Tango

E very beginning of a new chapter appears deceptive and murky, but once you have begun, you have to carry on, telling what happened next, and relating the whole story. Above all, you have to recover in your mind the details of events that passed over you, as they come back to you now. Okay . . . .

The floodwaters had finally retreated from the desert. They left behind them soil covered with a layer of salt whiter and thicker than the one that had covered it before the flood. Your old camp—from which the waters had driven you in the dead of night—looked like a fishermen's village that had been hit by a storm: ripped tents, rusty metal poles bent toward the ground, pools of white mud. The salt was the only thing that more or less stayed the same, drowning everything. Meanwhile, you began to feel constrained in your temporary lodgings in the work area, eating, sleeping, and working in the same place. So your move after about a month to the new camp was to be the beginning of a life that you could say was a little more comfortable. The prefabricated rooms were arranged in long rows looking over roofed balconies. Once again you were living together, Abu Jabbar, Muzhir, Istifan, Hussein; there was no other choice. But at least the rooms in the camp were bigger than the tents, and had little cupboards; so you could keep the pages of your novel in the drawer and lock it with a key, confident that no one would be able to reach it or read what was in it. We all became a bit happier; but Istifan was the happiest of all to move to the camp, for on the same day he had gone down to the village, bought a nightingale, and hung its cage made of palm leaves over his bed. Istifan was whistling to the nightingale, trying to get it to sing, when Muzhir, looking at the bird, said, "Don't waste your time with it! This nightingale will never sing!"

He looked at him in confusion. "This is a wild nightingale," Muzhir explained. "They caught it as an adult. Birds like that will never sing in a cage."

Istifan's face looked sad. "Be patient, perhaps he'll sing tomorrow," you said, to console him, without yourself believing what you had said.

Istifan died a few months later, with the bird watching the world—silent and alert—from behind the palm fronds, still refusing to sing. Fortunately, Istifan had prepared another method of amusement before his death. His friend Dankha, who lived with his friends in the room next door, had bought a gramophone and three records once (tango, waltz, and foxtrot) and, when it was nighttime, they would call to Istifan from the other side of the wall to dance with them (man with man) to the rhythms of western music.

One of Dankha's three records was playing on the turntable in the room next door. The sound of the music mingled with the voices of several men, while Abu Jabbar, in your own room here, was busy setting up the drinks table, helped by Muzhir, Hussein, and Istifan, each one of whom prepared something, while you sat on your bed trying to read (in reality, you were glued to your book so that you wouldn't have to join them for a drink, then complain of a headache all next day). Meanwhile, Dankha's voice rang out from behind the plywood wall, above the wave of men's shouting and the tunes of the music, calling out in Assyrian, "Istifan, come here!"

When Istifan heard the urgent call, he abandoned whatever was in his hand. "Excuse me, everybody—Dankha's got a party tonight!"

Then he left the room. Abu Jabbar shouted after him, "You didn't tell us if you'll be leading or following," and let out a resounding laugh that made his belly tremble.

The three men sat round the table getting ready to drink.

"In my whole life, and I'm now nearly sixty, I've never seen or heard of a dance party where a man dances with a man . . . no, by God!"

Abu Jabbar took hold of the bottle of arrack by its middle, lifted it up from the table and proceeded to pour it into his friends' glasses.

"This is life! What do you want them to do?" said Muzhir, watching the transparent liquid flowing from the mouth of the bottle and dropping into his glass.

Hussein gave him a sideways, distasteful glance, and said, "You can have your opinion. When there's no woman to be found, a man will do instead!"

Muzhir's hand started groping in a vague movement for something between the plates, as if he had forgotten what he had wanted to get when he stretched it out the first time. Then his hand found the plate of ice and his fingers took a small piece, which he dropped into the glass in front of him. Hussein watched his agitated movements and said insistently, "That's your view!"

Meanwhile, Abu Jabbar was busy getting his glass ready with the skill of a chemist mixing his elements in the laboratory, as Muzhir muttered, "In situations like this, I . . . ."

Hussein smiled sarcastically, "Only . . . ."

"Of course. Otherwise, where would they get women from? Do you want them to go down to the village, knocking on doors for Fadaa, Nashmiya, and Kharnaba?"

Abu Jabbar laughed in amusement, his eyes fixed on his brimming glass, but Hussein said to Muzhir sharply, "Are you making fun of the poor women of the town?"

Abu Jabbar looked at Hussein angrily and weighed into their tense conversation, raising his glass and his voice at the same time, "To the health of all the women in the world!"

Muzhir and Hussein raised their glasses and everyone drank a toast to all women, then returned their glasses to the table. A tense silence descended on the gathering, despite the shouting and the music that reached them from behind the wall. Meanwhile, the ceiling fan continued turning above their heads, making a soft squeaking sound against the ceiling supports, while the shadows from its three revolving blades fell on the wall. Some of the shadows were broken up by the palm branches that squatted in their place at the bottom of the birdcage, silently lapping up the downpour of light and shadows that rained down on the cage with no respite. Abu Jabbar fidgeted in his place. No, this wasn't the beginning he liked for his drinking sessions. When he sat down to drink, he liked to be surrounded by smiling faces that believed—or at least pretended to believe—what he was saying, and laughed at his amusing stories, regardless of whether the drinkers liked or disliked him in the depths of their hearts. But this Hussein, ever since he had come to share their quarters, had become like a thorn in the throat. He couldn't either swallow it or get rid of it and relax.

"A proper dance, my friends, would be the one I saw a week ago," he said in a jolly voice to break the silence. "When the managers celebrated the opening of their new club!"

They heard the sound of panting on the balcony, then a small white bitch passed in front of the door, followed a moment later by a pack of six or seven dogs. "They're having a party as well!" said Abu Jabbar with a laugh. But no one else laughed. He took a slice of cucumber from a plate and slipped it into his mouth. "The important thing is, I saw amazing things that night!"

Muzhir seemed relaxed at Abu Jabbar's attempt to change the direction of the conversation and break the siege of thorny questions about him, but Hussein carried on smoking with a frown on his face. "To be honest, I wasn't expecting to see the party. I went to the club on the orders of Engineer Sultan al-Imari. I took a number of workmen with me and went to supervise the place and move the furniture, and all the things that have to be done before a large party."

The sound of music behind the wall in the adjoining room had stopped, but the shouting continued as before. Abu Jabbar took another sip from his glass. At the start of an evening's drinking session, he always took three or four small sips at short intervals, a sip every few minutes; then after that he would drink slowly for the rest of the evening.

"An hour or so, perhaps less, before the start of the party, I finished the arrangements and sent the men who had come with me away. 'Abd al-Khaliq al-Mawla,' I said to myself, 'this is your chance. Don't waste it! Why don't you stay here and see with your own eyes how our English uncles dance?'"

Hussein interrupted him. "You mean your English uncles!" he said, disapprovingly.

"Okay, my uncles. But don't get annoyed, Abu Ali, don't get cross! The important thing is I asked Joseph the barman. 'Joseph, can I stay? To see the party?' But Joseph was . . . ."

Abu Jabbar's gaze fell on your face on the bed, with an open book in your hands and eyes that never left the page. "Muhammad, for God's sake stop reading now and listen to me!"

You told him you were listening to him. Abu Jabbar raised his voice to include you among his audience, as well as resisting the hubbub that was coming from behind the wall. The music had struck up again, though the dancing had not yet started.

"Joseph hesitated, then said, 'Okay, you can stay. But don't let Mr. Fox see you and make trouble for us. Sit with the guard outside. I'll send you food and drink later. Okay?'

"'Okay, Joseph,' I said, 'God preserve your wife.' First of all, the band members arrived from Basra, carrying black boxes, some big, some small. After they had eaten, they sat down in the middle of the large hall. They got out their instruments and each one started playing as they felt like, to tune their instruments . . . ta ta, dum dum, dum dum, those sorts of sounds."

Muzhir laughed, Hussein smiled too, and Abu Jabbar looked happy.

"The servants with their white waistcoats and black trousers were meanwhile moving between the tables, which were covered with white tablecloths, and which were still empty, waiting for the arrival of guests to sit around them and fill them with laughter and merriment. The servants put an ashtray here, and straightened a chair or the edge of a tablecloth there, things like that."

Muzhir took a sip from his glass and said, standing up, "Do you have to tell us all these details?"

"Where are you going?" asked Abu Jabbar, annoyed.

"To the toilet. Or do you want me . . . ?"

Hussein fixed Muzhir with a hostile, penetrating, sideways glance. (He had something against him.) Abu Jabbar turned toward you after his audience had become depleted.

"Hey, Muhammad, are you with us?"

You told him you were with them.

"At about eight o'clock, the guests' cars appeared, coming from Basra. Our own managers here in the area arrived on foot from their nearby houses, each one with his wife hanging on his arm, in her best outfit and walking just so."

From the next room came the sound of loud clapping and shouting. (At last, they'd agreed on something!) The wild nightingale became upset and began to flap its wings trying to escape, but without success. Every time it started to fly it collided with its prison wall and fell. When the applause behind the wall faded, the bird calmed down as well and stayed where it was at the bottom of his cage, panting, not knowing why those strange loud creatures should be frightening it during the night as well as the day. Abu Jabbar resumed speaking, "The big square in front of the club door became crowded with cars in less than half an hour. Some of the drivers got out and stood looking at the new club building, gazing at the colored lights everywhere, on the tree branches, on the palm trunks, on the wide windows, around the door frame, everywhere, as if it was a holiday evening! Other drivers stayed sitting in the darkness, inside their cars, smoking. They had a long evening's wait ahead of them."

"Where did they eat?" asked Hussein.

He looked at him in astonishment. "What do you mean?"

"The drivers you were talking about. Where did they eat?"

"I don't know, perhaps they went into the kitchen later," replied Abu Jabbar, annoyed. "I didn't pay any attention to them. The important thing is, I chose an unlit place for myself on the balcony, where the shadows from some trees fell. A place where no one could see me. Near one of the windows. I could see nearly everything from there. I think that it was around nine when the electricity engineer, Mr. Mark Doyle, came to the microphone and said something. I didn't understand exactly what he said but I heard the band strike up a dance tune. That was the beginning of the party. I wish you'd been with me, yes, really!"

In Dankha's room the tango record turned and the dancing really started behind the prefabricated wall, man dancing with man. Abu Jabbar laughed and shook his head, then continued the thread of his story, obviously enjoying himself.

"One minute, two minutes, three minutes passed, but no one moved. The dance floor in the middle was empty, the marble surface glimmering under the lights. The tables around the dance floor were all full of men and women, with bottles of whisky, brandy, gin, champagne, vodka, and beer, all the drinks in the world. Everything you could see was bright as a fish's belly. The women's arms, their round shoulders, their breasts and their bare backs; the bottles, the glasses, the plates of food and the ice trays, everything was shining! The whole world was bright!"

"Tell us something useful, Abu Jabbar, tell us something useful," said Hussein, interrupting once again.

"This *is* useful. Just don't be in such a hurry! The servants were continuously moving between the tables as the band continued playing. No one moved from their places, as if waiting for someone else to stand up. I saw Mr. Mark Doyle return to the mike and I heard his voice fill the space of the club as he called out the name of Engineer Sultan al-Imari, among other things."

Abu Jabbar made a sort of trumpet of his palms in front of his mouth and shouted at the top of his voice as if he were the party "sergeant," "Mr. and Mrs. Sultan al-Imari!"

After completing the announcement, he put down the trumpet.

"Applause and shouts from all sides. 'Yes, yes, Mrs. Imari! Mrs. Imari!'"

"And this Sultan, is his wife Iraqi or what?" asked Hussein with interest.

"His wife's English," said Abu Jabbar. "But what a woman! What a woman!"

"And did he bring her with him from Britain?"

These incidental questions from Hussein, which had nothing to do with the story of the party, annoyed Abu Jabbar. "No, they got married here," he said curtly, without interrupting the thread of his account. (Meanwhile, he was looking at you, the listener who seemed to be paying attention without interrupting.) "Let's stick to what's important. Sultan al-Imari got up with his wife. I'd seen her several times before. He sometimes sent me with some employees to do some jobs in his house."

"Like what?"

"Oh, for heaven's sake, do you have to know everything?"

Hussein took a sip from his glass and looked glum.

"The result was that Sultan and his wife both got up and started dancing to the music. But how they danced! I didn't know that my boss Sultan knew how to dance like that! Like a feather! And his wife was like a merry bird flapping her wings in the air!"

Muzhir came back in with his face and hands wet. Abu Jabbar stopped speaking and waited until he saw him sit down. Then he went on, "All the men's eyes were on her. The dance floor was theirs alone, for them to move over freely, clinging to one other, chest to chest, belly to belly, thighs intertwined, and her head on his shoulder. Then, with a slight gesture from Mr. Mark Doyle, the music stopped, and Sultan and his wife stopped dancing. Silence. Not a breath. Not a whisper. The whole dance floor was silent."

Meanwhile, someone was changing the disk on the gramophone in Dankha's room next door. The music played one of the other three tunes that were all that Dankha possessed. (We would continue for some time hearing these three records alternately, together with the dancers' feet scraping the concrete floor behind the wall, while Abu Jabbar went on with his story.)

"When the music stopped, Sultan and his wife went in different directions. He went to one of the English ladies and bowed to her. She turned to her husband and friends around the table, smiled at them, then got up with Sultan, who led her on to the dance floor. As for his wife, she seemed to be looking for someone, and afterward, of all the men who were at the party, do you know who she went to?"

Abu Jabbar looked at the expectant faces one by one, then answered his own question. "She went to that bastard, Husam Hilmi! She went to the table where he was sitting with his friends, took him by the hand, and pulled him up with her. The band played, and the four of them were dancing alone. After a few minutes the music stopped again. The dancers broke up. Each man took a woman for himself and each woman took a man. The bastard took the wife of the fire service chief. In a short time, perhaps a quarter of an hour or twenty minutes, the dance floor was packed from side to side. The music carried on playing as the men and women inside swayed about. And I, Abu Jabbar, betrayed my honor like a thief, as I devoured the women with my eyes."

His eyes shone (perhaps they were filling with tears). He became more animated as he tried to catch up with time, to make it cease its swift running, its harsh running, its uncaring running, then to go backward, to make it go backward just a week, so that he could relive the magic of that night again. Meanwhile, Hussein was looking at him without saying a word, with a mixture of contempt and astonishment.

"Believe me, kids, at that time I wished I could break the window and invade the place where they were. Could I take a woman for myself as well? Good God!"

"But you've got a wife!"

"You mean Umm Jabbar? The poor woman knows nothing about the world at all."

He was silent for a moment. He seemed sullen, as if he were thinking about his wife who was waiting for him in Basra, or maybe about something else. Then he started speaking again in a slightly sad tone. "I don't know how the time passed that night, it was astonishing. These accursed hours that creep up upon us here, minute by minute, and second by second, they passed there like lightning, praise be to God!"

"You're right," said Muzhir.

"It was nearly three in the morning and I was stuck to my chair, with my eyes on the window. The barman Joseph had sent me just one bottle of beer and some food with one of the servants at the start of the evening. After that he forgot me. The son of a whore!"

Hussein interrupted him with one of his incidental questions. "Tell me, Abu Jabbar, were there any other Iraqis at the party? Apart from your friend Sultan al-Imari?"

Abu Jabbar looked at him a little doubtfully. "What are you asking?"

"Just that!"

After a short hesitation, Abu Jabbar replied, most likely driven by a desire to boast of what he knew. "There were only a few Iraqi managers. You know. Let me think . . . there was Dr. Sami, yes, with his wife, an Iraqi lady, a real treat, may God protect her! I didn't see her dance that night. There was also the transport engineer, Akram Jadallah. He was dancing with his English wife. And I also saw him dance with Engineer Sultan's wife. Most of the men at the party danced with her that evening. I only saw her turn down one request. At the end of the night she took her shoes off and danced barefoot!"

Abu Jabbar stopped speaking and looked at the door. There, by the door, stood the little white dog that had passed by at the start of the evening. The pack of dogs, which had grown considerably bigger, were fidgeting behind her on the balcony.

"Come on, you lot, we're not in February! What's gotten into you?"

He raised his large arm, with its flabby flesh, in the face of the aroused bitch. "Go away, may God's anger be upon you!"

The bitch fled, followed by the panting pack. "It seems that the dogs' lust no longer knows the seasons!" said Muzhir.

"Let them mate as they will, you won't stop them."

"No, that's not what I meant. But haven't you noticed that there are more of them inside the camp than there are of us? Believe me, the day's coming when the dogs will be sleeping on the beds with us!"

"Abu Jabbar, please!" said Hussein. "That's enough of your dogs!"

Abu Jabbar smiled happily. "You mean, you liked what I was saying about the party? Okay, where had we gotten to?"

"You were talking about Engineer Sultan's wife." (You thought that actually Hussein wasn't so interested in the details of the dancing as about knowing the secrets of the people living there.)

"This amazing woman turned all the men's heads. She really drove them mad! But the best thing I saw and heard that evening, my friends, was when they started to dance to the tune of the Iraqi song 'Over the Palm Trees'!"

Abu Jabbar put his hands together, raised them over his head, and started to snap his fingers as he repeated the words of the song. The tone of his voice changed at once, turning sweet and mellifluous.

"Over the palm trees, high, how high!
Over the palm trees goes my eye!"

Muzhir gave a merry laugh and joined in the song, while Hussein continued smoking and drinking, looking at the pair of them without a word. Abu Jabbar and Muzhir's singing blended with the sound of the gramophone and the dancers' steps in the room next door.

Abu Jabbar seemed happy as he relived that evening's goings on, events that he had seen with his own eyes as he hid himself away in the darkness behind the window. Then he stopped singing, snapped his fingers, and wiped his eyes. "They were dancing like this!" he said.

He got down off his bed and stood in the middle of the room with his flabby body. He bent over a lady who had sat down with her husband and friends and asked her to dance with him. The lady got up at once, and he took her hand, then put his other arm on her bare back and tenderly drew her toward him. She laid her head submissively on his shoulder. He proceeded to dance with her, with half-closed eyelids, while the tango dance melody was repeating itself behind the plywood wall, from Dankha's disk. Muzhir applauded in delight, while Hussein sat smoking, his features unmoving, unaffected by all the hubbub and the emotions stirred by memories and drink. He carried on giving cool glances toward Muzhir, who was as happy as could be. (He had something in for him that night.) The woman lifted her head from his shoulder, and he smiled at her lovingly in gratitude, then took her gently by the hand to the table, to her husband and friends. He drew up her chair for her and whispered something tenderly as he said goodbye. "Tank you, tank you, madam! A thousand tanks, I am very grateful!"

Muzhir coughed as Abu Jabbar sat down again in his place. The sweat was pouring from his face and neck, and the wooden planks under his bed almost screamed. Abu Jabbar was pouring himself a fresh glass when the sound of a pipe rang out in our neighbors' room and the night air was filled with visions of mountains and valleys as the men started to dance the dabka. Their feet pounded the floor.

"This is perfect! Now go back to . . . !" said Abu Jabbar smiling.

The noise in the next room became louder, drowning out everyone's voices. They sat in silence, surrounded by an atmosphere of gloom. Perhaps none of them really knew the reasons. Shawkat, Daniel's assistant, passed by in front of the open door. A minute or two after he had gone by, the sound of the pipe in the next room ceased and the dancing stopped too. Then there was something like a quarrel. Raised voices and curses. Shawkat came back. The sound of the pipe that had stopped a little earlier could still almost be heard, still hanging in the air, like the dew after the rain has stopped. But the sound itself was fading . . . fading. On the balcony the men who had just been dancing the dabka dispersed, and their angry, vengeful voices dispersed as well.

"Basima, basima rabba!" That was Istifan's voice thanking his friend in Assyrian. Then he came into your room, red-faced, and glistening with sweat. Abu Jabbar looked at him in astonishment. "Hey, my boy! Your party ended quickly. Did you have a quarrel?"

"No," replied Istifan in a forlorn voice. "Daniel sent Shawkat to say that parties were forbidden in the camp after ten o'clock."

"And what's it got to do with him?"

98

"He says that even workmen have to sleep, and not be late for work the following morning."

"Never mind, come and drink with us!"

"Thanks, but I want to sleep!"

He started changing his clothes, so Abu Jabbar left him alone and went back to recounting his memories of the managers' party. The tone of his voice seemed loud in the middle of the silence that had recently descended. He was trying to gather together the threads of his intertwined memories, his wonderful memories of that night. But Hussein sat fidgeting—Hussein, the quarrelsome one who had something against Muzhir that night.

"After they got tired of dancing, they arranged some competitions: the prettiest lady, the prettiest dress, the nicest hair, the best pair of dancers, the best I don't know what! Strange and ingenious competitions dreamed up by the electrical engineer Mr. Doyle. That young Englishman was really the driving force behind the party!"

"Yes, indeed," said Hussein, interrupting him.

Abu Jabbar turned toward him and looked at him in silence. Perhaps he was trying to work out what he meant by that remark from the expression on his face. Then he said, impatiently, "Hussein, my boy, why are you angry at the whole world?"

"I'm not angry with the world, I'm just . . . ," said Hussein, stubbing his cigarette out amid the ash and butts in the ashtray.

"Just what, my boy?"

"Nothing, nothing, carry on talking!"

Abu Jabbar looked at you and then at Muzhir. "What was I saying?" he wondered.

"You're encouraging him," I told him.

"You were talking about the competitions at the party."

He looked at him gratefully. "Yes, yes, I was talking about the competitions."

"Goodnight," Istifan muttered quietly. He stretched out on the bed, then covered himself with the white embroidered sheet that his fiancée had given him on his last visit to his family in the north.

"Dr. Sami's wife won the prize for the most beautiful woman. A lady who'd come with her husband from the project base in Basra won the prize for the prettiest dress."

"It's getting cold, everyone!" said Muzhir, standing up. He went over to the ceiling fan switch, turned it off, and went back to his seat.

"As for the best pair of dancers, it was our manager, Engineer Sultan al-Imari and his wife. They were certainly the best dancers there!"

"So Sultan raised his standing that evening!" said Hussein.

Abu Jabbar ignored him and went on talking, looking at Muzhir.

"And your manager's wife, John Sullivan's wife, won the prize for the best hair. But she didn't dance much that evening. She was wearing a slightly loose dress . . . possibly pregnant!"

The fan stopped, and the shadows from its three blades stopped too on the plywood wall, and on the palm leaf cage where the nightingale sat in its place listening to Abu Jabbar's voice as he recounted his memories of that evening that had left him astonished.

"You mean, you even noticed that! You saw Madam pregnant from behind the window!" Muzhir exclaimed.

"I didn't miss anything!"

"She really is pregnant!"

"How do you know?" asked Hussein, jumping in.

"She's my manager's wife . . . she comes for her husband sometimes, so we see her."

"And what sort of relationship do you have with your manager, by the way?"

Muzhir was surprised and blushed. "My relationship? What do you mean?"

He didn't look into Hussein's face but lifted his glass and took a gulp. Then he looked at Abu Jabbar, who tried to change the subject. "Let me tell you what happened after that . . . ."

But Hussein interrupted him in a deliberate tone, "Thank you, Abu Jabbar. Please give brother Muzhir a chance to tell us what happened with John Sullivan."

"Perhaps it's amusing!" said Muzhir, putting his glass back on the table.

"What do you mean?"

"I know the truth about our relationship."

"There are lots of rumors!"

"Everything you've heard about me is a lie."

"Okay, what's the truth?"

"My relationship with him is like anyone's relationship with their boss at work!"

"That's right, Hussein, my boy!" shouted Abu Jabbar helpfully. "Like your relationship with Mr. Macaulay, or my relationship with Engineer Sultan al-Imari."

"Do you have a sexual relationship with Engineer Sultan?"

Abu Jabbar stared at him angrily and shook his head. Muzhir took the cigarette pack, and pulled a cigarette from it, but instead of lighting it he broke it between his fingers then threw the pieces onto the ground. Most likely, he didn't realize what his fingers had done. Then he stood up.

"Sit down, Muzhir," said Hussein, without emotion. "Where are you running off to?"

"Why should I run off? I'm not scared of anyone."

Muzhir sat down again in his place. Abu Jabbar was fidgeting, not knowing how to bring this critical argument to an end. As his bewildered, wandering glances fell on the cage hanging on the wall, he suddenly shouted out, "Quiet, everyone, please, quiet!"

He succeeded in turning their attention toward himself for a little, then said quietly, "Did you hear?" He proceeded to prick up his ears like a hunter listening for the sound of a bird from his hiding place, or for a movement among the bushes and thickets.

"What? What did we hear?" Hussein asked uneasily.

"It's finally sung! Istifan's nightingale has sung!" he said, pointing at the cage with his hand. "I heard it myself, tra-la-la, tra-la-la, like that. It's a pity Istifan's asleep just now!"

Hussein looked at him crossly. "Abu Jabbar, that's enough of these games. You mean . . . ?"

The he turned to Muzhir. "If these rumors are not true, then what are they?"

Abu Jabbar looked askance at him with obvious distaste. Most drinking sessions were spoiled by Hussein with his critical arguments. He was never happy with anything. And tonight he'd brought up the subject of Muzhir who was fidgeting as he defended himself.

"That means, you imagine that John Sullivan . . . he . . . ."

A triumphant smile suddenly flashed on Hussein's face. He hadn't been expecting this quick a confession.

"So it's not him it's you . . . ." said Abu Jabbar, his patience exhausted. "What Muzhir is doing is a real man's job. Enough, Hussein, my boy! Don't spoil the session! God spare your family!"

Istifan grunted a few unintelligible words from his bed. His voice— which no one had been expecting—suddenly intruded on the loaded atmosphere. They all turned toward his bed, and found him fast asleep. "The lad's sleeping!" said Abu Jabbar affectionately.

"No, Abu Jabbar, excuse me, you're mistaken!" said Hussein insistently. Abu Jabbar looked him, slightly surprised.

"It's you that's wrong. What Muzhir is getting up to is a whore's work, not the work of a real man! It's no different whether he's on top or underneath. So long as he gets his fee in the end!"

"Me . . . take a fee?" shouted Muzhir, angry at such an accusation.

"Of course, promotions, holidays, special treatment! What do you call riding beside the driver when the workmen go down to the city for a holiday?"

"A whore, a whore! I'm a free man, I'm your brother, your cousin!"

Muzhir jumped up and staggered out of the room, from drink and emotion combined.

Abu Jabbar shook his head sadly. "No, Hussein, my lad! No, you're quite wrong! It wasn't necessary . . . . If you had to talk to him about this, you should have taken him aside, by yourselves."

"Abu Jabbar," replied Hussein, without any feeling of regret. "I really intended to expose him in front of the two of you, you and Muhammad."

Abu Jabbar looked at him with something approaching pity. "We know, son, and everyone in the big camp knows."

"I know everyone knows, and he knows too, but so long as none of us blabs about what he knows, then everyone will be happy with his collective agreement to bury the secret!"

Abu Jabbar stared silently into his glass. Hussein had spoiled his evening, in spite of all the attempts he had made to liven it up. It was no use. This Hussein was like a thorn in the flesh with those big, fancy words of his. He always wanted to prove that he alone was in the right and that the others . . . he was responsible for all humanity! Abu Jabbar raised his head and looked at you. He was waiting for you to say something and give your opinion but you met his look with a disinterested gaze. You didn't like the confrontational way that Hussein had behaved, or his insults to Muzhir as if he was responsible for other people's behavior. Abu Jabbar looked away from you in despair and turned to Hussein, "How old are you now, my boy?"

For a long time he continued staring into the pitch-black night that had descended on the world outside the room.

10
Fox's Paradise

You said to yourself—as the palm trees, the edges of the track, the pipe lying on the ground, the salt of the desert, and everything else slowly receded—that the city was the story of a life, your life, and the lives of thousands of people that it enclosed between its walls, in its lanes, and its intersecting alleyways. It was layer upon layer of memories, sweet and bitter as colocynth, moments of joy and days of disaster, a complex mix made up of contradictions. You said to yourself that the city—to which you were then on your way—was, despite everything, your last refuge, to which you always returned when you were fed up with the world. You also said to yourself, as you looked at the desert on your left and the sun's fiery disc . . . .

"What are you thinking about?" asked Engineer Husam, who was sitting smoking at the other end of the seat. There had been a long silence between you.

"I'm thinking about the city."

"Didn't you go down to Basra last week?"

"Yes."

"Do you miss it?" he asked, astonished.

"Yes!"

He looked at you with his green eyes without saying anything. Perhaps at that moment he was saying to himself that this man, who was worn out by thinking about a city he had only been away from for a few days, was a nesting bird that hadn't quite gotten used to leaving his nest. But he smiled affectionately, "You'll be home before sunset!"

Perhaps, and this time I'll stay there a whole week! But we were at the start of the road. A few moments previously, the car had begun its journey, after Husam had collected his case from the house. The cook Abu Mahmoud had carried it out for him—that thin man with the pale face who seemed to be suffering from a continuing pain. I looked at the transport manager's house, Mr. John Sullivan, the man they were accusing Muzhir of sleeping with, but I didn't see anyone; the house was quiet. There was no one working in the garden, and no movement in the house. No curtain quivered, and no face looked out from behind any of the windows. Perhaps his wife, that enticing woman you had once seen in tennis gear, making advances to Husam, was now stretched out in bed, numbed by the drowsiness that began to overtake her in summer at midday since she had come to live in this burning climate that she wasn't yet used to. Or perhaps she'd gone to Britain to spend the summer there. It was possible. John Sullivan's private car—or perhaps it was his wife's—was parked in the garage. It was covered, and the house doors were locked. The white tulle curtains were hanging over the windows, glinting in the sunlight. The roads in the area seemed almost deserted, it was so hot. A servant emerged from the garden of one of the houses carrying something in his hand, then walked off somewhere on his own, through the deserted streets. The rays of the sun and the shadows of the palm trees colored his receding shadow. Perhaps the residents of the area were resting at that time of the day, inside their air-conditioned residences, or were drinking beer or playing billiards and darts in the club, or perhaps were reviving their bodies, made sluggish by the heat of this strange land, in the cool waters of the swimming pool. The sun—the sun of this foreign land— was striking the roofs and façades of the houses, the glass of the windows, and the roads running through the area, with a savage harshness. Everything outside was panting, even the hard stones. The burning air carried with it a mixture of smells and steam that rose up from the house gardens and from the asphalt roads, from the leaves of the trees and palms, from the warm air in the gardens and the papyrus clumps on the banks of the small rivers that fed into the Shatt al-Arab, and from the salt that covered the surface of the desert on the other side of the road. The managers' quarter, in the midst of all this sleepy, torpid silence, seemed to be nestling almost too humbly away from the prying eyes of strangers, the local population.

"And how is your life now? I mean, in the new camp," asked Husam, as he stubbed out the end of his cigarette in the little ashtray at the end of the armrest on his right.

He had asked you that sort of question before, but it seemed that he had forgotten, or perhaps he just wanted to start a conversation with you somehow.

"Better than the tented camp, of course. But we live four or five to a room. And then there's this dreadful heat in the rooms!"

"And the ceiling fans that we installed for you?"

"What can the fans do here?"

The heat was panting behind the glass of the window. The whole atmosphere was burning, though the air inside the car was cool and soothing.

"You're right," said Husam gently. "Nothing works here except for air conditioning. But you know, management can't . . . ."

He seemed glum as the palm groves on the right of the car continued to rush by like a green torrent pouring over the glass of the windows. The clumps of palms sped back to the village of Faw that we had left behind us, as the desert on our left stretched out in waves far into the distance, glowing white in the sun. The edge of the desert and the long black pipeline retreated, but the desert itself, if you looked into the far distance, you would find almost still, almost motionless in its place. But the more you shifted your gaze, the more the earth would appear to be creeping back, slowly at first, then with increasing speed until it reached the road, as if it was revolving on itself. The black pipeline rested on cushions of concrete at intervals; the body of the pipe was sagging with the heat, like a snake, as it touched the ground in the intervals between the supports.

"And Mr. Fox, how does he treat you?"

You turned your face away from the desert and looked at him.

"He treats us okay, those of us who work with him in the department. But he's harsh with the rest of the workmen on the project. Stuck up, most of the time."

"That's understandable, you're his tools. I mean, he thinks of you as his tools that he needs to look after."

Perhaps. Then I remembered my evening visit to Mr. Fox's room, and the three letters that had puzzled me. "Mr. Husam, what do the three letters "B-C-B" mean to you?"

"They might mean anything. Where did you read them?" he said, looking at me.

"On the back of a piece of news taken from a newspaper . . . in Mr. Fox's handwriting. I mean, the letters were in his handwriting."

"And what was the article about?"

"About a small-scale strike by some local employees, in the British army camp in al-Habbaniya."

"And you read just these three letters on the paper? On their own, like that?"

"No, it was a short phrase, with these three letters in it,"

"And this phrase, don't you remember it any longer?" he asked curiously, as he took out his pack of cigarettes.

"Yes, I remember it. The words, in English, were, 'Ask BCB for more details.'"

Husam lit his cigarette, took a puff from it then left the smoke to go up his nostrils as he always did. "B could be the first letter of Basra or Baghdad," he muttered to himself as he watched the gardens hurrying past. "Or of the word British, for example. C, Company, perhaps, or Committee, or Commission, or Consulate. Yes, perhaps that's it!" He turned toward me. "Perhaps he meant 'British Consulate, Basra.' Then the phrase would mean 'Ask the British Consulate in Basra for more details,' I think."

"And who is this asking?" I said, confused.

"Him. It's a note that he's writing to himself as a reminder."

"That means he's in touch with the British Consulate!"

Husam smiled and leaned toward me, then stretched out his hand and put it on my arm.

"Brother Muhammad, in my experience, every foreigner contacts his country's consulate. That's not the important thing. The important thing, if the letters really mean what I think they mean, is that the consulate is perhaps one of the authorities with which Mr. Fox is coordinating his dubious activities here."

"You believe that there are other authorities?"

"Perhaps. I don't know. You might come across some more evidence yourself."

"What's the use of that," I said disinterestedly, "if the project management, the consulate, and the government are all one thing at the end of the day?"

"At the present time there's no advantage, but in the future, who knows, it might be different."

But he fell silent. He looked at the back of the driver and said nothing, as if he had just then become aware of the presence of a third person with us in the car. "Abbas!" he said, addressing the driver. "You can spend the night in Basra, with your family. I've spoken to the transport manager."

"Thanks," said the driver gratefully. "My wife always says a prayer for you. Really!"

Husam relaxed in his seat and closed his eyes. It was easy to imagine that he was a European, so long as you didn't hear him speaking. The car shuddered as it passed over a bump in the road and he opened his eyes to stare at the road on his right through the window. "We've reached al-Siba," he said with a touch of satisfaction in his voice. But you can't see anything of the village while you're on the outer road. Its mud-brick houses are hidden deep in the gardens near the banks of the Shatt al-Arab, hidden from the eyes by a long curtain of palm trees. The road going down to them, which you passed through quickly, I imagined as a black dagger cutting through the green gardens then plunging inside. "Tell me, Brother Muhammad, how are you spending your free time in the camp these days?"

"I read, when I can find the opportunity."

I didn't mention any of my attempts to write. On previous occasions, after I had begun to establish a decent relationship with him, I had almost spoken to him about my novel. But something had stopped me. He had his secrets as well (secrets with women, if what Abu Jabbar said about him was true). Perhaps I would tell him one day.

"You're lucky," he said in a tone of regret. "I don't have the patience to read literature. Novels, in particular. I want to get to the end too quickly. What's happened to the characters, and things like that."

He noticed my look of surprise and smiled with a touch of embarrassment. "You're wondering, of course, what he does with all those books that he borrows from me."

I looked at him without speaking, waiting for him to explain.

"I was actually borrowing them for a friend."

How could I not have noticed that for myself? He'd never spoken to me, not once, about any of the books he'd borrowed from me. He'd never mentioned that he'd liked or not liked any specific book. So he . . . . I had the feeling of a man who'd given a present to a dear friend, then discovered that the friend had disposed of it before he'd even opened the wrapping paper to see what it was.

"I hope that hasn't annoyed you."

"Not at all. And if your friend wants . . . ."

"Thanks, I know, but he's left."

"When he comes back, then."

"I don't think he'll be coming back," he said, looking out of the window at the rapidly receding gardens.

I felt a tinge of regret in his voice. Then he turned to look at the moving palm groves as he smoked without speaking, immersed in his thoughts and fears. After a few minutes he said absentmindedly, "She's got two books."

He suddenly became conscious of the words that had escaped from him and he turned his face toward me. He sighed in resignation and said, as if to clarify things, "She's a real lady. A foreigner, the wife of a friend."

He stared at me questioningly in silence, as if he were trying to discover the thoughts and suspicions revolving inside my head after that confession.

"I'll get the two books back for you, don't worry!"

"That's not important."

"No, I'll get them back for you from his wife."

The wife of his friend! Was she that pretty filly, the tennis player? Mr. Sullivan's wife. But she didn't seem the type to waste time reading tiresome books. And he said "the wife of a friend," and I didn't think he'd be friends with someone like Mr. Sullivan. Who could that mysterious woman be, then, who had carried on reading my books for months at a time? "Your friend is a real womanizer!" Abu Jabbar had gone into the car and shouted his crafty words in my face, "A first-class womanizer!" Okay, what is a young bachelor like him to do, surrounded by all that temptation in that easygoing environment? It's a pity that Husam, after the unknown woman had left, had no longer needed that small service that I could give him. He considered me a friend even though each of us had his particular temperament and lived in a different world. He once invited me to visit him in his world. When I declined, he asked in surprise, "What's stopping you?"

"It's forbidden to go into your living area without a job to do."

"And who issued such a strange order?"

"I don't know, but all the workmen are aware of it."

"I've never heard anything like it," he muttered in astonishment, then added angrily, "This is one of Fox's orders, orders that he doesn't write on paper, but disseminates by rumor through his men, until they become a fact that you have to obey."

"Possibly."

"Anyway, you come, and don't take any notice! If anyone asks you, say that I invited you."

"I'd really like to," I said regretfully. "But I don't want to make difficulties with the manager."

"Okay, then I'll visit you in the camp. We'll agree on a date. Which room do you live in?"

What sort of a trap was this? I remained silent, not knowing what to say to him. When he noticed my hesitation, he seemed surprised and said, "Don't tell me that it's also forbidden for me to come to the camp!"

"No, it's not forbidden." I said shyly. "But they'll accuse you of collaborating with the workforce."

"Collaborating? Against whom?" he asked in astonishment.

"Against the management, of course!"

He laughed in disbelief. "But I'm part of the management, in a manner of speaking!"

His face, though, soon took on a look of despondency. "What is this? You can't visit me, and I can't visit you!"

He lit another cigarette.

While he was smoking in silence I related a story my father had recounted when I was small, a story about people in paradise that he had read in a book. My father said that God had created paradise of seven levels. On the day of resurrection, after throwing all the sinners and transgressors into hell, everyone would be placed in the position to which he was entitled through the deeds he had performed in this world. Those on the highest level could come down to visit those below them, but those on a lower level could not go up to visit those above them.

"But in Fox's paradise even this is impossible! Everyone has to live within his own private world, and no one can visit anyone else."

He carried on smoking in silence for a little, then said in a challenging tone, "I'm coming to visit you! Let him do as he likes!"

I didn't like this idea. He could challenge the director of administration; Fox didn't have the authority to terminate his contract. He could, of course, send in a bad report about him to Project HQ in Basra, saying whatever he liked, but Husam didn't seem to care about Fox's power to harm him. But what about me?

"Husam, really . . . I'm happy. But there's another thing that makes this visit impossible."

"What's that?" he asked, opening his eyes and looking into my face.

"On my first day of work, Mr. Fox warned me . . . ."

"Warned you about me?" he asked, confused. "How did he know that we would even meet?"

"No, no, he warned me about everybody. He warned me about making friends with anyone who might exploit me to find out office secrets."

The muscles on his face twitched a little. He looked at me without saying anything, as if he were weighing up what I had said.

"Do you think he doesn't know that you sometimes come down to Basra with me?"

"I thought of that. And I'm disturbed that he hasn't broached the subject with me up to now. I would have said that you were helping me get to the city, rather than having to ride in a truck, nothing more."

He looked at me and smiled. "You work with him but you don't know him very well! Anyway," he added, with a touch of annoyance, "he can go to hell, him and his warnings! Let's not talk about him!"

On our following trips, we never spoke about this subject again.

The air inside the car was thick with smoke. Husam put out his cigarette and wound down the window beside him. At once, we were struck by a blast of hot air that blew right through the inside of the car, burning our faces. By the time that Husam closed the window again after a few moments, most of the air had escaped from the inside of the car, carrying with it the smoke and the cool smell of tobacco, and leaving behind a smell of warm palm groves and the taste of salt on the tongue.

Three palm trees, which seemed from a distance to be growing from a single root, stood apart in the blaze of the sun at a distance from the line of gardens that stretched out to infinity. The trees told us that we had nearly arrived at the city, with no more than half an hour left. Then Basra appeared. There was a small bus coming toward us on the road. A dusty mass of old wood and rusty ironwork. On the roof, among the luggage, sat three or four men with their faces covered, shading themselves from the dust and the scorching rays of the sun with their kafiy-yehs. Their hands gripped the edges of the roof for fear of falling.

"Look, sir!" the driver shouted in alarm. "If one of them falls off in front of the car, they'll say that it's we who startled him! Come on, man, help me!"

As the bus drew closer, Husam looked at the men, but it was now impossible to see them. The bus flew past with a scream of the engine, creaking in the dust. For a second, one could see inside it row upon row of the top halves of men and women's bodies, packed together as they returned to their villages. For a fleeting moment, as the two vehicles came close to each other, some eyes in the bus tried to snatch a glimpse of the inside of the little car. The eyes glinted then disappeared, as emptiness filled their place. For a brief moment, dust remained hanging in the air, then quickly disappeared with the bus as it bore away its passengers. Meanwhile, the driver was still moaning, as if one of the men in kafiyyehs on the bus roof had really lost his balance and fallen in front of the car, to be crushed under the racing wheels. Policemen, arrests, and a trial. And if he had a tribe to support him that wanted to profit from his death, you would have to sell all the furniture in your house and still take out a loan.

Then we left the desert as we entered the palm groves at the village of Abu al-Fulus. The shadows of the palms spread out before us on the asphalt road. They split and piled up on top of each other in the gaps inside the gardens, as bunches of sun rays peeped through the branches and palm fronds, lighting up the grass and bushes on the edges of the road. The driver slowed the car down as he drove into the village of Abu al-Khusaib, and the landmarks in the village began to slip slowly past us: houses, gardens, cars, and people, some of them moving and others almost stationary, as they sat in the cafés and on the pavements, seemingly bewildered, or perhaps just dazed, watching the passersby and the vehicles with languid eyes, like mud statues. The village receded as we entered the palm groves, and the car hurried on, taking us through a winding tunnel of greenery.

"Muhammad, what do you think about marriage?"

It seemed a slightly odd question. What had prompted him to think of marriage at that moment?

"It's an adventure, I suppose, for both the man and the woman. An adventure that may be successful if one is lucky. But luck aside, most people only marry at the end of the road."

"That's the question," he said gloomily. "When will someone like me get to the end of the road?"

"Are you thinking of getting married?"

"No, not at the moment, anyway," he said defensively, as though it was on his mind.

"There's nothing in the whole world better than marriage," said the driver, who had been listening, while keeping his eyes on the twisting road for fear of suddenly meeting a vehicle appearing from behind one of the plantation walls. "Ask me!"

Husam gave a lighthearted laugh. "You believe so, Abbas?"

"Yes, sir, trust God!"

"God is generous, Abbas, God is generous," muttered Husam absentmindedly, in a tone that was no longer lighthearted, as he brought the conversation to an end.

We finished the journey in almost total silence, exchanging only a few passing words. For the rest, we were all preoccupied with our own thoughts, as the car approached the city.

"Muhammad," said Husam. "I'm going to Baghdad tonight, but Abbas will be returning tomorrow. You can go back with him."

I thanked him and told him that I had a week's holiday. A whole week! (I had several things to do in that period. First of all, I had to go to visit Fadlallah in hospital, and after that. . . .) When I got out of the car in al-Ashar, the sun's rays were painting the mountain peaks and coloring the treetops. The air had become a little cooler (or "broken" as they say here) before sunset. I was happy. Little things make you happy. Being away from the bother of work and the irritations of camp life for a bit; reaching Basra before evening; and cooler air, for example. You were happy then. You didn't know then, of course, that when you got back to the camp after your break you would receive some dreadful news that would bring you a lengthy period of sadness—a sadness that would from time to time suddenly return to you like a slap in the face.

11

A Mountain Bird's Journey

Sleeping inside was no longer possible, now that summer had come and the air was so hot. The ceiling fans were no use. So you took your beds and set them up in the empty spaces between the rooms, long rows of beds on which the men spread their bedding at sunset. In the morning, some considerable time before the work siren gave out its first penetrating shriek, everyone would fold up his bedding and leave it in place for the day under the rays of the blazing summer sun. When you unrolled your bedding in the evening to lay it out again on your bed, you would find it warm, as if you had lit a fire underneath it. The air would have cooled a little at sunset, and together with your own body when you lay down later, as night went on, it would gradually absorb the heat deposited by the sun in the folds of the bedding. Meanwhile you would see the men around you in various positions, sitting or lying, like dim shadows in the scatterings of faint light emitted by the lamps hung at intervals on the balconies. You could hear whispering, laughter, and curses as some of them smoked and drank. Then the activity would subside, and the bodies that had been moving and talking only a little while before would become still, all on their beds. Your eyes could no longer make anything out except for the rows of beds and sleeping bodies, as if you were sitting in a prison dormitory or a hospital. In the distance, the earth dam surrounding the camp appeared like a black wall in the darkness of the night. Meanwhile, you could hear their coughing and snoring, and a few snatches of their words as they mumbled through their sleep and their nightmares.

When the east winds blow over that place, laden with moisture from the sea, they make you wish you could escape from your body and flee without a backward glance. They cover you with a layer of sticky moisture that clogs the beads of sweat in your pores and makes you wander around in a state of tension. You don't know what to do with yourself; you spend the night awake, and in the morning you leave behind a sweaty bed smelling of damp cotton and material, as if you'd spent the whole night in the rain.

The winds were blowing from the east when I got off the bus in the evening at the camp entrance, as I returned from my break. I found the men wandering around like lunatics in an agitated, excited way, swearing at the world and the project management as well as the cursed winds. Some of them had left the camp and gone walking aimlessly along the deserted road, perhaps thinking that the air there would be kinder. You walked along the paths between the rooms, carrying your little bag weighed down by books.

You passed rows of beds and grumbling men. Almost everyone held a small fan in his hand. They were the sort of fans that villagers make out of palm leaves, decorating them with the names of God and his Prophet and saints, and with words of prayer, in blue and red. I saw Abu Jabbar standing by his bed, naked to the waist, with a small towel around his neck. He was wearing nothing but his underwear, and his swarthy torso glimmered in the fragmented light. He looked like a hippopotamus that had just come out of the water. He stood with his arm raised like the Statue of Liberty, while his other hand frantically waved a palm fan under his armpit in a vain attempt to dry the sweat that had gathered in the hollow. Hussein Tu'ma sat silently, despite all the frantic movement around him, in his flowing dishdasha, smoking in silence. You didn't see Muzhir with them. He had begun to avoid them since the day Hussein had revealed his dubious connection with the transport manager. But what really attracted your attention then was Istifan's bed, which was empty. Had he gone on vacation as well? You put your case down on the ground and said good evening to them both.

"Hello," replied Hussein curtly, while Abu Jabbar muttered an exaggerated greeting as he lowered his arm. "Welcome, my boy, welcome, you've come back!"

I was conscious of something odd, an odd tone, in their voices.

"Where's Istifan?"

"How was the break?" asked Abu Jabbar.

"Enjoyable, but tiring at the same time," you said, spreading your bedding out to rid it of some of the day's heat, before going into the room to put down your bag and change your clothes. "You know the demands of a home."

"Yes, yes, the demands of a home, of course, they're endless, I imagine."

He moved the fan nervously in front of his face, while Hussein continued smoking in silence, and looking at Abu Jabbar with hatred. Again, you nervously asked them, "Has he gone back to his family? Istifan, I mean."

"Why don't you tell him?" said Hussein, addressing Abu Jabbar.

"These cursed winds will kill me!" said Abu Jabbar.

At that point I felt that something terrible must have happened to Istifan. Perhaps the saw had cut off his hand, or a nail had gone through one of his eyes and blinded him.

"Has Istifan hurt himself at work?"

"Istifan is dead!" said Hussein finally. His reply was direct, and came like a thunderbolt, unambiguously: "He's dead!" That simply. So that was that. You were thinking of him as a living being, injured perhaps but still alive. Then someone comes to say one word, just one word, and that person you had pictured in your mind as a living being turns into a rigid corpse. "They killed him!" Hussein said angrily.

At that point Abu Jabbar stopped waving his fan and sat on his bed. "Your friend died suddenly," he said. "Who would have believed it?"

He was muttering in a trembling voice. You couldn't tell whether the trembling voice was sincere or false. You sat down on your warm bed. Your wandering looks fell on the men who were moving between the beds, shaking their fans to disperse the heavy air. Stray dogs were stretched out languidly on the ground, with open mouths, while the rig operator Fawzi's dog sat panting on its own, there at the edge of the balcony. In the sky above your head, remnants of white clouds could be seen (the east wind clouds, as they call them here), almost stationary in their places. Soon the winds would carry them away. So the kindly mountain lad was dead! He had died quickly. No, you were away for a whole week, with enough hours and minutes in it for millions of people to die, with time left over for even more to perish.

"Dreadful, just dreadful!" bemoaned Abu Jabbar.

Your voice sounded strange as you asked, "When did he die?"

"Two days after you'd left, on Monday morning," said Abu Jabbar sadly, while Hussein continued to stare blankly in front of him.

"How did he die?"

"In an accident. It must have been God's will!"

"A car accident?"

"No, no!" said Abu Jabbar, removing the damp towel from around his neck. "An accident at work. God's will!"

He started to wipe the sweat from his face with the towel. "They killed him, I'm telling you!" said Hussein again. "That bastard Sultan al-Imari, and the project management. They killed him—him and the other two men. Abu Jabbar knows, but he won't talk, because he's also in on it."

"Muhammad, my son," said Abu Jabbar, angrily. "Don't listen to talk like this! When one's day comes . . . I really advised him not to go down into the sewage tank. Engineer Sultan will confirm it."

You didn't understand anything. What was this about the engineer and the sewage tank?

"But what did Istifan have to do with the sewage tank?"

"An insult, for God's sake! No one will talk . . . and project management . . . ."

Hussein spoke loudly, to make his words heard by the men restlessly lolling around, worn out by that sticky heat that takes away the breath. Abu Jabbar sighed impatiently, "Here we are, back again to the heroics!"

"I'll tell you what happened," Hussein went on. "Istifan was working in the new managers' club, doing some joinery, widening the bar, or whatever. Outside the club, two maintenance workmen, Abu Jabbar's men, that is, were trying to clean a drain."

Abu Jabbar was fidgeting from the heat, and from Hussein's attempts to accuse him of having a hand in Istifan's death. But he was exhausted and unable to reply. He sat listening in silence, one hand wiping his damp flesh with the towel, and the other waving the fan continuously.

"One of the men went down into the drain and didn't come out, and when his colleague realized he'd been gone too long he went down after him. But he didn't come out either. The story is that when Istifan heard what had happened he left what he was doing and volunteered to help."

Hussein lifted his head up to Abu Jabbar. "Tell me frankly, which son of a bitch ordered him to go down there?"

"Hussein, please leave me alone!" said Abu Jabbar in a bored tone. "I'm dying of this heat. And you're torturing me!" Then he pulled himself together and got up from his bed.

"If I knew who that criminal was who . . . ," said Hussein in a threatening tone.

It no longer bothered you what they were saying. No words would be any use any longer. There was only one established fact, which would suffer no argument and no explanation: the death of the man who had left his village in the north to earn a living and who had choked to death in a drain in the far south.

Abu Jabbar went away huffing and puffing, dragging his feet with no energy. "I swear by all that is holy that he knows the details of what happened," said Hussein, watching him with anger in his eyes. "If he wasn't . . . ."

I watched his broad body move around the beds carrying the palm leaf fan and the damp towel, pursued by the heat pouring down from the sky and pursued also by suspicion.

"Where did they bury him?"

An unimportant question. His mortal remains could be anywhere in the country, it wasn't important anymore. But you didn't know what to say.

"They took him back to his village. Dankha sent a telegram to his father, and he came with some of his relatives and collected his body from the project hospital in Basra."

"So you didn't meet his father?"

"We saw him."

"He came here," said Hussein. "He wanted to know how his son had died. I don't know what that pig Fox told him. Then he took his case and other things and left. An old man of about seventy who had never left his village before. And didn't know a single word of . . . ."

You were lifting your case up from the ground when Hussein spoke to comfort you. "Keep calm, Brother Muhammad," he said. "We are not going to let accidents like this just pass. The project management has to take responsibility." You would have laughed if you hadn't been grieving so much. You picked up your bag and went into your room. You turned on the light and the ceiling fan, and the thick, clammy air inside the room almost shuddered. You were struck by the empty space as though you were seeing the place like that for the first time. Since the day when you'd taken your beds out of it, your room had appeared almost bare, like all the other rooms in the camp. Your little cupboards stood on their own next to the walls, with the coat stand in the corner with the shirts and trousers on it, and the two chairs that Abu Jabbar had got from Daniel each stood in its place (they were useful when the drinks table was set up). Abu Jabbar's trunk and your cases were still there, though the case that had been tied up with cord in the shape of a cross was not among them. Your few other possessions and some empty arrack bottles were scattered in the corners. In the middle of the room was spread a palm leaf rug, on which Abu Jabbar used to sleep every day after returning from work. When he got up, he would be bearing the marks—lines made by the leaves—clearly printed on his swarthy flesh. The room seemed emptier than ever, twice as empty if that is possible. But

Istifan's face soon appeared in front of you. It suddenly revealed itself, as you discovered him sitting beside you on the little bus that brought the pair of you, amid a throng of other passengers, here for the first time. You felt his shoulder touching yours, then saw him, when the bus had completed part of the journey, staring at the vast desert that appeared to the right of the vehicle. "Is this ice?" You heard him wonder in astonishment.

Some of the passengers were laughing at him. You couldn't see their faces, but you could hear them laughing. "Where are you from?" one of them asked.

"I'm from the north," he replied.

"You're right," said the stranger. "If you use your imagination."

"This isn't snow, it's salt," you said to him quietly.

"This is the snow of the south!" said another passenger, laughing.

"Salt, all this?" he asked in astonishment.

Then he nodded off. The monotonous landscape had made him feel sleepy, and his head nodded. He leaned toward you. You felt the young man's head finally come to rest on your shoulder. You stayed sitting there without moving for the rest of the journey, for fear of waking him up. So your concern to let him sleep for that hour had been in vain!

Then you noticed the cage hanging on the wall. This was all he had left behind. You will keep this bird for him. You try to challenge death by preserving what the dead have left behind, pretending to yourself that it is part of them. But the two of you will part, you and the dumb bird will be separated in the end.

So now he had become an issue and a topic for debate. How did he die? Who caused his death and the deaths of the two other men who went down with him? And on and on. Perhaps you alone—of all the people in the room—really grieved for him. Muzhir was in a crisis because of the scandal with the transport manager; and Hussein had found in the deaths of the three men a new excuse to incite the workforce against the project managers. Istifan's death was just one aspect of a case to be energetically pursued, with a view to stirring up the feelings of the men to resist management authority (or rather, Fox's authority). Feelings of hatred could only be aroused properly by shocking events. As for Abu Jabbar, he had wandered off into the night, for fear that Hussein's persistent questioning would drive him to reveal things he would perhaps prefer to keep hidden in his heart forever.

12

A Whispered Conversation

"May I share in your silence?"

This question, which never varied, with time acquired the character of a greeting. A question that Hussein asked every time he had the idea of visiting me on the new dam, as his hand reached for his pocket to take out his handkerchief.

"Please do!"

Sometimes he would take me by surprise as I wrote. I would gather up my papers and turn them over face down on the ground, while he looked at the papers silently, holding back the confused and hesitant question on the tip of his tongue. He would stay like that for a long time, burning to know the secret of those papers and the solitary sessions facing the desert. He spread out his handkerchief on the earth of the dam and sat down.

"My brother, Muhammad, what are you writing? Sufi poetry?"

You laughed. "What makes you think that?"

He looked at the turned-over papers. "Your remoteness from us and the rest of the human race, and your habit of gazing at the desert in a sort of Sufi trance."

I was annoyed by his words. "I can see better when I'm not looking at people and things. Faces distort and blur the vision. Other people's faces and things' faces too."

"Fine!" he said, smiling and taking out a pack of cigarettes.

I ignored the sarcastic tone in his voice. But my state of feeling at peace with myself and with the universe I had been living in before my solitude was disturbed had disappeared. The desert was at once stripped of its ghosts, its visions, and its continuous soft whisperings. Nothing remained of it before me except for its lifeless natural features, and the random changes that the hand of man had wrought there, just at the edges. The desert had turned into a colored carpet of lights and shadows, with all their varied refractions. There in the distance were some deep excavations, made by the iron jaw of a drill as it ripped through the face of the earth night and day. From afar, the body of the rig looked bright, from the rays of the setting sun behind it. Its black shadows spread themselves across the earth, and a row of three or four trucks could also be seen.

Hussein took out a pack of cigarettes, and found just a single cigarette inside it. He extracted it with his thin, yellowed fingers, then threw the empty pack carelessly into the desert. He lit his cigarette and began to smoke in silence for some time. Then he looked at the papers again, hesitantly stretching a hand out toward them. But his hand quickly retreated when he noticed my disapproving looks.

"Sorry, I don't want to intrude on your secrets."

I picked up my papers and put them on my other side, away from him. I saw his face glower. "I don't have any secrets," I said, to lessen the harshness of my action. "Believe me, all it is is that I have been trying for some time to write what might be called a novel."

His face relaxed and he turned his whole body toward me. "A novel?"

Perhaps I had exaggerated. "It's an attempt to use up my spare time in this outlandish place," I said, retreating a little.

"Okay, okay. And what is this novel of yours about?"

"People, of course," I said. "And the place where they live and work."

"Obviously about people. Does anyone write about anything else? I mean, the ideas."

"From what perspective?"

I knew where his interest lay, but I didn't give him a direct reply. "If you want to know," I said evasively, "you have to imagine a bird flying high in the sky over this small patch of land, seeing underneath it two worlds crossed by the public road leading to Basra, like a long black wall, like a barrier difficult to cross. On one side, next to the desert, lives a group of workmen, while the managers' quarter nestles on the other side, between the palm groves near the banks of the Shatt al-Arab. On that side the bird can also see the work area, the place where the inhabitants of the two sides (the bosses and the underlings) meet, when they undertake their shared tasks. As for the little village, it can see it out of the corner of its eye, nestling in the corner, on the banks of the wide river, like a scattering of seawater that the waves have carried forward then thrown onto the shore, where it has remained evaporating in the sun. You have also to imagine . . ."

He was smoking as he listened, but his eyes were smiling and sparkling.

"You have to imagine that this bird has an amazing ability to tear down barriers and uncover secrets. Everything that is woven and hatched in secret behind walls, and in wives' bedrooms, over a defined period of time. My story will be in two books, or let us say two 'faces,' one face for each side. These are the broad outlines, as they say."

"And you want to put all this in a novel?" he asked doubtfully.

"There's no harm in trying."

"Where have you got to?"

"The day when you confronted Muzhir about his scandalous relationship with John Sullivan, and made him leave the room in anger."

He was pleased to find that he was a character in the novel.

"And did you think I was right to do what I did?"

"Frankly, I didn't like your style," I confessed. "Defamation isn't to my taste. Then again, I was surprised. If you intended to expose him openly, as you maintained, why had you been patient for all this time, despite the fact that . . . ?"

"Before confronting him with what I had heard, I wanted first to convince myself that the rumors were true," he said, trying to justify himself. "Do you know that John Sullivan took Muzhir home with him to his wife's house? Did you know he took him on the pretext of repairing his car?"

"How do you know this?"

"From the servant."

I looked at him in astonishment. "Did you go into the managers' quarter?"

"No, you know that that is forbidden, except for work purposes. I met the servant in the village. The servants in the foreigners' quarters are all from the village. And I have friends there."

What do you suppose this thin young man was up to?

"Don't they spy on us?" he asked with a smile, as his eyes sparkled. "Then we must . . . ."

The black hair on his chin and cheeks had grown longer, with a few days' growth. He had no time to tend to his appearance. Like a child that had discovered a new toy and was trying to uncover its workings, he said, "Tell me now, what was your judgment on me? I mean, as one of your characters in the novel."

"I told you that I have been trying to take a bird's-eye view. Have you ever seen a bird making judgments on human behavior?"

"And what will your bird do when it meets with failure, for example?"

"Nothing. Flap its wings and fly away."

He let out a mocking laugh, then went on staring into the desert. The pale disk of the sun was descending slowly, and there was something like a pool of fog—or perhaps it was a dark cloud split apart—lying between the sun's disk and the edge of the earth. The sun's disk was pouring its lavish rays over it, lighting up its edges with a blood-red fire. Hussein stubbed out his cigarette on the ground and bent his head down. He started to draw circles in the earth with the tip of his finger around the extinguished cigarette stub. Circle after circle, as if to blockade it. There was a man calling from inside the camp to another man on the road, with a voice that penetrated the air: "We're waiting for you, we're waiting for you . . . don't be late!"

"It's time for supper," I said to him. "Let's go." But he didn't move.

"Listen, Muhammad, my friend. What you are doing is a good thing. Writing, I mean. Except that your way of doing it I don't see serving any useful purpose. I suggest . . . ."

His finger proceeded, perhaps unconsciously, to break up the circles he had just drawn in the earth, the blockade he had made around the burning cigarette stub.

"I suggest that you write about the struggle between the project management and the workers."

"What struggle? I haven't been aware of any struggle!"

He gave me a hostile, disbelieving look.

"The struggle exists, my friend . . . under the surface, and one day it will burst into the open. You don't notice it now because you're busy looking at your empty desert!"

"Perhaps, I don't know, I've only noticed subjection. The only rebellion I've seen was on the part of an unemployed man, an illiterate man."

"And who was that?" he asked with interest, as if he had discovered something new.

"You could regard him as a leader for the vagrants and the unemployed. His friends call him Farhan al-Abd. He comes to us every morning. And when Mr. Fox refuses to give him work he lets out his impotent shout from behind the fence then goes back empty-handed to the village."

Hussein seemed pleased. "And what does this Farhan say?"

"He curses Britain and anything that comes into his head. He used to curse George but since the death of the king he's been cursing the queen."

Hussein laughed, as if the curses were achieving something. "But his loud, hostile slogans have turned into something familiar and amusing," you said. "Imagine, even Mr. Fox, who at first punished him by sacking him, has recently begun smiling when he hears the queen being mentioned. He just says he's mad."

"Can I see him?"

"See who? Farhan al-Abd? Of course you can, you'll find him among the crowd of unemployed, standing by the fence every morning in front of our office. A very tall man, with a bald head. But why do you want to see him?"

"I just do," he mumbled obscurely. "Curiosity. Anyway, this isn't our subject. Let's talk about your novel."

I turned my head and looked inside the camp. I saw a number of men converging on the mess building while others were busy spreading their warm bedding, moving as fast as possible so as to catch up with their colleagues. I saw the stray dogs racing each other as well, chasing the smell of food.

"As I told you, I . . . I think you should write about the struggle between the workers and the project which is represented here by Fox, and by others in the project headquarters in Basra and the oilfields. You could start by describing the management's obstinacy, persecution almost."

"And the pressure that is increasing every day," I said, anticipating his next words.

He looked at me encouragingly and continued with enthusiasm: "Yes, insults, expulsion for the most trivial reason, sick men being sacked, demeaning methods of transport—haven't you yourself experienced the ride in a truck in the rain and cold? and rotten food."

"But the food's not bad," I said, a little annoyed. "By comparison, at least."

"Make it bad in the novel, make it bad. And write about the exploitation of temporary workers like Farhan and his crowd as well."

"And about sending spies among the workers, and stirring up the police against the workers, for example."

"Yes, yes, and make several men die in assorted work accidents through management negligence. You've got the death of Istifan and the other workers in the sewers, for example, or have you forgotten the accident?"

"No, no, how could I forget it? But . . . ."

"Then make the workforce stage a massive strike," he continued, heatedly, as he sketched out the novel from his viewpoint. "A strike that brings all activity to a standstill in the three work areas."

"And then the management will give in and surrender to the workers' demands," I said, to complete the suggestion.

"Of course," he said, as if certain of it, "if the men stay united."

"And you increase their wages, and work to improve their conditions, in the workplace and outside it as well!" he added, giving a free rein to his dreams and fantasies, as he stared into the empty desert. "And give them comfortable buses, warm in winter and cool in summer, to take them home."

"And then consult them about the management of the work. Yes, of course. They have to have a view about that."

But I took pity on him. I stopped playing the dream game out of annoyance. My God, how easily a man can become incapable of seeing the hidden aspects. I had been thinking that idealists were the only ones who could dream with their eyes wide open. Looking at a deaf reality! I didn't look at his face after he had realized that I was going along with his fantasies to make fun of him. Fawzi's dog in the drilling rig was barking wildly at the sun, which was half buried in the desert sand at the end of the earth. The mist, or broken cloud, had left a blazing line over the sun's disk, near the upper edge, like a broad brushstroke.

"I thought you were serious!" said Hussein reprovingly.

He wasn't angry, but seemed a little sad to see his sandcastle that he had built on the shore collapsing. A frivolous wave had emerged to destroy it from its foundations with the flip of its tongue, then retreated laughing. His face turned glum again, drained of the blood that his enthusiasm had sent into his cheeks.

"You're right, Hussein," I said apologetically. "I wasn't serious. For the simple reason that a novel of the sort you are proposing would appear contrived!"

"Let's say imagined on the basis of a certain reality!"

"What's the difference?"

"When you imagine something you are wandering inside your mind, then recording what floats to the top by itself."

"Chaos, you mean."

"You might say that it's organized chaos, for at the end of the day you won't be bringing in anything from outside your life . . . things you've lived or lived through. Now, let's go to supper!"

As we got up from the dam, the sun's disk was still almost half buried. It hadn't gone down much, as though it had disappeared halfway down the earth's throat, and the earth could no longer swallow it. I gathered my papers, and Hussein took his handkerchief, shook it out, and slipped it into his trouser pocket. As we went down I heard him ask, "Tell me, Brother Muhammad, why do you write?"

I was startled by his question. I had never asked myself why I wrote. "I really don't know," I said, trying to find a convincing answer, for him and for myself as well. "I've just told you that I'm trying to kill time. But that's not true. I could kill time by reading, which is enjoyable and doesn't cause me any suffering."

In the distance a number of men were leaving the mess building, while others were hurrying toward it. But he wasn't in a hurry to eat. He continued walking slowly and I was forced to walk at the same pace.

"Why, then?"

At that moment I remembered something from my childhood days. "When we were young, we used to compete by shouting," I said to him. "To see who could shout louder than the others. I used to tear my throat; it was a horrible game. The noise that we used to cause in the streets on summer afternoons was horrible. It would frighten the grown-ups and ruin their siestas."

"And what's this got to do . . . ?" he asked, looking at me in confusion.

"The thing is, Brother Hussein, that I can no longer shout in the streets now I'm this old. They'd think me mad and take me to the Shammaiya asylum in Baghdad. That's why I write. I think it's . . . ."

He was silent for a moment, thinking, then laughed. Up to this moment I hadn't known how this story of mine would be received.

We were getting close to the mess building. "You go in," I said to him. "I'm going to my room, to put away my papers."

"I'll come with you," he said, as he walked beside me.

I had the feeling he had something to say, but he carried on walking in silence. Most of the men had set up their beds in the gaps between the rooms before going to the mess. The smell of pillows, sheets, and warm covers filled the air, mingling with the smell of the food. We walked up to the balcony and went into the room. While I was unlocking my cupboard, to put my papers in it and lock them up, he opened his cupboard to take out a new pack of cigarettes. "Let's go," I said to him when we'd finished.

"One moment," he said, showing no sign of hurrying. He looked at the door opening, then started talking quickly and quietly. "Tell me, Brother Muhammad, if there was a strike against management, would you support it?"

His words came as a shock. When he had talked to me on the dam I had thought that he was making things up spontaneously. "A strike? It's really happening? But I imagined . . . ."

"Don't raise your voice," he said, looking at the door opening again. "Yes, it's really happening."

"When?"

"That's not important now. Just tell me, would you support it?" (If Mr. Fox knew that one of his men . . . .)

"If all the men went on strike, then of course I would join them."

"No, that's not what I mean."

What did he want from me, then? I looked at him for some explanation. "Don't worry," he said in a joking way, "I'm not asking you to do anything dangerous."

"What do you want me to do?" I asked him, puzzled.

He came closer and put his hand on my shoulder.

"If there's a strike, there'll be a confrontation between the strikers and the authorities who will be protecting the project management."

His whispering in my ear, as he spoke in a hushed voice while watching the door, made the thing seem dangerous, as if we were hatching a conspiracy together. "And will there be a confrontation?" I asked him in alarm.

"Certainly. And it will be at its most violent at Project HQ in Basra. That's where the men will gather from everywhere."

"But I'm no use at fighting or throwing stones!"

He gave a little laugh and tightened his hand on my shoulder.

"I never thought of asking you anything like that. Who told you that . . . ?"

"Then what do you want from me?"

"A simple request. Since you're so mad about writing, I want you, when the strike breaks out, to go to Basra at once, see what's happening there, and write for the opposition papers. Because the papers. . . ."

So he wanted me to attack the authorities and project management with words, instead of stones!

"Because the other papers will try to distort things."

"But isn't there anyone else?"

"Of course there is. But the more pens there are . . . ."

I began to fidget. He took his hand off my shoulder and said, as if to make light of it, "You can write under a false name, and tear up the drafts of your reports for the papers. And this conversation will stay a secret!"

We stood in the room for a long time. He seemed annoyed at my hesitation. He was afraid that someone else might disturb us.

"Didn't you say, just a few moments ago, that writing was for you an expression of a desire to scream? Then this is your opportunity!"

He was throwing my words back in my face, using them cunningly to his advantage. "What I meant," I said, trying to get out of the dilemma, "was turning the desire to scream into literary or artistic creation, something of that sort."

I felt that my words were useless, however, and I didn't look him in the eye. He realized that I was in a predicament and stood silently waiting. Finally, I said, "Okay. I can't promise you anything now, let me think about it."

"Think about it, then," he said resignedly, "but don't take too long to reply. Because the strike may . . . ."

Then he hurried out of the room in front of me as we left the balcony. We both prepared our beds and headed for the mess. We met Abu

Jabbar on the way, who put his hand on his belly and told us, "Today they've cooked us okra stew. Hurry up, before the meat runs out!"

His voice sounded happy and friendly, but his eyes looked at us suspiciously. Perhaps I was imagining the suspicion in his eyes because of my own fears, after the whispered conversation in the room. We walked past Abu Jabbar. I heard him belch freely into the early evening air. When the distance between us and his broad back had grown longer, Hussein explained what was on his mind. "I don't trust that man," he said. "I never trust him, I have a feeling about him."

The dogs, as usual, had gathered at the entrance to the mess. There was a large number of men coming out of the mess, and three or four stragglers like us, coming from different directions, and walking along briskly, faster than we were. I don't remember saying anything worth recalling. Perhaps we talked about the heat, which hadn't let up despite the approach of autumn, or about the dogs, whose number was increasing at an alarming pace. Something of that sort. Most likely, though, we walked the rest of the way to the mess in silence, with me thinking about the strike and the task that Hussein had asked me to undertake, while he walked sullenly along beside me, a bit annoyed, perhaps because he hadn't been able to persuade me as quickly as he had been hoping.

On that calm and peaceful evening, as I watched the men leaving the mess with full stomachs, laughing, smoking, and gossiping among themselves before they dispersed among the side streets of the camp, I could not imagine in the least that the strike that would take place before the end of the year would be a bloody event that would end in tragedy.

13

But It's Too Late

Finally, the heat broke—you thought that the blazing summer would go on until Doomsday!—and the temperature at night dropped. You could sleep indoors between four walls without feeling like you were choking. You picked up your beds and took them back inside. Some younger men in particular continued to sleep outside for a few nights under the open sky, savoring the cold snaps at dawn as they curled up under the blankets. But the number of beds set up outside began to decrease as autumn progressed, until finally the paths were deserted. Silence returned, and with it the packs of dogs that occupied the empty spaces throughout the camp. Your room recovered the familiarity of well-known places, after having been almost deserted during the summer. Its scattered contents gazed at you indifferently as if they were strange to you. Istifan's bed, which you had taken with you into the room, stood alone unmade in its place under the birdcage, with its rusty iron and black drooping wires. It seemed like a coffin or bier, not so much in shape as in the impression that such a sight leaves inside you—a sad, bewildering sensation that suddenly overwhelms you. It's rather like the feeling when you step inside a cemetery and are conscious of a stillness surrounding you: a constant, unchanging stillness, unshaken by anything in this world that gently envelops you. It leaves you silently thinking that you too could go at any moment, until you are roused from your musings by a car horn, some noise behind the cemetery wall, or the voice of someone beside you, reminding you that the time has come to leave the world of the dead and return to the world of the living. But your room's face changed after everyone had set up their own bed and spread their bedding on it. The room acquired new colors. Only Istifan's bed remained distant, emphasizing its occupant's absence more than ever before.

"Why did you bring this bed in?" asked Abu Jabbar, looking at it furiously.

"Because it's part of the furniture!" replied Muzhir. It was a weak reason. The fact was that no one knew why you—Hussein and yourself—had taken it upon yourselves to pick up the bed and bring it into the room.

"I'll talk to Daniel. He'll either take it away or else they'll bring us a new one in its place!"

Abu Jabbar left the room, his mind made up. I was surprised how disturbed he was at the presence of that empty bed. After a little while he came back with two men from rations, who lifted the bed up and took it out of the room. There was still some doubt up until then that you were one short. And any of you could still have persuaded yourselves that your absent friend had perhaps gone on holiday to visit his family and would definitely be coming back.

"Now, what do you think? Let's rearrange the beds! Muzhir, my friend, come and help me," said Abu Jabbar calmly, grasping the edge of the bed.

This time he attempted to cover the piece of floor that had become empty and open for all to see, like a large wound that refused to heal. Abu Jabbar wanted to bury the dead man and forget about him forever. You rearranged the beds. Abu Jabbar occupied the side facing the door to be able to move his enormous frame freely without bumping into anything. Hussein was on the left, while you and Muzhir put your beds and little cupboards next to the wall on the right . Your bed was under the birdcage, from which the bird would drop leftovers of food onto your bed, or occasionally a single small feather that would quiver in the air before falling. You would watch it as it hovered above your head and descended slowly before coming to rest, with its lines and colors, on the blanket, on the pillow, on the open page of your book, or in some other place where the breeze carried it.

You were wondering why Abu Jabbar hadn't proposed to get rid of the bird (perhaps it was because the bird was alive, despite refusing to make any noise, and flapped its wings to remind you of its existence). It was only the place that had regained its human warmth with the changing of the room's appearance; you yourselves, the room's occupants, had become lukewarm in your relationships, with Muzhir no longer talking to Hussein, after the night you all remembered. It was easy for him to avoid you all at rest times during the summer days and nights, but after you had gone back inside to sleep in your room again he could not avoid meeting Hussein and exchanging words with him when necessary. Muzhir had regained some of his composure and self-respect. The rumors said that he no longer responded to the transport manager's demands. They had started about a month previously, when the men began to see him going down to town on his days off, cramming himself between them on an open truck . . . one of them again, without any special favors.

On the other hand, the relationship between Hussein and Abu Jabbar had cooled some time ago, especially after the doubts that Hussein had raised about Abu Jabbar's connection with the death of the three men in the sewage tank. They talked to one another as before, but you could sense, from the looks and facial expressions, a mutual antipathy between them, disguised by what seemed on the surface to be the easy gossip between friends, or two people who had known one another for a long time. In reality, deep down they didn't want to see each other, but were forced to behave in a certain way because they shared a single room. In short, the two men were skilled actors, and you had a suspicion that each of them had hidden motives. Hussein would often leave the room. One day, while visiting the dam, he disclosed to you that the day of the big strike was approaching, but he didn't tell you the precise date, perhaps because he didn't know it himself. He told you that he and others were busy stirring up the men and preparing them for that day, and asked you to give him your reply to his proposal that you should write for the opposition papers. But you left him in suspense. You were afraid of the consequences. Abu Jabbar would also leave the room during the evening to drink with Daniel. He had stopped setting up an evening drinking table with his room-mates. Muzhir would go out to visit his friend Fawzi, the rig operator, or sit with you in the room, trying to read as well. It was as if he were trying, through his constant presence in the camp after work hours, to prove to you and the others that he was no longer just a man with an organ for John Sullivan to use to satisfy his perverted lusts whenever he chose. In the midst of all these strong and conflicting relationships, you were trying not to be influenced by what any of them thought of the others, and to remain friendly with them all—at the same time not letting this friendship reach the point of letting them intrude on your private life. You tried to leave enough space between yourself and each one of these characters to be able to observe what was happening, and to play your part as a storyteller and participant in events with as much neutrality as possible. The Indian clerk, Mr. Fadlallah, had advised you, before being struck down by illness and transferred to the project hos-pital in Basra, to look long into others' eyes if you wanted to discover anything about what they were hiding inside them; but you discovered that looking into other people's eyes didn't usually lead you to anything specific. And if you noticed, after that advice, that Mr. Fox's gray eyes changed color whenever he heard anything said in Arabic that aroused his attention, the discovery was due to having learned the secret from others: from the engineer Husam, then from the Indian clerk. When you caught Abu Jabbar at the beginning of that winter rummaging through Hussein's cupboard, he looked at you innocently, told you that his cigarettes had run out, and that he was looking for a pack to bor-row; but you remained confused, not knowing whether to doubt his intentions or to believe his eyes. Mr. Fadlallah had forgotten to tell you that trying to look for secrets in other people's eyes in the first place demands doubt. If its basis is trust (blind trust, as they say), all the wis-dom in the world will not help you and you won't be able to discover anyone's secret to save yourself from harm. But it was too late . . . too late, for events began to gather pace after that, as if they had simply been waiting for the arrival of winter, to lead you on, together with the characters in your novel, without your being able to resist them. You were like a small piece of wood or straw, carried on the surface of an overwhelming current, not knowing where it was going.

14

You Need To Be Strong

"Hello, yes John, how are things with you? . . . I caught two pigeons yesterday afternoon, near the river . . . . But I didn't see you at the Eagle's Nest! . . . Did you get any news from Maureen? . . . Good news. And how's the baby?"

It was late morning when you went in to Mr. Fox to ask for the afternoon off so that you could go to the village and catch a taxi to town before sunset. You were afraid that he might leave the office and not come back. But the telephone got there first and rang, breaking the silence in the room before you could speak. You wanted to leave and come back later but he gestured to you to wait, so you stood there waiting. The whole space of the room was dominated by his resounding voice and the foul smell of his tobacco. You obviously couldn't hear what the other person, John, was saying on the other end of the line. "I'm happy to hear that," Mr. Fox was saying, then added, "Yes, John, can I help you with something? . . . What did you say his name was? . . . But can't you try him in another job?"

"Don't worry, send him to me and I'll sort it out. I'll need a short note from you." As the other person was talking, Mr. Fox put his pipe in his mouth and took some short, quick puffs at it, then took it out of his mouth to speak himself, though usually he left his pipe in while he was talking. "Yes, John," he said, burying the fingers of his other hand in the hair of his beard, "the letter is essential for the records. You can send it later. A few words will be enough."

The daily ritual of selecting temporary laborers for casual jobs had ended some time ago. A large number of workmen were still waiting in the sun behind the fence, including Farhan al-Abd who had become even more uncouth recently. His swearing had developed to include new expressions that he hadn't previously employed. Mr. Fox no longer smiled in amusement when he heard him. His face would glower as he stood by the window for several minutes looking at him from a distance with a frown, for no one could mistake Farhan's build. He would see him standing there in the sun like a flagpole, surrounded by a bunch of workmen, spouting a jet of inflammatory words. The day that Fox discovered that Farhan's words were no longer just an expression of aimless and precipitate anger (an anger that flared up, then quickly subsided like a fire in a pile of straw), he firmly determined not to give him work at all in future, and ordered Abdullah to remove his name from the temporary laborers' register, which increased Farhan's anger and resentment even more.

"Okay," said Fox, bringing the conversation to an end. "I'll see you tonight in the Eagle's Nest." Then he put the receiver down and looked at you.

"Yes, Mohamet."

You told him why you had come. "Have you finished all your duties?"

"Yes."

"And you want to travel with Mr. Hilmi?"

His eyes were blazing. You had expected him to confront you with this subject one day. Engineer Husam Hilmi had told you that Mr. Fox knew.

"No, I want to travel from the village," you told him.

He took his pipe out of his mouth and put it on the glass ashtray in front of him.

"Sit down!"

He pointed to the chair by his desk. He didn't usually invite you to sit down, so you were a little tense, but he spoke to you calmly, almost kindly. "Tell me, Mohamet, what sort of relationship do you have with Engineer Hilmi?"

"I don't have any relationship with him," you said. "He saw me once lost by the roadside so he took me with him to town on the way. And he's kindly given me a lift three or four times."

"Seven times!"

"Possibly, I didn't count," I muttered, feeling confused.

At that moment Farhan's voice rang out, shaking the air outside. It had the most beautiful ring you had ever heard in your life. Farhan's voice really gave you support.

"And what about the books?" He wanted you to know that he didn't miss anything. But why had he kept silent for so long? You felt hemmed in then by everything in his room. You told him that Engineer Husam Hilmi had borrowed some books from you for someone else, then stopped.

"I know," he said, picking up his pipe and knocking the bowl gently against the glass ashtray. A bit of ash and a few leaves of tobacco, blackened but not burned, fell into the ashtray. You were wondering where all this would end. He wasn't angry, but his anger didn't usually appear on the surface anyway. He spoke again without changing the tone of his voice, "I hope that your need for a comfortable means of transport to your family is the only reason for this behavior." Then he took his tobacco pouch out of his pocket, a yellow leather pouch, so worn it was about to fall apart. "But I'm asking you to stop traveling with him. You know that . . . ."

This man was depriving you of your freedom to make friends with people and to live as you liked (to keep the office secrets, so he said). He'd warned you before and you hadn't objected: you needed a job and it had seemed simple to you. But you didn't know then exactly what the condition meant. He wanted to erect a wall between you and the others.

"I am perfectly happy with your work for me, and I don't want you to do anything foolish that will ruin your future."

He uttered this veiled threat in the same calm, kindly tone as before. Meanwhile, his fingers were occupied, at a distance from himself, with taking the tobacco from the pouch and filling the pipe bowl, with almost mechanical movements. Some of the smaller golden tobacco leaves fell through his fingertips and landed in the middle of the black ash in the tray. "You've got nothing to do with those men there," he said, pressing down on the tobacco in the pipe bowl with his thumb. "In future, when you want to visit your family, just tell me and I'll arrange for you to travel with the mail van."

"Thank you," I said, and got up. He put his pipe in his mouth and picked up his rusty metal lighter.

"As for today, you can go at any time, but just wait for a bit. They are sending us a workman who is stirring up trouble and I want you here to translate for me."

You tried not to smile. He was still pretending that he didn't know Arabic. A fresh cloud of tobacco smoke rose up to the top of the room, as you left and went back to your own place. Jirjis's chair was empty. Abdullah told you that he'd gone to Accounts. You sat at your desk with a slight headache, avoiding Abdullah's glances and the looks of the caretaker. But Abdullah noticed it. "Brother Muhammad," he said, cheerily, trying to relieve your annoyance, the reasons for which he didn't know. "Listen to what this man says in his application: 'Among my qualifications is that I have visited every city in Iraq except for the Amara province and the town of Tuzkhurmatu'!"

Abdullah always picked up on this sort of simple, innocent talk that some people wrote in order to get work on the project. But he left the application to one side and looked at you, "So, the boss didn't agree to the vacation?"

"On the contrary, he said that I could leave the office at any time," you said, smiling to dispel his doubts.

"Mr. Muhammad," said Mazlum, "if you visit Mr. Fadlallah in hospital, give him my greetings, I'm thinking of him!"

"They say that his days are numbered," said Abdullah. On your last visit to him you had found him wasting away, shriveled up like a corpse roasted by the sun. Just a heap of bones under burned, tatty, yellow skin. His eyes (those eyes!) were gazing at the world around him in silent reproach, as if to scream "Why?" in the face of some monstrous unseen force.

Outside, Farhan was yelling loudly, "Down with the Conservative Party!"

You stood at the window. The workmen were still standing in groups behind the fence near the small gate. Some of them had their eyes on the office building, while others were sitting or lying on the ground, resting their heads on their shoulders or their folded arms, sleeping in the sun. Farhan was gripping the top of the closed gate with his hands, shouting over their heads on his own, "And down with Churchill, Eden, and Attlee!"

"How long before Farhan puts himself forward for Parliament?" asked Abdullah, laughing behind your back. Mazlum laughed, but you didn't. Farhan had said all he had to say for that day. Tired of shouting, he left the gate, followed by the workmen who had despaired of waiting. Even the ones who had been sitting or lying on the ground got up, shook the dust from their clothes, and followed him back to the village. You stayed for a while watching the group of men move away from the road in their threadbare clothes, led by the dark-skinned man with his distinctive, towering frame and his bare head. Jirjis came in with some papers in his hand and you sat down again behind your desk. You told him that you'd asked permission from the boss to leave early, and he busied himself with his papers. You heard the caretaker talking to someone who was standing hesitantly outside, "Come in, come in and shut the door!"

Then Muzhir's face appeared. He was fearful and disturbed. He stood looking round, then when he caught sight of you he came toward you. You smiled at him to put him at his ease. "Greetings, Muzhir, come in . . . is there something I can do for you?"

His features relaxed a little as he approached you. He had found someone he could rely on. "You asked," he muttered in confusion. "The transport manager told me, he said you wanted to see me. He said, 'Go to . . . they want you.' Do you know why?"

So the telephone conversation I'd heard in Fox's room a little while ago had been partly about Muzhir, the man who was stirring up trouble, as the director had put it!

"Have you done something?" you asked, sensing what the reason might be.

"No," he said angrily, "but I refused . . . ."

He didn't know where to turn with his eyes.

You told Jirjis, who informed the director through the crack in the wall that Muzhir was there, then turned toward you.

"He wants you to go in with him!"

The pair of you went in. "Good morning, sir!" said Muzhir in English, trying to gain his favor. Fox looked at him carefully as if trying to recall where he had seen him before. Then he turned toward you, "Tell this man that his boss John Sullivan is not happy with him at all, so we have decided to sack him!"

Although you had heard of Fox sometimes taking harsh decisions like that about workmen, you were startled by his words, and Muzhir was stunned. His face turned pale and he looked baffled. Perhaps he was expecting some sort of punishment, a reprimand, or a warning, something like that. But to be sacked!

"But why? What have I done?" I heard him stammer, in English again. He spoke politely, folding his hands behind his back and keeping them there out of sight, so as not to make any stupid movement that might provoke the boss. Perhaps he was hoping that he might change his mind.

"You know very well why!"

"But I haven't done anything. Ask them!"

Fox took his pipe out of his mouth so as to speak more easily. "You don't obey your boss's orders and you are deliberately destroying the machinery. And furthermore, you have begun to incite other people to disobey orders!"

"Me? Destroying machinery? Inciting other people?" said Muzhir incredulously.

His hands had broken loose and his palms were pointing at his chest to reinforce his denial. You hadn't known that Muzhir could make himself understood in English. He didn't speak it perfectly but he could express what he wanted to in his own way, with the help of his hands. You remained just an onlooker.

"Yes, you!" said Fox sharply.

"That's not true, not true. He's demanding . . . ."

His voice was choked with anger, but he was reluctant to reveal the reason why his boss was displeased with him.

"You mean that your boss Mr. Sullivan is lying?"

"Yes, John is lying!"

You immediately realized that it was Muzhir who was being untruthful, not only because he had accused his manager of lying but also because he had made the mistake of using his manager's first name, as if he was his bosom buddy or someone of lower rank. You would have liked to help Muzhir in honing his rough and stumbling responses, but he was off, not knowing how to defend himself, dispatching his blows anyhow, like a desperate victim at the end of the road, bleeding to death. For a moment, silence reigned . . . a moment of tense silence. Fox got up from his seat and went out. His eyes were blazing. He stretched his arm toward the door and shouted in a thundering voice, "Get out! Get outside!"

You had never seen Fox so angry before. When you saw him move, you thought that he was going to strike Muzhir—who indeed seemed prepared for this possibility. But the manager opened the door of the room and stood to one side.

"Get out, you queer!"

This final insult was the one thing that Fox had said in Arabic, pretending that it was among the few words that he had learned. But where had he learned this word?

"You're the queer!" Muzhir replied, provocatively.

Perhaps Muzhir didn't know the meaning of the word that he had repeated to the director, but just didn't want to keep quiet about the insult and be chased out of the room. At this point Fox put his hand on Muzhir's back and pushed him out of the room. "You Arabs need force! You Arabs need Turks to control you, yes, Turks!"

You left the room with Muzhir, insulted as well. You heard him shut the door behind the pair of you, slamming it hard. Jirjis, Abdullah, and Mazlum were standing aghast in their places, startled by shouting of a sort that hadn't been heard in the office before.

"By God, I'll kill him! This bastard . . . this . . . !"

Muzhir began to shout agitatedly, leaving the tables behind and moving outside like a wounded tiger. "What happened? What's up with the boss?"

But you ignored Jirjis's questions and left the office. The distance between yourself and Muzhir had increased dramatically, for he had begun to hurry back to his place of work. He had evil intentions. You ran after him and grabbed him.

"Muzhir, calm down! Calm down, please! Let's talk!"

"I'll kill him! By God, I'll kill him, really! He imagines. . . ! Did you see, Brother Muhammad? Did you see?" he shouted, his tears welling from his eyes with anger.

"Come on, let's go to the camp, to calm down, and after that . . . ."

You took his hand. It was burning hot, but after a little, you were able to take him with you, and he walked along muttering beside you.

"I never imagined . . . ."

The guard opened the gate for the pair of you and you left the work area. His hand was still shaking in yours. His whole body was shaking with fear, like a threatened animal. You were also upset yourself, perhaps more than him. Mr. Fox, through that horrid outburst, had made you take a decision at last. Today you would say yes to Hussein. Yes, if the expected strike happened, you would support him by whatever means you could, whatever the consequences. You weren't bothered any more about an increase in pay or an improvement in working conditions. All you wanted was to see how the face of this fox looked when the men left their work and everything closed down. The important thing now was for the big strike to begin quickly!

15
A Stray Bullet

"You don't know how pleased I am that you've agreed at last!"

"I know, you told me that before."

"Muhammad, my friend . . . ."

We were coming back from the village. We had been attending the Qur'an ceremony arranged by the caretaker Mazlum for Fadlallah in the big tent set up by Mazlum on the patch of land near his house. A venerable sheikh sat reciting verses from the Holy Qur'an for the spirit of the deceased, while three or four loudspeakers broadcast his booming voice into the village air, thick with greasy fish and the smell of the river. Meanwhile, the mourners sat humbly inside, usually with gloomy faces. Some of them were watching the reciter putting one of his hands on his ear whenever he wanted to raise his voice, and noticing the movement of his lips. But the men were actually hearing the amplified voice being broadcast by the loudspeakers. As they listened to the reciter—or perhaps they were not listening to him—they would exchange general gossip among themselves in a low voice, though the dead man had not been a friend of any of those present and they only knew his yellow, burned face. Others, who had never entered the management office for any reason, did not even know his face, but had come to the Qur'an recital nonetheless.

Mr. Fadlallah had died two days previously. We were busy with our papers when Jirjis came out from the manager's office and told us the news, which we had in fact been expecting for some time. The boss, God bless him, had ordered his family to be supplied with a large tent, a microphone, and seats for the Qur'an recital, together with a grant for the funeral, twenty dinars in all.

"He hasn't got any family here," Jirjis had said, almost proudly. The caretaker Mazlum had told him so. "Then who will be responsible?" asked the chief clerk.

"I will, sir. The deceased lived with me."

"Okay, but in that case, the funeral expenses . . . ."

"It's easy, sir. We'll collect donations."

But Jirjis rejected that suggestion firmly. "Mr. Fox won't agree!"

"We'll collect them secretly, sir!"

"No, Mazlum!" Then he turned toward me. "Muhammad, don't worry, I'm going to the finance people."

As he was on his way to the door he told the caretaker to follow him. Mazlum wasn't outside long, but came back after a few minutes. In answer to our questioning looks, he looked cautiously toward the opening in the wall, then lifted his hand, but we couldn't see anything. His hand was clenched, but he opened first one finger, then another, revealing the side of a one-dinar bank note. He quickly dropped his hand again.

"Is this from . . . ?" asked Abdullah in disbelief. Mazlum bowed his head. "But he said . . . ."

Abdullah looked at me in surprise. "This man . . . I don't know in what . . . ."

The voice of the reciter filled the village air as sunset approached. Everyone was looking at his watch or asking his neighbor the time, then beginning to leave—the Muslims after reciting the Fatiha, and the Christians after making the sign of the cross on their chests while standing up. Everyone left the recital session more or less at once, for fear that the workers' canteen in the camp would close its doors and they would have to spend the night without supper.

We walked quickly along the long road leaving the village behind us. The large, pale disk of the sun was on the point of touching the face of the earth. As he walked beside me, Hussein asked, "Were you expecting such a large number?"

"No. A lot of people came!"

I really hadn't been expecting to see so many people at the memorial recitation for a retiring stranger with few friends. Perhaps they'd come as a courtesy to the caretaker Mazlum, but there was doubtless another reason. Fadlallah had been a kindly man who harmed no one. In his first few days in the office he'd seemed to me to be a servile person, who trembled in the presence of Mr. Fox, and who would cringe in front of him with hands folded, whispering, in reply to the orders given to him, the same English phrases time and again: "Yes, sir! As you say, sir! Whatever you say, sir!" Later, however, I became aware of his eyes. Whenever the boss was busy with his papers or with the telephone, for example, Fadlallah would give him sideways glances filled with an indescribable hatred. It wasn't so much a personal fear so much as a historical legacy, so it seemed to me. Perhaps this was the reason for all the hidden resentment that the dead man had borne in his heart for Mr. Fox.

"Muhammad, people generally . . . ," began Hussein, as he tried to explain the reasons that had driven all those people to come to the village and attend the funeral recitation. But I didn't have much confidence in his explanations, as he spoke about the motives of the human soul in the language of politics.

The sun's disk had chosen a spot for itself at the edge of the desert and had gone to rest there. The men lowered their voices spontaneously. The darkness that descended on them from the heavens quite suddenly was like a cloak, wrapping their hurrying bodies and covering their voices as well. But the noise of rushing footsteps remained the same, as it now turned into the sound that dominated the men's grumbling as they ambled along the deserted track, amid the silence on both sides—the silence of the desert and the silence of the palm groves where nothing could be heard except the chafing of the palm fronds at the top of the trees. "And you'll see them with your own eyes," said Hussein, in a voice that was more like a whisper, because of the darkness and the dangerous nature of the subject that he was talking about.

"But when?" you asked him, almost running out of patience. "You've been talking about it for ages!"

He turned to look at the faces of the men, which seemed impassive as they swayed along the road, then whispered, "Soon, soon!"

The darkness had fallen with remarkable speed among the tree trunks on the right of the road. But the desert on our left seemed slightly less dark, perhaps because of the emptiness and the whiteness of the salt that covered the face of the earth.

"This Saturday is the day," said Hussein, after a little hesitation.

"So it's been decided at last!"

"It may still be postponed for some reason. We're waiting for the signal from Basra."

The camp drew nearer, squatting at the edge of the desert, with its scattered lamps glinting at the ends of the paths and on the balconies. The big silver-colored tanks shone under the glare of the searchlights.

"And it seems that they know, for the arrests have begun."

I couldn't see his face clearly but I guessed that he would be frowning. Arrests from now on.

"This will be my last night in the camp," he informed me in a whisper. "After that, I'll be spending the night in the village, at a friend's house."

"But they can take you during the day, from work!"

"True, but they usually come at night, so as not to provoke an outcry."

The footsteps around us began to gather pace, as if the smell of food that the breeze carried toward us from the direction of the camp was drawing the men toward it. It was nearly six, and the canteen closed its doors at seven. The palm groves that had accompanied us like a black wall to the right of the road came to an end, and the work zone appeared in front of us—the high wire fence, and the open ground, with offices, warehouses, and workshops spread over it, with a group of tanks some way away. I saw a small number of men, four or five of them, moving in the distance between the lit-up hills. Small black creatures creeping over the ground. I was conscious of the frailty of my own body as we walked near those masses of iron that dominated the whole place.

When we moved away from them I felt that we had escaped from the clutches of some dreadful creatures. I never felt this sort of effect during daylight hours, perhaps because daylight gives a man a stature bigger than his own, while night turns him into a dwarf in the world of the creatures around him.

The men went down with us from the raised road and entered the camp yard. Under the light of the lamp hanging over the guard's kiosk, they regained the features stolen from them by the darkness of the road. At that moment, we were startled by a policeman standing in the entrance, the barrel of the rifle that hung from his shoulder glinting under the light. The man was deep in conversation with the guard. Hussein grasped my hand and said, exaggerating his unease, "We must behave naturally!"

We hurried past the men's outlines as the policeman turned his face to look at the men going in, but he didn't seem to be paying special attention to anyone in particular.

"Strange, just one man!"

"Perhaps there are others in the mess," I said, unconvinced.

"Or with Daniel," he added, looking closely along the camp paths.

The men began hurrying toward the mess, almost racing each other, but he suddenly let go of my hand and headed off toward the rows of rooms.

"You're not coming to supper?"

He shook his head.

"No, you go. And tell me if you see or hear anything."

He left me and went away with his head bowed as if wanting to hide his face from prying eyes. I didn't see any strange faces in the mess. Daniel was in his place behind the cooks, and there was a queue of men and the usual noise, the clinking of spoons and plates around the tables. Jirjis sat eating with the chief clerk in accounts. Abu Jabbar, who had finished eating, was still sitting in a corner listening to what the men around him were saying. I finished my food quickly to give Hussein enough time to eat his own supper, then went back to him. The door was ajar; I pushed it open and found him sitting on the bed waiting, having lit the heater, so that the air in the room was filled with warmth and a slight smell of paraffin. I told him there was nothing to worry about and that he could go and eat with his mind at rest before suppertime finished. He left the room; I changed my clothes and lay down on the bed. I was tired after traveling to the village and back. I had to attend the Qur'an recitation the following day, then everything would be finished. Mr. Fadlallah would become a thing forgotten, and after a time (short or long as it may be) it would be hard for me to imagine what his face looked like. His words might stay with me longer, but even his words would be erased by time in the end.

He had gone, like Istifan before him, though he had died in middle age, if that was any comfort. I looked at the cage hanging on the wall. I mustn't forget to put out food for the bird in the morning and to change its water, for this eternally silent creature would never complain, even if worn out by hunger and thirst. The room was quiet, and the three empty beds were standing silently against the wall. Muzhir's was still spread out on the bed beside mine, as if its occupant was still living with us. This was another person who had left us, though he at least was still alive. I could suppose that he was still alive, living somewhere in the country. Perhaps he'd gone back to his family in Nasiriyya, or gone to look for work somewhere else. I was looking at his bedding miserably, amid the silence of the room, when suddenly the air was shaken by the sound of shooting, like an explosion coming from somewhere not far off. The noise shattered the silence of the night. I jumped up from my bed and pushed open the door to the room, which was already ajar. I saw people standing by the doors to the other rooms asking what the shooting was all about. I saw Hussein coming toward me clutching his shoulder. "What's happened? What's going on?" I asked in alarm.

He seemed agitated as he brushed past me and went into the room. I shut the door and he collapsed onto his bed. His eyes were rolling.

"You're injured! What happened?"

"They want to kill me!"

"But who?"

He seemed stunned and confused, like someone who has been surprised by a danger that he hadn't reckoned on. The noise outside was getting steadily louder. I moved toward the door but he shouted a warning to me. "No, don't open it!"

I went back to him. "Let me see, let me see the wound! Don't sit like that!"

He lifted his hand from his shoulder, and I saw the color of blood on the palm of his hand. He began to look at his spattered hand without saying anything. The fabric of his jacket over his shoulder was singed, and stained with blood.

"Take it off! Take your jacket off!"

I helped him take it off. The spot of blood on his shirt seemed larger, and there were damp red lines extending in various directions down the fabric on his sleeve. I couldn't make out how deep the wound was under the soaked cloth, but when he had got his arm out of his clothes the size of the wound became clearer. It wasn't a serious injury.

"Thank God!" I said, to calm him. "It's a minor wound, just on the skin!"

"All this blood!" he said disbelievingly, turning his face toward his injured shoulder as he tried to inspect the site of the injury.

"Just a minor wound, believe me, but who fired at you? Was it . . . ?"

"I don't know. I was coming back from the mess. When I got near the row of rooms I heard the shot, and I felt a burning sensation. I didn't see . . . ."

The noise outside gradually began to subside, and then dispersed. "I'll get your clothes changed and go with you to the surgery," I said.

"No," he protested. "Dr. Sami will see that the wound was caused by a bullet and will hand me over to the police. And I . . . ."

"Okay, I'll go to Daniel, and get you some medicine and a muslin bandage."

"I've got some, in my cupboard, under the clothes. The key's in my pocket."

"Couldn't it have been a stray bullet?" I asked as I bandaged his wound. "Perhaps someone was trying to test a gun, and hit you!"

He looked at me in astonishment. "Here? Test it here? Who would dare?" He shook his head. "No, no, this is an attempt . . . quite certainly!"

I took his spattered shirt off him and put him into a dishdasha. He took his trousers and shoes off then sat on his bed and looked blankly in front of him. His body was shaking. I didn't know whether that was because he was feeling cold after being exposed to the air or because of his injury. I was picking up the heater to carry it closer to his bed when Abu Jabbar came in carrying a red apple in one hand. He didn't see the injured shoulder as it was hidden under his clothes, but he noticed that Hussein's face looked pale and that he was staring vacantly. He turned and looked in my direction. "Is he okay? What's wrong with him?"

"Someone fired a shot at him," I said. "And hit him in the shoulder."

Hussein raised his head and gave him a hostile look. "Your friends!"

"You mean, the shot we heard?" asked Abu Jabbar in alarm.

He went up to Hussein's bed and stretched his hand out to pull back the edge of his clothes to see the injury. But Hussein held his clothes in place and Abu Jabbar abandoned his attempt, pulling his hand back and muttering, "What a clumsy fellow this policeman is! They brought him in to get rid of the stray dogs for us but it seems that . . . ."

Hussein interrupted him firmly. "Get rid of the stray dogs? At night?"

"Night or day, my friend, the important thing is to get rid of them for us. But you're right, a man like this . . . . I hope the wound's not serious," he added gently.

"No, just a small wound," I told him. "The shot just grazed the flesh on the shoulder."

"Thank God he's okay!"

Hussein, though, paid no attention to his expressions of concern and looked at him suspiciously. Abu Jabbar moved closer to the bed. The wooden slats beneath it started to creak as he sat down. He wiped his apple on the pillow and said, "Hussein, my lad, you should sacrifice a sheep, for God's sake!" Then he looked at the apple, whose skin had begun to shine, and said, "Sacrifice a sheep and distribute the meat to the poor in the village, or to these out-of-work people who are gathering outside."

He bit a chunk out of his apple then carried on as he ate, "God most high has willed that you should be unharmed, that is, if . . . ."

But we didn't hear the rest of what he was saying, for the air was shaken by the ring of another shot followed immediately by the yelping of a dog. It was a short, intermittent howl of pain, like the final flicker of a fire before it goes out. Then the dog was silent.

"There, lad," said Abu Jabbar, turning his face toward Hussein. "Convinced now?"

A clamor had started outside again, together with hurried footsteps. There was general confusion, as though someone had been injured. Abu Jabbar got up from his bed.

"A fight, by the sound of it!"

"You believe that sort of talk?" said Hussein when we were alone.

"You mean, you still think . . . ?"

"Definitely!"

"And Abu Jabbar knows, you think?"

"Certainly!"

He was no longer shaking now that you had moved the heater nearer, and some of the blood had returned to his cheeks. But his suspicions seemed exaggerated.

"Have we become so depraved?"

He gave me an almost pitying look. "Muhammad, my friend, depravity is like a downward spiral!"

It was difficult to persuade him that the bullet was not intended for *him*. Perhaps he wanted to persuade himself, before persuading anyone else, that he was an important man and that other people ought to take him seriously. But then again, perhaps he was correct in his suspicions, for it would be equally baffling for the policeman to turn up after dark to kill stray dogs. Why at night?

The clamor outside became louder, then subsided, only to increase again. Sometimes the voices moved away and sometimes they drew closer, as if the people fighting (supposing that there was a fight) were carrying their voices with them to defend themselves. Then the noise subsided. Only one voice continued to resound outside. I asked Hussein whether the wound was hurting him. "Just a bit," he said, and smiled at me. That was the first time he had smiled since coming into the room, wounded and frightened. Meanwhile, Abu Jabbar was coming back to the room. We heard his heavy footsteps coming closer on the balcony, then he pushed open the door and came in.

"Another problem created for us by this policeman!"

"Has he hit someone else?" I asked in alarm.

"No, he hit a dog this time!"

I was sitting on my bed, while he was standing like a miniature wall in the middle of the room. I couldn't see the expression on Hussein's face, who was sitting on his bed on the other side.

"What's the problem, then?"

"The problem is that he left all the stray dogs inside the camp alone, then our friend killed the dog belonging to Fawzi, the rig operator!"

Hussein laughed. He didn't speak, just gave a little laugh.

Abu Jabbar moved from his place and examined him.

He had begun to calm down a little, and his features were less contorted. Abu Jabbar bent down over his trunk that he had placed under his bed. He had continued to keep most of his things inside that tin trunk despite having a cupboard like all the rest of us. He started talking, one of his hands holding it open and the other rummaging inside the trunk.

"Fawzi's mad. He went out of his mind when he saw his dog laid out on the ground, not breathing, completely lifeless."

Abu Jabbar got out a bottle of arrack from the trunk, then shut it, and stood up. His face was furious.

"Whenever they got him away from the policeman he would come back and attack him. We just couldn't get him back to his room. I left a group of his friends with him . . . he'd wrapped his hands round the man's neck and was on the point of . . . ."

Hussein laughed again, while I looked at him in confusion. I couldn't tell if he was laughing because he was pleased to have escaped a fatal blow while the dog had died, or if he was laughing in satisfaction because the policeman had created a new enemy for the project management by killing Fawzi's dog. Or perhaps the reason for his sudden satisfaction was a mixture of obscure feelings that he was unconscious of himself. Abu Jabbar looked at him in silence, then smiled, "This Fawzi's mad! The policeman's got an excuse. How was he to know that this scruffy dog had an owner?"

He transferred the bottle of arrack to his other hand.

"I would never have imagined this Fawzi . . . such a meek man! He was beside himself today! A dead dog! Find another one! Has the world got no dogs in it? The tragedy is here, with us!"

He spoke the last word looking at Hussein's face, then added in a fatherly tone, "If it weren't for God's mercy . . . ."

He approached his bed, almost touching the heater. "Imagine, Muhammad, this policeman couldn't have known that he had injured someone with his first bullet! I told him off; after we got Fawzi away from him I took him on one side and told him off. He seemed scared. He said, "I . . . .""

Abu Jabbar suddenly stopped speaking and moved away from the heater, looking at the fabric of his trousers. "He said he'd seen a dog running so he fired at it. 'I didn't see any man,' he said. I said, 'You're in luck, because . . . .'"

Hussein was looking at him the whole time, the look you would give someone you know is lying, while he went on talking passionately, trying to prove something.

"He wanted to come with me, to apologize to you, but I advised him to go away, to take his rifle and leave. Before Fawzi escaped from the hands of his friends. He refused at first, he thought it was an insult. But finally he went away. It's better he comes during the day."

He looked into my face, then into Hussein's face. He was looking for something in our eyes. Some trust, perhaps.

"Of course that would be better. He could distinguish things better by day," I said, trying to hide my embarrassment under his penetrating looks.

At this point, Abu Jabbar left the room carrying his bottle. "Most puzzling!" he exclaimed.

"A first-rate actor," said Hussein, looking at the door of the room, which Abu Jabbar had left ajar on his way out.

"Don't bother about him too much," I said, getting up. "Try to sleep now. It's been a hard day!"

I took his jacket from him and made him stretch out on the bed. He lay on his good arm. I drew up the blanket and covered his thin body with it.

"Muhammad, my friend," he said, before shutting his eyes. "Please don't let your tongue slip, and mention anything in front of him."

He was thinking again about his one nightmare, after convincing himself that his injury was superficial and wouldn't harm him.

I hung his jacket on the hook, picked up the paraffin heater and extinguished it outside the room. I shut the door and sat on my bed thinking about the day's events. Had they really tried to kill him? Most likely, it had been a stray bullet. But if his guess was right, I was a witness to a bitter struggle between the project management and the workers—a struggle that would end with God only knew what losses.

16

Diary of a Bloody Strike

Day One: The Challenge

Y ou are standing at the window, puzzled. It is Saturday today. Nothing has happened out of the ordinary. When the work siren gave out its metallic screech this morning everyone turned up as usual, answering its insistent summons. Had things been postponed? Hussein hadn't told you anything. You hadn't seen much of him since he'd started spending the night in the village with a number of other men. Outside, the sun spread its generous rays over everything—the almost-deserted road going down to town, the camp that seemed quiet from the distance, the burning desert, the outline of the rig standing alone in the desolate landscape, and the men without work, as they stood in their morning position that never changed (almost like a natural phenomenon).

And Farhan al-Abd, a man who never tired of waiting, even after Mr. Fox had slammed the work door in his face, was standing among them. Today, however, Farhan was standing unusually silent. Do you suppose he knew something as well? The machines and turbines that were busy all over the work area filled the air with continuous monotonous thuds, like the vibrations of a set of taut strings strummed by nimble hands in an unchanging single tune. Everything seemed peaceful, but nevertheless you felt that there was tension in the air. Perhaps your expectations were the cause of it, or perhaps it was how the others were behaving: Farhan's disturbing silence behind the fence; the questioning looks of the clerk, Abdullah, as he raised his head from the typewriter from time to time to listen to the noises carried on the wind; the behavior of the caretaker, Mazlum, who would slip out of the office occasionally, then resume his seat; Jirjis's unusual absorption in his papers, with a serious as he champed on his false teeth; or the silence of the manager sitting behind the wall, smoking his horrid tobacco. Mr. Fox hadn't moved from his place today to select the temporary workers as he did most mornings; he was expecting something too.

"Haven't you got any work today, Muhammad?" the chief clerk asked you drily, bending over his papers.

"Yes."

"Then get on with it!"

You left the window and sat down. It was nearly nine now. A man came in, one of Mr. Fox's plants among the workforce. He came in quickly, almost frightened.

"I have to see the boss," he muttered, without looking anyone in the eye. He didn't wait for the chief clerk to give him permission to go in to the manager. He crossed the room, knocked on the door himself, and went in. Jirjis's face seemed worried, while Mazlum, the caretaker, smiled where he was. A few moments later, another man came in to the office, just as frightened and agitated.

"Is the boss here?"

The chief clerk jumped up. Fear had infected him too. "Has . . . ?" he asked in alarm.

"Yes, sir."

At that moment the manager left his room, followed by the man who had been with him. The second man tried to give him the news he had brought with him, so that the first man wouldn't have a monopoly on the boss's approval.

"Sir, I . . . ."

But Fox interrupted him curtly. "I know, I know, now go away!"

He watched them with distaste as they slipped out of the office, a little stunned. Perhaps they had been expecting some praise for their timely reporting of events. But perhaps Mr. Fox was thinking at that moment that these two men and all his other spies had betrayed him and not communicated to him the true state of affairs at an earlier stage, so what was the point of getting news after the event? Who knows? Perhaps they hadn't been remiss in their duties and had told him everything hour by hour and day by day, but he had underestimated the situation because of his exaggerated self-confidence and his reliance on other people's submissiveness and fear. His face appeared dark and frowning as he stared out the window and chewed nervously on his pipe. His private world, for whose stability he had worked tirelessly, was on the point of collapse. He moved decisively; he snatched his pipe from his mouth and gave an order, "Mr. Jirjis, contact the district head at once. Tell him that some disturbances have occurred; and you, Mohamet, come with me!"

You walk behind him. What will the men say when they see you with him today? Despite that, you feel an unbounded pleasure when you see his troubled face. As the pair of you leave the office, you are hit by an intensely cold wind from the west, whose sharpness has hardly been blunted by the rays of the sun. As you cross the garden with the manager, you are conscious of the fact that the men without work behind the hedge have suddenly disappeared. Farhan al-Abd and everyone else had disappeared like birds before the coming of a storm. Even the guard who usually stood at the door was no longer in his place. He had left the gate open and gone off as well. The other gates used by the workmen, through which passed trucks, pick-ups, and various bicycles, were also open and unguarded, as scores of men flooded out through them. Others were heading for the gates, where more people kept appearing. They were coming out from corners, from office buildings, from the workshops, and from the stores. They had stopped whatever they were doing: each man had left what was in his hand, turned off his machine, given his back to the switchboard, gotten up from his typewriter, thrown down his pen, come down from the ladder—abandoned everything, in fact—when he received the signal, and left his place to join the others. Around fifty or sixty men were walking along the path toward the camp. Disbelievingly, Mr. Fox muttered in English between his teeth, "Bastards, bastards!"

This was the first time that the men had rebelled against the management's authority and left their places of work before the work siren had given them permission to leave. The gray Rover was waiting at the end of the garden, but where had the driver gone?

"Abdul, Abdul!"

The place was deserted. No one answered his call. Was the car driver with them as well?

"Get in!" he said angrily.

He sat behind the wheel himself. The car took you both out of the work area. He was trying to catch up with the bunch of men moving away on the path.

"Did you know?" he asked without looking at you.

"I think that everyone knew in the last couple of days."

"Yes, yes, everyone knew, but why didn't Basra do something?"

He seemed at a loss. It was the first time he had seemed so confused, not knowing what to do.

"I don't understand. I, I mean we, made sure they had everything . . ." (wasn't it odd that this man should be complaining of his troubles to you, an employee of his?), " . . . housing, free food, and their wages."

He seemed to be in a real dilemma, from which he didn't know how to escape. The whole work area had become like a pail of water that had suddenly sprung a leak. You could see lots of men hurrying along the path, but he took no notice of them. He wanted to catch up with the large bunch of men who were now moving through the camp work area in the middle of the road. Perhaps he thought that the leader of the rebellion was there. He pressed his foot harder on the throttle, and the noise of the car engine grew louder amid the strange silence that had come over the entire work area. The incessant buzz of machinery had stopped, to be replaced by a silence like the silence that falls over the ground when the rain stops. That sort of feeling did not even happen on holidays, for there was always someone busy operating a piece of machinery and making the air pulse. Mr. Fox caught up with the group of men and overtook them. The glowering faces—dozens of them—turned and looked at the pair of you. He stopped the car on the mud by the side of the road, about thirty meters away, opened the door and got out. You got out hesitantly too (this wasn't the position you would have liked to see yourself in; you should have stayed away from work, but they hadn't started yet). What was this man trying to do? It was like his own personal battle! The bunch of men continued to hurry along the path, silently and carefully, and a little more slowly; the group had lost its cohesion and become more stretched out. Behind them was a sort of long tail of men, their frames spread out the length of the road, for the gates were still spewing more of them out. As the faces of the men in the front rows started to get closer to you, the air was filled with the sound of approaching steps. In the first row you could make out the faces of Hussein, Fawzi the rig operator, a man who looked like a wrestler (you had seen him once whispering with Hussein near the washhouse in the camp), and several others that you'd seen in the mess. You were astonished to see Farhan al-Abd's face shining in the sun above the level of the others' heads. The distance between the bunch of men at the front and Fox's frame standing in the middle of the road with you beside him was becoming shorter. The men stopped warily about three meters away. Some of them looked uncertain, a little afraid perhaps.

Mr. Fox took his pipe out of his mouth. "Tell them, if they don't go back to work this minute, I will sack them all!"

He spoke angrily and decisively. "Sack us all?" replied the man who looked like a wrestler. "Even those who . . . ."

A noise erupted, drowning his words, then subsided again after a little. The manager spoke again, a little more gently this time. "Tell them that I'll forget the fact that they left work without permission."

Some of the men laughed. Sarcastic comments could be heard from the ranks, while in the meantime their numbers had increased as the stragglers arrived. Mr. Fox noticed and realized, perhaps, that the attempt to get them back to work was becoming more difficult as time went on. You noticed something like pride in the glint of their eyes as they blocked the road (was that because they were enjoying their inner feelings of power for the first time, hearing Mr. Fox himself begging them to go back?).

"By God, everyone," shouted the man who looked like a wrestler. They moved, but Mr. Fox raised his hand. "Please, please!"

What was he trying to do? Delay them while he waited for something to happen? While he waited for someone to come to help persuade them to go back?

"Don't let him make fun of you!" shouted Farhan al-Abd over the heads of the men.

"What's this black man doing here?" asked Fox, his soft voice concealing a sense of distaste.

Farhan's voice rang out again, "Down with Britain!"

Voices were raised asking him to be quiet. You yourself were trying not to smile.

"Tell them that they mustn't let people from outside the project interfere in their affairs!"

"We all. . . ." shouted Farhan.

"Tell them I suggest that they go back, and send me two or three men to tell me their grievances."

A few small waves of laughter could be heard from the men. When they had died down, Hussein said in a calm, unemotional tone, "Our colleagues in Basra are the ones who are negotiating with the top management, and when they come to an agreement. . . ."

Mr. Fox lost his patience. "I am warning you. Anyone who leaves now will have to take his things and leave the camp. I don't want to see him here."

"No one is leaving, we are staying!"

But this threat had some effect, for a noise could be heard at the back of the ranks, something like an argument. Mr. Fox noticed the first signs of a split, the first signs of a split caused by his words.

"Tell them to think of their families. How will they live if. . . ?"

You could see some backs retreating, not many, just five or six people, walking along the edge of the road, returning to the work area.

"You know, we won't give any wages, or food, to anyone"

He was interrupted by the sound of the horn of a wooden bus approaching from the direction of the town. As the horn rang out without a pause, Mr. Fox stepped aside, taking you with him. The crowd of men was split into two halves. The bus pushed its way through with its cargo of men, women, baggage, and animals, covered with dust from the road, while its horn continued its long-drawn-out wail, until it had left the throng of men behind. Only then did the noise of the horn die away and the bodies come together once more and move forward, as if the bus that had passed between them a moment before had woken them from a state of temporary numbness—a numbness whose causes they did not know—with its motion, its noise, and the faces of the despondent people inside. Why had they continued listening to Mr. Fox all this time? But then they carried on without hesitation, paying him no attention, like a river following its course, a river whose gushing waters could not be stopped by a small stone squeezed into the bottom of the mud in the middle of the channel. Mr. Fox shouted in English at the faces that had started to bob before him, "I'll speak to Daniel; he won't give you food!"

But the faces continued to exchange glances. He shook the tobacco from his pipe and put the pipe in his pocket, then hurried over to his car, opened the boot, and took out the rifle that he used to hunt wild pigeons in the palm groves on holidays. Had the man gone mad? He raised the rifle and fired into the air, over the bobbing heads.

The men stopped when they heard the sudden noise behind their backs. They turned toward him startled, with astonished faces. He quickly loaded the gun and shouted at them from where he was standing. "Come on, everyone back to work!"

It was the first time you had heard him speak Arabic. But where had he learned this strange dialect?

The man who looked like a wrestler shouted an imitation of the dialect Mr. Fox was using (perhaps it was a sarcastic imitation, or perhaps he thought that Mr. Fox didn't understand any other dialect, or perhaps it was an unconscious imitation). Then Farhan broke through the ranks and emerged with his tall body, undoing the buttons of his dishdasha with his hand and baring his swarthy chest to the sun. "Fire, Mister, fire!" he shouted as he advanced toward the manager.

Farhan's suicidal behavior inflamed the feelings of the others and a number of them rushed forward, everyone baring their chests and shouting "Fire!" and some shaking their fists threateningly. Fear appeared on Mr. Fox's face and he retreated. He aimed his rifle at their chests, perhaps intending to scare them, but his finger pressed the trigger and a bullet escaped, hitting one of the men in the hand. A stunned silence ensued. Even the man who had been hit didn't make a sound, but merely grabbed his bleeding hand, as he tried to suppress the pain. No one could believe what had happened, perhaps not even Fox himself. (Sometimes events create themselves without your consciously willing them, like moving a small stone on top of a mountain with the tip of your toe, and causing a dreadful avalanche that destroys a whole village.) But the stunned silence didn't last longer than a fraction of a second, during which everyone tried to grasp the significance of what had happened. Then angry voices were raised, and Mr. Fox turned to run toward his car. But they caught up with him. Farhan snatched the rifle from his hands and smashed it on the ground while others grabbed him from every side. It seemed that matters were completely out of hand, beyond the grasp of reason. (Could a little blood do all this?) Hussein, the man who looked like a wrestler, and three or four others were trying to release Mr. Fox from the angry hands.

"Leave him, everyone . . . it's not him . . . !"

Fox himself seized the opportunity presented by their attempt to save him, and the moment of hesitation that followed it, to run to his car, get in, and try to escape. But Farhan al-Abd, Fawzi the rig operator, and a number of other men who couldn't be easily restrained surrounded the car and blocked its path, while others hovered around, eyeing you suspiciously. Hussein noticed them and rushed toward you before they could touch you. He grabbed your arm and spoke quickly, "Go away, go to Basra now! Don't stay here a moment longer!"

His thin face seemed flushed, and his expression suggested an inner agony, some inhibition, and perhaps some embarrassment as well.

"We've had news that they started before us there … you must travel now!"

Then he let go of your arm and moved toward the surrounded car, to see what he could do. The wounded man was now standing to one side, near the fence, out of range of the general chaos. He was surrounded by a number of men who were trying to find out how deep the wound was. He seemed quite proud of his wound, although it had been just a moment of enthusiasm that had made him stand at the front, driven on by the mad shouting around him.

You went off on your own in the opposite direction, toward the camp. When you turned round in a few moments you found Mr. Fox's car upside down on its roof. Its black tires were in the air at the edge of the road, and there were men moving away from it. You didn't know whether he was in it or not. At the same time, you noticed two police vehicles moving toward the camp. Daniel and his assistant were staring in confusion at the agitated bodies moving along the road, and were trying to work out exactly what was happening, but from a distance. "Muhammad," asked Daniel, as you approached them, "I heard shots and could see a disturbance over there! Has something happened?"

"No, Daniel, nothing's happened!"

You left him confused and went down to the camp. The room was empty. (Where could Abu Jabbar have gone today? You hadn't spotted him anywhere.) You put your little case on the bed, and put some dirty clothes in it. You left behind the books you had finished. You mustn't load yourself down with things that would slow down your long walk to the village, from where you would take your transport. Don't forget the manuscript of your novel! Where had you put it, it wasn't in the cupboard! Perhaps you had put it under the pillow, or stuffed it under the bed. Perhaps you'd hidden it in your big case. Where had it gone? It wasn't like you to mislay it! It must be somewhere in the room, but now you were getting agitated. Through the open door of the room you could see men rushing around as though trying to avoid some imminent danger. You spotted Dankha passing across the balcony, so you followed him to his room. "Hey, Dankha, what's happened?"

"The police arrested Fawzi and several . . ."

"And Mr. Fox? What?"

"They got him out of the overturned car."

"Is he seriously hurt?"

"I don't know, I only saw them from a distance."

What sort of a beginning was this? Anyway, whatever happened in the next few days, you had to travel to Basra now, to the center of confrontation between the management and the workforce, to observe how events developed at close quarters, and to write about what was happening there. You asked Dankha to take Istifan's nightingale and look after it while you were away. He looked at you in astonishment. "Are you traveling?"

"Yes."

"And if they go back to work tomorrow?"

"No, Dankha, I don't think they will be going back that quickly."

Days Two and Three: Hope
Project HQ in the City

A rectangular piece of land, with buildings scattered over it, surrounded by a fence of ordinary wire, about two meters high, with a number of small and large gates in it. If you are coming from the city center, then the long side of the HQ lies on the left of the road, facing a stretch of land with some palm trees on it (the remnants of a large abandoned plantation). The other long side is situated on an unfinished road that separates the HQ from a soccer pitch and some tennis courts belonging to the project. (This road remains uncompleted to this day, as a result of a difference of opinion between the city council and the project management, with each side maintaining that the task of paving the road falls to the other party. Each party has its own logical reasons, of course: the council takes the view that the road passes between facilities owned by the project, while the management believes that the road is actually a part of the city used by everyone.

The British managers of the project haven't adopted their stubborn position with regard to this little road out of a need to save cash, for they spend a lot of money on other things, but it is a matter of principle, so they say.) As for the first short side, it faces a large plantation, while the farther short side is situated on a paved road, behind which there is an open piece of wasteland on which boys sometimes play barefoot. Except for those people with some connection to the project (people with a son, brother, or relative working there, for example), the city population usually showed no interest in this place when they passed it, for they didn't think of it as any different from any other place in the city that didn't concern them. But now, they had started looking at it curiously, watching the angry men congregating at its gates, and the local press and radio (even the BBC!) had started discussing what was happening there.

A summary of what the newspapers and radio were saying:

"Man fired on by the British submits complaint!"

"Workers prepare to send delegation to negotiate with management."

"Minister for Social Affairs arrives in Basra and seems optimistic."

"Arrest of British man who fired on worker." (So they had got Mr. Fox out of his overturned car safely.)

Meanwhile, the men standing at the gates whose numbers had greatly increased during the day were relaxed, chattering, exchanging jokes, and laughing, like men who were confident of certain victory in the end. Had Hussein exaggerated his estimate of the possible dangers? Everything here appeared calm, completely calm.

Day Five: Anticipation

The management repeats its well-known slogan, "No work, no pay!"

In response, the workers try to resist this threat. They organize a fund to support their poorer members, and collect donations from the better off, and from other sympathizers. Meanwhile, the minister of social affairs is forced to return to Baghdad and declare that a settlement is imminent, as the police arrest a number of men on a charge of incitement, and the strikers continue to mount a guard on all entrances to work areas, for fear that the management may persuade some of them to go back.

Day Six: First Signs of Weariness
Conversation at one of the gates

First man: "Have you got a cigarette?"

Second man: "No, I smoked my last cigarette yesterday evening."

Third man: "I've got one. Take it and divide it up."

First man: "And you?"

Third man: "I've decided to stop smoking."

Fourth man: "A decision dictated by your bankrupt state, presumably!"

(They laugh, but after a few moments a look of dejection appears on their faces.)

Scene: On the empty lot where the boys sometimes play ball, near Project HQ, a number of workers (porters, sweepers, office boys, servants, and others of that lot) are filling the air with noise and dust as they circle around, shaking their kafiyyehs, and stamping the dusty ground excitedly with their feet. They are surrounded by a large circle of passersby who have stopped to watch. What these people are saying is unintelligible to anyone who doesn't know the southern dialect. One of the onlookers turns to the man standing beside him and says, "Do you know what they're saying?"

"Yes, they're saying, 'How can we have our overtime pay cut?'"

(They laugh.)

"Do you think they'll succeed?"

"With this sort of mad frenzy?"

They move away as the noise and the movement continues.

An announcement on behalf of the management:

In a statement to the local press on behalf of the project management, it was announced that news of an impending settlement was mistaken and that the strike situation had not changed. As for the British man who injured one of the workers, he was a minor official who injured the man accidentally. End of statement.

Day Eight: Patience Runs Out
Live scene
Beginning of the day. A large number of men congregate on the empty lot near project headquarters, then walk toward the city, wanting to reach the provincial governor's building to support their negotiating delegation by standing there. The men charged with guarding the gates have not left their positions. The long line on the road is hindering the traffic. Cars are starting to drive along the edges of the road, stirring up the dust, while the screech of their horns mingles with the cries and shouts of the men. Halfway along the road to the city center, police cars appear and block their path. The policemen jump out and a fight ensues between the two sides. The policemen use their rifle butts and fire into the air, while the men use their arms and stones from the road. One of them tries in a moment of frenzy to snatch a rifle from a policeman, and the bayonet pierces the palm of his hand. Amid all this chaos no one can say definitely whether the injury was caused deliberately or happened by accident. After that the men disperse of their own accord. Perhaps they did not want the scuffle to turn into a bloody battle while their delegation was still negotiating with the management. The policemen move away, taking with them the man who tried to snatch the rifle, and traffic resumes its normal course on the road now strewn with stones.

Day Nine: The Edge of Despair
A scene and a conversation at one of the entrances
At midnight, four men are squatting around a fire that they have lit on the ground. They are wrapped in their kafiyyehs and have raised the collars of their jackets or coats to protect their necks from the sting of the cold winter's air. Their swarthy faces and their rough outstretched hands are lit up by the glow of the fire. Beside them is a small pile of firewood. Inside and behind the fence, the management buildings,

stores, and repair shops are enveloped in darkness and silence. From time to time the lights of approaching cars on the road can be seen shining, sweeping the darkness of the night from their bent backs and revealing their crouching figures to the eyes of anyone in a passing car. Then darkness returns to envelop the road again and cover their backs, while their faces remain lit up in the glow of the fire. Strange figures wander in the night on the other side of the road. The men are aware of the existence of these creeping shadows that you can see from a distance, for they occasionally turn their heads and stare into the darkness without speaking. One of the four men takes a dry stick from the pile of firewood and throws it onto the fire. The eyes watch the stick in silence. You can see it turn black, bend and crackle in the flames, then smoke rises up as it begins to burn.

The man who has thrown the dry stick into the fire breaks his own silence and the silence of the night, "It's a war of nerves. They want to exhaust us."

He speaks angrily. The glowering faces say nothing for some time. The hands remain stretched out at a distance from the flames. Another man is constantly putting his hands near the fire then taking them away, in an attempt to always have them in the right place, somewhere between the maximum bearable temperature and the edge of burning. "I think . . . if . . . ." he says.

The three faces turn toward him. "That is, I say, if we accept . . . what they've given us."

The man who had spoken angrily: "But they haven't given us anything important."

A third man shows signs of despair: "And they won't. Especially now that the minister of the interior arrived in town this morning."

The fourth man, who seems confused: "Perhaps, by God I don't know. The problem's become . . . ."

The man in despair: "No, definitely. You all heard how they threatened our delegation."

The man who was afraid of burning his hand: "But the minister told them, 'You're free men'!"

The man in despair: "He told them, 'You're free to work or die of hunger. That's your business. But you're not free to stand in the way of anyone who wants to return to work'!"

(The dry stick collapses in ashes amid the glow of the other pieces of wood.)

The angry man (staring at their faces): "And who is this that wants to go back?"

The other three men: "No one, obviously."

"It's logical, after all this!"

"No one, until . . . ."

A silence descends, in which you can almost hear the struggle flaring up in different degrees, in the soul of each one of them. Meanwhile a car passes by on the street, for a brief moment laying bare their backs in its quivering lights.

The despairing man: "I read today that they released the Brit who fired on one of our men. They said he was killing stray dogs."

The confused man (in surprise): "But before that they said he was shooting birds!"

The despairing man (sarcastically): "Birds, dogs, no difference."

The angry man shakes his head. He looks at the blazing fire then feeds it a large piece of wood.

Around one o'clock in the morning.

A taxi stops at the closed entrance. The doors open and four men emerge. They have come to take over guard duties from the men squatting around the fire. The sitting men get up, looking relieved. The taxi stands waiting with its engine running, waiting for the men who are due to depart, but the men do not move in its direction. The driver stares at them from behind the car window. He sees them all hovering around the fire as they stand, their dirty boots, legs, and chests lit up by the fire as they stretch out their hands seeking warmth. The fire also lights up their faces, though less clearly. The faces of the newcomers seem sad and desperate; the faces of those who have finished guard duty seem exhausted and confused.

The man afraid of burning his hands asks, "Hey, what's the news?"

One of those who have just arrived replies hesitantly, "The most important thing isn't a piece of news, it's just a rumor."

He looks at his colleagues as if asking permission to divulge his information. The men who have finished their shift look at him expectantly, with some dread. "It's just gossip. We heard it just now."

He looks at his colleagues again while the men about to leave fidget.

"They say that a delegation met the minister and told him that they were speaking on behalf of the men who wanted to return to work."

Consternation appears on the faces of the men whose guard duties are over. The angry man asks, "And do you know who they are?"

"We'll find out. This isn't our concern right now!"

"And what is our concern right now?" asks somebody else.

"The minister told them to tell anyone that wanted to go back, to go to work in the morning and he would find the gates open to him."

Meanwhile the fire has completely enveloped the large piece of wood that the man has thrown into it—the man who has spoken angrily the whole time—and has quietly consumed it. The men stare at the blazing fire dumbfounded.

"So this is the situation then! Tomorrow everything will be decided!" says one of them, his head bent , in the voice of someone who feels that the battle has reached the point of a decisive clash, and that the project management has finally pushed them to the wall. None of the others says anything, as if everything has been decided and further discussion is pointless.

The four men whose guard duties have finished move away from the fire and go up to the waiting taxi. It turns and takes them off toward the city center. The others squat around the fire to continue guarding the entrance until the following morning.

Day Ten
The Scene Outside

Time: Dawn, about half an hour before sunrise. The pale light in the sky has made it possible to see things around us clearly.

Place: The crossroads. In front of us we can see a track about thirty meters wide, unpaved. Within the track, to the right, there is a wide rectangular area surrounded by a high fence. Inside this area we can see some buildings scattered here and there, though most of the area appears empty and deserted. Some palm groves appear in the distance on the far side of the track.

On the left is the rear side of Project HQ and the entrance that is usually used by people to enter and leave on workdays. The wide gate, now closed, is situated at a point in the fence not far (about sixty meters) from the beginning of the track. We can see a large Christ's-thorn tree spreading its branches over the entrance. Inside we can see a two-story structure and some other buildings (workshops, stores, and offices).

We can see about twenty men guarding the shut gate on the left, and more than fifty others standing in small groups near the fence, on both sides of the entrance. There are small piles of stones on the ground here and there at the bottom of the fence. The men's features cannot be seen clearly, and when they speak their voices cannot be heard as they are too far away. But we can see that they are standing uneasily and sometimes gesturing nervously when they speak. Generally, though, they seem to be standing there in silence as if waiting for something. Inside, behind the fence, the place seems quiet and completely deserted. No sound can be heard at all. Meanwhile we can see people continuously moving on to the path to join the men who are gathered at the entrance to Project HQ. Some of them pass quickly in front of us , while others come from the end of the track, from the direction of the palm groves.

From outside the scene, so to speak, we can hear a vehicle approaching from the left of the road, then a small taxi passes us crammed with more passengers than usual (building workers, it appears). The taxi goes off in the opposite direction, leaving us once again faced with the spectacle of men congregating at the entrance, some of them crouching on the ground in front of the fence, while others look for stones, which they pick up from odd corners and put on the existing piles.

Most of them, however, remain standing in almost complete silence. A group of vehicles approaches. There is a heavy screeching, which the men hear, turning their faces toward the start of the track, though they can't see anything yet.

We turn our eyes in the direction of the noise.

We can see a line of four large vehicles, covered personnel carriers, escorted by a jeep. The convoy heads slowly toward us. Before the jeep has completely caught up with us it turns and moves onto the track. As the vehicle is turning we can quite clearly see the figure of a police officer sitting next to the policeman who is driving. The police officer looks like a middle-aged man. We can see him staring at the track in front of us, almost absentmindedly.

Return to the men at the entrance.

When the men the convoy making its way on to the track, an anxious movement sweeps through them. Those who are sitting start up, and those who had been searching for stones return to stand next to their colleagues. Their faces are tense. All are turned toward the approaching convoy.

Return to the convoy, the first part of which has made its way onto the track: In front of us we can see the back of the first vehicle as it turns. We notice policemen sitting opposite each other, with their rifles in their hands, their rifle butts on the floor of the truck. We can't see all of them, we can only clearly see the two men sitting opposite each other at the back of the truck with the barrels of their rifles gleaming in their hands. We can can only see a little of the two men sitting after them, whose rifles glint slightly. After that, the details become gradually less distinct, until finally the outlines of the rest of the men disappear in the darkness. The impression we gain of the faces that we can see well as the truck turns in front of us is one of tension, perhaps also of fear.

The convoy from the point of view of the men gathered at the entrance: The jeep approaches followed by one of the trucks. A second truck is turning onto the track, followed by the front of the third truck, which in turn is followed after a few moments by the fourth.

Then the convoy moves forward in a single line. The air is filled with the hum of the engines.

Return to the men at the entrance: The men follow the convoy with angry, glowering faces as it moves along unhurriedly (off scene), then drives by in front of us. We are aware of each passing truck by the sound of its engine above the rest of the din; the noise then subsides a little, and the drone of the next truck's engine rises as it passes in front of the men.

From the direction of the men's startled faces, and from the drone of the vehicles that have eventually stopped, we realize that the convoy has come to a halt on the other side of the track, close to the entrance.

An uneasy silence descends on the men. From the distance, we can hear birds chirping in the branches of the tree above the wide entrance. Then we can make out the top part of the tree in a broad patch of clear sky. We will continue to hear the birds chirping, and their quiet movements as they enter and leave the tree, as well as the distant noise of the town, so long as the place is free of other sounds.

Return to the convoy of personnel carriers now standing on the edge of the track: The police officer gets down from the jeep. He moves slightly away from the small vehicle and faces the stationary trucks. He lifts his arm and gives the order to get out of the vehicles.

The front door of each truck opens and the officer in charge jumps out then runs to the rear to hurry the men up. We watch as the men get out of the four vehicles. We see a movement as someone else gets out of a truck, then pause to look at a policeman jumping from a truck. We see him in the air, his back a little arched, bending his legs, his rifle in his hand away from his body. Then we see him landing on the ground and running to catch up with his colleagues.

Return to the men at the entrance, whose numbers have increased as others arrive: The group are standing in silence, almost still. A few of them are fidgeting nervously, looking at their colleagues' faces. Their hands are at a slight angle, and their eyes are fixed on what is happening on the other side of the track. From outside the scene, we can hear the sound of dozens of anxious feet, the scraping of shoes on the ground, the crack of weapons, and high, repeated commands. "Come on, quickly, forward, wait in line! You, there! Your rifle! Forward, you idiot! Now stand in line, stand in line! Move, you! Are you asleep? Don't drag the rifle! Hurry up!" The noise being made on the other side seems a bit exaggerated, perhaps to instill terror. From the branches of the tree over the men's heads some birds take flight, and fear appears on a number of faces, but most of the men simply glower more as they hear the preemptory commands. Finally the voices are quiet and then you can hear (from outside the scene) the quiet, intermittent buzz of the city that has slowly begun to awaken.

Return to the policemen: The police superintendent is standing alone beside the jeep. He slowly turns his head to reconnoiter the place, while the noise of the city is carried on the breeze. We follow what he sees. At first, he looks at his men, drawn up in a long line formed of four shorter lines, at the head of each of which stands an officer. The men are holding their rifles with their butts to the ground. The sun, which has risen a few minutes ago, throws their shadows and those of their weapons onto the ground in front of them. The long, intertwined shadows appear like a large black net, covering the surface of the track and climbing up onto the bodies of the striking men on the other side. The police superintendent looks toward the entrance to the track: the long line of policemen is still in his field of vision. With him, we can see the beginning of the track, then open ground. Meanwhile, we can see people going in, either individually or in small groups of two or three, walking hurriedly and purposefully. They are surprised to see the large number of policemen with their weapons and trucks.

(A quick scene, from the perspective of the people who have just moved onto the track, toward the line of policemen standing with their weapons at the ready facing the men at the entrance. We return to see, with the police superintendent, the men moving slowly onto the track. Two of them stop then turn to go back to where they had come from, while others come forward slowly and cautiously. The police superintendent continues to reconnoiter the place. He turns his back to the men standing at the entrance, and surveys the broad piece of ground on the right of the track. With him, we see a soccer pitch behind the fence, with its goalposts, and some tennis courts enclosed in their own fence inside, and a few scattered buildings here and there. We cannot see anyone inside. We look as far as the end of the fence. We can see the palm groves, and see people going in quickly, then being surprised when they see the policemen, and slowing down or going back. The reconnaissance operation undertaken by the police superintendent does not last more than a couple of minutes. The police superintendent is now walking in front of his men and looking at them as if to inspect them. He looks hard at their tense faces and wandering gaze, then reaches the front of the long line, stops and turns to the bunch of men on the other side, examines them for a short moment, then starts to cross the track toward them. He walks slowly, but with firm, confident steps, and we follow his back as he moves away toward the men, whom we can see looking at him suspiciously. Those who are standing on either side of the entrance move nearer.

We see the police superintendent—from the perspective of the men gathered at the entrance—coming forward, with a line of policemen standing firm in the background. The impression that we have of the chief's face, as he comes closer, doesn't suggest any hostility or desire to cause harm, although he seems somewhat rigid. (Off scene, we can hear a car horn nearby.)

Cut to the men looking at the police superintendent as he approaches them. Our eyes move over their anxious, questioning faces. They are surprised and disturbed. The police superintendent arrives and stops, and the men form a large circle around him, silent and expectant. The circle remains open on the side nearest to the policemen, as if the men are afraid to turn their backs on armed men. We see a number of men trying to impose some order on the behavior of the agitated group.

The police superintendent speaks in a friendly tone. "Good morning, everyone!"

The men look at him doubtfully but their usual greeting in reply: "Good morning, sir!"

179

Some faces relax a little.

The police superintendent: "Brothers, who's your leader here?"

Several voices speak: "There is no leader. It's our delegation that . . . ."

"Why do you want . . . ?"

"The delegation's going today" (and words of that sort).

The police superintendent seems a little confused. He raises his arm and interrupts them, but gently. "Brothers, please listen to me. We're not collaborating with . . . ." He corrects himself. "I'd like to speak to one of those present here."

The men's faces show signs of confusion, hesitation, and doubt. Some of them look at each other but no one speaks. A silence descends, through which we can hear the distant noise of the city, and the movement and chirping of the birds among the tree branches above the entrance.

The police superintendent looks at the workers. "Okay, don't you have a senior man among you?"

Hesitation appears on the men's faces, then a man of about sixty comes forward from the ranks.

Elderly man: "Yes, sir."

Police superintendent: "Your name?"

Elderly man (we can see his startled face; he turns to look at the faces of the men around him; the faces look at him in silence). He approaches the police superintendent and says: "No name is necessary."

The police superintendent smiles, trying to appear understanding. "Don't worry, the important thing is I don't want any harm to befall you. It's not right for you to be standing here in front of the gate!"

Off scene, we can hear voices asking, "What is he saying?" "What does he want?" "We can't hear, folks!"

A nearby voice replies to the questions: "He's saying that he doesn't want us to come to any harm!"

The police superintendent continues his speech: "So I advise you—you're a mature and sensible man, as I can see—to take everyone away and go home, if you don't want any trouble!"

(The shouting gets louder.)

Cut to the elderly man, who raises his hand, asking the men around him to be quiet. The voices subside a little. Then the elderly man addresses the police superintendent: "Why don't you take your own men, son, and go away and leave us to deal with it?"

(Voices are raised in support. We see the faces of the men speaking all at once.) "Leave us to reach an agreement with the management!" "What's it got to do with you?" "Why. . . ?" (and similar expressions).

Cut to the police superintendent. We see him looking at the faces without saying anything. Then he lowers his head, waiting for the voices to subside.

The elderly man shouts angrily: "Leave us alone and we'll be able to reach an understanding, my friends!" (The voices become quieter.)

The police superintendent raises his head. We can see his face with all its features now. We can see the white hairs in his fine black mustache. But his handsome face is showing signs of impatience. Despite that, he tries to remain friendly until the last moment. We hear him speaking in an unthreatening tone, in the tone of someone who is announcing a tangible fact: "Sir, for your information, I have orders to fire if you continue to blockade the gates!"

The elderly man speaks (we can see all the details of his face: a small, lined face, with drained eyes that betray fear, for the man now clearly understands the seriousness of the situation that they are in—but he is surrounded on every side by angry, challenging shouts from the men provoked by the words of the police superintendent, and is left with no choice). He seems to be surrendering to an irresistible fate. "Do as your conscience tells you, my friend, we won't budge from here, so long as the management doesn't agree to . . . ." (He speaks with a raised voice, though his words can hardly be heard amid the increasing clamor from the men.)

Cut to the policemen on the other side of the track. We see them waiting in their same places. Their bayonets are glinting in the sun. The platoon commanders wear anxious expressions as they see their leader surrounded by all those angry faces.

Cut to the police superintendent. We see him standing inside the circle of men that has contracted around him and is almost squashing him. Then we see his face break into a smile of pity and he shakes his head in despair as he backs away from the men. The men immediately close in on the elderly man who is lost among the angry bodies.

The police superintendent returns to his men. We follow his back as it moves away from the men agitating by the entrance and approaches the policemen who are ready on the other side. We see him stopping roughly halfway between the two groups. He stands in the tangle of shadows made by the men's bodies and weapons. The shadows have shortened and now appear like a long fence thrown to the ground. We can hear, off scene, shouting from the men at the entrance, who seem to be arguing among themselves, then the voices become quieter. A hum of traffic and car horns in the nearby streets.

Cut to the men at the entrance: We find that they have made their bodies into a long, thick wall in front of the gate, in a desperate attempt to prevent any breach. Their faces are more expressive of anger than of fear: perhaps the friendly tone of the police superintendent speaking to them has made them imagine that the man wouldn't order weapons to be used against them.

The police superintendent stands opposite the men with their swarthy, sunburned faces. We see him standing on his own. In the background we see the silent, expectant wall of men. The police chief seems a little hesitant, but that only lasts for a short moment, then his face changes and becomes stern. He raises his head and shouts in a sharp voice that for the first time sounds annoyed and angry: "Platoon leaders, get ready to fire!"

A quick cut to the men gathered at the entrance. Some faces seem startled. The men move about in confusion, moving apart in an uncoordinated fashion, running here and there toward the piles of stones. Some of them take out the missiles they have been hiding. They stand warily holding their stones and artillery. Offstage we hear the shouts of the platoon commanders ordering their men to prepare to fire. The air is filled with the crack of more than a hundred rifles being fired at once, and the flock of birds flies off from the branches of the tree over the closed gate. At first we see them flying off aimlessly, each bird in a different direction, but they quickly regroup and head to the east in the clear sky, then are swallowed up in the daylight.

17

End of a Dream,
Beginning of a Dream

Just twenty-four hours in terms of time, from yesterday morning at around this hour, but how far away yesterday seems now. In fact, it seems another age completely. It was a bright and beautiful day, like today, and the warm sunbeams had taken the chill off the air a little. It was a wonderful time to travel or take a stroll. The battle had been short-lived, a few minutes, then people's dreams had ended, changed into a frightening nightmare, as the ranks split apart and dispersed. They had picked up their wounded and withdrawn from the battlefield, leaving behind them lifeless corpses strewn here and there on the ground in the sun. Despair had set in men's eyes in place of the glorious dream that had fired them for such a long time (the dream created by optimistic words). Most faces that I had seen in the camp yesterday evening or this morning seemed dumbstruck, unable to believe what had happened. Today you can see the signs of despair and frustration on the face of Mazlum the caretaker, who is sitting by the door smoking gloomily, and on the face of the clerk Abdullah, sitting behind his typewriter staring absentmindedly in front of him. Jirjis is the only one to seem happy with the way things turned out, for what the men did seemed absolute madness in his estimation: anyone that imagined that they could impose their conditions on the management must have lost their mind, and must also be lacking in loyalty, for they were biting the hand that feeds them and their children. Jirjis is now bent over his papers, not saying a word. Despite his satisfaction, though, he seems extremely pale, as if he is ill, a bad pain in the stomach, a splitting headache, something like that. Behind the wall sits Mr. Fox, smoking his pipe and filling the air with the stink of his tobacco, looking like the victor. I see him stretch out his hand to pull back the pane of glass from the square opening in the wall and order the head clerk to come to him. Jirjis goes in and shuts the door. I hear Mazlum the caretaker muttering quietly from where he sits, "God preserve us from this day!" Abdullah looks at him without speaking. Mazlum continues his pessimistic words as he snatches furtive glances at the director's room. "I have a feeling about today and the next few days!"

The minutes pass slowly while the vague noise behind the wall continues. Abdullah, who has finally woken up from his torpor, asks me, "Muhammad, my brother, wouldn't you like to drink some tea?"

He speaks in an almost jolly way, trying to appear unconcerned. Perhaps he has just decided to ignore the defeat that everyone (except for a small number of people like Jirjis) has suffered.

"Yes, please!" I say to him.

He turns to the caretaker. "Please, Mazlum, bring us some tea."

"Okay," replies the caretaker, his eyes on the manager's office, "but please wait a bit!"

Abdullah looks at him enquiringly. "I want to find out the secret of this long meeting!" continues Mazlum.

"What are you expecting?"

"I don't know. But you've seen the mark the incident left above his eye. Do you believe that a man like this will forget?"

"What are you afraid of? Did you help Farhan al-Abd when he overturned his car? Go on . . . "

The caretaker got up wearily and left the office. I picked up a pile of local newspapers from Jirjis's table, wondering who had brought all these papers to Mr. Fox while work was at a standstill.

I busied myself flicking through the papers and scanning the headlines. Nothing new. News of incidents in Basra: I knew them all, indeed some of them I had written myself under false names. I was scanning the pages looking for news unconnected with what had happened, news items like the following: "Did you know that men with beards and mustaches are the healthiest?" A really nice news item! "Experiments have demonstrated that beards and mustaches prevent a large proportion of dirt found in the atmosphere from entering the mouth, as they act as a filtering device." Mr. Fox was the healthiest of us all, no doubt about that, even without his light, pointed beard and his handlebar mustache. He must be very happy now, smoking his loathsome tobacco and feeling satisfied. But what had been going on between him and the chief clerk all this time? It had been more than half an hour since Jirjis went inside. There'd been intermittent whispering and periods of silence, sometimes long drawn out. Perhaps Fox, in these periods of silence, was writing or reading something, while Jirjis sat submissively in front of him, awaiting orders. Finally the door to the manager's room opened and the chief clerk emerged with a glowering face, even paler than before, as if he had been insulted or reprimanded inside. He spoke to me in a dry tone that was almost hostile: "Mr. Muhammad, the boss wants to see you."

I felt anxious. "About what?" I asked him, uncharacteristically.

"Go in and you'll find out," he replied, retrieving the newspapers from my desk.

As I made for the manager's room, Mazlum the caretaker came in carrying the tea tray. I knocked on the wooden door with the back of my finger, then opened it quietly and went in. Immediately, before he had said a single word, everything became clear, and I realized that my secret had been uncovered. So they'd managed to get it to him! It was definitely Abu Jabbar, no one else. The draft of my novel that had mysteriously disappeared was now lying on the cold glass top that covered Fox's desk. I had conflicting feelings—the feelings of someone who has lost a loved one then suddenly stumbled upon him again, but found him in captivity . . . bound . . . in trouble! But how could you entrust to paper everything in your heart, knowing full well that paper was fragile and insecure and that its great weakness was that it could easily fall into

186

untrustworthy hands and turn into a weapon that could be pointed in your face by your enemies?

"I'm astonished!"

His voice hit you. The small bandage over his left eyebrow looked pure white. You thought he had been killed when they overturned his car, or at least been badly injured, but this bandage that was no longer than your little finger, that was stuck slightly at an angle over his brow, and which perhaps hid beneath it a small scratch this was all that there was to show for the incident. After that they had detained him for a day or two because he had wounded a man with a bullet from his rifle; they had detained him to stop the opposition papers talking, then released him. And now here he was, sitting in front of you behind his spacious desk in all his majesty, smoking his pipe and addressing you with quiet anger, a suppressed anger that was only apparent in his blazing eyes.

"This is the first time that anyone . . . ." You could sense in his voice a mixture of astonishment, disappointment, and bewilderment. "I warned you on the first day, but you didn't just ignore my warning, you actually . . . ." What could I say to him to refute the hard evidence lying on his desk? "You were a quiet person who worked well."

I saw him lift his large hand and feel the place of the wound over his forehead with his fingers, as if by this apparently unintentional movement he was wanting to say to me, "Look! Do you see this injury? Do you know how it happened?" and thus make me feel the gravity of my error.

He brought his hand down from his brow and continued what he was saying. "For this reason I looked on you with favor and trusted you, and paid little attention to the reports about you."

Despite the fact that we had both discovered each other's secret he insisted on speaking to me in English as he explained (perhaps for his own benefit) the reason why he had turned a blind eye to me for such a long time. But I had to defend myself somehow, however weak the defense might be. "But this is a novel," I finally said to him in a weak voice. "Pure imagination, with no connection to . . . ."

His eyes blazed even more than before. "Do you think I'm an idiot?"

Probably nothing in this world made him more angry than an indication from someone else that they thought little of his intellectual abilities. With his keen intelligence, he was now pained by the fact that he had been remiss with you and not discovered what you were really up to earlier. But you yourself didn't know that you would be swept up by events like this. "Pure imagination!" you heard him say sarcastically. "Do you really believe that by altering a few names and changing the dates and places of the events a bit, you can . . . ?"

The telephone rang in the big room. The chief clerk pushed the glass pane across, and stuck his pale, lined face through. Mr. Fox, however, indicated angrily that he did not wish anyone to interrupt him at this moment. Jirjis closed the window while Fox looked at you. "Tell me, do you know what would happen if I handed you over to the police now, with this fictional novel of yours?"

I felt drops of cold sweat dripping over hot flesh all the way down my arm. It came from a place under the armpit then flowed all the way down the arm, one drop after another. But where could all this sweat be coming from in winter? He continued to glare threateningly for some time at my astonished face, enjoying the sight of my terror after having boxed me into a corner. Yes indeed, what would happen if he handed me over to the police after writing all this? Finally he looked away from my face. He took a piece of paper and a pen (he had apparently gotten them ready before I came into the room) and pushed them across the desk. "Take this and write your resignation!"

Incredible! So he wasn't going to send me to . . . I thought he would keep his promise! What had made him take this decision?

"And make it as from today," he ordered. "There's no need for a period of notice!"

I took the pen and paper, and wrote my resignation from work on the project without any elaboration or explanation, and without giving any supporting reasons. I wrote it quickly before he could change his mind. I still couldn't believe it. His eyes gazed at me like an eagle's eyes, reflected on the glass pane, watching my trembling hand as it penned the words on the paper. So this was how it ended. I hadn't expected it like this! He took the paper from me and wrote something in the margin, then pulled back the window and pushed it toward the chief clerk, before shutting the window again.

"I want you to leave the office right now, this minute! You can collect what is owed to you tomorrow!"

When he noticed signs of pleasure on my face, he became angry again. "Don't think for a moment that I am treating you like this out of mercy!" he said. "No, I just don't want anyone to say that Mr. Fox harbored a spy in his office and only uncovered him when it was too late. Now, get out!"

But I didn't budge. He looked at me in astonishment. "What are you waiting for?"

"The manuscript of my novel!"

I spoke these words in Arabic. I was no longer an employee of his; I was finally free of him. He raised his enormous fist then brought it down on the bundle of papers like someone bringing a heavy stone down on the back of a bird that has settled quietly on the ground. "No," he said firmly, "this stays with me!"

May God make your soul burn in the fire of hell, Abu Jabbar! May God make your soul burn! All that effort wasted, and now I had to try to write it again. Time, and a loose imagination, would play with the events and personalities, and it would be another novel. But what could I do? I left Fox's room, trying to smile at the waiting faces. Jirjis knew everything, both the reasons and the result. Abdullah and Mazlum didn't know anything yet; they looked into my face in confusion, sensing that there was something suspicious. I went toward the table holding myself upright. The glass of tea that Mazlum had brought had gone cold while waiting for me. "I've submitted my resignation," I said in an unconcerned tone as I sat down.

Abdullah and Mazlum would know the news anyway. "The boss forced you to, that's for sure!" said Mazlum at once.

The chief clerk scolded him, "Mazlum, do you want to. . . ?"

"But you were happy here. Why?" asked Abdullah the clerk in astonishment.

"Everyone knows his own circumstances," said Jirjis, less sharply this time.

Mr. Fox came out of his room. He saw me gathering together my few possessions from on top of the table but pretended to ignore me. He gestured to Abdullah the clerk to follow him, to choose the temporary workers that the work would need for that day.

After he had gone out Jirjis turned to the caretaker. "Come on, Mazlum, take these papers to accounts." He handed him two or three pieces of paper and watched him as he left, then turned his whole frame toward me. "Muhammad, did you have to mention me in your papers?"

I tried to remember what I had said about him in my novel. I had once compared him to an old country woman who had lost her teeth, and I'd perhaps mentioned him by chance in some other places, but I couldn't recall saying anything scandalous about him.

"I'm sorry, Abu Basil. Believe me, I didn't say anything bad about you."

"And what you said about my donating money to bury Fadlallah?"

So that was his secret that he didn't want exposed in front of the manager!

"But your donation of money was a good deed!"

He shook his head in a worried way. "Good from your point of view, but the boss has a different perspective!"

"I'm sorry if I've put you in a difficult position with him," I said.

"Imagine, he told me you're not trustworthy, you're not trustworthy! I, who took such a risk!" Suddenly he was silent and stopped complaining. What had this wretched man risked, do you suppose?

"I wish you could have stayed with us," said Jirjis more sympathetically, changing the subject and looking at the door. "Believe me, by Jesus, I really mean it!"

"Thank you, Abu Basil, but we can't always choose our own destinies. Look after your health!"

"Do I look ill?" he asked in a worried way.

"No, no, you're fine, completely fine!"

I could hear the noise of the out-of-work men behind the fence as my hands gripped the papers that were no longer of use to me. The men's voices seemed subdued today, like a fire that has died down. These men were also feeling defeated, for one of the strikers' demands had been to employ the temporary workers on a permanent basis. Far-han al-Abd, whose voice would boom out among them every morning, cursing Britain, its queen and its political parties: the rumors that I'd heard about him in the camp canteen this morning were not consistent. Some people said that they'd arrested him the first day and taken him to Basra bound in chains, while others (the majority) said that Farhan had not been arrested, for he was slippery as water and could escape from anyone's hands; a man like him couldn't be easily detained and he was now hiding deep in the palm groves that stretched along the banks of the Shatt al-Arab from Faw to the village of Saraji overlooking Basra. He was moving, light as an uncaged bird, between the houses of the peasants, fishermen, and smugglers, who opened their doors to him and gave him food. (One of the men said that he'd spoken to someone who'd seen him in one or another of the Shatt al-Arab villages.) He was bound to turn up again. Perhaps this particular rumor was just a precautionary one, for disappointed men to hang on to—men whose hopes hadn't lasted more than a few moments in the face of the bullets. Or perhaps it was the truth. Who knows, for there is nowhere better to hide from prying eyes than the thick palm groves or the hundreds of small villages lost in the depths of the orchards. Everything is possible, and no one knows anything for certain.

Face Two
The Eagle's Nest

1

He stood alone in the middle of the large courtyard. Dark concrete rectangles lay on the ground in front of him like a row of enormous graves of dead giants. Agitatedly, he said to himself that the building of the camp would be delayed, since work had continued to proceed so slowly. Then he walked toward the dam and climbed up on it. He could see the workers' camp on the left, like a great basin, into which were crammed tents lit up with the color of the setting sun, so that they looked like a herd of sleeping spotted cows. The sun's disk appeared large and pale as it slid down toward the earth on the distant horizon, its blood-red rays coloring, in varying degrees of light and shade, the face of the white desert that had been ripped open by the drilling machine and left with deep scars. He could see the oil rig standing at a distance from the dam with a number of trucks beside it. He could hear the drone of its engine and the hum of its enormous jaw as it went up and down. He could hear barking too for a few moments. He stood looking at the desert and smoking in silence. He couldn't see a sight like this over there—sunset in the desert! Of course, during the few hours when the clouds cleared, he could see sunrise or sunset—possibly standing on the shore with a girl hanging on his arm or standing behind his back to protect him from the cold winds blowing on them from the North Sea. But the sun was feeble when it appeared, and it hung in the sky overhead for a long time. Night would come and it would still be hanging there, reluctant to move. Slowly, slowly, it would creep away like an old invalid. That was an ailing sun, not like the healthy sun here in his own country. But despite the gloomy sky, covered with clouds for most of the hours of daylight; despite the sick sun and the rain and cold and snow; despite the almost-always gloomy face of nature, he felt himself as free as a bird, as light as a feather, untroubled by anything except for a feeling of exile and longing for his country and his family. Every day there his life had a special flavor, special features that had stayed in his memory. His days had not been sterile and empty like his days here, days that passed heavily then piled up like a clump of figs, or a heap of dung (the present eats the future, like a herd of elephants devouring a field of clover, then turns it into the dung of the past) as he got older, year by year, and his life passed uselessly. It hadn't occurred to him as he climbed the steps of the aircraft in London's Heathrow Airport to go back home after his long absence—it hadn't occurred to him that he would end up here in this wilderness, this outpost that he himself had chosen, because he had found it the best option open to him when he had started looking for work. And now that work has finished for the day, the work that had occupied his thoughts during the daylight hours, what could he do with himself to fill the hours of this long winter's night?

He lit a second cigarette from the stub of the first one, which was about to burn his fingers, then threw the stub into the desert and got down from the dam. He left the tombs of the dead behind him. The guard sitting at the entrance to the work site stood up as a sign of respect. He said goodbye to him with a wave of his hand and made his way up to the public road, which he crossed quickly, then turned his back on the track that headed down to the town and proceeded to make his way along the dirt shoulder of the road, avoiding the plantations whose green color filled his eyes. He walked for some minutes then turned off on a side road lined with palm groves that led to the managers' area, with one side of the long wire fence that surrounded the work area stretching out on his right. He passed a patch of waste ground in the middle of which was a Christ's-thorn tree that cast its lengthening shadows over a carpet of grass colored by the rays of the setting sun. His ears were filled with the familiar gentle hum that he had grown used to hearing whenever he walked back home, the chirping of thousands of birds flocking together and hopping about among the thick leaves and branches, as each bird tried to find a perch for itself where it could sleep before evening came. The noise of the birds inside the enormous Christ's-thorn tree drowned out the sound of the rig, which now seemed far away. He began to feel the depth of the silence and peacefulness around him, a rural peace that felt like a cloak enveloping his body. Some minutes passed as he walked along shrouded in the silence and calm that filled the whole place. Then he heard the low hum of the engine of a small car approaching him, and the grinding of its wheels on the ground as it quickly approached from behind. He didn't turn around. The new arrival in the car might be anyone returning a little late from work. He was aware of the car slowing down, then saw it stop beside him. He saw the mechanic Akram Jadallah sitting behind the wheel and heard him shout, "Get in!" as he drew his smiling face closer to the window.

"Thanks, but I like to walk," he replied with a smile.

Akram waved and drove off. He seemed happy in this place; he couldn't feel fed up in his off-duty hours, for he didn't really have any hours off duty; he would fill them with anything, like a man creating his own private world even in the midst of disaster. He would see him in the club in the evening, and hear his raucous laugh in the billiard room when he scored a lucky hit and shot the balls into the pockets. He would see Suzanne, Akram's wife, hiding away in her usual corner in the club hall, a lonely, neglected wife, like an abandoned possession that has been stored away, trying to fight her anger by reading novels and drinking beer. Her book and glass were as much of a trademark as Charlie Chaplin's hat and stick. He would also see Dr. Sami and his wife Mona there, trying to fill the emptiness of their monotonous days with word games that neither of them could win. He would catch sight of

Fox's face, the pig who spied on everyone, and he would scan the other faces, foreign faces that he was used to seeing in the club night after night. He would also hear the same old conversations, which hardly ever changed.

He carried on walking quickly along the road. In the work area he could see men busy painting the storage tank walls a silver color that reflected the rays of the setting sun. He could see men hanging from the high walls here and there, like migrating birds that had settled on the tank walls to rest, worn out from flying vast distances. Seas, mountains, and valleys! Then the fence turned, so that he was now surrounded by palm groves on both sides. He felt at peace, and started to sniff the pure air that wafted over him from the direction of the Shatt al-Arab, carrying with it the smell of cultivated land, of the water of small streams, and of palm trees.

There wasn't much that he liked about this place, but he liked walking and inhaling the smell of the river and the plantations—and of course, loving Maureen. But she had gone to see her family, leaving him to face the loneliness and monotony of life on his own. The houses scattered among the plantations looked as if they were inviting him to come closer. His black shadow on the ground was growing paler and longer. Before long, it disappeared into the darkness of the evening that had descended almost of a sudden. He could see some windows already lit up, and others now being lit, but he heard no voices or other sounds; it was as if the houses were deserted, as the silence enveloped everything. The first day that he had arrived at the managers' quarter here, he had been dazzled by the place. He had arrived at midday one summer's day to be greeted by small white houses with sloping roofs and square windows, behind which hung curtains of embroidered white silk. He had seen gardens full of colored summer flowers and found a network of clean paved paths joining one house to another. If it hadn't been for the palm groves in front of him, the salt desert behind his back, and the midday heat that set the air ablaze, he would have imagined that he was somewhere else. But this place that at first glance seemed to him an ideal haven of rest and peaceful living had quickly lost its magic and after a short time become like a beautifully built prison.

There was John Sullivan, busy with his private car in the garage of his house, wearing khaki shorts and exposing the rest of his naked, sun-burned body to the evening sun. (Our sun burns their skin, but our cold doesn't affect them much.) The car hood was up and a small lamp dangled there, lighting up the inside of the engine. It occurred to him to ask when his wife would be returning from visiting her family. He was desperate to find out the date of her return. But he had to be cautious and choose his words carefully when asking, for Mr. Sullivan liked to pretend that he didn't know anything about the unusual relationship that had quickly formed between himself and Maureen his wife.

"Hello, John!" he said, as he approached his bent back.

Mr. Sullivan took his head out from under the hood. "Hello, Awsam, I didn't hear you coming, you walk like a cat!"

He saw him take a rag from on the car fender, and wipe off the oil that had stuck to his fingers. "Has it broken down?" he asked, walking closer to the car and looking into the engine. He didn't know much about repairing engine faults, but he wanted to start a conversation with him somehow. "No, just a slight vibration in the engine," replied Sullivan, still preoccupied with cleaning his fingers.

He looked over his head at the lighted house that stood there silently. "It seems you're still living alone!" he said, in a tone that didn't indicate any great concern.

Almost all the house lights were on, and the threshold and garden path were illuminated by lamps. Lights could also be seen in the windows peeping out from behind the curtains, but despite that the house seemed as gloomy as an unlit tomb.

"Yes, I'm still alone," said Sullivan, turning his hands over to inspect them, then added, looking at him rather coldly, "but Maureen will be arriving soon."

He couldn't detect any sign of pleasure in his voice at his wife's return, though he himself was immediately overwhelmed by a transforming happiness. He no longer felt lonely. "You mean, she'll be arriving this evening?" he asked, trying to keep his voice neutral as far as possible.

"No, not this evening," replied Sullivan, putting the oil-stained rag back on the car fender and removing the little lamp from the hood. "She's not coming back by air; she's coming back in the car she'd left behind over there."

"All that way?" he asked, astonished. The exhilaration and happiness he had felt inside him had slightly subsided.

Sullivan undid the two ends of the wires from the car battery and the little lamp went out. "She can take care of herself!" he replied, twisting the black wire.

"But at this time of the year?"

He immediately realized that he had to stop asking so many questions of this sort, which were giving away his personal interest in her return. He saw Sullivan gather up his tools, take the rag from the car fender, and move away in silence. His ample body disappeared behind the outline of the car. Sullivan was bending down to open the trunk and put the tools back in their place, so he could no longer see his face. He saw his red fist grasp the side of the trunk lid and saw the side of his bare arm. Finally he heard him say from behind the car, "You don't know her very well!"

His voice sounded harsh, with something like a challenge in it. "Well, I hope she arrives safely, anyway!" he said, putting an end to a conversation that had begun to take a difficult turn.

"Thanks," replied Sullivan, his face still hidden in the boot of the car. He said it out of habit, out of politeness rather than gratitude. He could hear a faint clicking coming from inside the trunk. The man was still rummaging around or rearranging his tools, or perhaps he was just pretending to, so as not to have to be bothered with him. When his wife was here, he used to deal with him in a different way and didn't treat him with such blatant coolness.

"Okay, John," he muttered, feeling embarrassed at standing on his own talking to a man who was hiding his face from him. "I'll see you tonight in the Eagle's Nest."

He didn't hear a reply. He was already crossing the track heading for the house on the opposite side when he heard the sound of the trunk being closed, and he thought that Sullivan must have slammed it in anger.

———◈———

He pushed the bell with his finger, and the door of the house was opened by the cook, who stood on one side with his lean frame and pale face, muttering a greeting, "Hello, sir!"

"And hello to you too, Abu Mahmoud; how are you today?" he replied cheerily, stepping inside.

After discovering that she would be coming back soon, he had suddenly become happy. Wasn't it strange how a few words could have all this effect on a man's heart? As soon as her husband had said, "She'll be coming back soon," the world had changed and his depression had left him.

"All in God's hands," the cook replied. He could see Robert Macaulay sitting on the sofa in the living room in a white short-sleeved shirt and white shorts, as if it were summer, his legs stretched out in front of him on the table beside a collection of old English newspapers and magazines. In his hand was a glass half-filled with a clear liquid that looked like vodka, gin, or local arrack that hadn't been mixed with water yet, but which in fact was a salt mixture solution that he used to drink from time to time to strengthen his soft bones, so he said.

Macaulay raised his head and looked at him. "You're late, old man!"

He sat himself down at the other end of the sofa and stretched his legs out on the table as well. "I was inspecting the work on the new camp site."

"And how is it going?"

He told him it was going slowly. Macaulay put his glass down on the table and turned his attention to him. "Why?"

He told him that the contractor was not meeting deadlines, and was cheating them out of materials.

"And this 'foreman' Abdul, what's he doing there?"

A bored smile appeared on his lips as he pictured the foreman, who resembled an inflated balloon. "This Abu Jabbar is a useless individual, and what's more I think he's in league with the contractor."

He spoke without anger and without rancor toward anyone. When he had been at the work site a little while ago he had been upset, but he'd calmed down and become more sympathetic the moment he'd discovered that she'd be back soon. He would have liked to tell Macaulay, but the senior engineer seemed preoccupied at that moment with discussing the measures necessary to speed up the work.

"Do you want to warn the contractor? Should we dismiss Abdul?" asked Macaulay.

"Let's warn the contractor, yes. As for Abu Jabbar, it would perhaps be better to transfer him to another, less important position, the maintenance branch, for example."

He didn't want to be the cause of his losing his livelihood, so long as he had no definite proof of his complicity with the contractor, and so far, he had only suspicions. Macaulay took another sip of the salt solution with a gloomy face and turned his head to face the cook, who was standing nearby waiting in silence. "Yes, Abu Mahmoud, do you want something?"

"Would you like to drink your tea here or in your room?" the cook asked in a feeble voice.

He told him he would drink his tea in his room, then turned to Macaulay. "Bob, we need another engineer. You know, to supervise the building of the new club, and the swimming pool, and the maintenance work."

Macaulay promised him he would ask Project HQ in Basra to send a new engineer, then took his feet off the table and got up. He was now going back to his room, to his solitary confinement. He turned round to look at the furniture in the room, and saw a collection of clean shirts, which the cook had brought from the laundry, lying on his bed. He wanted to carry them to the cupboard but he was afraid that they might get dirty from the dust that still clung to his fingers from work, so he left them where they were. From the pocket of his leather jacket he took a notebook with his observations about the progress of the work. He put it on the writing table in the corner of the room, then took off his watch and put it on the glass surface of the rectangular table in the middle of the room. Then he emptied his pockets of money and other things and put them all on the table beside the watch. All these small movements, which he always performed before going into the bathroom, were undertaken almost mechanically, while his mind tried to calculate the days that a small car would take to cover the long distance between the city of Exeter where her mother lived, so she had told him, and the city of Basra (for if she reached Basra, she would have arrived). The polished walls of the bathroom shone under the light; everything in the bathroom appeared spotless. He couldn't compare his room to a prison cell, he just felt bored, but soon she would be back, ten days, perhaps two weeks. Her husband hadn't told him on which day she had left Britain, nor which route she was taking. A brave woman! Her husband didn't seem to care. How could he have let her come back on her own? A beautiful woman on a long road that was almost deserted for much of the way, as it wound through the countries of the East. But why should her husband care? What was the difference between her being raped by some adventurer on the way, and she herself letting someone like you sleep with her when she felt the urge? But why was he so concerned about her, as if she was his own wife? She would arrive safely, even if she had been raped by someone or had let men sleep with her in the motels along the way. Neither he nor her husband would notice anything about her when she got back. "You don't know her very well," he had said to me, but I don't think he knows her very well himself: he's got other things to think about.

The warm water pouring down on his naked body had washed away the tiredness of the day. Meanwhile, he could hear the sound of the door to his room being opened quietly, followed by the clatter of the tea tray being set down on the table. He had better not stay too long in the bathroom, or his tea would grow cold. He turned off the tap, dried his hair, then wrapped a bath towel round himself and went out. He sat on one of the two wide stools in front of the table, lit a cigarette, then poured himself a cup of tea. While he was smoking and drinking his tea, he heard Bob Macaulay getting rid of his surplus gases in the living room while humming the opening bars of Beethoven's Fifth Symphony: Dee-dee-dee-dum! Dee-dee-dee-dum! Then the combination of sounds came nearer to the door of his room; he heard a knock on the door and Bob Macaulay entered, naked. His red private parts hung between his thighs under a knot of pale, faded hair; drops of water still clung to the flesh of his chest and slightly bloated belly; while the light-colored hair on his head, now tinged with gray, which he usually cut short, seemed to be sticking up, as unaffected by the water as a bird's feathers. He watched him step into the room, his bare feet leaving a trace of dampness on the carpet.

"Can you lend me a razor blade?" asked Macaulay.

He left his glass on top of the table and his cigarette on the edge of the ashtray and got up. "I told Abdul to buy me some from the village," Husam heard him say behind his back, "but he's very forgetful these days, because of the wretched pills that he's swallowing. He left us without supper tonight!"

"Let's eat at the Eagle's Nest," he suggested, going into the bathroom.

"Where else do you want us to eat? At Maxim's?"

The air in the bathroom was heavy, still full of steam from the hot water. As Macaulay's naked body moved nearer, he tried to avoid colliding with it or looking at it. In spite of all the years he had spent among them there, seeing so many of them naked without embarrassment, he still tried to look away from the sight of men's bodies when they were so embarrassingly bare.

Bob Macaulay held the razor blade carefully between his thumb and forefinger, as if he were holding a bird he feared would escape from his fingers and fly away. He went out humming again. Anyone hearing him would think that he had a happy life.

When Husam had finished drinking his tea he put on some clean clothes. But now, what to do? It was still too early for the club. He stood uncertainly in the middle of the room, moved over to the fireplace and looked at the picture of his parents in a silver frame that was on the mantle. His mother had given it to him when he had last visited them, "So as not to forget us," as she had said. "Get married, my boy!" he heard his mother say, "That would be best for you, you're past thirty!"

"Listen to what your mother is saying, my boy!" said his father in her support.

But he had shaken his head and said, "Not now."

He returned his framed parents to their place on top of the fireplace, where they would stay sitting quietly, watching him in silent reproach as he aimlessly frittered away his life in a relationship with a fickle, foreign, married woman. He left them and walked across to the window. He pulled back the curtain and stared into the night that had lowered its curtains over everything outside. On the work site, the searchlights had created an enormous patch of light in which the silver tanks were scattered under a dark sky. Men were still working there, but he could not see them from his room. He saw lights twinkling in the workmen's camp at the edge of the desert on the other side of the public road toward the village. He turned to look in the other direction, toward the distant city. He could see three or four lamps spreading their dusty yellow glow in the middle of the place where the new camp would be built. Then he saw lights moving. There was a vehicle coming along the road from Basra. He couldn't see it clearly as it made its way toward the village. He followed its yellow headlights as it crept through the darkness of the night. The vehicle crossed the track leading down to the managers' quarter and continued on its silent passage, its rear lights like two small embers dancing on the road. Then he thought he saw the vehicle stop near the workers' camp—stop for a short time then move on; perhaps it had dropped off someone in the camp returning from leave, or brought someone new to work in this Godforsaken place. How on earth could people live proper lives there in that camp?

The long night was still just beginning. He heard a knock on the door to his room and when he turned round he saw Bob Macaulay coming in again, fully dressed this time, ready to go to the club.

"Are you ready?"

"You want to go right now?"

"What else do you have to do here?"

"But we'll only see Fox and Durham playing darts there now, with their ugly wives sitting at the bar waiting for some man to arrive so that they can bore him with their endless chatter!"

Macaulay laughed. "I used to be like you. I couldn't stand looking at their faces. But can you believe it, as time went on, and with no other women around, their faces began to change and I then discovered a beauty in them I'd never noticed before."

"You must be joking!"

"I'm not joking, believe me. It's really what happened. It's as if some magician had put a spell on them. After a number of months the ugliness disappeared and I began to see them as the prettiest and most refined women in the world. Time and deprivation, old man, time and deprivation will make you appreciate anything!" he added with a sigh.

"I don't believe that they would look any different to me," he said, "even if I lived a lifetime without a woman."

"That's just talk, because you really haven't tried to live without a woman for a long time."

"And what happened after that? I mean, after some really pretty women had arrived here? Did you still regard Jenny and Hilda as pretty women, or did the old ugliness return to its place?"

"It returned again," said Macaulay a little sadly, walking toward the cold fireplace. "A pity, isn't it?"

He saw him look at the picture of his parents. "Your mother must have been an attractive woman in her youth!"

"Yes," he replied curtly, then drew the curtain over the darkness outside and left the window.

"Well, that's life, one pretty, one ugly, and in the end . . ." said Macaulay, raising his eyes from the picture of the old couple.

He grasped his arm. "Come on, I'm starving. I could eat a whole horse at this moment!" And he turned out the light in the room and went out with Macaulay to the Eagle's Nest, the last lap in another day of his voluntary exile.

If only that wretched woman would come back quickly, his life would be changed!

2

As he turned to leave the work site he saw the engineer's black Humber coming up the road, its windows glinting in the afternoon sunlight. "God's anger has come!" he said to himself. He glanced quickly at his watch and found it showing ten past four. What could have made him linger and be so many minutes late? Why hadn't he picked himself up and left, as soon as he heard the work siren cleaving the air with its final call of the day? He stood where he was, waiting anxiously. His day, which had passed quietly, with no irritations, would end badly, as it did every time this bastard came to inspect the work.

The contractor's workmen had gone away exhausted. Some of their backs still dotted the edge of the road, having covered part of the track toward the village, while the men who had left the work site on the other side had begun to turn down to the camp to recover from the day's exertions. Only the man was left with him, the guard who was the reason he had left later than the others. First, the guard had asked him for a cigarette (perhaps it was just an excuse), then started to complain about his personal problems, and so made him face his own biggest problem! The guard now stood innocently beside the concrete pre-fab store smoking his cigarette, while he hoped that the approaching black car would not be carrying his boss. But he was dreaming, for he could see the head of the engineer sticking up in the back seat behind the driver's back when the car slowed down as it approached, then turned off the public road and slowly rolled along the dirt track that led to the work site. This time he could clearly see the face of the engineer, who seemed to be moving behind the window, and his nervousness increased. He saw the car stop a short distance away, took a deep breath and prepared for the confrontation. He tried to step lightly and open the car door for him, but his heavy body let him down. He saw him alight with his tall body and called a greeting, making a noise that he knew full well would be of no use whatsoever.

"Welcome, sir, welcome, I've been thinking of you, I've been really waiting for you. I said we must . . . ."

The engineer didn't look in his direction. His green eyes were intent on examining everything around him. He saw him throw the stub of his cigarette to the ground and turned toward him reproachfully.

"Abu Jabbar, the work is late!"

"You're right, sir, by my honor you're right, but the rain . . . ."

"What rain?"

The sky above was clear, with not a cloud in sight, and the ground below was dry. There were some small pools of mud and water in the hollows, but they weren't affecting the progress of the work. The drilling machine that roared in the desert as it bore into the ground was more proof of the futility of his excuse.

"Sir," he said, trying to placate the engineer, "yesterday morning we finished pouring the floor for the fourth block." Immediately he wished that he hadn't spoken those words. He saw him walk forward with his massive strides and he followed him apprehensively (he's up to no good!). The engineer stopped at the concrete rectangle that had been completed the previous day. It was wet, as the workmen had sprayed it with water before leaving. He saw the engineer bend over the ground and pick up a small pickaxe that he had found thrown onto the ground beside a pile of stones. He knew at once what the engineer had in mind , for it wasn't the first time that he'd seen him watching out for mistakes and faults in the work. The engineer's movements after that were in complete agreement with his expectations. He said to himself that he would now hit the pickaxe in his hand on the edge of the wet concrete floor (which son of a bitch had left his pickaxe here? It was as if someone was conspiring against him!). The engineer struck the pickaxe against the edge of the floor and an earth colored piece the size of a fist fell off. Now he would break it into two pieces. The engineer threw the pickaxe from his hand, took the piece off the ground and broke it in two between his fingers, as if he were breaking a piece of fresh cheese. Then he threw one of the two halves onto the floor and turned toward him. "When did you say you finished this?"

"Yesterday morning, sir," he replied hastily, "it's still moist, sir!"

The engineer gave him a strange look that he could not decipher.

"Abu Jabbar, do you think I'm stupid?"

"Heaven forbid, sir, heaven forbid!"

He hid the short black stick that hung from his hand behind his back and let his shoulders sag, hunching himself up so far as his enormous body would allow. He stood there submissively. He would tell him that he hadn't been there when the contractor poured this floor; he'd gone off to do something else. No, better to tell him that he'd gone to visit a sick worker, a reasonable excuse. He followed the movements of the engineer's hands carefully, as he rubbed the dark piece of concrete between his long fingers. He saw it crumble easily, then the fragments fell to the ground. Sand and pebbles with a little cement. He lowered his eyes as he heard the question that he had been expecting: "What is this?"

He tried to meet the engineer's disbelieving looks with an innocent expression.

"Really, sir. I was away for less than an hour, maybe. By my honor, a sick worker! You know it's essential."

The engineer left him to speak freely, without interrupting. He simply went on looking at him quietly, his looks indicating that he didn't believe a single word of what he was hearing. This didn't surprise him, for the scoundrel was suspicious of everything. But he had to say something to justify the fact that as the foreman responsible, he had failed to prevent this sort of blatant deception with regard to the building materials. When he had finished giving his flimsy excuse he stood silently like a naughty schoolboy.

"Listen, Abu Jabbar," said the engineer. "This floor will be ripped up from its foundations first thing in the morning. Understood?"

He was angry, but despite that he didn't raise his voice. Why should he raise his voice when he knew that his orders would be obeyed?

"Yes, sir," he replied, "but . . . ."

The engineer fixed him with blazing eyes. "But what?"

"Nothing, sir, nothing. I just wanted to say, at your service, sir!"

God damn you, Hajj Subayh! The whole day's work has been wasted, not to mention the materials. I told him, "Work as you see fit!" and he goes and uses a lot of sand without thinking of the consequences! How many times have I warned him! I told him this bastard had eyes like a hawk!

The engineer now began wandering all round the extensive work site. He tried to keep up with him with his slow steps and panting breath. He felt tired, very tired. Even a full day's work had never made him as tired as this.

If Engineer Husam had come a bit later, he would have stripped off his clothes by now, washed his face, arms and legs, and be lying in his bed in the quiet of his tent. A breeze carried to him the smell of the food that was being prepared for supper in the camp kitchen. Part of his thoughts—a small part of his thoughts—wandered off of its own accord as he tried to guess the sort of food that was being cooked for that evening. He couldn't make out anything in particular; the smells were a mixture of spices and the odor of burnt fat. That small part of his mind obsessed with food was trying to puzzle it out when he was surprised by the voice of the engineer, who stopped and turned toward him, interrupting his train of thought.

"Abu Jabbar, you can't believe that I don't know what's going on here. I will warn Hajj Subayh once more. As for you . . . ."

He waited apprehensively for the rest of the sentence but the engineer did not complete it. He left his threat hanging ambiguously in the air, inducing a sense of unease. His brain began to hurriedly think of all the possible penalties as he panted behind him from one place to another. If he told him what sort of penalty he had in mind he would spare him the torment of his worry and unease. But what did he mean when he said that he knew what was going on? What exactly did he know? He saw the engineer go back to the concrete floor that he hadn't approved and kick the side of it with the edge of his rubber sandals, then step up and walk on it. He seemed gloomy. Perhaps he was hesitant about implementing the decision to rip the floor up and lay it again. But the engineer just got off the floor and looked at him angrily. "First thing in the morning, Abu Jabbar!"

"Anything you say, sir," he replied submissively.

The engineer's face, originally fair, seemed bronzed by his constant tours of the work zones under the sun's rays, and the triangle of skin where his shirt opened at the top of his chest was the same. He was wearing gray trousers, a white shirt, and a leather jacket. He was amazed how this man could keep his clothes so clean as he spent the whole day making the rounds among the dirt and building materials in the various work areas. His own clothes were always filthy. He saw him look away from him and wave his hand to the driver, who hurried over to him at once. He heard him speak to him in a different tone, a quiet, friendly tone, as if speaking to a younger brother, and he felt jealous of the driver and even angrier with the engineer.

"Abbas, you're tired today," he heard him say to the driver. "I don't need you any more. Take the car back. I'll walk home."

Once again he saw him give him that same disturbing, ambiguous glance. He didn't feel comfortable with suspicion and contempt in his eyes. God, how he hated him! He couldn't recall ever loathing anyone in his life so much as this conceited young man.

"Abbas, wait!" he heard him say to the driver, who was walking toward the car. The driver came back to him. "Take Abu Jabbar to the camp on your way!" He couldn't believe his ears and his face lit up. He thought that this gesture on the part of the engineer must indicate a sort of pardon. He started prattling away, using all sorts of random expressions of praise and supplication. "May God preserve you, sir, you really deserve the best, by my honor, I always say. . . ."

But Husam the engineer simply turned his back on him and walked away in the direction of the earth dam, dragging his long shadow behind him. The rest of his words remained unspoken as he followed the driver anxiously. He bundled himself inside the car, which slowly carried them away. It left the work zone and climbed up to the road, then increased its speed and headed off toward the camp. He sighed as he complained, "This engineer, may God preserve him, is very difficult, he's quite inflexible!"

He saw the driver smile. He felt as though he had been forced into a corner without being able to do anything to defend himself. He was angry with the contractor too. He had to speak to him and tell him to be more discreet in his swindling, rather than expose him in front of this young man who was the same age as his son.

"A man should be tolerant of other people and not make enemies for himself. Otherwise, he'll get hurt later and regret it."

"What's the problem?" asked the driver, keeping his eyes on the road. "Who's going to get hurt later and regret it? You mean Husam?"

At once he realized his mistake and immediately backtracked. "No, no," he said, "Husam is a gem! I'm talking generally, in general terms! I mean, everybody should cooperate, that's all I mean. Everyone with everyone else, as they say. Is what I'm saying right or wrong?"

"No, you're quite right, Abu Jabbar," the driver muttered in agreement, having lost interest in the subject of the conversation.

What devil had made him open his mouth and sound off like that about the engineer? This tattle-tale could easily report what he'd said to his boss, and make him even more prejudiced against him. These days a man couldn't feel safe with anybody. "Brother Abbas," he said in another attempt to dispel any effect his thoughtless words might have left in the driver's mind, "I've seen all sorts and conditions of men during my long life, but by God, by my honor, I've never seen anyone as decent and upright as Husam. An upright man, straight down the middle, better than the British, a thousand times better!"

He waited for the driver to say something to show that he'd absorbed these last words of his but the driver said not a single word. He remained as silent as if his lips had been sealed with reinforced concrete. Could he have heard him properly, or was he daydreaming, thinking about his own personal problems? When they reached the entrance to the camp, he got out of the car feeling dejected. His fear that the driver might convey to his boss his implicitly threatening words had added a new load to his existing worries. Why hadn't he held his tongue? Tonight even a full bottle of arrack wouldn't be enough. But despite his feeling of dejection he perked up when he saw the workmen moving around inside the camp, moving between the tents and the washrooms, or from one tent to another. He started to walk purposefully toward his tent, his short stick under his arm, as cocky as a victorious general.

The ground in the camp had dried out after the heavy rain that had fallen more than a week ago, but the stones that the men were laying on the paths to walk on were still scattered along the road, and he had to avoid stumbling on them as he cut through the camp paths while at the same time retaining his strong and purposeful walk. He had to preserve his dignity in front of the others, for what was the value of a foreman whom no one respected? The air in the camp was full of cooking smells. This time he could make out the smell of cooked rice, meat on the fire, and onions frying in fat, and his mind turned to the joys of the evening meal to come. He wouldn't be able to enjoy his food today, with the same appetite as usual, though, for that bastard had given him a knock. God curse him and the day they brought him in as his boss! He went inside the tent and found it empty, as it usually was at this time of the day, between the end of work and the time when supper began. His tent mates would come in a few minutes to wash their faces and limbs with water from the cold taps near the camp fence; some of them would change their clothes and some not, and then they would disperse. Muhammad, that strange lad who didn't smoke or drink, would go to sit on the dam facing the desert, staring silently into space like a crazed lover. Muzhir would tell you if you asked that he'd been to the village, or had been with Fawzi the drill operator, or—and this was what usually happened—that the transport manager had asked him to mend his broken-down car. As for Hussein, the lad with a tongue like a saw, no one knew where he spent this time of the day. Istifan didn't go far; you could find him in his fellow villager Dankha's tent, as they exchanged memories about life in the north, perhaps. But there was no one in the tent. He wished they had been with him just then. Of course, he wouldn't talk to them about what the engineer had said or about that vague threat. No, that would perhaps diminish their respect for him—but if they were there in the tent with him, just being there would calm him down. He stayed sitting on his bed absentmindedly; for a long time, he sat there without moving, a thickening bundle of worry. He looked at the empty beds, at his belt on which the mud had dried, and at the empty arrack bottles scattered under the beds and by the walls. Everything in the tent looked miserable as if it was sharing in his sorrow and confusion.

He hadn't achieved anything in his long life except for a son whom he saw only occasionally, and a job as project foreman, but no house and no money. All the money he had earned had turned into empty arrack bottles, empty like his life. And now this bastard had come to finish him off completely. If he had him sacked, it would destroy him. He hadn't made his intentions clear. He had said to him, "As for you. . . !" and shut up. What sort of evil could this stuck-up young man have in mind for him? Why didn't he himself trump up some charge against the engineer and convey it to Mr. Fox, the boss, as part of the information that he gave him about the workforce from time to time? It was true that the boss hadn't entrusted him with the task of spying on the managers and engineers, but he would welcome any news he could give him. But what could he say about Husam? His relationship with John Sullivan the transport manager's wife wasn't a secret, and these sorts of things weren't a big problem for them. The charge against him had to be connected to politics, yes, but this bastard had no interests in his leisure hours apart from women. He had to think of something and plan slowly. The charge had to be convincing; then one report from Mr. Fox to Management HQ in Basra and this reckless engineer's presence here would be at an end. He might even go to jail! Then his worries would end. He felt happy to have finally arrived at a solution and taken a decision. He saw everything around him in the tent brighten up and look at him encouragingly. He felt himself ready for eating. He slipped off his shoes, shoved them under the bed with his foot then put on his sandals and got up from his bed with a new sense of purpose. Even the creaking of the planks under the bed, which usually annoyed him, sounded sweet in his ears. He would wash his head and limbs, enjoy his short daily snooze after work, then make his way to the mess tent early, cheerfully and energetically, to enjoy his evening meal in peace. Yes, there was no other solution; this was the knock-out blow from which that bastard would not get up in one piece!

3

"Get in, old man!" shouted Macaulay, opening the door of the car that had stopped near him on the side of the road. "Get in!"

He moved aside to clear a space for him beside Husam on the back seat. The driver was looking at him as he waited.

"Thanks, Bob," he said, putting his hand on the door to close it. "I'd like to walk for a bit."

"Forget walking today and come with me. I've got some good news for you!"

He got in and closed the door. The gray Rover continued on its way toward the small white houses tucked away between the palm groves.

"What is this good news?"

"Basra's going to send us a new engineer!"

He felt that Macaulay had deprived him of his daily exercise for no good reason. He could have given him this piece of news later when they met at his house. "They're going to send him to us from al-Zubayr," said Macaulay, looking at him to see the effect on his expression.

"Why would they transfer him? Perhaps he's no good!"

"Let's see him first, and judge him afterward."

He said nothing. The arrival of a new engineer would make his own workload lighter, but news like this could wait. What had happened to Macaulay?

"You don't seem happy!" he heard him say. "It was you who asked for an additional engineer!"

He saw him smile, smile with a vague twinkle in his eye.

"Bob, you're hiding something from me, this isn't the good news."

"No, it isn't," Macaulay confessed.

"What is it then?"

He saw Macaulay look at the driver's head. "I'll let you know when we get home."

After a few minutes the car stopped in front of the house. Macaulay asked the driver to wait for him and the two of them got out.

"Are you going back to work today?"

"Yes," replied Macaulay. "There's some work we have to attend to on the loading quay."

The cook opened the door for them and stood against the wall in the entrance with a drooping face.

"And now, what is this good news?"

"Your friend has arrived today," said Macaulay as they went into the light of the living room.

"Maureen?" he exclaimed delightedly.

"Who else have you been waiting for?"

"I thought that she would take longer than this. So . . . ."

In fact, he had been expecting her to arrive before now. Every day that had gone by he had recalculated the distances and days that the journey would take, though calculating the distances and time on their own wouldn't produce a result, for Maureen with her whims and her erratic temperament was the variable factor that one could not rely on or measure properly. But now she had finally arrived and surprised him.

"When did she arrive?"

"Before noon. Shall we go and visit her this evening?"

He was eager to see her, of course. He looked at Macaulay uncertainly. "She must be worn out now after the journey!"

"No, she's not worn out. She spent a night in Basra, and her husband sent a project car that brought her here today."

Macaulay sat down on the sofa in the living room, while he remained standing. "And what did she do with her car?"

"She left it at HQ in Basra to be serviced. Now, aren't you happy?" asked Macaulay, looking into his face with a smile.

He laughed and said nothing. Macaulay knew all his secrets inside out. "Shall we go to see her tonight?"

"Yes, let's go."

"Okay, you wait for me in the Eagle's Nest." Macaulay turned to the cook, who stood waiting for their instructions, and spoke to him in Arabic. "Abdul, make some tea quickly!"

Then he turned to Husam. "Would you like to have your tea with me?"

"No, I must take a bath first."

"Of course, of course, a real bath today!" laughed Macaulay.

He left him laughing with amusement and went into his room. So she had finally returned, she had returned! What would her face look like now, tanned by the blazing eastern sun behind the car window as she drove the long route through Turkey and then across the desert of Syria and Iraq?

<hr />

The cook took the tea tray off the table but didn't leave the room and remained standing hesitantly.

"Yes, Abu Mahmoud?"

"Sir, I'm ashamed even to raise my eyes to you and the boss!" muttered the cook in a confused way, holding his hand to his forehead.

"Ashamed, why ashamed? What have you done?"

"I haven't done anything," replied the man in a feeble voice. "It's just this pain, and today . . . ."

"What's happened today?"

"I couldn't go down to the village for the shopping and I haven't cooked anything for supper."

"No problem," he said sympathetically, "we'll eat at the club."

"For how much longer, sir?"

219

"Until you get better!"

"By God, sir, I can't see any hope!"

The man seemed to him completely desperate, in the grip of a savage and all-embracing pain. "And what did the doctor that saw you in Basra say?" he asked gently.

The cook shook his free hand in a confused way. "He says . . . he says, if you want the headache to go, have your teeth taken out!"

"All of them?" he asked in astonishment.

"All of them, sir."

He heard Macaulay humming, "Dee-dee dee dum, dee-dee dee dum!" His voice was accompanied by the sound of footsteps as he walked across the living room toward the outer door. He heard the sound of the door banging, then silence reigned in the house. "And what have you decided?" he asked the cook, who was standing there submissively.

"It's a dilemma, sir. I'm afraid of having them all taken out and the pain carrying on. But if I don't, I'll still be . . . ."

He wished he could do something for him. "Listen, Abu Mahmoud. Don't have them out. Wait, I'll speak to Dr. Sami and he'll examine you."

The cook didn't seem happy with this suggestion. "Sir, Dr. Sami examined me before and said he couldn't see anything wrong with me. All this pain, and he tells me . . . ."

"Perhaps he meant that you didn't have anything physically wrong with you, that your body's in good shape," he said, trying to cheer him up. "Anyway, don't worry, I'll speak to him and ask him to send you to a good specialist in Basra, or even in Baghdad."

"God prolong your life, sir!" murmured the man more cheerfully and left the room.

He stayed sitting with a grave expression on his face and recalled the first day he had seen this ailing cook. When he had pressed the doorbell the man had opened the door for him and stood there looking in astonishment at him and at the driver who was busy unloading the cases from the car. It was clear that no one had told him that a new resident would be keeping Mr. Macaulay company and living in the house. When he realized that he was an Iraqi, and not British as he had imagined at first, his astonishment had turned into a sort of loathing. It had never ever occurred to him that it would be possible to accommodate a local and a British manager in a single house. When he saw him striding through the yard followed by the driver carrying some belongings he rushed to the door and stood blocking both their paths.

"This is Mr. Macaulay's house, the boss's house!"

He had been tired from the hassle of the journey and grumpy from the blazing weather outside. He stretched out his hand and shoved him aside a little harshly, then ordered the driver to bring the cases into the house. The man was stunned. He retreated without resisting, like a soft branch that you push out of your way; then stood against the wall terrified, his small, restless eyes watching him and the driver both in astonishment while they put the things down in the living room. He heard the driver telling the man off: "What is this, Abu Mahmoud? Does the house belong to the boss or to the project?"

He didn't hear him reply, but saw him sink to the ground and sit on the floor in the corridor, leaning his back against the wall and holding his head between his hands. He left him where he was. He wasn't surprised by the man's behavior, though, for since returning to his home country he had sadly noticed that a lot of people here looked at foreigners as if they were demigods. Why should this wretched man, who had probably spent his entire life working as a servant in foreigners' houses, be any different?

He would have to speak to Dr. Sami about him this evening if he saw him in the club, and so as not to forget, he strapped his watch on his right hand instead of his left.

———

As he went through the entrance to the Eagle's Nest he heard the familiar buzz of men's and women's voices, the steps of the waiters moving briskly to take the club patrons' orders, soft music mingled with the noise of small, solid balls striking each other in the billiards room (bak, bak!), and laughter. The air was heavy with a mix-ture of smells: of drinks, grilled meat, and cigarette smoke. As he was about to make his way across the lounge to the bar room he spotted Suzanne, the wife of Engineer Akram Jadallah, sitting on her own in her usual corner under the standard lamp with the decorated shade, reading a book, oblivious to everything around her. On the table in front of her stood a bottle of beer and a mug with some yellow liq-uid at the bottom of it. This was Suzanne as he always saw her, trying to find comfort in her solitude with her two companions, a glass and a book.

He went over to her. "Hello, Suzanne!"

She raised her head from the book and her honey-colored eyes lit up. "Hello, Awsam!"

Her pretty face seemed gaunt. It had not been so tightly drawn when he had met her four months ago but it had begun to droop slightly as day succeeded day. "Where's Akram?"

She pointed toward the billiards room. "He's there with his friends as usual, can't you hear him laughing?"

There was considerable bitterness in her voice, despite her attempt to make her tone seem devoid of emotion. She didn't want to become bogged down in the details of her domestic life.

"What are you reading?" he asked, changing the subject.

She showed him the title of the book without losing the page she was reading. "Haven't you got new books from home?" he asked.

"No," she replied.

He promised he would bring her some books from Baghdad when he went to visit his parents at the end of the month and she seemed grateful. "Please do," she said, "I'm fed up, as you know."

Akram's laughter could be heard ringing out in the billiards room, followed by shouting. He saw her staring into the dregs of beer at the bottom of her glass. "It seems he's won a game! He'll be in a good mood for a bit when he's won a game!"

He stood for some minutes looking at her long hair shining under the light. It was blond but she had dyed it black. She had also used henna, as some of the women do here, but her hair had not turned out as she had wished: it had turned an odd color, almost bright red. The pale skin that she used to expose to the sun had not turned brown as she wanted but had turned a burnt coppery color. Perhaps she thought that by changing the color of her hair and skin, she could build bridges that would link her to the world in which her husband had lost himself since returning to Iraq—for all the bridges that linked them while they were living together over there had been broken.

"Won't you sit for a bit?" she asked.

He would have liked to have sat with her for a little. She didn't like gossiping to women but at the same time she avoided sitting with men of her own race so as not to stir her husband's anger or jealousy. But he wanted to have supper while waiting for Macaulay to come back so that they could go to visit Maureen together, so he looked at his watch and murmured an excuse.

"Thank you, but I have an appointment and I must finish my supper quickly."

Then he left her with her glass and book, and went into the bar lounge.

The lights fastened behind the wooden shutters threw their beams onto the ceiling; then the beams split and fell faintly onto the drinkers' faces, on the ashtrays full of ash and stubs, on the glasses of beer and whisky, and on the hands of men and women fondling their drinks on the polished surface of the bar counter. Meanwhile, Joseph the barman was moving nimbly, cleaning the glasses and getting the orders ready. The large mirror covering the bar wall behind the rows of bottles of whisky, gin, vodka, and various other spirits reflected everything—the rows of bottles and glasses, Joseph himself with his constant activity, and the upper parts of the bodies of the people sitting at the bar counter, those sitting around the tables, and the empty chairs further away that stood silently waiting for someone to come and occupy them. They also reflected the white pipes of the radiator along the walls at a height of about two and a half feet from the floor, the dartboard hanging on the far wall of the lounge, and some players who were aiming their small colored arrows toward it. The mirror created an illusion of spaciousness and breadth in the minds of the Eagle's Nest patrons. Music soothing to the nerves echoed through the air of the club from loudspeakers cunningly distributed throughout the lounge and rooms, as well as hidden places that were not easy to discover at first. Bob Macaulay had told him once that the mixture of sound and light sources had been devised by the electrician Mark Doyle, the young man who had come to work here a few months before his own arrival. It was he who had given the little club the name "Eagle's Nest" and had hung a sign with the two words written on it over the door.

Perhaps Doyle has wanted to gradually turn the club into one of London's Soho underground taverns, to convince himself and his compatriots that they weren't very far from their native country, and that this salty land—where the temperature sometimes climbed to 120 degrees in the shade in summer—was just a natural extension of that group of cold and always cloudy islands. He had only forgotten to hang an inn sign at the entrance to the club, something out of the ordinary that would attract attention, to make the Eagle's Nest's resemblance to the bars he'd left at home complete. Perhaps he hadn't yet come across the right skeleton.

He stood looking at the people in the club. He spotted Dr. Sami al-Nashwan sitting with his wife Mona at a table in the corner and remembered the cook's illness. But they were eating supper, so he didn't think it right to talk to him about a subject like that. It would be better to visit him tomorrow in the clinic. At one of the high tables next to the bar he saw Tom Fox with his light-colored, pointed beard and mustache. He felt upset as he immediately recalled what Abbas his driver had said to him at midday. Fox's wife Jenny was sitting on another seat beside him, while on his left sat Hilda, the wife of Barry Durham, the fire chief. He walked over to the bar, asked Joseph to bring him a bottle of beer and stood waiting. Fox didn't look in his direction, as if he hadn't noticed him, but he became aware of Fox's wife staring at him with her small eyes. When their eyes met she nodded her head in his direction and smiled, so he smiled back, then quickly turned his face away, but was surprised to find her looking at him through the mirror behind the barman's back. She had a face like a horse, protruding teeth, and hair the color of sun-baked bricks. Macaulay said that time and deprivation had made him see her as beautiful after some time had elapsed. Could this be possible? He realized, though, that the appearance of this woman, who was blameless toward him, could not excuse all this dislike of her. Perhaps he had stumbled on the wretched woman without realizing the feelings of hatred welling up inside him against her husband, the pig now sitting beside her who was constantly sticking his nose into other people's business.

Joseph arrived with a bottle of chilled beer and a large glass. He took it and hurried away from the bar. He found a servant standing to one side with a tray in his hand, waved to him as he put down his bottle and glass on an empty table, then sat down. He heard Dr. Sami's voice calling behind his back, "Hey, Husam, bring your beer and come and sit with us!"

He turned toward Dr. Sami and his wife, who had sat down at a nearby table. "Sorry, I don't want to intrude!"

"Come on, my friend, come on!"

He picked up his bottle and glass and stepped toward their table, then hesitated and stopped.

"Hello, Mona!"

She smiled in his face. "Hello!"

"I'm afraid you may be having a private conversation."

"Sit down, for God's sake," she replied, laughing. "Forget the formalities. Does Sami ever have private conversations?"

Her husband pointed to an empty chair between them. "Sit down, my friend, sit down!"

He put the bottle and glass on the table between their empty plates and sat down. Dr. Sami looked into his wife's face with a smile. "My dear fellow, we finished our private conversations some time ago."

"Yes, the learned doctor has nothing left to talk about except so-and-so with a hernia and someone else who's complaining of a swollen bladder."

"And she gets annoyed."

"I'm not surprised."

He poured his beer into his glass. Dr. Sami offered him his pack of cigarettes.

"No thanks, I'm going to eat."

Dr. Sami offered the pack to his wife and asked her gently, "And you, my dear?"

His wife took a cigarette and the pair of them started to smoke contentedly. He wondered whether they were really as happy as they seemed to be. Or was it a show they put on for other people? No one knew, for there was no one more skillful than husbands and wives when it came to playacting; he himself had discovered that, both from his relationships with women and his friendships with men. He took a large gulp from his glass and carried on waiting for the servant to come back with his supper. Dr. Sami let out a small puff of smoke away from his wife's face then turned to him.

"Husam, tell me, is everything okay?"

"Yes, fine! You may sometimes see some odd medical cases but I only have the problems of workers and contractors: this building's wrong, that wall's not straight, and so on and so forth."

"Right, Husam, you've reminded me. When will the new club be finished? We're tired of this cramped place, my friend!"

The subdued chatter continued around them. The darts players at the far end of the lounge were continuing their game, but without too much noise.

"Soon, God willing. A few months and it will be ready."

"A few months? I mean, from what you say, we won't be able to have a dance party at New Year's!"

His wife looked at him disapprovingly.

"Why all this enthusiasm for dancing parties, my dear?" she asked. "Do you have someone you want to dance with?"

"No, my love, no! Believe me! But one needs a change of atmosphere. We're tired of cocktail parties."

He was tired of cocktail parties as well, and the present club building wasn't large enough for organizing a dance. When the

226

management decided to put on a cocktail party for some occasion or other it would tell the maintenance men to remove the portable wall between the bar and the lounge to make the place a little more spacious. He noticed the servant bringing the supper tray as the doctor asked again, "Okay, but when will the swimming pool be ready?"

The doctor's wife gave a small laugh but said nothing while the servant was there. He lifted his glass of beer off the table and bent slightly to one side to allow enough room for the servant's hand to maneuver, as it laid out first the plate of kebabs, then the bread basket, bottle of sauce and salad dish, and finally the knife and fork. The hand then took away the plates and bottles and glasses from in front of Sami and his wife. When the servant had finished its task and withdrawn, he straightened up and said, in reply to the doctor's question, "The swimming pool will be completed before the summer, with the club."

Dr. Sami grabbed the arm of the servant, who was on the point of leaving, and looked at his wife. "What will you have to drink, my love?"

She emptied the smoke from her lungs while the servant waited submissively, holding the tray now loaded with dishes and empty bottles. "Tea, please," she said finally.

"One tea, one coffee!"

Dr. Sami let the servant go.

As he set about eating he heard Mona guffawing quietly and looking at her husband.

"Anyone who heard him asking about the swimming pool would think that he was a world champion swimmer!"

Her husband looked at her reproachfully. "And who taught you to swim, my dear?"

"We won't disagree," she replied, backtracking a little. "But you have a habit of thinking about something when it isn't there, then when it comes . . . ."

Husam laughed in agreement. "Mona's right. Remember how you got on our nerves about the tennis courts? But now the courts have been available for a while and everyone is playing, while you haven't played a single day!"

"I don't have time, Husam, my friend, I don't have time!" said Sami, as if to excuse his laziness. "You know that I'm the only doctor here. And tennis makes different demands."

"How are they different?" asked his wife, puffing the smoke from her cigarette into the air. "Enlighten us!"

"If there is an urgent case and I'm in the swimming pool," he said, in an attempt to explain the difference, "I can get dressed quickly and go off, without causing any inconvenience to anyone else. But if I am engrossed in a game of tennis with someone else . . . ."

Mona laughed and shook her head in despair. "My God, this man's brilliant at concocting excuses!" she said.

He saw her raise her hand and pass it over her hair, then bring the cigarette to her lips and draw on it for a long time with her eyelids lowered. Her long black eyelashes looked like a pair of small Andalusian fans. Her skin was pure white, and her wine-colored hair was gathered up on her head. Her broad face was completely full on display. She was the prettiest wife in this godforsaken place. Prettier than Maureen (whom he was longing to see at that moment), prettier than Suzanne, Akram's wife. Mona, though, like her husband, was on the plump side, from too much food and too little exercise. They were like chickens bred for the table, chickens that they keep the lights on all the time, so that they can't tell night from day, eat all the time, eat and grow fat. Even he had begun to put on weight, despite the fact that he walked every day and sometimes played tennis. He rubbed his hand gently over his belly under the table. Yes, he too had begun to put on weight; he'd turned into another chicken, a chicken patronizing the Eagle's Nest.

Mona puffed at her cigarette and looked at the faces of the people sitting at the nearby tables, then gave him a special look and said, "Maureen arrived today!"

He carried on eating, pretending that he hadn't noticed her revealing glance, while her husband tried to play down the news, "Yes, we heard she'd arrived."

"And what else did you hear?" she asked him provocatively.

"Is there something else?"

He raised his head from the plate of food. She put out her cigarette in the ashtray in the middle of the table, as her eyes moved from face to face, enjoying the sight of their expectant glances. Then she said slowly, "Maureen has brought another woman with her!"

"Another woman? Who could that be?" asked her husband with interest.

"I've no idea," she said, shrugging her shoulders disinterestedly.

Bob Macaulay hadn't told him that a second woman had arrived with Maureen. Perhaps he didn't know himself.

"Amazing," said Dr. Sami, as if to scold his wife. "Why didn't you tell me from the beginning?"

"And why all this interest on your part?" she retorted. "I mean, who could she be? God knows. A waitress in a bar, or at best a salesgirl, or are you interested because she's a foreigner with colored eyes?"

She reached for his pack of cigarettes while her husband laughed cheerfully.

"Husam, my friend, do you approve of this attack? I didn't say anything, just a question! Now you can see how persecuted I am!"

He lit her new cigarette for her from the stub of his own, then threw the stub into the ashtray, still laughing. "Persecuted and defeated!"

He seemed happy with her feelings of jealousy, though. He was about forty, but his gold-framed spectacles, his thick hair that was graying early, and the slight swelling under his eyes all made him look older than he really was.

The servant came up to the table, put a glass of tea in front of Mona and a cup of coffee in front of Dr. Sami, then stopped and asked, "Anything else, Doctor?"

Sami shook his head and lifted his cup. This time the waiter turned to Husam. "And you, sir?"

He asked him to wait, paid the bill for his food with a generous tip, and the waiter went away happy. Dr. Sami looked at his wife who was sipping her tea slowly with her cigarette in her other hand and asked her sarcastically, "This woman who's come from Britain with

Maureen, what business has she got here? Has she come to see Nice or Cannes?"

"But who wouldn't want a free trip to Iraq? Warm sunshine at this time of the year, food and drink to suit any taste, and we've got men (praise be to God) who will spend thousands of dinars on her and women like her!"

"Don't humiliate me like that! I'm not prepared to spend a single piaster on any woman except for my beloved wife. We left those sorts of things to bachelors years ago!"

He gave him a wink, and she seemed happy to see him backtracking in front of her. He had the impression that they were enjoying the verbal contest, which he had witnessed on several occasions. It was a sort of sport to keep away the feeling of boredom. He started to eat, following the amicable spat between the married couple in silence, smiling occasionally but without intervening. The fire service chief, Mr. Durham, and his wooden wife Hilda, who had been at the bar a short time ago, were sitting at a nearby table drinking beer, while at another table sat the stores manager, Mr. Carnie, and the accounts director, Mr. Johnson, with their wives. Akram Jadallah's booming laugh could occasionally be heard from the billiards room. He was playing with some friends of his who were employed by the Port Authority and whom he brought to the club from time to time, despite the fact that the British project workers disliked people from outside coming there; they regarded them as intruders. Whenever the noise from Akram and his friends in the billiards room grew louder, signs of irritation appeared on their faces.

He heard Dr. Sami continuing the subject of the conversation. "Yes indeed, you bachelors are the lucky ones!" he was saying, but Husam didn't comment on his words at all, for he didn't want to take sides in their game. He saw Mr. Fox lift his wife Jenny by her waist off the high bar stool, like someone picking up a small child, put her gently on the floor, then she started walking in front of him as he followed her with his enormous frame and his handlebar mustache. How gentle the man appeared as he walked behind his ugly wife, like any henpecked husband, how gentle and content with his life he appeared to be, having drunk his fill of alcohol that evening, perhaps at someone else's expense. Before leaving the bar lounge with her husband, Jenny spotted them, smiled, and raised her small, pale arm to wave to Mona in the distance. Mona smiled at her until she had left the hall, then lowered her head.

"Poor woman, she's not pretty at all, though she's got a good heart."

"Unlike her husband!" commented Dr. Sami.

Husam pushed away the empty plate in front of him and spoke angrily while taking his cigarettes from his pocket, "This morning he was asking the driver about me, wanting to find out from him where I went, what I was doing, who I was speaking to and so on. Imagine, the bastard!"

"His usual behavior," said Dr. Sami, without seeming the least bit surprised. "He was a policeman in Palestine prior to 1948, so what do you expect?"

They heard shouting and laughter, then Akram and his gang came into the bar lounge. He had with him two older men, who lowered their voices when they saw how quietly people were sitting. Akram, however, stayed cheerfully raucous. As he passed near them, he joked noisily, "Dr. Sami, mind your dick!" Mona gave him an angry look then turned to her husband, "Won't that Akram ever stop repeating that stupid expression?"

"Don't let him get on your nerves, my dear, be patient for a little while and I'll make him stop."

When Akram had seated his two companions around a table near the darts area at the end of the hall he came up to them and apologized to Mona, "Sorry, Mona, I didn't mean you!"

Mona raised her head to him angrily. "Stop that stupid expression, whether it's me you mean or not! Then come and tell me, instead of wasting your time with any old person, why not sit for a bit with your wife? You leave the poor woman on her own and more or less lock her up, so that she can't speak to anyone, and no one can speak to her!"

Her words took Akram by surprise and his face glowered.

"Who told you that I'm locking my wife up? She's a free woman but she always prefers to sit on her own reading. Even at home, she leaves the children to the servant and sits reading . . . and drinking! What am I to do with her, Mona? I just don't know."

He was trying to reinforce what he was saying with hand gestures but his words had started to falter on his tongue. He stopped trying to persuade Mona of the error of her perception and, without looking any of them in the face, suddenly muttered, "Excuse me," and angrily left them.

A lengthy pause ensued during which no one spoke. Then Dr. Sami looked at his wife reproachfully, "Mona, my dear, you didn't have to speak to him in that tone of voice!"

Her black eyes seemed disturbed by her husband's reproach while Husam was there.

"Honestly, I hate the way he behaves," she said angrily. "Like an adolescent!"

Sami gave him a look, spreading his hands out submissively. For some time they did not hear Akram's voice, but before long his laughter rang out again, quietly at first, then booming a few minutes later. "You imagine he'll take any notice of what anyone says?" asked Mona mockingly, looking at her husband. She took a puff on her cigarette then sullenly blew out the smoke and left the rest of the cigarette to fall from between her delicate fingers into the middle of the tea glass in front of her. He heard the faint hiss of the little firebrand being extinguished in the dregs of the tea in the glass. He wished she hadn't made that ugly gesture, which didn't fit well with her delicate beauty. Why in the tea glass when there was an ashtray in front of her? He tried not to look at her for fear that she would see in his eyes a sign that he was displeased by her action; instead, he looked at his watch and found that it was nearly nine. He turned toward the bar and looked inside. Bob Macaulay was late. He heard Dr. Sami jokingly ask him, "What's this, Husam? Is this a new fashion, wearing your watch on your right hand?" and he remembered the cook's illness.

"Actually, I put it on that hand so that if I saw you I'd remember something."

He took his watch off to put it back on his left wrist. Sami sat up straight and looked at him attentively. "Remember what?" he asked.

Mona was looking at him expectantly, thinking that he might have some news for her. He looked at her in some embarrassment then turned to her husband. "Don't worry, I'll speak to you later. I don't want to spoil your time sitting together by talking about illness. I'm afraid that Mona may be cross with me."

Mona smiled consentingly. "No, please talk as you need to, illness is our stock in trade!"

Dr. Sami looked him in the face curiously. "I hope everything's okay, Husam. What's ailing you?"

He laughed. "No, no, I'm not ill! I just wanted, I mean, you know the cook Abu Mahmoud? Anyway, it's better if I bring him to the clinic tomorrow."

The doctor's interest in the subject faded. "As you like. If I recall correctly, I examined him once, but never mind. Bring him after ten o'clock, after I've finished my dizzying workload."

He noticed the first signs of annoyance on Mona's face and handed her the pack of cigarettes. She took one out and put it between her lips. Her husband gave her a disapproving look as he took a cigarette for himself from the pack he'd offered her.

"My love, you're smoking too much these days!"

She shrugged her shoulders to show she didn't care, and he gave in and fell silent. Husam lit her cigarette for her, followed by her husband's, and began to feel annoyed at having to wait so long. Macaulay hadn't appeared yet and it wouldn't be right to visit Maureen at home too late in the evening, especially as she had a guest with her about whom he didn't yet know anything. Akram and one of his friends were playing darts, and his other friend was sitting watching them, commenting on their style of play, while a waiter moved nimbly between the bar and Akram and his friend, bringing them their various orders. Their noisy chatter at the end of the lounge—occasionally punctuated by Akram's uninhibited laughter—seemed extremely loud by comparison with the subdued hum of the other bar patrons sitting quietly around the tables. He heard Mr. Durham, who was sitting at a table behind his back, say to his wife, in a voice that he intended to be audible to the people sitting round the nearby tables, "All they need now is bananas!"

"That Akram," said Mona angrily. "He behaves like an ape!"

But her husband wouldn't back her up. "No, my dear, if you want the truth, these foreigners, most of them anyway, at the bottom of their hearts think we are *all* like monkeys, and just need a few bananas for us to get excited , and shout and jump around."

"When I was living with them over there," Husam said, embarrassed, as his hand lit another cigarette from the stub of the one that had burned out, "I used to think that they were extremely nice people, but when I came back to Iraq and saw them here I was struck by their behavior. I saw most of them behaving with a strange arrogance and sometimes in an almost depraved way!"

"It's natural, for here they are representatives of their government!"

"I think Mr. Macaulay is a good man," interjected Mona, "not like an Englishman!"

He smiled and looked at her. "He's not an Englishman!"

She thought he must be joking but her husband explained, "Bob Macaulay is a Scot, my dear, a Scot!"

Her eyelashes trembled with a slight embarrassment as she looked at her husband. "Anyway, I think their women are nice and friendly!"

He husband smiled and winked at her. "Their women, yes, God knows, they're nice and friendly!"

Mona blew cigarette smoke in her husband's face. Laughing loudly, he quickly bent his head to avoid the cloud of smoke then sat up straight again. "Since you're talking about their nice women, tell us a bit about Maureen's new guest. What's she like? Big, small, pretty, the opposite? English beauties are real beauties, as our friend Husam knows, but their ugly ones—God preserve us!—well, you have Jenny as the best example."

"Pretty or ugly, I don't know," she replied in a languid tone. "I haven't seen her yet. Tomorrow or the day after, she'll bring herself to the clinic or they'll ask you to go and examine her, and then you'll be able to see her properly, from head to toe!"

"Is she ill?" he asked with concern.

"No, she's not ill now. But she'll get ill. You yourself told me once that these people don't have sun like us, so when they come here they strip like idiots and lie in the sun, then their temperature rises and they get ill."

"You're right. But I thought . . . anyway!"

Mona was saying something to her husband, but Husam's mind was elsewhere, for at that moment he had spotted Bob Macaulay coming into the bar lounge. He picked up his pack of cigarettes and his lighter from the table and hurriedly got up.

"Excuse me!"

Dr. Sami looked at him in surprise at his sudden decision to leave. "Where are you going?"

"I've got some urgent business."

Mona smiled, staring at him from under her black eyelashes. "Sami, my love, don't stand in his way! Husam's got important business tonight that can't be put off!"

He hurried away before she could say anything else.

They walked in silence, each carrying his own gift. He had bought a bottle of whisky, while Macaulay had bought a bottle of gin from the club bar. They left behind the din and smoke, the food smells, and the drink and music, and went out into the open air and the silence that reigned over the quarter outside. The fronts of the white houses and their little gardens were illuminated by the lights that shone on the paths and over the house entrances, forcing the darkness to gather itself up and retire to the palm trunks that stood in the empty parts of the area. The sky above their heads, though, appeared deep black and overcast, and there was a sluggish breeze that scarcely moved, in which one could detect the signs of imminent rain. He could smell the aroma of the rain to come. From the far depths of the palm groves surrounding them; from among the trunks of the palms standing silently, as their upright trunks awaited the downpour of rain to wash them; from among the peasant villages that crouched in the darkness, he could hear the insistent barking of dogs shattering the silence that extended along the banks of the Shatt al-Arab. Had they perhaps been disturbed by an intruder, or the cautious, stealthy footsteps of a nighttime wanderer, that their barking had become so loud? The atmosphere outside was miserable, yet at the bottom of his heart he felt happy—the serenity of a man who was finally at peace with the world and had forgiven it all its faults. The return of a woman after an absence had made him content with the world; he saw the world as happy, and saw this far-flung place, which usually induced a sense of malaise, as a wonderful oasis of life, where he could spend all his years!

He heard Bob Macaulay hurrying him on.

"She's waiting for us now. I telephoned her to say we were coming."

Could Macaulay have guessed his feelings at that moment?

"And did you know that she's got other guests?"

He was disturbed by the suspicious looks in some people's eyes when they saw him with her.

"I saw Mark's car at the door. If you don't want to see him, I can go on my own."

Macaulay was joking, of course. Mark Doyle was one of the very few Brits in this place that he felt comfortable with.

"Mark is a nice person, I sometimes play tennis with him, you know that."

"Don't try to play with him tonight, he's there for the girl!"

"But you didn't tell me that Mrs. Sullivan had brought a girlfriend of hers back with her."

"I didn't know."

They started to make their way along the path through John Sullivan's garden, walking between two low green hedges before entering a patch of ground illuminated by the lamp over the front door. The lawn, lit up on either side of the path, stretched silently over the face of the ground in the quiet of the night, awaiting the first spots of rain. The grass had been carefully cut, the rose bushes pruned, and the stray twigs on the hedges trimmed in a way that made them look in the night as though they had been built of some green material, rather than springing from under the ground. Mr. Sullivan took good care of his yard and didn't rely on the gardeners used by the project management, as the other people living there did; it was his good fortune that Sullivan didn't look after his wife so well.

He left Bob Macaulay to press the door bell so as not to appear too anxious to see Maureen in front of him, but after waiting for some time he wanted Bob to press it again. He saw him smiling under the light by the door; he seemed to be enjoying seeing him fidgeting on the threshold. Macaulay was not much bothered about this visit; he had come with him to pass the time, and perhaps also to see this new girl with his own eyes, after finding out that she was here.

"Perhaps they've gone to bed!" he sighed, annoyed.

He looked at Macaulay. "At this hour? And Mark's car is still here."

He smiled, understanding full well his tone of voice.

"Patience, old man, patience!"

Finally they heard footsteps approaching hurriedly, and Maureen opened the door to them herself. When she caught sight of him she surprised him with a tone of voice that was more than a mild rebuke. "At last, the aristocrat has come!"

He looked at her longingly, quite dazzled by her charms. She says "aristocrat!" What a thing to call him! She thinks he is being standoffish because he hasn't rushed to see her before now. But it was Macaulay who. . . .

He smiled at her awkwardly and she turned her eyes to Bob Macaulay, while making way for them to go in. "Hello, Bob! I'm sorry, I was in the kitchen."

She led them inside where they were met by warmth, music, and soft feminine laughter. In the living room, at the end of a low, wide sofa, sat Maureen's new guest with a glass of whisky in her hand. Mark Doyle, the electrical engineer, was sitting at the other end of the sofa, smartly dressed in a blue jacket with gold buttons that glinted in the light. They were sitting with their backs turned to the entrance, facing the wood fire whose tongues of flame licked each other in the fireplace in front of them. They were facing it, but they were some distance from the blaze, for on either side of the sofa there were two easy chairs, and a teak table in the middle, with an ashtray on either side of it. Mark Doyle's glass was in front of him on the table, beside his cigarette pack and gold lighter, and there was another glass, which Maureen had left on the table when she came to open the door for them. As they came through the entrance, the new woman laughed at something Mark said to her, but she stopped laughing and turned her head toward them as they came into the lounge. He could see one side of her face. She looked like a woman of about twenty-five, though the light freckles scattered over the skin of her face perhaps made her seem younger than she really was. Her hair was a whitish blond, almost the color of silver, cut quite short. She had blue eyes—pale blue, like the sky at midday.

Maureen took their presents from them ("Wow, you shouldn't have!") then quickly relieved herself of the two bottles, putting them down on a metal serving trolley with a glass top that was parked in a corner of the room with two or three bottles, an ice bucket, and some glasses on it. She turned toward them with a touch of pride. "And now, let me introduce you to my dear friend!"

She went up to her guest and pointed to Bob. "Mr. Robert Macaulay, senior engineer. You can count him as a bachelor if you like, even though he's a married man."

The young woman's face registered some confusion but she smiled, thinking it was one of Maureen's jokes. She smiled delicately and offered her hand to Mr. Macaulay, still sitting comfortably on the sofa, while Maureen was speaking about her.

"Diana Cortzen. She works as a fashion model with Harrod's. The best, of course!"

What had a fashion model come to do in the village of Faw at this time of the year? Perhaps she was just a waitress in a bar or a store salesgirl as Dr. Sami's wife had said. Anyway, now that Maureen had arrived, what did he care who she was, so long as her presence here spread a little more joy, in this desolate place. Meanwhile, Maureen was putting her hand on his shoulder. "And here is Mr. Awsam Hilmi. He's overseeing the construction of our new club. He's a bachelor and wants to stay like that until the Day of Reckoning!"

She looked into his eyes. "Am I right?"

"You're always right!" he replied submissively.

They laughed and he gently pressed the warm, soft hand the young woman extended to him. "I'm very pleased to meet you, Mr. Hilmi," he heard her mellow voice say.

This time he looked at her face to face. Her features were not beautiful by conventional standards but there was something difficult to define (her smile, her bold eyes, her slightly wide mouth, or perhaps her voice when she spoke) that made her an attractive woman. She had the figure of a fashion model: he could see that in her upright pose and in the length of her legs as she sat on the sofa. As he noticed her penetrating looks, he said to himself that this young woman, if she stayed here for a time, would stir some sluggish waters and there'd be more than one story to tell. He and Bob sat on the two vacant chairs on either side of the sofa. He sat near Diana while Macaulay took his place beside Mark on the other side. Maureen brought a small chair from beside the telephone table at the entrance and sat opposite him next to Macaulay. The fire continued burning in the fireplace, sending a pleasant heat into the room, and in a corner a record was turning on the record player, filling the place with sweet sounds. No one said anything as they sat down. He saw Mark take his glass from the table, then look at Diana as if to say, "We'll finish our story later," and he saw her smile to show she understood.

Maureen pointed to the drinks trolley. "Everyone help themselves!" she said, then took her glass that she had left on the table and looked at him. "My mother wanted me to stay with her for a few days longer but I told her it wasn't fair to leave my husband on his own for so long." She gave him a little smile full of meaning. She had changed noticeably and become more attractive. He wanted to tell her so at once, but an eastern reticence, retained despite all the years he had spent over there, made him say, "You seem to be in very good health after your long journey!"

Mark agreed and said that he had noticed that as well and had said the same thing to her when he saw her. Maureen's face lit up, "That's what everyone says!"

He thought she was a little thinner than before she had left. Her soft skin, sunburned during the journey, was a color like bronze. She had let her long brown hair tumble down over her back and shoulders, and her green eyes sparkled with happiness. She seemed to him like a beautiful gypsy, a beautiful gypsy lover! He wished he could be alone with her right that moment, away from other people's eyes. He heard Macaulay, who was standing by the drinks trolley, ask him, disturbing his train of thought, "Awsam, what would you like to drink?"

"Whisky, please."

Then he looked at her again, until Mark roused him from his dream this time, by saying, "I don't see you at the tennis courts these days!"

Before he could construct an excuse to justify his absence, Macaulay, who was busy preparing their drinks, said, "He's gotten lazy!"

Maureen then looked at him menacingly, "I'll make him play again even if I have to drag him to the tennis courts!"

He saw Diana smile, smile and look at him for a long time. He realized that she had gathered from Maureen's frank words that the relationship between them went deeper than a mere friendship between people living in the same place.

He avoided her looks and turned his attention to Bob Macaulay, who came back with two glasses and put one in front of him.

"But where's John?"

Macaulay wanted to find out the reason for her husband's absence. "Oh, John!" she muttered, slightly irritated. "He's gone to the workshop. He says he's got some work there."

Once again he felt a burning desire to be alone with her away from the others. The music had stopped, and nothing could be heard from the record player in the corner except for the hiss of the record as it turned round under the scratching of the needle.

His desire for her was not love this time; it was a kind of animal attraction. He was aware of a strange magnetic force emanating from her like a sort of black magic. There was something like a mesmerizing smell filling the air around him and drawing him to her. (Perhaps her body was emitting the giddying aroma without her being aware of it.) He said to himself that this was how one animal was attracted to another, with no emotions, no preliminaries, no stimulation except for a sensation of the presence of the other creature's body in the vicinity. But the burning desire to immediately possess her subsided when she left her glass on the table, stood up, and moved her body away from him to change the now-silent record. He would be alone with her tomorrow; for now, he had to behave like a civilized human being. The mad desire spun in the cells of his body for just a few minutes before passing. Perhaps her body had stopped sending its signal spontaneously when she got up and transferred her attention to something else, something inorganic and unfeeling, thereby releasing him from her spell. Or perhaps she had also said to herself that she had to behave like a civilized woman.

"I'll play you some records that I brought back with me."

She returned after a little to sit in her place while the sounds of music poured out again, filling the air in the living room, but gently. She took her glass from the table and held it between her two hands like someone holding a child, then played with it, tossing it in the air then catching it. Through all this, her hands stayed still, and the liquid at the bottom of the cup was also still—its surface tilting a little, but nonetheless still.

After a few moments, the voice of the singer could be heard through the strains of the music:

From the land of rain,
From the land of ice,
I journeyed to you
Seeking the warmth of your heart.

Maureen was looking around at the various faces. They were silent for a few moments, respecting her wish to listen to her new song. Meanwhile he started to look at her collection of glass figurines carefully lined up on top of the stove. She adored statues like that—birds, animals, and historical figures—all standing silent and gloomy, gazing submissively at what was going on in front of them.

Macaulay broke the silence by asking, "How was the journey?"

"Oh, it was wonderful! We drove the length of the French Riviera, then Italy, then . . . ."

Diana gave a sorrowful sigh. "But the beaches were all deserted, nothing except for waves and sand and seagulls—and empty hotels!"

"And what would you expect at this time of the year?" commented Mark, laughing.

The two women started to tell them what they had seen during their long car trip from Britain to Iraq. The journey had been exciting, like one of Sinbad's journeys in Diana's view, especially after they had left Europe behind them. She had been seeing the countries of the East—their people, clothes, and customs—for the first time. "I couldn't have imagined it!" she declared. They had stayed in Istanbul for three days. And had they seen the Great Mosque? Of course they had seen it, though Diana spent most of the time in the bazaar.

"And Diana bought herself an oriental slave girl's clothes!" laughed Maureen.

Mark suggested that Diana put the clothes on in front of them so that they could see how she looked , but she excused herself, promising to put on the dress one day when there was a suitable occasion, a party, for instance.

They continued drinking, smoking, chattering, and listening to the music and songs that Maureen had brought with her, everyone sitting relaxed, not moving except when necessary, to pour a new glass, to change the record, or to add a new piece of wood to the fire blazing in the fireplace. At midnight Maureen, helped by Diana, brought them in a light snack. They were eating when they heard a noise from the kitchen: footsteps and the clatter of utensils. Bob Macaulay turned to look at Maureen, "Is that your servant?"

She listened hard and her face froze. "No, Abdul prepared supper for us then went home to the village."

She turned her head toward the kitchen and called from where she was sitting, "Is that you, John?"

They heard her husband's voice reply to her slightly hurriedly, "Yes, yes, don't worry. I'll be with you in a minute!"

Her husband had come into the house through the servants' entrance and no one had noticed him. They tried to resume what they were saying, but the sporadic murmur of a conversation between two people reached them from the kitchen and aroused their curiosity.

He saw Maureen fidgeting where she sat, then she abandoned her food and stood up. "Please excuse me for a moment," she said and rushed off to the kitchen. Shortly afterward, he heard her talking softly to her husband. Their conversation seemed tense but her precise words were unclear. Then, in a moment of anger and at the end of her tether, Maureen could be clearly heard saying, "Did you really have to bring him here?"

Suddenly their voices stopped and silence reigned. Mark got up and went over to the record player to turn up the sound of the music, to conceal any subsequent conversation in the kitchen. Macaulay occupied himself prodding the embers in the fireplace with a black poker that had been hanging on the wall. He saw Diana look at him in a confused way, not understanding what was happening or why they all seemed embarrassed. "I hope you're finding the place here enjoyable," he said to her with a smile.

"I'm sure I'll find it amusing."

A woman was singing in Spanish on the record. After a few moments Maureen came out to them, trying to smile, but her face seemed flushed. She perched her body on the arm of the chair where he was sitting.

"John will take a shower then join us."

He felt her soft backside press on his arm, while her breast hemmed him in, and one side of her hair fell over his shoulder. After her critical argument with her husband in the kitchen, Maureen had begun to behave rather carelessly, almost recklessly, while he was confused in the presence of the others. He saw Bob Macaulay look at his watch, then at him. Mark walked over to the window, drew back the side of the curtain, and looked into the night.

"It's raining!"

They would get soaked if they left now but their house was only a few steps away, and he and Bob Macaulay had only to cut through the yard then cross the road. It would be better to go now. Macaulay was right, the atmosphere inside the house was no longer congenial. He shifted his body a little to let Maureen know that he had made up his mind to leave so that she wouldn't lose her balance on the arm of the chair when he got up.

"John must be tired from work and probably wants to rest!"

Mark supported him, leaving the window and downing what was left in his glass with a single gulp. She lifted her bottom off the chair and his arm.

"Wait until it stops raining."

"It might not stop all night."

She didn't insist on their staying, and he got up from the chair. "Tomorrow, then!"

She smiled. "All right!"

At the door, Maureen took him by his arm and held him back after Mark Doyle and Bob Macaulay had gone out.

"I've got a little present for you!"

"What is it?"

"Come tomorrow at four and you'll find out."

She let go of his arm. "And your guest?" he asked her flippantly, in a low voice.

She gave him a warning look. "She's not your business."

Mark Doyle had gotten into his car, started the engine and driven off, illuminating the trickles of falling rain with his car lights. As Macaulay hurried off, he looked at her with passion. He was about to do something rash, there and then, as they stood next to each other on

244

the threshold under the lamp. He was about to seize her violently and clasp her to his chest, but she guessed what was going on in his head and gently pushed him away. "Go away now!"

He left disappointed, hurrying away in the rain, pursued by the voice of the Spanish singer that came from inside the house. Before he left the yard he turned to look at her. He saw her still standing, framed by the house, despite the cold air and the raindrops that the breeze was gathering up and spreading over her. She stood watching him leave, clasping her arms across her breasts, penetrated by the light pouring over her by the lamp above the door as well as the one from inside the house, accentuating the lines of her shapely body. He looked at her as he hurried between the walls of hedge that her husband had carefully trimmed. The cool raindrops fell on the burning flesh of his face. The singer's voice rang out behind him as he walked out into the night, mingling with the hiss of the rain falling on the rooftops, cars, the turfed ground, and the rosebushes in the little gardens, on the low fences and paved paths, and the palm trees in the surrounding planta- tions. The voice of the Spanish singer that continued to pursue him— stronger even than the night and the rain—held within it something of that eastern sorrow, the heritage of eastern sorrow that had continued so rooted despite the years.

4

"**D**o you know who asked me about you today?"

Macaulay was sitting at the end of the sofa in the lounge at home with a chilled herbal drink in his hand. He turned to him, "Who asked about me?"

"Mr. Reynolds, the general director of management and personnel for the project."

"You didn't tell me you were going to Basra!"

Macaulay frowned after drinking a small mouthful of the solution.

"I didn't go to Basra. He came here. As you know, he makes surprise visits to the work zones from time to time, to inspect his flock, so to speak."

Macaulay's sarcastic tone surprised him.

"It seems that you don't care for him."

"I don't think anyone cares for that man!"

"Strange. When he met me on my appointment to the project he seemed a nice, understanding man to me."

"Snakes can be nice too!"

Macaulay stared at the liquid left at the bottom of his glass. The grains of salt that had sunk to the bottom had left a pure white layer at the base, which was covered by an off-white liquid. He saw him push the glass away on the table. He appears to have had enough. He's had his dose of calcium and his bones will get a little harder, Husam thought.

"And what did he say about me?"

"He wanted to know if you'd gotten used to the conditions of work and life here."

An incidental question that didn't mean much. As his job required, he wanted to establish if he'd selected the right person or not.

"And did you say I'd gotten used to them?"

"I told him you were trying hard."

He laughed and went into his room. While he was washing the dust from his body, Husam tried to remember his meeting with Mr. Reynolds at Project HQ in Basra. It had been a long meeting. The man asked him all sorts of questions, most of them having no connection with his work as a civil engineer. He couldn't now recall the conversation they had had. It had been in the summer, more than five months ago. The only things to have stuck in his memory were the questions he had thought odd or confusing. He had also retained in his mind a picture of Mr. Reynolds sitting behind his wide desk with a large picture of King George VI above his head on a white, bluish wall, in a dark navy uniform, with rows of brightly colored medals and decorations embellishing his chest. A few minutes after the start of the interview Mr. Reynolds had said to him, "You usually use first names here in conversation, which is fine, so do you mind, Mr. Hilmi, if I call you by your first name?"

He spoke fluent Arabic, with a slight, almost imperceptible accent. He told him he didn't mind. But his next question came as a surprise. "Mr. Husam, do you believe in God? Do you pray and fast?"

He told him that he did believe in God.

"But you don't fast or pray?"

He saw his blue eyes twinkle as he smiled.

When he had called on Mr. Reynolds' secretary at the time arranged, she had asked him to sit down and wait for a little, while the manager finished a conversation he was having. He sat down to wait, while she went back to her typewriter, a woman of about forty with stern features and a worn-out body. He didn't know how the general director of management and personnel could have chosen her to be the face through which he received people. The central air-conditioning system was sending an invigorating breeze through the whole building while the June sun burned everything outside with its scorching rays—the asphalt on the roads, the walls of the houses, the glass in the windows, the cars and pedestrians on the streets; indeed, it was burning the air itself. He saw some English magazines on a small black table in the secretary's room and picked up one of them. He started to flick through the pages in a disinterested way, casting his eyes quickly over the headlines and pictures. He wasn't in the mood for reading. He had the same feeling that comes over a man about to sit an examination of which he knows neither the subject nor the results. Meanwhile, the secretary carried on working without paying him any attention, as if she were alone in the room. Then he heard the telephone on her desk give out a soft ringing noise, and he knew that the conversation the manager had been having had finished. He threw down the magazine in his hand and looked at the secretary expectantly. He saw her lean over the intercom, press a button, and wait. Then he heard Mr. Reynolds's voice inside the small black box with the white front ask, "Yes, Julie?" His voice was loud.

"Mr. Hilmi has arrived. Do you want to see him now, sir?"

Her voice was rough, and could almost have been the voice of a man. Mr. Reynolds replied with what seemed like eagerness, as if he were expecting a close friend he hadn't seen for ages.

"Certainly, at once!"

She looked at him with an impassive face. "Mr. Hilmi, you can go in now."

He got up to go in but was surprised to find Mr. Reynolds open the door to his office and come out himself with a cheery face.

"I'm sorry, have you been waiting long?"

He shook his hand warmly. The flesh on his hand was warm, soft, and smooth, but his grip was strong. He seemed to be about forty as well, but unlike the emaciated secretary he had a ruddy, laughing face, and handsome, well-proportioned features. He saw him turn to his secretary.

"Julie, please don't let anyone interrupt us. We will be talking for a bit."

He gripped Husam's arm in a friendly way and led him into his room.

"Please, please, sit down! No, no, not here. Sit in this chair by me." And he pointed to a leather chair with a raised back that had been put next to his big desk. As Husam sat down his eyes noticed three scenes on the wall opposite; different views of the British countryside in winter: gloomy skies, mountains covered in snow, and lakes with water the color of lead—depressing images of a country thousands of miles away. They seemed strange here, in this country where the sun shone the whole year round. But they weren't strange to him, at least.

Mr. Reynolds noticed where he was looking. "You lived there for a long time, didn't you?"

He told him that he had lived there for about seven years, studying and working.

"And did you complete your studies at state expense?"

He told him that he had studied at his father's expense.

"Mr. Husam, tell me frankly, why did the state refuse to send you to study at its expense?"

He was startled by this question. What made him think that the state had refused to sponsor him? Or was he just wanting to make sure?

He explained to him that he had not applied for state funding because his father hadn't wanted to make him wait a long time and preferred to send him to study at his own expense.

"Your father must be a rich man!"

Mr. Reynolds's desk was clean, with no papers or files on it, and its surface, which was covered by a thick pane of glass, shone under the light. There was just one small piece of paper in front of him, the size of the palm of a hand. He saw him give it an occasional passing glance, without appearing to be reading from it. He couldn't see him writing down anything of what he was telling him in his replies. It was as if the interview, which he himself had been rather nervous about, was just a meeting between two friends.

"Mr. Husam, what are you reading these days?"

When he tried to reply, he found that he hadn't read anything important since returning from Britain. He told him that he'd read some magazines and would look at the daily papers in the same sort of half-hearted way as one awaits a response to a job application. He thought Mr. Reynolds seemed more interested now.

"And what are the names of the papers that you usually read?"

"I don't read any papers in particular, just those that I find in front of me. After being away for so long I'm trying to catch up on what's going on here."

"Of course, you have to. But you know well, Mr. Husam," he added, looking at him steadily with his blue eyes, "every newspaper makes the news differently. For example, if you read a paper that doesn't like the government, you might get incorrect ideas about what's really happening in the country."

A lengthy pause ensued, during which Mr. Reynolds looked at him in silence, and Husam discovered that his eyes were not blue, as he had thought at first, but dark gray. Mr. Reynolds was waiting for him to say something, but he said nothing. After returning home he had learned to be careful with what he said. When he was in Britain, he could say whatever was in his head without fear. He had been a lively member of student groups while he was studying, especially in the early years. He was one of a large group of Arab and foreign students who rebelled against everything they thought was wrong with the world, whether it concerned them or not. With them, he felt that he was fulfilling himself and enjoying his life at the same time, for political activity there was a sort of amusement. Besides the demonstrations, seminars, speeches, and signing of petitions, there were also trips to other cities, drink, and girls, while here . . . .

"What sort of political books do you read?" asked Reynolds.

He told him that he had nothing to do with politics.

"Mr. Husam, you're an intelligent man."

He didn't know how or when he had taken his pack of cigarettes out from his pocket. He was aware of the pack in his hand, as the fingers of his other hand tried to extract a cigarette from it, and hurriedly put it back in his pocket, but Mr. Reynolds saw what his hands were doing.

"You can smoke, Mr. Husam. I don't mind smoking."

"Thank you," he muttered, a little embarrassed, "but it's not necessary."

"As you like. I'm afraid that my questions may have upset you." He smiled as if to apologize. "We're enjoying a conversation and getting to know each other."

He had the sense that the man, with his kindly smile and uninhibited words, was actually trying to attack him somehow, trying to find out what sort of person he was, and that if he revealed anything about his past activities in Britain he would probably refuse his job application without further discussion. He was therefore cautious in framing his replies, and a little tense. His hands annoyed him: they seemed to have developed a life of their own, embarrassing him as they had done just now, but he forced them to be still and remained waiting in silence with his palms resting on his knees.

The next question surprised him.

"Tell me, Mr. Husam, have you read Jurji Zaydan?"

He found himself laughing, laughing with pleasure, laughing from the bottom of his heart. Mr. Reynolds had eased the pressure on him and suddenly switched the conversation from the labyrinths of politics to the world of literature. Jurji Zaydan!

"Why are you laughing, Mr. Husam? He's a good writer and his books teach us a lot. I've read almost all of them, *The Bride of Farghana*, *The Maid of Karbala*, *History of the Arabs before Islam*, *History of Islamic Civilization*. I've also read the Holy Qur'an and *The Path to Eloquence*. The Imam Ali used to say to you Arabs, 'Come, let's make war,' and you would say, 'It's summer now, it's too hot!' or in winter you would say, 'It's too cold!' But that was a long time ago! You people have changed, you've changed a lot.' You're not cross that I'm talking like this, Husam?"

He smiled but said nothing. Mr. Reynolds' questions and remarks sometimes provoked him and at other times amused him and made him laugh. Most of the time, though, they induced in him a sense of foreboding and put him on his guard. He was surprised and confused, listening to his words, which seemed on the surface like idle chatter.

He felt a rise in temperature of the water pouring on his naked body in the bathroom, moved away from the shower, and turned on the cold-water tap a little. He stretched his hand out under the spray, and when he found that the temperature of the water had moderated, went back to standing in his previous position. He realized that he had not heard the sound of the door to his room being opened. Perhaps his preoccupation with recalling what had happened at the interview had made him fail to hear the noise the cook always made when he brought his afternoon tea to the room.

"Mr. Husam, I'm sorry I didn't ask you before what you'd like to drink. Would coffee suit you?" Mr. Reynolds had asked.

He turned his body toward the intercom positioned between three telephones on a side table to his left, switched it on, then said, "Julie, make us coffee, please, if you don't mind."

Then he turned to face Husam again, "Husam, tell me, why do you want to work with us?"

He told him he'd finished his studies and training abroad and that he had to find a job.

"That's fine, but excuse my asking, why do you want to work with us in particular, rather than somewhere else?"

"Because your project has more opportunities to apply what I learned over there."

"Just for that reason?" he asked, with a crafty smile.

Husam smiled as well. "And because you pay a good salary, so I've heard."

Mr. Reynolds let out a little laugh. "No, no, what you've heard about a good salary is—how should I put it?—exaggerated, yes, greatly exaggerated. Anyway, that is a point we can discuss later. First, the chief engineer has to agree to you, and then . . . ."

In the short periods of silence (periods that lasted no longer than a fraction of a second, during which he was thinking how to steer the conversation deliberately vaguely toward one subject or another) the general director of management and personnel was gazing at the sky through the large window opposite him that looked out onto the cross-roads. The sky was spread out before his eyes. There was an area of empty ground with no crops or buildings on it in front of the project management building, and beyond it a number of small houses whose walls were not much higher than ground level. The whole sky in front of him shimmered in the sun.

"Husam, you're a bachelor like me, I know. Have you left a fiancée behind in Britain? Some of you choose your wives from our people, I know."

This question of his aroused some memories, bringing to light in his mind the faces of girls he had gotten to know during his stay in Britain. He had been on the point of marrying one of them until he had discovered that she had slept with some of his student friends. After that he had started to base his relationships with girls on a principle of mutual interest: she would supply him with sex, while he would supply her with food and shelter, occasionally with some small presents, but without any ties or obligations, and neither imposing conditions on the other; and if either of them felt bored, they would say goodbye and leave with no hard feelings.

He told him that he hadn't left any fiancée behind there.

"Aren't you thinking of getting married?"

This time it was his mother's face that appeared. Since he had come back, she had been urging him to marry her sister's daughter, a pretty, well-educated girl whom he liked, but he hadn't made his mind up yet. His mind was still confused after the life he'd led there and he needed some time to be able to feel comfortable with conditions of life here again.

"Not now. Perhaps I'll get married when I've settled down."

"That's fine. You know, Husam. . . ."

Hearing a knock at the door, Mr. Reynolds stopped speaking. He watched his secretary, who pushed open the door and came in with her dry face, carrying the coffee tray. "Thank you, Julie, thank you, that's very kind, thank you!" he heard him say, with what seemed to him excessive politeness. (Had the cook, Abu Mahmoud, brought the tea without his hearing him?)

The secretary put the two cups of coffee in front of them then left the room without saying anything. Husam noticed that there was something strange about Mr. Reynolds's relationship with his secretary, whom he treated with a mixture of courtesy and wariness, as if he was afraid of her for some reason.

After she had left the room and closed the door behind her, he turned his attention back to Husam. "What was I saying? Oh, yes, we were talking about marriage. I was really asking because the accommodation we have reserved for married people is in short supply at the moment. Bachelors live two or three to a house. Suppose you were working for us, would you agree to share with someone else? You wouldn't object? Fine, fine. That takes care of that point. Husam, drink your coffee before it gets cold."

At that moment he was in dire need of a cigarette; so he drank his bitter coffee without any appetite, while on the other side of his wide desk Mr. Reynolds drank his with obvious pleasure. As he put his cup down on the pane of glass, Husam heard him say, "I forgot to tell you, if we agree to appoint you, we'll be sending you to work in Faw. You have to be prepared to go anywhere, Husam. No objection? Fine, fine."

He turned off the hot and cold taps then put on his bathrobe, dried his hair with a small towel and left the bathroom. He didn't find the afternoon tea tray on the table where the cook usually put it. Had Abu Mahmoud forgotten? He pressed the service bell and sat down to wait. He heard Bob Macaulay humming Beethoven's Fifth in the living room, dee-dee dee dum, dee-dee dee dum, then the voice moved away and disappeared. Someone who knew nothing about him would think the man was a happy-go-lucky type. He was amazed how these people could put up with a life of exile in this place. Perhaps they endured the hardship for the sake of their high salaries, or perhaps some of them felt they were soldiers in the service of the mighty Empire overseas. Bob Macaulay didn't seem to be one of those. Mr. Reynolds was one without a doubt, though, for quite apart from his Arabic this man knew a lot about the country, small details that no one else would bother about.

"Husam, your family live in al-Wazira. Where's al-Wazira? No, no, don't tell me, let me try to remember."

As he covered his eyes with the palm of his hand, he noticed the lined pink skin on the back of his hand, while amid the soft golden down and the gentle patch of freckles he saw some prominent blue veins, which made him think Mr. Reynolds must be nearly fifty. Some people are given away by their hands, not their faces, he said to himself. He heard Mr. Reynolds describe al-Wazira's location with his hands covering his eyes. He described its location precisely and mentioned the names of other places in the vicinity, as if he was a Baghdadi. Then he uncovered his eyes and he saw the marks from his coarse fingers— pale lines on his brow and pink skin at the top of his cheeks. The blood soon restored their normal red color, however. When the interview had finished, after more than an hour, the general director of management and personnel escorted him out himself, took him through the secretary's room and to the door, then said goodbye to him as to a friend. After that he met the chief engineer, a taciturn man of about sixty, who asked him some purely professional questions, and after about a week he was appointed to the project. So Mr. Reynolds wanted to know if he'd gotten used to the place by now?

His window overlooking the desert was a black rectangle studded with pale lights in the distance. He got up and went over to the window, drew the curtain and covered the face of the darkness outside. Then he moved over to the fireplace and stood looking at Maureen's present. What do you suppose the damned woman had meant by choosing this feeble bird as her present for him? Or hadn't she meant anything in particular? Just an elegant statue that she'd taken a fancy to. The glass penguin stood quietly on top of the fireplace beside the picture of his parents, shining under the light, staring out with its small glass eyes. He lifted the bird up, felt the cold glass on the warm flesh of his palm, and looked at the milk-white chest, the little head, and the wings; it had all the attributes of a bird except that it could not take off from the earth's surface as other birds could. He put it back on top of the fireplace then took his watch from the table. What sort of afternoon tea was this when it had gone five o'clock and the cook hadn't brought it yet? He dressed quickly and left the room to find out why.

He found the kitchen in darkness and silence, with steam from the tea and the smell of something burning in the air. He pressed the light switch and hurried over to the electric stove. The water in the teapot had totally boiled dry, and the tea leaves were burning at the bottom of the pot. Abu Mahmoud, the cook, was lying curled up in the kitchen corner where he usually used to sleep, his green blanket covering his body. He turned off the cooker and was about to switch off the light and leave the kitchen when he heard the cook's feeble voice say, "Sorry, sir, tea's ready!"

He saw him gather up the blanket and stagger upright, resting one arm on the wall, with an extremely pale face, and tears glistening in his eyes. Could the man be crying, or were they the tears that well from the eyes when the pain gets to be too much? He looked at him sympathetically and said, "Go back and rest, rest, don't worry about the tea!"

He grasped his shoulder blades and put him back where he had been. But the cook would not rest. He sat in his bed and wrapped the blanket around him.

"Forgive me, sir!"

"It's no problem. The important thing now is to rest."

The man sighed in pain. "I can't find any rest, sir!"

"And the medicine that the doctor in Basra prescribed for you?"

"It didn't work, sir!"

The cook held his head and said, "There's nothing but to have my teeth pulled out and see what happens."

He stood looking at the cook at a loss, paralyzed by his inability to do anything useful.

"The important thing now is to try to rest. After that. . . ."

He switched off the light then left the kitchen and found Bob Macaulay waiting for him in the living room.

"How is he now?"

"Worse than ever!"

Macaulay bit his lower lip with a grave expression. "And what can we do? That's life!" then he moved toward the front door.

He didn't go back to his room but sat on the sofa in the living room as silence descended on the whole house. He could no longer hear a sound from inside the kitchen. Perhaps the man had finally gone to sleep; perhaps the pain had relaxed its grip so he had been able to rest. He looked at his watch; the night was still young. But it would be better to go to the club than stay at home and put up with his feeling of impotence. Maybe Maureen would come to the Eagle's Nest later. He got up from the sofa, took his pack of cigarettes and lighter from his room, and went out.

5

Diana came into the bar lounge at about nine o'clock. He glimpsed her in the mirror behind Joseph, who was busy cleaning the top of the bar table with a damp rag. She was wearing a green dress with a plunging square neckline showing the top of her breasts and a short, white jacket with wide sleeves over the dress. The dress was tight-fitting, hugging her body, and revealing her prominent hips and the curves of her bottom. She stepped carefully in then stopped. (Perhaps she really was a fashion model, as Maureen had said.) She came in with two men who also stopped when she stopped. One of them was the electrical engineer, Mark Doyle, and the other was a swarthy young man of about thirty with a round face, carrying a tobacco pouch in one hand. He hadn't seen him before. He remembered what Bob Macaulay had said to him that afternoon, "The engineer we requested from Basra has arrived, and they've housed him with Mark Doyle." This was the new engineer, then. He and Dr. Sami had been sitting at the corner of the bar for more than an hour, leaning their elbows on top of the counter, drinking beer, chatting and smoking continuously, filling the ashtray in front of them with charred stubs and ash. Dr. Sami noticed his wandering looks, raised his head, then exclaimed cheerfully, "This is Lady Diana!"

She was standing exchanging opinions with the two men about the best place to sit while her slightly superior glances (the glances of a

woman conscious of the effect her magic may have on others) sur-
veyed the faces of the club regulars — some of whom were looking at
her carefully.

"This girl doesn't waste her time, she wants to sleep with the men
from east and west all at once!" Dr. Sami seemed to be enjoying looking
at her. "But who's this swarthy individual with her beside Mark?"

"I think he's the engineer we'd requested from Project HQ."

He spoke without turning his head. He didn't want Diana to think
that he was paying her any special attention. Finally Diana took a decision and led the two men to the bar. He felt her small hand alight on
his shoulder.

"Hello, Awsam!"

He turned round, pretending to have seen her for the first time, and
got down from his high stool.

"Hello, Diana!"

The he greeted Mark, and looked at the new arrival. "I believe
that . . . ."

"I am Sultan al-Imari."

The young man offered him his hand. When Husam tried to introduce himself, Sultan told him he already knew him, as Diana had
told him his name when they came into the bar lounge. Al-Imari was
smartly dressed, and from his navy jacket pocket peeped the bowl of
a large black pipe with a single black eye, like a submarine periscope
scanning the surface of the sea looking for hostile navy units. He spoke
in English, trying as far as possible to imitate native speakers in their
pronunciation of the letters — which Husam attributed to his desire
to impress Diana, perhaps. Mark took a seat at the bar, leaving two of
the tall stools vacant on his right. Sultan sat on one of them, while she
continued chatting to Dr. Sami, who had got down from his stool and
squeezed her small white hand between his palms. He heard her say to
Dr. Sami with a hint of surprise, "I don't see Moona with you tonight!"

He saw Dr. Sami quickly release his grip on her hand and mutter
in an embarrassed way, "Mona's tired today, she preferred to stay at
home."

"I heard that she . . . ."

"Yes, yes . . . ."

That wasn't the conversation Dr. Sami wanted to have with Diana, but the crafty woman knew how to ward off anyone who didn't appeal to her. She moved away to take her place between her two companions, and Husam and Dr. Sami took their seats again, as Joseph came up to the new customers. She ordered a gin and tonic, Mark Doyle ordered a bottle of beer, while Sultan wanted a glass of whisky, stressing to the barman that it had to be Black Label as he didn't like any other sort. He saw him then take his pipe from his jacket pocket, open his pouch, and begin to fill the bowl of the pipe carefully with yellow tobacco leaves. Meanwhile, Dr. Sami was drinking in silence and looking at himself gravely in the mirror, perhaps examining the ravages that time had wrought on his face. He had been hoping for a warmer welcome from Diana, but the wretched woman had reminded him of the wife he had left at home enduring the trials of the first months of pregnancy.

Husam turned to Sultan. "What do you think of this place?"

Sultan smiled happily as he looked at the faces of the British club regulars sitting with their wives at the bar or grouped around the tables in the lounge.

"I haven't seen much yet, but I think that I'm going to be happy here, yes, I'll be happy."

Husam saw Dr. Sami smile at last. Sultan was busy lighting his pipe and Husam lit a new cigarette. Diana was looking at him. "I'm surprised."

Husam looked at her, puzzled. "Why are you surprised?"

Her talking to him like this at the bar, with the new engineer there was embarrassing. He hadn't seen Maureen for more than three days. He had gone to Baghdad to visit his parents and when he returned he had tried to phone her but her servant Hasan had told him she was asleep. "How is she?" he asked Diana in an offhand tone.

"She's got a bad cold."

The she looked at Dr. Sami as if to tell him off. "You didn't tell him, Doc!"

"I don't talk about my patients," said Dr. Sami in a neutral tone. "Also, she's not that ill. Two or three days and she'll be recovered."

"I hope so . . . ." she said in her sing-song voice, looking at Husam and not at Dr. Sami.

Sultan had continued smoking his pipe all this time like a European, clutching his glass of whisky between his hands, happy to find himself in the Eagle's Nest and enjoying having Diana sit beside him. He watched her as she talked, and felt her breath on his face, while Mark Doyle sat on the other side patiently listening to the chatter of Jenny, who was sitting beside him by chance. He noticed the face of her husband, Fox, watching her carefully; his face was redder than usual because of the drink, but he didn't seem to be interested in his wife's chatter. His foxy eyes were watching the faces carefully, trying to fathom from the lip movements and facial expressions the conversation that was taking place between those sitting at the bar counter, particularly what he and Dr. Sami might be saying. Dr. Sami was asking Diana, "And how is your own health?"

"I'm completely fine!"

Then she picked up her glass and took a small sip from it. Dr. Sami lowered his head and spoke to him quietly in Arabic, "Did you hear, Husam? My wife, God preserve her, was expecting her to get sunstroke, so they asked me to examine her. Imagine! And she says she's perfectly fine, the bitch!"

He laughed, but avoided looking in her direction. Meanwhile she had started talking to Sultan, who was giving her his full attention. After a little, he saw her fidget, then heard her say uneasily, "I feel hot here!"

He saw her breasts under the fabric of her dress jump forward as she took off her white jacket, apparently fed up with it. Sultan left his glass and got off his stool. He took the jacket from her hand and took it to hang up at the entrance. She lifted her bare, lightly freckled arms, and with a few quick movements of her hands tidied her hair that had become a little disarranged. Then she turned to Husam, "Will you come to the tennis courts tomorrow? The weather's wonderful these days, it's as if it were spring!"

"Yes, the weather's really wonderful at the moment," added Dr. Sami in agreement. "Winter is like spring in this part of the world, while our real spring is boiling hot—like spring in Calcutta!"

She smiled. She thought he must be joking, so she looked at Husam. "Is what the Doc says right?"

"More or less."

"Then take this opportunity, come on, let's play tomorrow!"

He heard Dr. Sami mutter something beside him, with his head bent, staring into his cup.

"Go on, my friend. The girl says, take the opportunity!"

"Don't worry," added Diana, "she won't be cross with you."

Sultan al-Imari went back to his place after hanging her jacket in the entrance and she looked at him gratefully. "Thank you, Mr. Imari!"

Sultan's face lit up with happiness, like a child who has been given a box of sweets.

Dr. Sami finished what was left in his glass and got down from his stool. "Come on, Husam," he said in Arabic, "let's sit at a table. We're out of place here. Also, I'm hungry!" He looked at Diana and Sultan and said in English, "Excuse us!"

Husam pushed away the remains of his beer that had turned warm in his glass. Sultan said he would see him at work the following day. He said goodbye to Diana then followed Dr. Sami. He noticed that Sultan seemed pleased to see him go. He had the feeling that this new engineer would not be making his work any easier, even if he didn't cause problems.

This smooth, elegant young man had left a confused, unsettling impression inside Husam. But perhaps he had judged him too quickly. The next few days would show whether he was right in his suspicions or just imagining them.

———

They sat at a table well away from the bar. Dr. Sami saw a servant gathering up empty plates from a nearby table, waved at him, and ordered some grilled meat. Then he turned to Husam and said, "And what will you have to eat?"

"I ate at home."

"It seems your cook has recovered with the new treatment."

"No, he's not recovered, not yet, anyway," he replied absentmindedly.

Dr. Sami looked toward the bar. "Have you heard, my friend?" he said, changing the subject of the conversation, "They say he's going to be happy here!"

"Okay, but tell me, Sami, do you think that if he has his teeth out he'll get better?"

"If who has his teeth out?"

"I'm talking about our cook."

Dr. Sami didn't reply at once. He seemed hesitant. Then he said slowly, in a professional tone, "Of course, if it's his teeth that are the cause of it; I can't tell definitely." He took a long puff on his cigarette, blew out the smoke, then added, "But if they advise him to have them out, let him have them out."

He was amazed at the ease with which Dr. Sami had delivered his final verdict, but said nothing. The Eagle's Nest was gradually filling up with its usual customers and the air was swirling with cigarette smoke and a continuous chatter that surrounded them on every side, mingled with soft music from sources hidden in the corners. From a coal fire in the kitchen, the air wafted a smell of grilling that whetted the appetite, sneaking it through doors, windows, and cracks to the lounge, billiards room, and bar, and to every corner of the club.

"And if he has them out and he doesn't get any better?"

"If he doesn't recover, that's his fate. Or do you think a doctor can breathe life into dead bones?"

He didn't like Dr. Sami's slightly morose tone. Then he heard him add with a laugh, "You know, if Mona had been here, she would have been cross with you for talking about illness in the club."

"I'm sorry, forget what I said!" he replied, annoyed.

Dr. Sami saw the servant bringing the tray of food and pushed the ashtray aside to make room for the plates in front of him on the table.

"If you take my advice, you'll leave this sick man to go on his way, and look for a new healthy cook."

He gave his advice quite quickly then threw his burning cigarette butt carelessly into the ashtray, and started to help the servant arrange the plates of food on the table. Husam looked at him for a long time as he bent over his food, eating with a startling appetite. Then he heard him ask, without raising his face from the plate, "Won't you have something else to drink?"

"No, I've had enough," he said, irritated, and looked at his watch. It was gone ten. He picked up his pack of cigarettes and lighter from the table and put them in his pocket. "Excuse me, I'm going."

Dr. Sami stopped chewing the food in his mouth and looked at him in astonishment. "But the night is still young!"

"I want to go for a walk."

Dr. Sami finished his mouthful as he looked at him. "I'm afraid I may have made you angry!"

"No, no, why should I be angry?"

He got up to leave, but Dr. Sami held him back, looking toward the entrance of the bar lounge.

"Wait a minute. Here's Akram. Let's listen to his news!"

He noticed Akram standing near the bar, looking at the faces of the people sitting in the lounge, trying to find someone. When he caught sight of them he smiled but stayed standing where he was for some time, turning around, then came up to them and shouted his favorite phrase: "Dr. Sami, mind your dick!"

Dr. Sami smiled indulgently. "Come, come and sit down, and tell us what's going on!"

Akram replied, still looking around absentmindedly, "They say that the managing director will be coming from London to inaugurate the project."

"I'm asking about news of interest to *us*! A general salary improvement, new allowances, things of that sort, on such an important occasion."

"There are rumors about an increase in the foreigners' salaries. Perhaps some of it will trickle down to us."

"Okay, sit down."

But Akram declined to sit down. He said that he was waiting for some guests and left the bar lounge. Dr. Sami started eating again, shaking his head and laughing quietly.

"God curse you, Akram, you're an itinerant radio station! I don't know where . . . ."

"Goodnight," he said, bidding him farewell and leaving hurriedly.

As he walked through the lounge he saw Suzanne sitting in her usual corner. Her book was not in her hand, though, but turned over on the glass surface of the table beside her empty glass and an ashtray full of stubs. He would send the driver, Abbas, to the camp the following day to pick up the books that Muhammad Ahmad had promised him—the translator he'd met on the road and whom he'd taken with him to Basra when he was going to visit his parents in Baghdad. Suzanne would like those books. Akram was sitting near her on the edge of the chair, listening to her as she talked in a low voice, moving her hands around; meanwhile, his own eyes were darting back and forth to check the door, watching for his guests, who were late. Husam didn't approach them, but left them to their domestic problems and went out of the club. The cold night air began to lick his warm face, loaded with the smell of the earth in the orchards, and the waters of the Shatt al-Arab that flowed calmly behind a thick, dark wall of palm trunks, silently eating into the soil of the banks to lay bare the tangle of roots that the trees had extended through the soaking ground toward the river.

He thought of visiting Maureen to check on the bad cold that Diana had talked about, but it wasn't a suitable time. It would be better to phone her in the morning and visit her after that. He started to walk into the night, turning his face toward the desert.

6

He collected his plans, put them back in the map cupboard, and left the office about an hour before the work siren announced the end of the shift. As he entered the house he was surprised to find Bob Macaulay sitting in the lounge, drinking his afternoon tea. He didn't usually come back from work at this time. He saw him raise his head. "Hello, old man!"

His voice lacked its usual good humor and he noticed an absent-minded look in his eyes. "You don't look happy!" he said with concern. "Has something happened?"

Abu Mahmoud, the cook, had come out of the kitchen and was standing waiting to one side. Macaulay gave a faint smile. "No, no, nothing's happened. Sit down, drink your tea with me."

He told him that he'd promised Maureen he would play and didn't want to keep her waiting, then turned to the cook and told him not to bother making tea because he wouldn't wait. The cook went back to the kitchen as Bob Macaulay handed him a small piece of paper.

"This is for you!"

It was an invitation card of the sort sent to staff by the project management when they are organizing a function on some special occasion. He saw a similar card on the table in front of Macaulay with an opened letter beside it. Perhaps the contents of the letter were the reason for the unhappiness plainly visible in Macaulay's eyes, and for his early return home. He'd spoken to him once about his problems with his wife. He and Husam had been drinking alone at a corner of the bar that night; it was nearly midnight and Macaulay had been drinking heavily that evening and revealed some of his secrets. He told him that he had separated from his wife because there was another man in her life, but he wasn't sorry to have lost her; he was grateful to her in a way for being honest with him and telling him frankly, soon after the beginning of her relationship with "that man," that she was meeting a lover behind his back. She suggested to him that they should separate and he wasn't angry. He would have been angry if she had hidden it from him. He was only upset for their only daughter (Sally) who was still a child of no more than eight. He made it a condition that her mother should not meet "that man" at home in the child's presence, though it was okay to meet him elsewhere. She agreed, so he left the child with her. He heard news of his daughter via his elderly mother, who lived alone and wrote to him constantly. Perhaps that letter had come from his mother with some disturbing news.

"Is Sally okay?" he asked anxiously.

"She's fine, she's fine," muttered Macaulay absentmindedly, then changed the subject and asked, "Won't you read your invitation card?"

He looked at the piece of paper and read: "The project management has the pleasure of inviting you to a cocktail party, to be held in the Eagle's Nest in honor of the Management Director of the Companies, and on the occasion of the inauguration of the project, on Friday, January 11, 1952 at 8 p.m."

"The day after tomorrow," he said, looking at Macaulay.

"You'll be going, of course?"

"Can we do anything else?"

He left him to his tea and thoughts, went into his room, quickly washed the day's dust off himself, and put on his tennis outfit. He put a can of balls with a small towel, a hairbrush, and a pack of cigarettes with his lighter in a small bag, took his racket, and went out. He didn't find Macaulay where he had left him. The cook had taken away the tea things. The invitation to the cocktail party was lying abandoned in its place on the table, but the letter that had caused Macaulay's gloom wasn't there.

He left the house and crossed the road to Sullivan's house. He pressed the doorbell and stood waiting. It was a sunny day and the sky above his head was a clear blue; a cool breeze was blowing, carrying with it the smell of salt and the sound of the drilling rig, busily biting into the desert sand and emptying it into trucks. He had a sudden tinge of conscience about leaving work early, for the men were still working, though not all of them of course, for he had spotted some people playing tennis through the dark palm trunks. He couldn't recognize them from a distance but he could make out, on the green surface of the tennis court, the figure of a woman with her short white skirt moving about between the men. Her movements were supple and graceful, a ballet dancer, unlike the men playing with her who were hitting the ball savagely, moving from one place to another with clumsy movements and tense nerves.

He heard the door being opened from inside, then Maureen's voice came from behind the door, asking, "Awsam, is that you?" She had left the door ajar rather than opening it fully.

He was surprised by this reception. "Why don't you open the door properly to check?" he asked.

"Come in quickly," she replied hurriedly. "Don't let me catch another cold!"

He pushed the door and went in. He saw her hurry away, her body completely naked, her wet back glistening under the light as she slipped through the living room back to the bathroom. Strange! Where had her servant Hasan gone? Where was Diana? The house was empty. He walked over the damp patches left by her bare feet on the carpet, and put his bag and racket on a chair. He heard the sound of water splashing over her body and the bathroom floor. He went into a small corridor and stood near the bathroom door. Raising his voice above the sound of the water, he asked, "Where's Diana?"

The noise of the water stopped, then her voice came from behind the door.

"She's gone with Sultan. He invited her for lunch at the club. Then they'll play tennis."

So the woman he'd spotted among the tennis players was Diana, he said to himself with surprise.

"I didn't know that Sultan had a day off today!"

"He has a day off every day," she replied sarcastically.

The water resumed its splashing over her body, but more gently. He had to speak to Bob Macaulay about Sultan. It seemed he'd abandoned all responsibility for the maintenance work to that rascal Abu Jabbar. He heard the sound of her movements as she busily rubbed something, or washed something, behind the closed door, then he went back to the living room and sat down on the sofa.

He took out his pack of cigarettes and lit one, then started to smoke voraciously as he waited for her to emerge. Perhaps her husband would come in at that moment! He had shown no objection to his being in the house while he was away, for he had his own private life and wanted her to have something to occupy herself with apart from him. But to see Husam sitting in the living room while she was naked in the bathroom might perhaps disturb him slightly. A little annoyed, he shouted at her to hurry up.

"You said you wanted to play before it turns cold!"

"I'm finished, don't be so impatient!"

Then he heard the bathroom door open and saw her emerging into the corridor, wearing a long orange bathrobe. Her hands were drying her long hair with a small white towel.

"Why didn't you wait for your shower until you'd finished playing?"

"I felt fed up."

The fragrance of her scented soap spread through the house, enveloping him. She was a bundle of beautiful colors exuding perfume. He looked at her, bewitched.

"Where's your servant Hasan? Why didn't you leave him to open the door, if you were afraid of the cold?"

She stood drying her hair with the towel beside him.

"Abdul isn't here. I sent him to the village to buy me some hanna."

"Buy you what?"

"Hanna, hanna for my hair, you idiot!"

"You mean henna!"

"Yes, heena," she said, trying to imitate his pronunciation.

She stretched her hand out to his head and stroked his hair with her delicate fingertips. He grasped her wrist and pulled her toward him. She fell into his lap, and the edge of her bathrobe fell from the side of her thighs that were scorched from the hot water. He let her hand go and planted his fingers in the hair on her head from behind, then drew her face toward him while his other hand started to feel the exposed parts of her thighs before creeping under the fabric of the bathrobe to feel the secret parts of her warm body. But she managed to release herself from his hands, snatched the towel which had fallen to the floor, and fled out of range of his hand.

"Are you mad? John is on his way!"

Then she left him in his aroused state and went to her room. He heard the gentle noise made by an elegant woman dressing, then combing her hair in front of the mirror and making herself up, totally absorbed—the small, clipped sounds made by makeup implements, a hair comb, lipstick, powder, a bottle of perfume and the like being lifted up or put down on the table. But the drawn-out shriek of the work siren that clove the air at that moment deprived him of the pleasure of listening to those quiet sounds that were coming from inside her bedroom.

He looked at his watch; it was exactly four. The day's work had finished and he had started to live in "free time," his own time that was owned by nobody else. After a little he heard the roar of a fast car entering the quarter, its wheels screeching on the asphalt at the corners between the houses. This had to be Akram Jadallah, Akram the Mover as Dr. Sami called him. No one else drove a car so recklessly.

He saw Maureen coming to him at last. "I'm ready!"

She looked like a pretty girl with her tennis outfit on, and her hair plaited under a white cap. She had hung her small bag over her shoulder and was carrying her tennis racket in her hand. As he got up and collected his things he heard a car approach, then stop in the house garage. John Sullivan, her husband, had arrived. As he walked behind her toward the door he heard the sound of the car door closing. They walked out into daylight and he saw her husband coming from the direction of the car park carrying a black briefcase. He was about to enter the house but stopped when he saw them.

"Hello, Awsam!"

His tone was neutral, not expressive of anything in particular. He saw him pause on the green surface of the garden; his shadow, which had lengthened as the sun's disk had dropped toward the west, was touching the walls of the house. He looked at them and saw them standing side by side in the narrow path between the low walls of hedging. Then he spoke to his wife, "Hello, my dear, are you going to tennis? Fine, is Abdul inside?"

"No, I sent him to the village. Won't you come with us?"

She didn't mean what she said and her husband knew it, but they were superb at keeping up appearances. Husam saw her husband shake his head and excuse himself from accompanying them.

"No, my dear, I'm a little tired, you go and enjoy yourself."

He left her and went toward the house. He had the feeling that Mr. John Sullivan, despite his occasionally cold looks toward him, was deliberately leaving the two of them alone.

Maureen walked in front of him along the garden path without saying anything. She walked quickly as if hurrying away from something, and he followed her, bewildered.

7

The Morning Hours
Revert to the Servants

The clock on the kitchen wall showed it was past eleven in the morning. The chicken would be ready by now. He turned off the electric oven but didn't take the chicken out. He took a clean, empty glass, filled it with water, and put a spoonful of the boss's medicine in it. He stirred the spoon in the water for a time then put the glass in the fridge. He stood looking around him. He had nothing to do until the boss and Mr. Husam came back to eat lunch. He had everything ready: he had boiled the vegetables, fried the potatoes, and prepared the salad. He had put a clean tablecloth on the dining table in place of the old one, and arranged plates, knives, and forks for two people on the table. Before that, he had cleaned the whole house, changed the linen, and rearranged the covers on the beds in the two rooms. He had time to rest a little before they arrived. He left the kitchen at ease with himself, went out of the house and sat down on the front doorstep in the sun, looking at the shrubs in the garden, and gazing over the hedge to scan the paths and houses in the quarter. He felt the heat of the sun hidden in the doorstep spreading through his body through his clothes. He felt happy in himself for he hadn't had a headache for a week. But he knew that this happiness was under threat. He knew that well from his long experience with this crafty pain; he had had years to get used to that rotten game. The pain would sometimes leave him for days at a time until he imagined it had finally left him and would not come back, then it would suddenly hit him unexpectedly sometime as he was sleeping, like the Angel of Death. He had started this journey of torment after an unfortunate incident when he had fallen into the sea from the deck of the Greek ship he was working on as a cook while it was sailing in the Gulf. When the coastguard picked him up on the Ras Tannoura shore two days later, he was unconscious and on the verge of death; his flesh had been mangled by fish, which had left several injuries to his face, chest, and limbs. Even people who had known him before thought that he must have suffered some childhood illness when they saw his face. But the disfigurement that clung to him afterward wasn't a visible physical disfigurement, it was of a different order. From that day he had tried all sorts of treatments without success. He had continued to take tranquilizers, which did not help much when the pain got hold of him. Despair drove him to submit to his fate, so he tried to live his pain-free hours without hoping for any happiness to come. But advice from a friend, or a news item that he or his wife had heard, would again drive him to look for a cure. This time they had told him, "The pain will leave you if you have all your teeth taken out; your teeth are the cause of it!" He lifted his hand and felt the empty spaces on his gums. They had taken out six teeth in the project hospital in Basra ten days ago and the doctor had told him to come back in two weeks to have more out. Was there hope for a complete cure or was it just fantasy—an experiment that they would do on him, and that was that? God alone knew. At that moment, however, as he sat enjoying the warmth of the sun, having finished all the housework, he felt happy. He was alive, and his eyes were lapping up the things around him as greedily as someone discovering the world for the first time. The manager's quarter was quiet, and the white houses with their little gardens shone under the rays of the sun; there was a gentle breeze from the direction of the Shatt, bringing with it the smell of the palm groves and the food being cooked by the servants for their masters. The network of paths that linked the houses was empty, for the women were now tucked away inside their houses behind lowered curtains, sleeping in their beds or amusing themselves with problems that had nothing to do with cleaning or preparing food;

and a few of them were playing tennis. The smaller children—those who hadn't reached school age yet—had been left at home in the care of the servants, while the elder children lived far away over there beyond the sea in Great Britain, where they were pursuing their studies. He only saw them when they came for the Christmas holidays or summer break to visit their families. Then the paths in the little quarter would be filled with the activity of girls and boys with flushed white faces and shiny fair hair—quarrelsome, beautiful creatures amused by everything, who ran in every direction and stared in bewilderment at the people, palm trees, river, and all they saw here. The mothers would shake off their idleness, not sleep in too late, and appear in the mornings lightly dressed in their private gardens, in the paths of the quarter, in the club, or in the surrounding palm groves, chattering, exercising their dogs, or pushing their children's strollers, with their children who had arrived from Britain not far away. Then a day would come when the paths would be empty and the little devils would suddenly disappear, driven off in cars by their families to the city, where they would board the planes that would take them back to Britain. As the quarter was emptied of their cheerful hubbub, it returned to its former calm. Once again, the morning hours would revert to the servants alone.

Abd al-Bari, Mr. Durham's cook, was hanging out clothes in the sun on the washing line in the garden of the house at the corner, while Sahi, who cooked for Mr. Johnson, the stores manager, was pushing a cart toward the club (perhaps he was going to buy a bottle of wine for the lady of the house, who was always drunk). Hasan, who cooked for Mr. Sullivan, the transport manager, was sweeping fallen leaves from the garden paths in the house opposite. He saw him stop sweeping and wave him a greeting then return to his work. Soon he saw Fox's maid Wasima coming along the path with a bulging bag in her hand. He heard her call "Good morning, Abu Mahmoud!" in her sharp, high-pitched voice as she left the road and approached the garden gate.

"Good morning, my girl!" he replied without raising his voice.

She walked up the garden path with her full, squat figure. She was one of only two women working as housemaids in the quarter. She had been employed by Mr. Fox to save money on expenses, since women were content with a lower wage than men, while Safiya, the housemaid employed by Dr. Sami, had been taken on because the doctor didn't want another man in the house—so the servants said—with his pretty wife.

Wasima stood in front of him but her shadow didn't hide the sun from his face. She spoke with the affection of a dutiful daughter talking to her sick father.

"You're okay today, I hope? No pain?"

He looked at her with gratitude. "No, I'm fine, thank God! Long may it continue!"

She put her bag down between them and sat on the warm doorstep beside him, then spoke in a serious tone, like someone making an important statement. "Abu Mahmoud, I have some information that may be of use to you."

He turned toward her attentively. Looking into her face made him miserable. He always looked at something else when he was speaking to her. But this time her words made him lift his eyes to her face for a brief moment.

"And what is this news that may be of use to me?"

"Yesterday evening," she said eagerly, "I heard our neighbor talking to my mother about a holy man who lives in the Bihar region. He cures all the sick who visit him. They say he knows the secrets of the unknown!"

"Really?" he asked cheerfully.

"Really! Our neighbor says that the sick come to him from everywhere, Baghdad, Mosul . . . . Why don't you go to him and he'll get rid of this pain for you?"

He said nothing, remembering the six teeth they had taken out for him in Basra.

"Go to him, please!"

"I wish you'd spoken about this man before!"

She gave him a puzzled look. "What's stopping you, then?"

He sighed sadly. "It's too late, my girl. I've started a new treatment. Look!"

He stuck his thumb and forefinger into his mouth and showed her the black holes in the pale flesh of the gums on each side of his lower jaw. She seemed stunned.

"What's this?"

"They're taking my teeth out. They say this is the treatment for me."

"And you agreed?"

"I'm ready to drink poison, if necessary. So this is nothing!"

She gave him a pained look and muttered in a broken voice, "No, no, let me say it, you've done the wrong thing, it wasn't necessary!"

He saw her eyes glisten with tears. How quickly this woman cried. "Everything is in God's hands," he said, soothingly. "And what's this you've got in the bag?" he asked, trying to point her thoughts in another direction.

It was a paper bag, with damp patches, and he knew what was in it.

She looked at him dejectedly. "This is food for the mistress's dog."

She used to go occasionally to the workmen's camp to bring back meat and bones collected by the cooks in the mess there for her mistress's dog, on Mr. Fox's orders. He smiled at her, showing the remains of his teeth.

"All this for that black pup?"

"You know!"

She remained sitting beside him in silence, staring into space in front of her. He hadn't succeeded in diverting her thoughts away from his illness. He saw Hasan, Mr. Sullivan's cook, cross the road and head toward them. He was watching him walk slowly in the sun when Wasima spoke to him again, more quickly this time.

"Abu Mahmoud, I think you should keep the rest of your teeth and come with me to that holy man."

"God is generous; what God wills will be!" he said, putting an end to this discussion before Hasan reached them. He had the feeling that he'd made a mistake taking the doctor's advice. Who knows? Perhaps he could have been cured by a man like the one Wasima had talked about. But it was too late to turn back the clock, and he didn't want to hear anything that would dent his conviction of the value of a treatment that would cost him all his teeth.

Wasima picked up her damp bag and got up. "I'm going to finish the housework," she said, "before Beardy comes!"

But Hasan blocked her way. "Where are you going?" he asked. "Wait for a little!"

"Let her go!" he interrupted. "Don't make the mistress angry with her!"

"No, the mistress is a good, understanding woman," said Wasima, defending her employer." But my God, that husband of hers, when he's at home, he doesn't let me rest for a single moment, he makes work appear from under the ground! Imagine, he's got only two jackets, one for work and one for going out, winter and summer, and he wants me to clean them every day!"

Then she changed her tone of voice to imitate Mr. Fox's way of speaking Arabic: "Waasiimaa, clean my jacket now, Waasiimaa, touch this up, Waasiimaa. . . ."

Hasan chuckled and he laughed, while Wasima forgot that she had made her mind up to leave, and stayed there gossiping. "If you could see his underclothes, heavens!" She screwed her face up to express her revulsion at his underclothes. "His vests are all holes . . . rags only fit for wiping windows."

He saw Hasan listening to her in amusement and chuckling. He stopped smiling. "Wasima, my girl, don't talk like that about our masters. It's nothing to do with us."

"Anything you say, sir. But who would believe it? All this power, and under the clothes . . . !"

"Why don't you get married again and stop being a maid in this uncivilized fellow's house?" asked Hasan.

"Marry me yourself, then!"

Hasan was taken by surprise by her suggestion. He stopped laughing, got out of her way, and sat down on the doorstep beside Abu Mahmoud, as if seeking his protection.

"You know I've got two wives!" he said.

"And I also know that you're looking for a third," she said angrily.

"That's just a rumor."

"And what does it matter to me?"

Before leaving she turned to Abu Mahmoud. "Listen to what I'm saying, Abu Mahmoud, come and I'll show you."

"God is generous!"

Hasan followed the outline of her body as moved away, then turned to Abu Mahmoud. "A miserable woman, that! Perhaps her virginity could excuse someone marrying her the first time, but now . . . ."

He said nothing. He understood her predicament. They sat silently in the sun, then heard the roar of a vehicle approaching, and after a little, a small truck loaded with crates passed the entrance to the garden. They saw it stop at the entrance to the club.

"These crates are all drinks for the party tonight!" said Hasan. "The boss asked me to go to help the club servants. Sahi and Abd al-Bari will be going too. A big party; do you want to come?"

"No."

"Why? I don't think the boss or Husam would object to your earning a few dinars over and above your wages."

"No, they wouldn't object, but my health isn't up to it, you know that."

"Come on, my friend, it's only a few hours, and aside from the money, you can watch them as well!"

"I don't want to watch them anymore," he said, indifferently, unmoved by such temptations. "I've seen enough things in my life already!"

Hasan was saying something when the work siren let out its sudden screech, making the air vibrate in their ears. The lunch break had begun. Hasan jumped up and quickly left, before his master returned. Abu Mahmoud jumped up too, but before going into the house he stayed for a few moments standing on the doorstep looking at the club servants, who were busily moving the crates of drinks from the small lorry into the club under Joseph the barman's supervision. It was going to be crowded tonight! Lots of guests would come from Basra and al-Zubayr with their elegant wives, and the club would be packed from wall to wall with men and women, just like every other time. And tomorrow morning his colleagues who'd helped with the serving tonight would tell him, without needing to be asked, what they'd seen and heard, and what had gone on between the British. Tomorrow he would know all the secrets.

8
Cocktail Party

I t wasn't particularly cold, but he took his coat with him. Perhaps he would want to go for a stroll after leaving the party. Bob Macaulay waited for him at the door, smart as always on this sort of occasion. He heard the sound of the front door being closed behind them by the cook after they had left. They walked on along the empty paths. It was still early, and there was nothing to show that a party was being held nearby except for a few cars whose roofs he could see glinting under the light in front of the entrance to the club. They wouldn't be the first to arrive, anyway.

They didn't hear any noise as they approached the club garden. A number of drivers had left their vehicles and gathered in their colleagues' cars to chat behind closed windows. He glimpsed their dark heads sheltering behind the glass. Other drivers had stayed where they were, smoking. He saw a small glow of a light at the end of a cigarette of a driver sitting alone behind the wheel of his car. He would have to wait a long time this evening. They made their way between the parked cars, passed through the club garden, then went in. He saw three or four men's coats hanging on the coat stand on one side of the entrance, and on the opposite side some women's hats and coats. He hung his own coat with the others and followed Macaulay inside. While Macaulay was shaking hands with the welcoming party, Husam cast a quick glance over them. He saw Fox's face first of all, with his trimmed light-colored beard, his mustache, and his devious look. He felt a little annoyed. Whenever his eyes fell on this man's face he felt annoyed. It wasn't strange for Fox to be standing alongside the guest of honor for the evening, for he usually had the task of introducing the guests by name to important personalities visiting the region. The company managing director was a tall, thin man with a gleaming bald pate, fringed at the back by a crescent of light gray hair. Macaulay had told him that the man had been an admiral in the British Navy before his retirement and appointment to his new position, and that King George VI had knighted him for his important services to the Empire. He also saw Mr. Reynolds, the general director of management and personnel, who had come from Basra with the managing director. Mr. Pullman, the director of operations in the region, was standing at the end of the reception line. When his turn came, he stepped forward and shook the lined hand with the long fingers extended to him by the aging man, who smiled solemnly at him, while Mr. Fox at his side politely murmured, "Mr. Hilmi, sir, construction engineer, sir!" He left the managing director and shook hands with Mr. Reynolds, with his merry smile that he recognized from the time he had interviewed him in Project HQ in Basra some seven months previously. He also shook hands with the director of operations, mumbling his usual words. As he walked in, he heard Mr. Reynolds's voice explain to the managing director, "He's one of the young Iraqis who . . . ," but he couldn't hear the rest of the sentence. He didn't need to hear them, for he knew what Mr. Reynolds would have said: they were always boasting of the young men that had studied with them over there.

The place seemed to him very spacious. It had been prepared for the party by removing the wooden partition that divided the lounge from the bar and emptying both rooms of chairs, stools, and tables. A large white curtain had been lowered over the bar corner, with its rows of bottles, mirror, and long counter, hiding it completely from view. They hadn't left anything on the walls. In place of the dartboard, which had been removed from its position, there was a pale empty patch on the wall. He saw a couple of dozen men and women arranged in small groups around the place. He recognized among them the elderly chief engineer who had given him a short interview before agreeing to his appointment, and Mr. Reynolds's secretary with her worn-out face. The others were people he had never seen before, departmental heads and section managers with gray hair and red faces, some of them obviously overweight. They had all come from Project HQ in Basra with their wives, most of whom were over fifty. He saw Dr. Sami standing apart from the others in a faraway corner with his wife Mona, so he left Bob Macaulay and went over to them to mingle with his fellow countrymen.

"Come on, man, why are you late?" shouted Dr. Sami cheerily.

"Is it me that's late or you two who came early?"

"Yes, tell him, Husam!" said Mona in his support. "He got me in a terrible state, I don't know how I got dressed!"

She looked at her husband angrily. She was wearing a long sleeveless jacket of black silk that left her shoulders and smooth arms bare, with shoes of the same color. On her chest she was wearing a diamond brooch in the shape of a small bird sitting on a branch, while from her ears dangled earrings, also diamond, so long that they almost touched her shoulders.

She had arranged her hair in three circles that sat one of the top of the other like a little pyramid. Her black hair looked golden brown because of the henna she used, and she had gotten some of the British wives in the quarter to use it as well. She was made up only lightly, with a fine layer of foundation on her face and slightly wide white neck, a light touch of rouge on her cheeks, slightly bluish lipstick, and a new perfume that smelled like lilies. She seemed more elegant and attractive than the other women at the party, of course. She stood holding a glass of tomato juice in her hand, while beside her stood a happy Dr. Sami, clutching a glass of whisky in one hand and holding a cigarette in the other. The place was still quiet, and the guests were exchanging conversation in a subdued tone, occasionally letting out cautious, polite, small laughs as if afraid that their voices might wake somebody sleeping nearby. He saw Hasan, Maureen's servant, approach him with a tray full of glasses and drinks. He took a glass of whisky and said, "I see you're here tonight!"

"Yes, I came to help!"

"At last," said Dr. Sami with satisfaction when the servant had left. "At last! So they've given us a cocktail party for a visit by the managing director to inaugurate the project in our place of exile!"

The entrance was now overflowing with guests, as if they had all arrived at the club at that moment. Each new arrival stood waiting his turn to step forward and shake hands with the managing director and the members of his entourage, then mingle with the rest of the guests. The noise inside began to get louder despite the guests keeping their voices subdued and controlled.

"Akram the Mover has arrived!"

Dr. Sami had been looking toward the entrance. After a moment Akram stepped into the hall with his wife Suzanne on his arm. They were smiling—an attractive picture of marital harmony on display to everyone. Suzanne was wearing her long white jacket, the jacket she always wore on special occasions. Akram looked around the faces of the guests, looking for friends or acquaintances. Dr. Sami raised his hand with a glass of whisky overhead and gestured to him, and Akram and his wife made their way over to them.

"Hello Moona, hello Doc, hello Awsam!" muttered Suzanne as she greeted them. "You're late, you two!"

"I'm the cause, really. I had work in the village," said Akram, turning around.

"His work's never ending," smiled Mona.

"What can I do, Mona? Obligations!"

He cast his eyes over the guests' faces, trying to size up everyone at the party. Then his gaze stopped at the faces of three men standing in a corner away from the others, and he touched his wife's arm.

"Wait here, my dear, I won't be long."

He turned to the others. "Excuse me for a moment!"

He left his wife with them and went off. Mona let out a little laugh, which she cut short when she noticed the sadness in Suzanne's eyes and said in English, "I'm sorry, I didn't mean. . . ."

Suzanne gave her an indulgent smile, then looked at Husam. "Awsam, I want to thank you for the books. I wonder if you could get some more?"

Dr. Sami smiled as he looked at her. Everyone knew her great passion for reading. But was it a passion for reading for its own sake, or an attempt to escape from a boring life? "I'll try," Husam said. "I actually . . . ."

At that moment he heard Mona's voice speaking beside him, as if she were directing her words to him but not to the others. "Here's Maureen; she's graced the party with her gallant husband!"

He restrained himself from turning toward the entrance, but Mona's words had confused his train of thought for a short moment.

"Actually, I borrowed these books for you. I borrowed them from someone I met by chance. I was on my way. . . ."

"Sami, look how she's clinging to her husband's arm!"

Mona was intent on letting him hear her comments, but he continued explaining to Suzanne, "He's a young man who works as a translator for Mr. Fox and lives in the camp. When I give him back the books . . . ."

He couldn't carry on pretending not to care, so he turned to look at the new arrivals. He saw Maureen clinging to the arm of her husband who was walking along, showing her off as they cut through the clusters of guests, smiling at friends and acquaintances.

Maureen spotted Husam standing with his group and led her husband toward their little circle. She greeted them, smiling sweetly, "Good evening, everyone!"

"Hello Maureen, hello Maureen!"

Suzanne smiled at them without saying anything. She could no longer speak freely about the world of books that she loved.

Maureen looked at Mona's hair, which was sparkling in the light. "Moona, your hairstyle is fabulous!"

"Really?"

Maureen turned to Dr. Sami. "And you, Doc, you seem younger tonight!"

The wretched woman was pretending to ignore Husam as she distributed her generous words of praise around the others. He saw Dr. Sami's face light up with genuine pleasure and heard him say, with a laugh, "Was I old before?"

Mona pinched her husband. "He's a forty-year-old adolescent!"

The smile vanished from Dr. Sami's face and he looked at his wife with suppressed anger amid a wave of laughter. Meanwhile, Mr. Sullivan stood there sullenly, listening submissively to the words being exchanged, with a polite smile frozen on his lips in the direction of the others. When the merriment had subsided, Maureen spoke to Dr. Sami in a serious tone. "Dr. Nashwan, I know that it isn't polite of me to discuss medical problems with you in a place like this . . . ."

Mr. Sullivan was looking at his wife anxiously. It looked as though he didn't know what she wanted to talk about. Medical problems?

" . . . but in the last few days I've started," continued Maureen amid the attentive silence, "to feel dizzy when I get out of bed."

Her husband looked at her in slight alarm and Dr. carefully Sami noted her rosy face.

"You're in perfect health!"

"And this headache!"

"Perhaps you're oversleeping in the morning, or . . . "

Dr. Sami looked at her husband, who appeared thunderstruck, while she asked, laughing, "I what?"

Husam distracted himself by taking a large swig from his glass. Mr. Sullivan's face became even redder and he stared at his wife. "Impossible! I mean, you never told me you've had a headache!"

She put her hand on his arm to calm him down. "Don't worry, my dear, don't worry, the doctor's joking!"

Husam saw Suzanne look at her coldly as Mona gave a wicked smile. What was Maureen doing? Was she playing with *his* nerves or her husband's?

Dr. Sami smiled, conscious of his importance. "Anyway, if you want to be certain, I can examine you."

Maureen laughed. "Later, doctor. Try and visit us at home!"

She gave her husband a fleeting glance and saw that he was speechless. Husam was also at a loss to explain what he had heard. A servant approached them carrying a tray full of drinks, and Maureen and her husband took two glasses of whisky, while Dr. Sami exchanged his empty glass for a full one, and Mona put her empty glass back but didn't take anything. Suzanne looked for a glass of beer but couldn't find one, so she spoke to the servant in the heavily accented Arabic that she had learned here, "One beer, please!"

"Yes, madam," murmured the servant, and slipped away. Then another servant came carrying a tray with little pieces of red meat on it, with wooden cocktail sticks stuck into them. Maureen took a piece, holding the end of the stick with her fingertips, slipped the little piece of meat into her mouth, then threw the cocktail stick back on the tray, as Suzanne did the same.

Seeing his wife about to stretch her hand out as well, Dr. Sami warned her quietly in Arabic, "It's pork!"

She took no notice and took a piece of pork anyway; the servant stared at her in silence, then picked up the tray and went away.

The managing director had left his place by the entrance and started to mingle with the guests, stopping at each group for a couple of minutes to say something and listen to what they had to say, before excusing himself and going on to another group.

The place had become packed with guests, and the air was heavy with the smell of women's perfume of every kind, mixed with cigarette, cigar, and pipe smoke, smells from the glasses of different drinks, and the aroma of food carefully arranged on silver trays, which servants in white jackets and black trousers were bringing from the kitchen. They carried the trays skillfully on the palms of their hands as they took them round the circles of guests, their unspeaking faces etched with polite smiles; what thoughts or feelings were going on behind them no one could possibly know. There was whisky to drink, of course, as well as gin, cognac, brandy, Russian vodka, sherry, and beer. There was also orange, pineapple, and tomato juice for those not wanting to drink alcohol. For snacks, there was kofta in the shape of small balls the size of a hazelnut, fish, stuffed vegetables the size of dates, and small, rectangular pieces of pork. There was also caviar. Each type of food was arranged on a tray on white paper, and each piece had a small wooden cocktail stick planted in it so that the guests could eat what they liked without touching the food with their fingers. As a servant approached a group, the circle would open up for him at once, and hands would stretch out to leave their empty glasses and take full ones; then one of the hands would gesture to him to go away and take the empty glasses, fill them again and bring them back. If the servant was bringing some sort of hors d'oeuvres, though, they would detain him for longer, until everyone standing in the group had taken what they wanted as they continued telling their amusing tales.

The servant brought the glass of beer that Suzanne had ordered as Jenny, Mr. Fox's wife, approached them. She was wearing an old blue jacket, extremely carefully ironed, with a white carnation on her chest. Her face was spattered with powder, though none of that had done anything to alleviate the ugliness with which she was cursed.

"Nice party, isn't it?" she said cheerily.

"Even nicer since you arrived!" said Dr. Sami with a touch of flattery.

"Oh Doc, you're too kind!"

Then she gave Mona an admiring look. "Moona, you look splendid in that dress!"

"Thank you, Jenny. You too, this dress of yours is beautiful!"

Jenny's face lit up. "Really? Everyone tells me that, although it's not quite new!"

The men smiled and occupied themselves drinking, smoking, or gazing at their drinks. She turned to Maureen, "Maureen, what is it that you are doing to look prettier every day? And this dress that you're wearing really suits you!"

Then she looked at Mr. Sullivan and said in her languid voice, "John, you should be proud of your wife!"

"I am proud, I am proud," muttered Mr. Sullivan absentmindedly, then leaned over to his wife and whispered something in her ear. "Excuse us," he said, making their apologies.

Maureen smiled at them, threw Husam a quick glance, then allowed her husband to take her arm and lead her away. Jenny followed them with a puzzled look as they made their way through the guests. A confused silence ensued, which Dr. Sami quickly broke by saying, "Husam, do you like this big crowd?"

"Was it me that invited all these people?"

"That's not what I meant—if you'd only finish the new club!"

Suzanne looked at him. "Sharif and Umar are always asking me whether the swimming pool will be ready for the start of the summer."

He assured them that the swimming pool would be ready for the summer season, as would the entire club. Perhaps in May.

Jenny shouted for joy. "Oh, wonderful! My son Patrick will enjoy staying here when he comes for the summer holidays!"

"I'm sorry, everyone. That was the district head and the deputy chief of police and the head of customs. I saw them standing on their own and thought I should go and flatter them a bit until the whisky had had its effect on them," said Akram, apologizing as he came back to them with his empty glass in his hand.

"It would be better for you to flatter your wife a bit," said Mona in Arabic, reproachfully.

Suzanne smiled at her with appreciation, while Akram started to look for a servant to return his glass to and take a new one.

"Mona, I know that you are angry with me because I sometimes tease your husband, but believe me, I love him!"

Dr. Sami was not listening to Akram's conciliatory words. He was staring, bemused, at a spot in the middle of the hall that had entirely captured his attention. Husam followed the direction of his gaze, and saw Diana standing with a laughing face in the middle of a large group of captivated men. Among them were Mark Doyle and Sultan al-Imari with his greasy black hair that gleamed in the light. Diana was wearing the clothes she said she had bought in Istanbul—an oriental slave girl's clothes, as imagined by western film directors. He heard Dr. Sami mutter quietly, as if talking to himself, "So elegant, that bitch! She certainly knows how to dress!"

"Who?" asked his wife, provoked by his words. "Who is this elegant woman that's dazzled you so?"

"The caliph's slave girl," he muttered, utterly bewitched.

She looked over to where he was gazing, then gave him a chastising glare.

"Shame on you, doctor, shame!"

"Hello, Hilda!" shouted Jenny in welcome, clearing a space for her friend.

"Hello, everyone!"

The wife of Mr. Durham, the fire service chief, joined their circle.

"What a crowd!"

"And where's Barry?" asked Jenny.

"He's over there, talking to the chief engineer."

He heard Dr. Sami say to his wife, "Shouldn't we circulate a bit? To see some people?"

But she replied firmly, "Stay where you are. I know the people you want to see!" Then she turned to Husam for help, "Talk, please, defend me a little!"

Akram noticed a servant carrying a tray of drinks and waved to him. As he was exchanging his glass, he suddenly gave a warning to the others: "Hey, everyone, the managing director is quite close! I think he's coming over to us."

A few seconds later, the elderly man came toward them. All at once, their faces took on serious expressions, and an atmosphere of caution gripped them as they made room for him between them.

"A splendid party, isn't it?" the man said slowly, standing between them with his tall frame. He had a deep, dominating voice. Jenny and Hilda replied, as if with one voice, "Yes, very. A wonderful cocktail party, sir!"

The others murmured similar expressions. Husam also said that it was a fine cocktail party, as he had to say something. The man seemed to him to be around seventy, perhaps more, but his body was ramrod straight. A picture of his father passed through his mind. His father was younger than this man, but already he leaned on a stick when he walked. What was it, do you suppose, that made people age so quickly in this country?

The managing director looked at him with blue eyes that flashed like a cat's eyes in the dark. Then he started to speak. "I arrived here before dusk and walked to the river. You're really lucky with this beautiful weather!"

He stared into their faces to see if they realized the value of this blessing that God had granted to them and not to anyone else.

"In our country, they call your wonderful weather a millionaire's climate, because the very wealthy are the only ones who can afford to travel whenever they want, to enjoy weather like this. It's wonderful! Really wonderful!"

"Only at this time of the year, sir!" said Dr. Sami.

The managing director gave him a patronizing look. "Yes!"

He wasn't prepared to start an argument with anyone, and seemed a little tired. These sorts of social occasions must irritate him. Only yesterday, so Husam had heard on the radio, as well as from colleagues on the project, that the managing director had attended a grand banquet arranged by the management in al-Zubayr to inaugurate the project. The prime minister himself had turned the wheel of the oil pumping station so that the black liquid could start on its way through pipes laid out in the desert to the loading quays, and from there to Europe. He had delivered a speech detailing the sacrifices that the management of the project had borne to reach that decisive point. It had been an exhausting task, of course, but it was necessary, and he had to undertake it for his country's sake, as well as for the group of companies that he had been entrusted with chairing. Since arriving in Iraq five days ago, he had attended some sort of function every day, sometimes here and sometimes somewhere else, with all the discomfort of travel that this entailed, whether by plane or by car on roads that were usually bad. Then he had to stand on his feet for an hour or two trying to look happy, exchanging polite conversation with important people and with the project workers—although the local employees most of the time did not understand the significance of his words of inspiration. This phenomenon in itself invited some reflection. Could the reason be that they didn't understand the language well enough, or was it because they thought in a different way from people in Europe? Perhaps this was what was going round inside his shiny bald head, but Dr. Sami had objected that the weather here was not always nice, and so he had replied curtly "Yes" and concluded that subject.

He saw Sultan al-Imari quietly approaching them and standing at the managing director's shoulder, with a glass in his hand and the top of his shiny black pipe clearly visible from the opening of his breast pocket. He heard the old man ask, "Does anyone know why they call the area near the river in Basra 'al-Ashar?'"

His question was directed at the Iraqis in the group. He noticed Fox standing beside him with his wife as if he had appeared from nowhere. He was standing respectfully, enjoying seeing the signs of confusion and embarrassment that had appeared on their faces, for he liked seeing the Iraqis bewildered about their own affairs. Husam didn't want to increase Fox's enjoyment by subjecting himself to that ludicrous examination, so he watched the scene in a detached way, without exercising his brain to find an answer that would be of no importance to him anyway.

He heard Sultan al-Imari give a sort of shout of victory. "Because, sir, that is where they used to collect the tithe tax, the ushr, on goods entering the city."

"Bravo!"

The guest of honor turned to Sultan, who looked very happy at that moment, then addressed himself to the whole group, "Enjoy the party!" He nodded his head to the ladies, then quietly moved away, having favored them with more than two minutes of his time.

Husam watched him as he moved his tall upright frame to stand with another group, whose voices grew quiet as he approached. "A millionaire's climate!" muttered Dr. Sami sarcastically in Arabic, "Just let him come here in summer!"

His wife gave him a warning look, as Sultan al-Imari excused himself in English and hurried away. Hasan, the servant, now approached them, this time carrying a tray with rows of kofta, small balls of meat on thin sticks. Everyone helped themselves, then sent him away and busied themselves savoring the food. "Maureen's lucky!" said Hilda, pointing at the servant's back. "This Abdul's a fine fellow! Our Abdul's thick. Just imagine, two months ago he asked us to lend him money to buy a bicycle. But he hasn't used it yet. He says he's still trying to learn."

"Perhaps he didn't buy a bicycle," said Fox sarcastically. "Perhaps he used your money to buy a new wife."

He laughed, and Akram, Dr. Sami, and Mona laughed with him. Suzanne smiled but it was obvious from her looks that she was generally not pleased with the conversation.

"I'll tell you a story about a man and a bicycle," said Fox.

The word "story" aroused their interest, like children. Even Suzanne looked at Fox in some anticipation. Fox seemed unusually at ease, perhaps because of the large amount of free whisky he had drunk, or because he had seen the managing director have a relaxed conversation with the guests and thought that he would imitate him.

"After I'd finished working in Palestine," Husam heard him say in an intoxicated tone, "I sent Jenny home and went to work in railway management in Nigeria . . ." (this was new information he was hearing about Fox!) " . . . in a suburb of a city called Kano, in the north of the country. We had a middle-aged African there who worked as a caretaker. He lived in a village about three miles from the station. He asked us to help him buy a bicycle. But despite all attempts, the man persisted in not learning how to get on it and didn't know how to make it stop."

He saw the women listening to Fox more attentively, their curiosity aroused by these small details.

"We put two large stones for him in front of the building. When work had finished, he would cram his bike between them, then get onto it like someone getting onto a donkey. Then someone who was around would give him a push on his back, and he would take off on the bike amid laughter and whistling."

He heard Akram chuckling, and saw Suzanne give her husband a disapproving look. The others were smiling. They were anticipating an amusing end to the story that Fox had brought with him from his time in Africa.

"When he fell off on the road, people would help him on and push him on his way again. This became a common sight for people living in the huts on both sides of the road, who would see him sitting happily on his speeding bike, with his white frizzy hair and his lined black face. His children and grandchildren, and the wives he still had left (he had had a lot of them) would wait for him near his house in the village, and when they saw him approaching helter-skelter down the hill in the road—happy with his toy, but terrified at the same time—they would quickly block his path and grab him from all sides before helping him down from the bike. He sometimes came to us as though he had just been through a bloody battle!"

The smile disappeared from Jenny's face, while Suzanne's face glowered. "But despite all these difficulties," continued Fox, "he wouldn't give his bicycle up. He loved it. One day—I don't actually know how this happened—they were unable to stop him when he reached the hut. Perhaps they thought that he must have learned a bit so they left the task of blocking his path to a small number of lads. But he was going so fast that he went past them. The bike, whose equilibrium had been disturbed when the clumsy hands reached out to grab it, started to wobble, with the old man screaming in terror on top of it, and a band of his children, grandchildren, wives, and neighbors running noisily along behind it, trying to catch it up and stop it. But because they couldn't catch it he and his bike fell into a large ditch behind the village huts."

"And did he die?" asked Jenny with concern.

"No, no, he didn't die, we found out next day that they'd gotten him out of the ditch alive but with some fractures to his ribs and legs.

That was the last we heard of the man, and it's the last time he rode his bike as well!"

He started to laugh, and Akram laughed cheerfully as well. Dr. Sami and his wife smiled, while Suzanne looked at Fox with disgust and at her husband with something like contempt.

"These local servants behave in the same stupid way everywhere!" said Hilda in annoyance.

"But Tom, you should have stopped him hurting himself!" said Jenny, reprimanding her husband.

"What could we do? Deprive him of the fruits of civilization? They would have said we were imperialists if we'd done that. No, no!"

This man aroused his distaste more every day. What stories would he tell about the locals here when he went back to Britain, or went to work somewhere else? He saw Suzanne press her forehead with her small, thin hand. Dr. Sami noticed and asked with concern, "Is there something the matter?"

"Nothing important," she murmured, flustered by the others' stares. "Just a slight headache I've had since this afternoon."

"Shall I bring you something?"

"No thank you, doctor, it will get better when I sleep."

The women looked at her sympathetically, and Jenny said, "Akram, it's best you take her home."

"No, I'll go on my own," Suzanne objected. "I want to check on the children as well."

But Akram took the glass from her hand and grasped her arm. "I'll take you home, then come back."

As soon as Akram had gone, and before anyone in the group could start a new topic of conversation (forcing him to listen to the end out of politeness even if he was dying of boredom), Husam murmured his apologies and left. He paid no attention to Dr. Sami, who was trying to make him stay. He didn't want to listen to more of those stories. He saw Diana standing in the middle of another group of people, but Mark Doyle and Sultan al-Imari were with her too. The managing director had left the party some time ago, and the guests were chattering freely

294

and more loudly, the noise occasionally punctuated by raucous laughter at a joke someone had told. The district head, deputy chief of police, and head of customs were still standing in the same place. They were drunk and their tense faces had relaxed. He saw them laughing, with their glasses in their hands, but they weren't trying to mingle with the other guests. None of the guests tried to approach them, except for Akram Jadallah, who knew them from before, and Fox, who was always keen to strengthen the management's links with the local symbols of authority, so that he could seek their help if needed. Perhaps the foreign guests were avoiding them because of the language barrier, or because of their excessively formal appearance (they hadn't been able to shed their work clothes), or because they had come to the party without their wives, or quite simply because no one was bothered about them. As they stood there on their own amid all the crowd and noise, he pictured them as a small patch of oil floating alone on the surface of a roaring river, never mingling with the river's flowing waters.

A servant passed close to him with a tray of drinks so he stopped him and put his empty glass on the tray. He didn't take another. He wanted to light himself another cigarette. He made his way slowly between the circles of guests, looking at the inebriated faces amid the continuous chatter. He took a glass of whisky from the tray of a servant beside him then started to amuse himself listening to the mixture of conversations coming to him from every side. He was standing at the edge of the groups so as to be able to sneak off when he wanted to and not be forced to listen to conversations he didn't like. The words rained down on him as he wandered freely among the guests, standing for a moment here and a moment there without showing any particular interest in what was being said. "My dear, henna doesn't suit your blond hair!" "This fish isn't cooked, it's just soaked in vinegar," "I imagined . . . ," "Thank you, Abdul," "Have you tried the local arrack? Horrible!" "I've had enough to drink," "No, no, give me your empty glass," "Abdul, do you have a gin and tonic for the lady?" "This meat's delicious, take a piece," "Tell me, how do they make it so tender?" "Simple, cover it with . . . ," "Sir, the beer you ordered!" "And how is your heart these days?" "Okay, but the doctor warned me . . . . you know," "And what's this?" "The locals call it dolma," "Wait, Abdul, don't go!" "I really don't see anything wrong with a man sleeping with his friend's wife," "That's because you're not married!" "Ha, ha, ha, ha!" "I think I've got a cold," "Abdul, bring me a brandy," "Yes, sir!" "Tell me, where did you spend the vacation this year?" "Akram, you know that having several wives is reckoned a crime punishable by law where we live," "I know, that's why your men marry just once but keep two mistresses!" "Ha, ha, ha, ha!" "Imagine, this Abdul has three wives and every night he sleeps with one. These orientals are never satisfied . . ." (the last speaker was a woman whose face he had never seen before). He hurried away from the group before they became aware of his presence. He remembered the emaciated African he had heard addressing a crowd of Englishmen and foreign tourists at Speaker's Corner in Hyde Park in London, condemning them for their sexual frigidity. "You Europeans sleep with a naked woman in your arms from sunset to morning, and ply her with kisses, and that's all. You kiss her all night and don't do anything else. As for us (here he pointed at his emaciated chest, whose bones were visible through the opening in his dirty shirt), we men of Africa and Asia, we can hardly touch a woman's body with our fingertips (here he raised his hard black index finger in the air to show them), with this fingertip, without the volcano erupting and spewing out its lava!" He was boasting of the virility of the men of the two continents in front of that European audience, and they were listening to his insults and laughing.

"And you, aren't you proud of your virility? Have you got anything else to do?" "Diana, is it true that you're on your way to getting married here soon?"

He regained control of his senses, then turned his head, found Diana looking at him, and heard her say to Jenny, who had moved from the place where he had left her, "Who told you that?"

He turned his head away so that she would not think he was eavesdropping. Getting married, that was what she had in mind! At that moment he felt a hand grasp his arm and heard a voice behind him say, "Oh, Husam, I want to see you!"

It was Mr. Reynolds's voice, the general director of management and personnel.

"How do you do, sir," he said in English.

"Come, come, there's no need to speak in English. I want to speak to you, Husam!"

He led him gently from the crowd of guests, and they stood in a corner next to the wall.

"Tell me, how are things going here so far?"

"Not bad, I've gotten used to the place."

"That's good. And your problems with the workforce?"

"There aren't any problems."

Mr. Reynolds looked at him, slightly surprised.

"Is that possible, Husam? Everyone I've spoken to here has a complaint."

"In fact, most of my problems are with the contractors."

"And the workforce?"

He told him that he always tried to understand the reasons for their complaints and to find suitable solutions for them. He saw Mr. Reynolds give him a long stare, and noticed an ambiguous glint in his eye.

"And have you succeeded?"

"I can say that I have won their affection."

Mr. Reynolds smiled in a way that Husam didn't like. He thought there was a touch of contempt in it.

"Fine. It's nice for others to like you. Every one of us wants others to like them, Husam. But an Italian philosopher once said that it is better for others to fear you than to like you. Do you know why, Husam?"

"Why?"

"Because their affection depends on their own free will. They can love you today but hate you tomorrow, according to circumstances. But the reasons for people to fear you are in your hands alone." Then pointing at the crowd of guests, he added, "Anyway, this isn't the right time or place for this conversation. I just wanted to know how things were going for you here. Tell me, have you decided to get married? If you make up your mind to, tell me; perhaps I'll be able to find a house for you."

He thanked him and told that he hadn't decided yet. Mr. Reynolds looked him straight in the eye. "So, it seems that you're having an enjoyable life here, and are not feeling lonely, like some bachelors!"

He noticed him casting a quick glance toward Maureen, who was standing with her husband, Mr. John Sullivan, among a group of guests not far away. He felt the blood rush to his head. He was infuriated to discover that there were people spying on the private moments of his life. That scoundrel Fox, he muttered under his breath.

"The important thing is that how I live my life outside work hours shouldn't harm the interests of the project."

"Husam, believe me," replied Mr. Reynolds with a laugh, to soften the impact of his frank words, "the moment that we hear you are doing anything in your private life that will harm the interests of the project, we will simply terminate your contract of employment with us. Don't frown like that, come on, let me introduce you to my wife; I've gotten married before you. You've seen her before."

He felt his warm, flabby fingers as he took him by the hand and led him to a group of men and women, among whom he recognized Mr. Reynolds's secretary. He heard him say in English, "Julie, my dear, Mr. Husam Hilmi would like to say hello to you. You remember him, of course!"

Julie turned her dried-up face toward him and held out her hand, which was like a man's hand. "Oh, yes, I remember. How are you, Mr. Hilmi? I'm delighted . . . ."

She seemed a little less stern to him now that she had become Mr. Reynolds's wife. He smiled and touched her hand. "I hope you will both be very happy!"

Meanwhile, Mr. Reynolds had left him, to lose himself among the guests, listen to the news, and ask searching questions in a light-hearted way so as not to arouse suspicion. "Thank you, Mr. Hilmi, thank you!" said the secretary who had become his wife, then went back to listening to what the other men and women who had come from the city were saying. He didn't feel any desire to listen. He was fed up with all this chatter. He stayed for a few moments then excused himself and left them. He leaned his back on the wall, feeling annoyed. How quickly he had become annoyed! A few words spoken by Mr. Reynolds had upset his mood.

The noise continued. He looked at the corner where he had been standing a short time before with Mr. Sami and his wife and the others, and found that the group had turned into a women's group, all chattering excitedly about their own personal secrets, while the men had gone their individual ways. He was amazed that Mona had finally released her husband. He saw him standing in Diana's group. That was what he had wanted. He saw Akram again standing with the district head and his colleagues, flattering them, as he called it; this man had a remarkable ability to flatter and to gather information and friends! But his relationship with his wife was crumbling day by day. He noticed Diana break away from her group and make her way between the crowds of guests, smiling at everyone who looked in her direction, that same sweet, attractive, ambiguous smile, like a Byzantine slave girl from the *Thousand and One Nights*. The crowd meant that she had to maneuver as she walked between the circles of guests, and he couldn't work out where she was heading for, but when she got closer and he noticed the way she was looking, he realized that she was making for him.

"Why are you standing here on your own?" she asked, with a hint of surprise.

"I just am."

She stood beside him and leaned back against the wall like him. He felt her arm touch his arm. "What did Mr. Reynolds want from you?" she asked in her melodious voice.

"Nothing. He was talking about work."

"I hate that son of a bitch," she said, in a disturbed tone.

He turned toward her in astonishment. "Why should you hate him? You don't work on the project!"

"He thinks he's God Almighty!" she said, angrily.

Her anger toward Mr. Reynolds aroused his curiosity. "What's he done to you?" he asked.

"He says that my stay here has lasted for too long, with no logical justification, and that it's time for me to go back to Britain. I know who's putting him up to it."

"Who?"

"It's not important. I'll make him swallow his words."

"How?"

"You'll see!"

He felt a little calmer. He was glad to have found someone else cross with Mr. Reynolds for trying to interfere in the details of their private life.

A servant approached her carrying a tray with small pieces of bread arranged in rows, covered by what looked like a paste made of fine black granules. There were about a dozen pieces left on the tray. Her anger quickly subsided. "What's this?"

"Caviar."

"Oh, I love it!"

She took a piece with her fingertips, put it in her mouth, and threw the cocktail stick back on the tray, eating the caviar with relish. "How tasty!" She took a second piece, then a third. He watched her eating without opening her mouth, her moist lips glowing. When the servant wanted to leave she held him back. "Wait, Abdul!" Then she turned to him, "Why aren't you eating?"

"I don't eat anything connected with fish."

She laughed. "Say it, you're afraid!"

"Why should I be afraid?"

She looked at him mischievously. "Because caviar makes men hungrier for women."

He looked at her in astonishment. "I never heard that before."

She gave him a seductive look. "Anyway, don't worry. You can eat as much as you wish, I'll sleep with you tonight."

He wasn't totally surprised by her words. For some time now, she had been hinting that she would like to sleep with him. But that was the first time that she had let slip the flimsy veil of false shyness that she hid behind and spoken to him frankly about her desire. He gave a confused glance at the face of the servant who had stayed waiting submissively, but he didn't notice any change in the deaf-mute expression on the mask of his face, as if he hadn't heard anything. "Thank you, Hadi, that's enough," he said, sending him away for fear that he might hear more.

The servant bowed, then went away without saying anything.

Husam turned to her. "You shouldn't have talked like that with the servant there!"

She laughed like a naughty child. "He didn't understand what I was saying."

"The servants here understand everything."

"You're changing the subject," she said, indifferently.

What was he to do with this woman? He had a feeling that there were eyes watching them. He looked at the faces in the middle of the hall and noticed Maureen eyeing him in the distance.

"I think we should go our separate ways."

Her eyes gave a smile of cunning. "I know. Alright, as you wish. I'll go now. Ciao!"

She slipped away in front of him and started to make her way between the chattering bodies, back to her admirers.

The atmosphere had become heavy, laden with the cigarette smoke that had swept away the fragrance of all the different perfumes the women had put on. Despite that, none of the guests seemed to want to leave the place. They were enjoying the party. The women were sizing each other up and exchanging carefully formulated words of praise, or relating the latest scandal, while the men were repeating their witty and amusing stories, anxiously seeking smiles of approval and encouragement in the eyes of the others' wives. The place was no longer tolerable, so he decided to leave. He drank what was left in his glass and started to look around for the servant to give him back his empty glass but couldn't find him. The servants had vanished from sight, now that all the food and drink in the kitchen had been finished.

He put his glass on the ground, next to the wall, away from the movement of feet. He was straightening his body up when he noticed

Maureen coming up to him. "What did that whore want from you?" she asked in a low voice, moving closer to him so that no one else should hear her.

"Nothing, she was just chattering, like everyone else here."

"Just?"

"Just. But why are you angry with her? Isn't she your friend?"

But Maureen interrupted him angrily. "I don't think so. She has no qualms about sleeping with any man, at any time, in any place! I'm amazed that idiot wants to marry her!"

"And who is it that wants to marry her? Mark Doyle?"

She looked at him suspiciously. "Don't tell me you don't know she's going to marry Sultan!"

"Sultan al-Imari?"

"Who else?"

He saw Mr. Sullivan looking at him in the distance as the two of them were speaking.

"It seems John is looking for you."

She went off with a bright smile on her rosy face to meet her husband. So Diana and Sultan al-Imari were getting married! What a piece of gossip! They'd be an unusual couple amid the variety of other couples in this paradise! He looked around for Diana on his way out. He saw her saying something and laughing among a group of men near the entrance, with Sultan standing beside her and looking at her adoringly. (A western body in eastern clothes!) It seemed that what Maureen had said was correct. But what could this idiot know about her?

Diana saw him making his way toward the exit. He was looking for his coat among the piles of coats hanging one over the other on the rows of hooks at the entrance, when he became conscious of her approaching. She didn't look in his direction. She started to look for something in her black fur coat pocket, then took out a silver cigarette lighter, but did not move away. Instead, she stayed loitering near the coat hooks, looking around her. Then she came up to him, and he heard her whisper a challenge, "You won't escape from me. I'll get you one day!"

He laughed at her rashness—laughed with pleasure—while she quickly moved away carrying her lighter.

—⁓⁓⁓—

As he left the Eagle's Nest, he heard a driver start his engine, thinking that it was his employer leaving the party and so getting ready. When he discovered that it was Husam, however, he turned the engine off again. He must have been fed up with waiting that long, and started to see his master in every man leaving the club. There were a large number of cars waiting, some of them standing in the empty spaces between the palm trees on the other side of the road. The drivers inside were still waiting for their masters to emerge. The breeze had become cooler, but it was invigorating after the oppressive atmosphere inside the club. He would feel warmer after he had walked for a little.

He raised his coat collar and started walking alone between the houses. He felt a sort of headache. His mind was stuffed full of everything he had seen and heard at the party—all those men and women's faces with their varied features and expressions, all those garrulous mouths, and that sea of words. The houses were quiet at that time of night, all of them empty except for small children who had been left in the care of local servants. Thick curtains hung over the windows. The lights at the corners of the paths and in front of the houses were all lit, and the ground was also illuminated by the moon; palm trees cast their black shadows, making lines on the paths and the white walls of the houses. He could see the silver tanks glistening in a sea of light from the searchlights, behind the long stretch of barbed wire that surrounded the work zone on his left. Then he approached the large Christ's-thorn tree that he passed on his way back home in the afternoon after work had ended, standing on its own in a patch of grassy ground. He would often hear the chirping of the birds that came from everywhere to shelter in its branches before nightfall, but the tree itself stood silent, in all its majesty and vastness, uttering not a sound amid the all-enveloping silence, despite the fact that it held inside it at that moment innumerable small bodies throbbing with life. Sometimes a

303

bird would flap its wing, or rub its head against the head of its mate sleeping beside it on the branch, or let out a chirp of protest because another bird had disturbed its sleep. But those soft, clipped sounds never left the nests hidden from the eye among the leaves and intertwined branches. He could never hear those sounds himself, but only imagine them.

A car light shone behind his back. Then he heard the roar of its engine approaching, and it flew past him—a black car with a roof that glinted in the moonlight. He saw it move away, then slow down and turn to the right in the direction of the city. So the guests who had come from Basra had finally begun to return home.

He found the public road deserted, with no trace of the car that had passed him a short time beforehand. It had disappeared into the night with its lights and its drunken passengers. He himself was sober, having resolved not to drink too much. He stood hesitating, not knowing in which direction to walk; he was aimless, he just wanted to stretch his legs, take in some clean air, and restore his clarity of mind. The salt that covered the surface of the desert on the other side of the road shone with a strange whiteness, a gentle whiteness, not the burning white that the sun produces during daylight hours. From afar, at the edge of the road leading down to the city beside the desert, he could see the camp, not yet fully built, looking like the remains of a small deserted village. He decided to walk down the road to the village, for the sight of the camp, with its rows of roofless rooms, disturbed him. The building had begun to progress better after getting rid of the dishonest work supervisor. Sultan al-Imari had seemed happy with him, for one suited the other. And now Sultan wanted to marry that flirt! He would have a unique wife and a unique foreman! He started to make his way along the track between the white desert and the work zone, walking on the side next to the desert. There was a steady rhythmic beat of machinery in the work zone, but the desert on his right was a vast expanse of peace and quiet.

The headache that the loud talking had given him at the party had dissipated after his solitary walk. The sights he had seen and the words he had heard—those that left any impression on him—had subsided into the ambiguous world of memory, to burst forth one day unexpectedly, stirred up by another sight he would see or a word he would hear. But there were things that remained floating on the surface of his consciousness.

The news of Diana's marriage to Sultan, then her threat to him that she would "get him" one day. It was an exquisite threat, which stirred his pride, but it was also a strange threat, for those sorts of words might well be uttered by an insistent man to a stubborn lover, but for a woman to utter them to a man? How did she think that she could carry out her threat? Anyway, that wasn't what was preoccupying him now. There were only two things still seriously worrying him: Maureen's hints that she might be pregnant, and Mr. Reynolds's conversation, from which he had deduced that there was someone observing the details of his private life here. He was not going to change his lifestyle because there was someone watching him. What disturbed him more than anything else was Maureen's words, when she had said that she had been suffering from headaches recently. If she really was pregnant, that meant that the son she was carrying was most likely his, for her husband's secret was known to everyone. But if she had a girl? You'll be holding your head up, Mr. Husam Hilmi, as a daughter of yours grows up over there. Mr. Sullivan, her "stepfather," would proudly present her to his friends: "This is my daughter, Patricia"—or Sylvia, or Clara, or any other name the pair of them may choose.

Then your mother will rejoice when she hears the news. It's what you've been wanting! This wasn't what you had in mind, but as you sow, so shall you reap! And you have sown in strange soil! But you used to sleep with them over there as well!

True, but over there, I was careful, I protected myself, I always kept a supply of condoms and carried one in my pocket. Then again, Maureen said that she was taking pills and that she didn't want her body to be disfigured by the effects of pregnancy. Perhaps she wanted to provoke her husband, who seemed stunned. He'd try to find out the truth from her tomorrow. But would this woman tell the truth?

As he wandered absentmindedly, he reached the workers' camp squatting in the depression between the edge of the road and the desert. He looked at the tents scattered around the camp area, which stood silently, their insides in darkness. Which tent do you suppose that the translator, Muhammad Ahmad, was sleeping in? He would ask him for some more books for Akram's wife. The camp paths seemed deserted now, an open arena for stray dogs, now that the men were sleeping in their beds, resting ahead of the next day's work. The whole camp was sleeping quietly, or so it seemed at this late hour of the night; and the jagged moon, from its dominating position in the sky, was pouring its cold light over the tents. Several minutes went by as he stood where he was, his thoughts incoherent, then headed back again.

Tomorrow he would ask her.

9

The four of them sat on a mat made of palm leaves that he had bought that afternoon in the village market. Sitting on a mat on solid ground was more comfortable for him than sitting on his bed, whose planks creaked whenever he moved his body even a little. He sat alone on one side of the carpet, not sharing it with anyone, for his broad bottom occupied a wide area when he sat down. His three companions all sat on the other side. Everything was ready for the start of the evening session—glasses, dishes of mezze, ice and water, all lined up on a newspaper that they had spread between them. In the middle of the newspaper stood a tall bottle of arrack, a monument to freedom and release from the cares and troubles of the world. He reached for the bottle of arrack.

"Hey, Istifan, my lad, when are you getting married? The fiancée's available, thank God!"

When he started a drinking session he liked to leave all the cares of the world outside the tent. He would leave them to the wind and night and to the barking of the dogs, then talk about anything that seemed witty or amusing. Generally, he would talk about his wife. Tonight, however, he preferred to start a conversation with Istifan, for this lad from the mountains had touched his heart: he seemed honest and straightforward, unlike the others—different from Muzhir, who was insolent, like himself; different from Hussein, who was argumentative; and different from the strange Muhammad, whom no one knew what was going on in his head, with all those books that he read and the papers he wrote and then hid out of sight.

"I'm waiting for enough money to do it properly," said Istifan.

"Don't wait, don't wait too long, my boy!"

In the meantime, his fingers had been trying to open the bottle, whose smooth body glowed in the light from the lamp in the tent. He removed the stopper from the magic liquid, the elixir of joy and happiness. His fingers moved deftly, as if he were unveiling a bride, while Hussein sat smoking, watching him in silence, and Muzhir bent over the newspaper, trying to read the words that were framed between the glasses and dishes. Only Muhammad Ahmad stayed perched, like a strange bird, on the bed, with a book between his hands. He started by pouring a quantity of the clear liquid into his glass, then gave the bottle to Hussein and lifted the jug of water.

"To marriage, my lad . . . ."

Suddenly, however, Muzhir's voice rang out, "The World in a Week!" He was reading from the newspaper spread out under the dishes. "Since the announcement of the news of the death of King George VI . . . ."

Muzhir lifted up the dish of buttermilk that was hiding the rest of the words, and continued reading loudly, paying no attention to his looks of disapproval.

". . . king of Britain, on Wednesday afternoon . . . ."

Hussein passed the bottle of arrack to Muzhir, then interrupted him and said, "That's right, Abu Jabbar, why haven't you put on your mourning clothes for King George's death?"

"Why should I wear mourning clothes when the king of another country dies?"

"But you always say that they're our uncles!"

"Hussein, for God's sake," he said angrily, "Don't start the session with one of your annoying topics." The he turned to Istifan, who seemed confused. "Marriage is a blessing from God," he said.

Hussein put a piece of ice in his glass, and Muzhir laughed as he continued reading in silence. His hand was still holding up the bowl of buttermilk as far as he could while reading the hidden lines, while his other hand grasped the arrack bottle that Hussein had just handed him.

"They're saying in the paper . . . ."

Muzhir put the bowl back.

"They're saying that it's fortunate for the monarchy in England that the late king will be succeeded on the throne by a woman."

"Woman, man, tortoise, it makes no difference. Fox will still be the master of the show," said Hussein.

Abu Jabbar paid no attention to what Hussein had said, but looked at Muzhir.

"A woman's better, that's for sure. There's nothing in the whole world better than a woman. That's why I say to Istifan that he should get married quickly."

"Marry the Queen of England?"

"Marry his fiancée, Matilda."

Istifan smiled shyly, as Muzhir began to get his glass ready.

"If the fiancée is available, the worst mistake is to wait."

"Abu Jabbar, please leave the boy alone. Why do you want to bother him about marriage right now?"

Muzhir poured some water onto the arrack in his glass. Istifan was busy with the bottle of arrack, trying to pour himself a glass.

Abu Jabbar stopped and gave Istifan an embarrassed look. "Don't take any notice of this talk, my lad," he said. "Muzhir here doesn't need a woman to sleep with, because . . . ."

Muzhir dropped the piece of ice between his fingers, then tried to pick it up again from off the newspaper, but it slipped out of his fingers like a small fish. Eventually, he managed to retrieve it and drop it in his glass with a clumsy movement that made some of the liquid spill out of the glass. Abu Jabbar was watching his confusion with delight. Hussein was waiting for him to elaborate, but he was satisfied with what he had said already. Knowing other people's secrets is a lethal weapon, which you can brandish in their faces when you like, on condition that you merely hint at what you know. If you tell all you know, then you will have used your weapon just once, and rendered it subsequently useless.

So he didn't elaborate. And anyway, he didn't want to turn Muzhir into an enemy, for he had been his tentmate before the others came.

He addressed Istifan again, who had finally succeeded in sorting his glass. "Waiting is a waste of life because time, my lad, is like God: you can't see him, but he is there."

Muhammad looked up from his book and gave him a searching look. He liked that. Muhammad had covered his body with a blanket, for the breeze during the last few nights of February had a cool feel to it as it blew into their tent, but despite that he was damp with sweat. He wished he had a more agile body, like these young men. He also wished he were young again, but that was of course impossible.

"Don't imagine that time is static and still. No, it is like a stout cable, dragging us to the grave, day by day, and hour by hour!"

He wiped the sweat from his face and neck with the palm of his hand.

"For that reason, a man should not let his life go to waste. He should enjoy his life, marry, sleep with women, drink, sing, and make merry!"

Muhammad went back to looking at his book, a faint smile playing on his face.

"So don't waste time talking!"

Muzhir raised his glass. "Your health!"

They raised their glasses. "And to the health of Istifan's bride!"

He drank remorsefully. Then Shawkat, the camp clerk, put his head through the opening in the tent. "Abu Jabbar, Daniel wants you!"

"Now?"

"Yes, now!"

He looked at his friends, then at Shawkat. "Do you know what he wants from me?"

"No, he just said come urgently!"

"Where is he now? In his room?"

"No, he's waiting in the rations room."

Shawkat left. He took another swig from his glass, a large swig, then put the glass on the newspaper and looked at it regretfully. God curse you, Daniel! What a time to summon him! He took a slice of tomato and slipped it into his mouth, then placed his two palms on the mat, lifted his weight on them, raised his bottom into the air and then stood up straight.

"I won't be long."

As he moved toward the door of the tent, he heard Muzhir shout after him: "Don't forget us when Daniel gives you some tins!"

He walked out into the night, chewing his mouthful. He saw a group of dogs around a bitch behind one of the tents, jostling together, agitated but silent. He passed them by. What did Daniel want at this late hour of the night? Perhaps he wanted to drink with him. But Shawkat had said that he was waiting for him in the rations tent. He was heading toward the big tent whose door he could see was open, with a tongue of yellow light streaming from it, when he noticed Fox's Rover standing at a distance in the darkness near to the camp fence. So that was the reason! The boss had come to hear the news from him, and entrust him with some new tasks. But he hated meeting him here amid the workmen's tents. What if someone should spot him? He started to look around cautiously. He would suggest to Fox some other place to meet.

He had been walking in a carefree mood, his head held high in the face of the night and the cold breeze, feeling happy, though conscious of a slight numbness flowing through his veins. After seeing the car standing there quietly near the hedge, though, trying to hide from prying eyes as far as possible, he began to feel scared and his footsteps became uncertain. He started to move like a thief, trying not to let anyone see him. He walked off at an angle, pretending that he was just going past the tent, at the same time turning around to check the paths. When he was confident that no one could see him, he plucked up his courage, climbed the two steps at the door, then walked inside. Immediately, the thick curtain fell over the opening, and the tongue of light that had stretched over the ground outside the tent was cut off.

He saw Mr. Fox sitting in Daniel's place behind the table, pipe in mouth, while Daniel sat to one side. He couldn't see Shawkat, the clerk. He'd brought him the summons and disappeared. It's better that way. He didn't want witnesses to his secret activities. Even Daniel's presence—the link between him and the boss—he found distasteful and constricting. He bowed to show his respect, and raised his hand to his head. "Good evening, sir!"

He muttered his greeting in the English that he had learned from them when he had worked at the Shabiya camp. He saw Mr. Fox take his pipe out of his mouth. "Hello, Abdul!"

Mr. Fox spoke in the Arabic he had learned while working as a policeman in Palestine. He stood in front of Fox submissively, wrapping his arms around his chest. They were separated by the iron table, on one side of which Fox sat comfortably, while he stood with drooping shoulders on the other side.

"How are you?" asked Mr. Fox in a friendly tone.

"I'm very well, especially now that I'm in your presence, sir!"

"Good, Abdul . . . now, let's see, what's the news?"

He didn't know why he insisted on calling him Abdul, as if he were one of the servants, though he knew his real name very well. He looked at Daniel, who was sitting silently with a neutral expression, the face of a person who has nothing to do with the conversation going on in front of him. He was still hesitant. What he wanted to say this time could not be heard by anyone except the boss. Mr. Fox noticed his hesitation and turned to the camp superintendent, "Daniel, you can go now. Come back in half an hour!"

Daniel got up obediently, lifted the curtain on the door enough to let him out, and slipped into the night. He was free of another witness.

"Please, Abdul, sit down."

He made for the chair that Daniel had vacated, and cautiously lowered his large bottom onto it.

"Tell me, what have you got for me?"

"Well, sir, you didn't tell me to watch the managers, but . . . ."

He stayed silent, not knowing how to phrase the words to make them convincing.

"Come on, tell me. There's no one listening."

"Sir, I'm not one-hundred-percent certain, but I have doubts . . . doubts about this engineer."

"Which engineer? What's his name?"

"Mr. Husam Hilmi, sir."

Fox seemed interested. "You have doubts? What do you mean? I want to understand . . . ."

"Sir, I believe that he has some links to the workforce. But, as I said, I'm not completely sure. If you . . . ."

He had to appear not to be in a hurry, or prejudiced. If he told him right away that the bastard was engaged in political activity against the management and against the government, Mr. Fox might interpret that as an attempt by an employee to take revenge on his boss, and he wouldn't like that. Obedience and order went before everything else in their eyes.

"How do you mean, links? Explain to me properly!"

"Sir, it may be that I'm imagining it. But I saw him exchanging books with Muhammad. Abbas, the driver, takes the books back and forth between the two of them."

"Who's Muhammad?"

"Your translator."

Mr. Fox looked astonished. "Are you sure of what you're saying, Abdul?"

"Yes, sir. He lives in the tent with us . . . I mean, the translator."

Fox put his pipe in his mouth again and started to take a series of short, consecutive puffs, to stop the lighted tobacco in the bowl of the pipe from going out. Meanwhile, he could hear the sound of footsteps outside. His heart quaked. He was afraid that someone might come in suddenly and take them by surprise. But the footsteps moved away and disappeared in the night.

Mr. Fox spoke without taking the pipe from his mouth. "Listen to me carefully, Abdul. The first thing is, I want you to keep a watch on Engineer Husam. And after that, I want you to see what books the translator has."

"But sir, I can't read them!" he said, embarrassed.

"You don't have to read them. I just want to be brought the name of the book and the name of the author and then I'll know everything."

"Whatever you say, sir!"

He was delighted. He had paved the way for the next blow. But he kept a face that did not betray any particular joy, the face of a servant who was simply carrying out the orders of his masters. He made a movement to get up, but Mr. Fox held him back.

"Wait, Abdul, there's another job."

He stayed sitting, waiting.

"Tell me, Abdul, do you know the drilling machinery operators well?"

"Yes, sir, Fawzi, Ulwan, Jasim, and Khudair."

"Excellent! There are some people saying that they're slandering the project management. I want you to keep a close eye on them."

"Yes, sir."

An easy task, for these were his friends and Muzhir's friends, Fawzi in particular. He could visit them in their tent at any time and drink with them, and listen to what they were saying without arousing any suspicions.

He saw Mr. Fox looking at him closely. "Abdul, you've been drinking arrack!"

He had been given away by that wretched smell on his breath that hung around in the air of the tent and dominated every other smell, despite the fact that he had only had two swigs of it.

"Sir, I didn't know that you would be honoring me with .... It was ...."

But Mr. Fox merely smiled at him kindly. "No arrack, that's all. It's not good for the health. You must only drink whisky!"

"And where is the whisky, sir?"

"It's here, Abdul. We have everything you could want."

He watched him as he opened a drawer and took from it a bottle of whisky with a decorated label attached to it, stamped with a round red seal. (This whisky kingdom is a complete empire in itself, with its own ceremonies and seals!) He looked in delight at the gleaming bottle being passed to him across the desk.

"Take it, you deserve it, Abdul. You're a faithful servant!"

Like the genie in the story of Aladdin's lamp who brings you what you want before you can blink an eyelid!

He took the bottle in both hands. "Thank you, sir, a thousand thanks!"

He got up from the chair, but did not leave the tent. The present, and Mr. Fox's friendly words, had encouraged him to ask for more.

"Yes, Abdul? Do you want something else?"

"Sir, you know well how devoted I am to you . . . ."

He saw Mr. Fox look at him, but without saying anything. "After all this service, sir, they've transferred me to the maintenance branch. Could you get that reversed?"

"Through whom?" asked the director in a voice that had lost its friendly tone.

"Through the new engineer, Sultan al-Imari."

"Listen to me, Abdul. We are all working on the project for a single purpose. You mustn't disobey orders. Just do as you are told."

"I know, sir, but . . . ."

But Mr. Fox would not let him finish. "You're working for Mr. Sultan al-Imari now. Work hard. If you're not happy, I'll see if the problem can be resolved later."

Mr. Fox seemed a little annoyed.

"Anything you say, sir!"

He had not succeeded in persuading Mr. Fox to intervene, but he had gotten him to promise to find a solution if he didn't like working with Sultan. Abu Jabbar moved away from Fox, walking backward and bending his head toward him, not turning his back until he was at the tent door. He hesitated before drawing back the side of the curtain a little and peeking into the darkness. The camp paths were deserted, and the tents stood black in the heart of the night. He shifted his whole body outside. He went down the two steps in front of the door and hurried to his tent, carrying his spoils with him. They would be astonished when they saw what was in his hands. He would tell them that he'd ordered one through Daniel and that he'd brought it to him today.

He saw his friends on the mat as he had left them, with Muhammad still staring into his book. They turned around as he entered, and Muzhir shouted a cheery welcome: "Whisky, for once!"

He walked over to the side of the mat. "I bought it from Daniel. I was . . . ."

Hussein blew out cigarette smoke and raised his head in his direction. "Are you sure that you bought it, and that it wasn't a present from the group of . . . ?"

He gave Hussein a look of pure loathing. "Go and ask him."

Muhammad let his gaze drop to his book again without saying anything. I'll find out what's in these books that he reads day and night. I'll copy their titles and the names of the people that wrote them, as the boss told me to. He bent down over the chest he had placed under the bed, pulled it forward a little, opened the lid, then slipped the bottle in amid his meager possessions.

Muzhir looked at him in disappointment. "Why are you hiding it?"

"I'm keeping it for special occasions."

He pushed the box back under the bed and went back to sit in his place. He raised his glass with pleasure. He would continue digging quietly until the hole that Husam Hilmi would eventually fall into became large enough. Perhaps Muhammad would also fall into it with him, but there was nothing to be done about it: in every battle, men perish who have no connection with the reasons for the struggle.

10

So her husband had gone to Basra, to stay there for a couple of days to take delivery of some new trucks. He wouldn't find a better opportunity to be alone with her and try to discover the reason for her strange behavior toward him. From the day she had found out she was pregnant, she had been avoiding him. Could she have found a new lover? And who could he be? Mark Doyle was still preoccupied with Diana, who hadn't severed her relationship with him, even after her wedding to Sultan al-Imari. No one else sprung to mind. He had to find out the reason for this perplexing behavior on her part. He would go to see her, go to her house, today.

It was nearly ten o'clock. He had returned from work a few minutes ago. He wished he could have come back before that. But after the floodwaters had inundated the desert and submerged the workmen's camp, they had begun to work overtime to speed up completion of the building of the new camp, so that they could move the workers there from their temporary refuge in the work zone. He had to be there most of the time. He also had to put the finishing touches to building the club, as management had just decided that Saturday, March 3 should be the date for the dance to inaugurate the Eagle's Nest in its new building.

He heard a knock at the door, then the cook came in.

"Sir, would you like me to make you supper?"

"And Mr. Macaulay, where is he?" He hadn't seen him when he came into the house.

"He had supper before you and went out."

The cook seemed younger, perhaps because of the false teeth—bright white and neatly aligned—they had been fitted that day, in place of his own teeth that had all been removed.

"Abu Mahmoud, are you happy with those teeth?" he asked.

"I had no choice, sir!"

"That's not what I mean. I don't think they're fitted securely."

When the cook spoke, his teeth wobbled inside his mouth independently of the movement of his jaw.

"True, sir, they won't stay still. Imagine, sir, I was busy cooking around sunset and I sneezed. And what should I see but my upper row of teeth flying through the air!"

He laughed.

"Abu Mahmoud, be careful that they don't fly into a cooking pot or salad bowl!"

"No sir, of course!"

"I think you should go back to the doctor and let him repair those teeth, or fit some different, stable ones that don't fly into the air whenever you sneeze."

"I told the doctor that they were acting up, but the doctor, God preserve him, said they were still new, and that I had to be patient with them until they had settled down."

"No, no, go back to him."

"Quite honestly, sir, I'm tired of consulting doctors, tired of being patient and seeing what happens. Who knows, perhaps the teeth will settle down as the doctor said. Do you want me to get supper?"

"Yes. But give me ten minutes. I'd like it ready when I've finished in the bathroom."

When he had finished his supper, he went back into his room, and lifted the telephone receiver on the writing table. His parents looked down on him from the top of the fireplace as he turned the dial to speak to Maureen. He waited anxiously to hear her voice at the other end.

"Hello, yes?"

Her voice finally came through, sleepy and a little irritated.

"Maureen?"

An oppressive silence ensued. Then she spoke, "Yes, Awsam, what do you want?"

Her voice sounded far away. He thought she had yawned.

"I heard that you were alone in the house today."

"So?"

What was this offhand tone? He pulled himself together. "So I'll come over soon."

"Why?"

Her question hit him like a slap, but he tried to remain as calm as possible.

"I want to talk to you."

"Just talk?"

He could hardly believe it. Could feelings change this quickly? Where had all that passion gone, all that concern? His eyes fell on her present to him when she had come back from Britain. He saw the penguin, with its useless black wings, staring at him coldly with its glass eyes. He saw his mother looking at him too, but with tired eyes full of sorrow. He looked away from the bird's face and from his mother's face.

"Yes, just talk."

"Nothing else?"

What had happened to the woman?

"No, nothing else. Calm down!"

"Okay. I'm about to go to sleep, but never mind."

He heard the sound of the telephone being put down at the other end. He slowly lowered the receiver in his hand, but he didn't terminate the call at his end. He stared dumbfounded into the unlit fireplace. He saw some old ash and the remains of charred sticks. Meanwhile, his fingers were pressing hard on the neck of the receiver, wanting to strangle it. Then he came to again, put the receiver back in its place, and released his fingers from its neck. He got up and left the house.

The residential quarter was peaceful, as usual, and the clean paths were deserted. He didn't notice anyone as he crossed to her house. In the distance, in front of the club entrance, two or three cars were standing, their polished roofs gleaming in the light. He made his way through the garden between the walls of hedges. The atmosphere was spring-like, yet the refreshing breeze did not calm his soul. He was seething. He pressed the bell and stood fidgeting around on the door-step, glowering. He heard the sound of her footsteps approaching, then the door opened and her face looked out at him. He saw her smile, the smile that he knew and was used to.

"Come in quickly," she said hurriedly.

Her voice surprised him. It was quite free of the harsh tone he had heard her use on the telephone. She was wearing a short, white, sleeve-less dress. He put his hand on her bare arm and led her, somewhat roughly, into the living room. She walked with him obediently. When she was in the full light, she turned her face to him.

"Your face is frightening in a comical way! Look!"

She released her arm from his grip, then grasped his hand and dragged him with her to the bathroom.

"Look at your face in the mirror!"

His face looked melancholy and grave beside her own enchanting face, with its relaxed, contented features.

"Hey, do you like this barbarian?" she teased.

He saw the mask of his face break, as his features—which always became softer in her presence—began to reappear. His mask was a flimsy one, his savage anger born of a moment, brittle and swift to dis-appear, like fire in a bundle of straw. It was a fine covering on a sub-missive face, devoid of will. He cursed her secretly and cursed himself, then turned his face from the mirror. She took him back into the living room, leading him this time.

"Sit down!"

He sat down at the end of the sofa.

"What would you like to drink?"

"Anything."

320

He was trying to reinvent an anger that had been dissipated, but without success. She went inside, and he stretched out his legs, as if he were returning from a long journey. After a little, she came in again, carrying a bottle of whisky and two glasses, which she put down on top of the table. Then she sat down at the other end of the sofa, away from him. She opened the bottle, poured him a glass, and another for herself. He took out his pack of cigarettes and lit two, one of which he gave to her. They smoked in silence. He was still confused, not knowing how he had weakened before her so quickly. She looked at him in amusement.

"What did you want to talk about?"

He stared into her eyes for some time. They were like two colored beads looking at him innocently.

"Maureen, what game are you playing with me?"

Her face registered surprise. "Is that what you believe?"

"Then how do you explain your avoiding me recently?"

She took a long puff from her cigarette, then slowly blew the smoke out, one puff after another. She looked miserable.

"And why should I avoid you of all people?"

"I don't know. That's what's upsetting me."

"Actually, I asked Abdul, your cook, about you once. He said that you were coming home from work late every day."

"I'm not just talking about this week. Can you recall the last time we played tennis together?"

She avoided his looks, as she concentrated on her drink. "It was more than two months ago," he continued angrily. "Before the cocktail party."

He stopped drinking, and tried to reignite the first signs of the anger that had raised its head again, with the tobacco from his cigarette. He took a long puff, but she would not be shaken, and her nerves seemed steady.

"And do you not know the reason?"

"I came here to hear it."

"Quite simply, I'm afraid for my unborn child."

She touched her belly. Damn it! This was another embarrassing topic, on which he wished she would give him an honest answer. She was the only one who could know who was the real father of the unborn child inside her; even though he himself believed that she was carrying his son, she was still the only person who could know for certain. He had asked her once about the child's paternity, after she had hinted at the subject of her pregnancy in front of Dr. Sami at the cocktail party. But her answer had been vague and evasive. "Who would people expect a married woman to be pregnant by?" she had asked him. "By her husband, of course, wouldn't they? Or would you be happy for them to say that I was carrying another man's child?"

He looked at her belly. He had not noticed any swelling under the fabric of her dress. He stretched out his hand to touch her belly but she blocked his hand's path and grasped his wrist.

"What do you want to do?"

"Touch your belly."

She looked at him apprehensively. "Why?"

"I just do."

She left him to feel her belly behind her dress without releasing her small hand from around his wrist. When he pressed on the flesh with his palm, she pushed his hand away quickly but firmly.

"That's enough now!"

She took her glass, and he looked at her in frustration. "Didn't I tell you you'd changed?"

She stared at her glass, then raised her head to him. "In the autumn, I'll be a mother."

She seemed proud of being pregnant.

"And you'll also get married, and a day will come when you'll be a father. And then you'll know."

"If I haven't become a father already."

But she ignored his words, blowing them into the air with her cigarette smoke.

"Everything changes in this world." She stubbed out the remains of her cigarette in the ashtray. "That's life."

He recalled Bob Macaulay, who used to repeat this expression in the face of the inevitable, but Maureen had changed the way she behaved with him purely by choice. He looked at her sadly. "And everything between us is at an end?"

His cigarette was eating itself up between his fingers. He saw her get up—pick up her glass and get up. She stood opposite the clock on the wall, then murmured in what seemed like panic, "It's nearly midnight!"

He looked at her indignantly. "It's not polite to mention the time when you have guests! Come on, sit down!"

"I'm sorry, I didn't mean to be rude."

"Maureen, please tell me, do you still have any feelings for me?"

She laughed, but he didn't understand what her laugh signified. "Do you want to know?"

"Yes, I want to know."

She looked at him gloomily. "The fact is, I find you an attractive man. Usually kind, and sometimes delightful."

"And that's all?"

"And what were you expecting? Have you forgotten that I'm a married woman?"

She knew well what was going on inside his head, but she was steering the conversation in a different direction. Had she only now discovered that she was a married woman?

"Don't you still enjoy sleeping with me?"

She looked suspiciously into his eyes. "Yes, from time to time." Then, when she saw his eyes light up, she added, with what seemed almost like fear, "But not now!"

She tried to get up again, but he put his hand on her bare shoulder and forced her to stay where she was. She wriggled under the pressure of his hand. "No, Awsam, please!"

He had to put her words to the test to see how she would behave then. He left his place at the end of the sofa and came closer to her. "I told you, not now. I'm in a bad mood today."

He took the glass from her hand and put it on the table, then took her in his arms. At first, she tried to push him off her, but he locked his arms firmly around her and started to kiss her passionately. She stopped her resistance. He thought that she had given in to his desire, so he lifted her from the sofa and carried her into her bedroom. "But you promised not to touch me!" she said angrily, seesawing in his arms.

"Of all the promises you hear, don't believe a promise like that from a lover alone with his beloved!"

He put her down on the bed. She stayed lying there where he had placed her, while he sat on the edge of the bed and began to undress.

"You're like a naughty child, destroying everything he can lay his hands on!"

He waited for her to undress as she usually did, but this time she didn't move a finger. He proceeded to undress her, a little roughly. She had said that she would be giving birth in the autumn, meaning that she was now in her third month, or perhaps the fourth. But the hollow of her navel was still sunken, and the slight swelling in her belly was no higher than the level of her hip bones. Previously, when she had slept naked, her belly was so depressed that it seemed to almost touch her back, like a small valley between two hills. The sight of her belly in its new form made his blood run hot—this belly that held his child inside it. Yes, his child, he was certain of it. He advanced toward her with passion, but she lifted her arms in his face, before he could bring his body down on her. "Please, for the sake of the child, be gentle!"

After that, she submitted to him to do what he liked with her, though without sharing his mad frenzy. Her hands, which at moments like this in the past had almost ripped him to pieces, lay lifeless on the bed at her sides. At the moment when he penetrated her, her gaze was elsewhere. Only her body was with him, while she herself seemed removed from what was taking place. As the final moment approached, he found himself panting alone, as if he were making love to a corpse. He got up off her quickly, disappointed, insulted, and frustrated. He saw her sit and cover her nakedness with a white sheet, her brown hair falling over her chest and touching the top of her breasts. She looked at him as he quickly put on his underclothes in confusion, for his nakedness seemed to him at that moment shameful, disgusting, and inexcusable. He heard her say, in a conciliatory tone, "Listen, Awsam, don't misunderstand me!"

The whore was lying to him. All this time, she had been lying to him!

"This wretched pregnancy has turned me off a lot of things that I used to like."

Yes, the pregnancy, she had changed after the pregnancy had been confirmed. Like the sun, which sometimes shines through a small chink in a mass of dark clouds after a long period of darkness, the truth suddenly appeared to him. Only then had the truth appeared to him! He almost shouted to himself, "What a fool I am! What a fool!" (A shirt button came off in his tense, clumsy fingers.

"Some food I used to love is now making me sick."

But she said that she was taking the pill. She didn't want pregnancy to spoil her elegant figure. And I believed her, I thought that love . . . .

"I can no longer stand myself. I've even begun to hate . . . ."

Has the air of Iraq made me become a romantic, believing in talk of love and the like from a woman like Maureen? How come I have forgotten the sort of relationships I had with women like her over there? Give her food and lodging, and she will give you unlimited sex. But Maureen isn't in need of food or lodging. She wanted you for . . . .

"All the same, it's a nice feeling a woman has when . . . ."

But why me? She could have slept with her servant Hasan, if what she wanted was a man to make her pregnant. He tightened his belt around his waist, tightened it more than usual.

"I will be going home! I think that . . . ."

Hasan the servant would be no use. Hasan would leave her with a child who could well have dark skin and black hair, and be stigmatized from the day he was born. She would no doubt have thought of that. She couldn't think of anyone better than you as a father for a bastard who would look like you, with fair hair, and be lost among them over there, lost, lost, lost!

"John suggested that I travel early, so as . . . ."

Her husband had become important now! He will suggest, he will get things ready, he will make arrangements for the birth, he will send a telegram to tell his family the good news, he will enquire about the best hospital, and await the happy day! As for you, you were just a bull to fertilize her, you have done what was required of you, and your role has ended.

"I told him I would travel after the party for the new club, in May. John will come in September, so that he can be with me, when . . . ."

She continued speaking at length, with remarkably calm nerves, quite unconcerned. She spoke about her happiness and John's happiness and about how they intended to deal with the child that was on its way, the child whom they were openly stealing from him without his being able to do a thing. He was putting his shoes on at that moment. He had the idea of throwing one of them at her, but what would have been the use? She has taken from you what she needed, and left you with your futile anger, a barbarian's anger, as she described you.

As he left her bedroom she was still sitting on the bed, her back and thighs covered with her white nightdress, a goddess of purity and innocence. He slammed the door behind him, then made his way through the garden of her house, across the path, and through his own garden. He entered his house feeling the bitterness of a deceit uncovered too late.

11

A shimmering point of light, made by the sun's rays on the surface of the water that had lain stagnant in the desert for more than a month, accompanied the car as it traveled toward the city. He felt as if the tiny vehicle were carrying them along a coast road. Palm groves kept them company as well, to the right of the road . . . endless palm plantations on one side, a sea that had gushed into the heart of the desert on the other, while between them stretched the almost empty road, that always seemed to him extremely long, because it made the city far away. The heat of the air had begun to dissipate as afternoon set in, and the breeze coming from between the palm trees seemed cool. Engineer Husam Hilmi, who was sitting at the other end of the seat, half opened the window beside him so that the smoke would not be trapped inside the car, then started smoking, totally absorbed, while staring gloomily at the road. He seemed preoccupied today, and lacking in enthusiasm. What could be on this man's mind, who lived such a comfortable life?

"Muhammad, my friend, are you comfortable now? I mean, after your move to the new camp?"

"It's better, of course. You can't imagine how bad the old camp was! Especially in winter!"

"I know, I know!"

"Imagine, sir," said the driver, who was listening to the conversation, "if anyone spoke in his room, the whole world could hear him! Those walls were like cardboard . . . ."

Husam laughed, and his face relaxed a little. "In fact, I suggested to the management that we should coat the walls with plaster to reduce the noise, but they said it wasn't necessary."

"Of course, sir, they don't want to spend a single penny on us."

"Keep your eyes on the road, Abbas!"

"Yes, sir."

"The problem (here Husam turned toward him) is that management has never taken employees at your level, like office managers and foremen into account. They should have provided you with better living conditions. In fact, Husam, sir, the management should have provided that sort of thing for everyone." He looked at the road, which was slipping behind them under the car.

"True."

He said nothing more, perhaps not wanting to speak too much in criticism of the management's behavior in front of the driver. He liked this Husam Hilmi. He had liked him since the first time they met, when, seeing him standing in the road with his little case in his hand watching the trucks take the men toward the city, Engineer Husam had stopped his car and given him a lift. They shared a feeling that things around them were not going as they ought to—even though Husam's concern with the workmen's problems was a product of his instinctive belief in justice (and perhaps some thoughts and ideas that he had read about in books at some time or other, about socialism and human rights and the like), rather than a concern arising from real experience of injury or injustice. Husam lived another life, a different life; it was impossible for a man like him to comprehend the feelings of a person living in a tent on the edge of the desert, who relieved himself squatting in a latrine open to view, and who, when he traveled to see his family, crouched like an animal on the roof of a truck, exposed in winter to the cold and the rain, and in summer to the sun and the dust. For all that, it made him happy to discover a sincere concern to understand other people's suffering in a man like that, despite the enormous distance between Husam's life and his.

328

Husam stubbed out his cigarette in the small ashtray fixed to the side of the armrest beside him, then turned his face toward him. "And how do you keep yourself busy among all those people in the camp?"

"I try to keep clear of them as far as possible, and keep an eye on what's going on from a distance."

Husam gave him an absentminded look. "In this day and age, no one can keep clear. You're involved, even if you live in a cave!"

The desert sea had reached its limit and stopped. The floodwaters had not come further than this point. The surface of the earth was exposed again, and the point of light, which had grown longer as the sun's disk dipped, had receded. From the stagnant waters emerged the black pipe that the project management had stretched out in the desert, to set out on its long journey creeping over the earth, like an endless black snake. They were now nearly at the village of al-Siba, tucked away among the palm groves to the right of the road.

"In the afternoons, I sit on the dam, facing the submerged desert, thinking, reading, and sometimes writing."

"But where do you go at night?"

He saw him looking at him carefully.

"And writing? What do you write?"

Until that point, he hadn't mentioned to Husam that he was trying to write, and he didn't know how the phrase "sometimes writing" had slipped from his lips. He seemed a little nonplussed, as if the act of writing was a shameful activity. "Actually, I'm trying my luck at writing a novel," he said, almost apologetically.

"A novel, really?"

"Something of that sort, just to kill the time. What can a man do, in this sort of place?"

The plantations were passing rapidly as the setting sun extended its tongues of light into the empty spaces between the palm trunks near the edge of the road. Farther away, however, the shadows were thickening in the depths, making him wish that he could sit there to rest a little from the day's exertions, in the lengthening shadows.

"I wish I could do the same as you. I've got lots of things I'd love to write about. But I can't get away on my own for long. Things about women, about . . . ."

He didn't finish. He looked at his watch, then started to note the landmarks on the road. He seemed hesitant. Finally he turned toward him. "Muhammad, my friend, I don't know what your novel is about, but I think you should put a woman in it. Make it revolve around a woman, or a number of women."

Muhammad laughed. "If Hussein could hear you!" He saw Husam looking at him, not understanding what he meant. "Hussein wants me to make it revolve around a struggle between the workforce and the British management: a strike, fights, deaths, informers, things like that. He wants it to be a gloomy novel!"

Husam looked at the driver's head, then back at Muhammad. "And who is Hussein?"

"One of the four people with me in the tent."

"Muhammad, my friend, don't get involved, beware of getting involved. You can't write about everything that comes into your mind here. Don't forget that we . . . ."

A large truck was advancing on them from the direction of the city, dragging behind it a cloud of dust. Husam hurriedly raised the window beside him, but despite that, as the truck sped by, they did not escape the dust. Husam waited until the air inside was clear then lowered the window a little.

"What were we saying?"

"We were comparing women and politics as a subject for a novel."

"Yes. Look, Muhammad, a novel without a woman will be very boring, like life without a woman."

"You're right. Woman is an important element, even if she is sometimes the cause of suffering."

"You're telling me, my friend, you're telling me!"

He watched him as he lit himself a new cigarette. So he was a supporter of women in a novel, unlike Hussein. The question now was which of them was the more suitable subject, women or politics?

330

But why should he not combine them in a single novel with two faces—one face dominated by politics and things connected with politics, and the other face dominated by women. Then there would be the links between the two faces, the shadows, people being trampled underfoot here and there, anything borne on the winds coming to us from the west, and other things, some of them still obscure, with unclear features, and some that had not yet occurred to him at all.

"And what have you made the focus of your novel?"

Husam had woken from his daydreams to ask him the hard and disconcerting question that left you embarrassed, not knowing how to formulate his response—the question that only the novel itself, when it is finished, can answer at all convincingly. Anything before that would just bes idle chatter.

He hadn't considered getting into all those details, but his secret had been exposed. Who knows, perhaps Husam Hilmi had something that might be useful to him for writing his novel? Abbas, the driver, was steering the car skillfully along a road full of potholes and ruts without interrupting. He didn't understand that sort of idle talk.

He tried to explain to Husam one side of his concerns in his writing. "When I started to write, I had an obscure idea. My life in the camp was the starting point, the spark, so to speak. I didn't have a focus for the novel in my mind, I mean there wasn't a clear focal point you could put your finger on and say that's it. There were several intertwined things, threads that hadn't yet become clear, scenes and some ideas. Things of that sort."

Husam was listening to him with interest.

"Perhaps you find what I'm saying strange. But that's the truth. As I wrote, I was feeling like a man lost at sea, buffeted by the waves. Sometimes I would see lights glimmering, and would start to swim toward them to reach dry land. But these deceptive lights would soon disappear, only to appear again, in some different place, on another imaginary shore. But despite the confusion, and the feeling of something like despair, every sea has a shore, and the day must come when we reach it, or else," he added with a laugh, "someone comes to save you from your dilemma with a suggestion or an idea."

Husam looked at him with some surprise."

"Perhaps it's not difficult, I just see it that way. The delightful thing about it is that as you write, you discover things that had never occurred to you at all, and doors open in front of you of whose existence you were completely unaware, but they open of their own accord, one after the other."

The sun was setting toward the earth, its rays pouring down through the window beside him, filling the width of his body.

Husam said nothing. He saw him simply smiling, smiling at all those words that had escaped from him in a sudden burst of enthusiasm as he spoke about his novel. Who knows, perhaps fate had brought them together so that he could open a door for him to look through onto a new horizon that would help him to write.

"Husam, sir, what would you suggest? What sort of woman would you like to see in my novel? I don't mean her external shape."

"Look, Muhammad, you shouldn't underestimate physical shape. We deal with people initially on the basis of the impression that their external appearance leaves on us."

As he listened to him, he thought it was unfortunate that Husam didn't have the necessary patience for writing.

"Women, in particular."

Engineer Husam gave him a thoughtful look. "If a woman is attractive, her shape is a trap, a hole you can fall into like a blind man. But I understand what you mean, I understand what you mean." The he fell silent and started to smoke. "So you want a woman for your novel." He was silent for a moment as he looked at him. "Okay, let's imagine an attractive woman, a married British woman who seduces a young Iraqi. After he has fallen in love with her, he discovers that she only wanted him to sow the seed of a child inside her. That was what she had been wanting—though perhaps she wanted to amuse herself with him a little too."

"But you said she was married!"

"Yes, but her husband is a homosexual."

"Why did he marry her, then?"

Husam smiled. "Don't you think you're asking too many questions?"

"The novel has to be convincing. And the reader has to know why the events happened in the way that the author has told them, and not in some different way."

"Okay. For the sake of the reader who wants to know every last detail, you say that he married her for appearance's sake, to hide the secrets of his sexual life, and to get the project management to give him a house where he can live freely, and receive guests at home with their wives without embarrassment. He can appear with her at parties and public functions; if he meets an important person he can proudly introduce her as 'my wife,' and so on. There are many privileges, not available to a bachelor."

"But he doesn't sleep with her."

"No."

The sun was gathering up the remains of its rays from the face of the earth, taking them with it as it disappeared at the furthest point in the desert. So this man didn't sleep with his wife. He slept with men like himself, or else they slept with him.

"But why did she marry him if he wasn't going to sleep with her?"

"You mean why didn't she leave him when she'd become convinced beyond a doubt that . . . ."

"Yes, why?"

"Muhammad, my friend, a question like that would have occurred to *us*. But *they* are practical people, who look at the reality of life in a different way. Abbas, don't go so fast!"

"As you say, sir!"

The driver slowed the car a little. They were now speeding through the groves in Abu al-Fulus village, having put the desert behind them.

Husam continued his description of the imaginary woman. "And why should she leave him if she can combine the privileges of a wife with the lewd behavior of a whore?"

His tone was sarcastic as he uttered these last words. When he looked at Muhammad, he saw him staring at the road.

"I mean, she can have sex with any man she fancies, and she can also become a mother. She just chooses a suitable man to make her pregnant, just like she chose that idiot, that idiot."

Husam repeated the final word with passion, in a voice weighed down with emotion, his eyes on the receding road. Muhammad had the feeling that Husam Hilmi wasn't actually speaking about a woman who was a product of his imagination. He saw him light another cigarette from the stub of his burned-out one; Husam then threw the stub out the window and continued smoking in silence. He respected his silence, and did not ask him anymore questions. The car took them past Abu al-Fulus police station without stopping or dropping its speed. (Cars carrying villagers stopped here to be searched for smuggled goods and fugitives.) The sun had disappeared a short time ago. Abbas turned on the car lights, and after a few minutes the car began to make its way along the street that passed through the center of the village of Abu al-Khasib, moving slowly amid the throng of people and cars, as the packed cafés and shops, with their lamps now lit, receded on either side of them. Husam was smoking and looking at everything in silence. When the car had left the village, with its bustle, its clatter, and its lights, to resume its journey on the winding road between the palm groves on which evening had now descended, he turned his face toward him.

"Hey, Muhammad, do you want a second woman?"

He couldn't make out the expression on his face, for the inside of the car had turned dark.

"Do you have a second woman?"

"I have as many women as you need. A second, a third, a fourth if you like."

"Okay, let's imagine the second one."

"She's a cunning catcher of men, who comes to Iraq driven by a love of adventure. She's heard about Baghdad and the *Thousand and One Nights*, and King Shahryar and all that, so she comes to see with her own eyes. But when she arrives she sees another world before her, a world that has no connection with the world of those strange stories and fables, though despite that she finds it pleasant, enjoyable, generous, as well as (and more important than all that) filled with males. This woman succeeds, with astonishing speed, in making a young Iraqi take her as his wife. But even while she is dependent on our friend, she continues her hobby of looking for other prey."

"And what about the third?"

"No, she's different. She is a good and virtuous woman, who has also married a young Iraqi, while he was studying in Britain, after which he had brought her to Iraq. After his return, however, he slips back into his old life, among his family and friends, and leaves her. He leaves her to her exile, a woman surplus to requirements."

Husam fell silent, and did not elaborate further. He noticed that the so-called imaginary women were all British women who had formed attachments to young Iraqis who had studied over there, that is, they were from the place where he himself had lived and knew well. Were they really imaginary, then?

He saw masses of black palm trunks standing peacefully in the silence of the groves, which were wrapped in what looked like a dark fog (perhaps what looked like fog was the smoke from ovens lit by peasant women to make bread for supper). The darkness was rapidly thickening, as the driver skillfully maneuvered his car over the bumps that followed one after the other. The car headlights illuminated a short space of the road in front of them, lighting up the edges of the plantations and the oleander bushes with their large flowers that emerged from the darkness and flung themselves toward them, almost into their faces, like colored splinters hurled toward the speeding car by dozens of hands.

"This road's beautiful, I like it a lot. You can't see anything in the night, but during the day . . . ."

"But it's dangerous, sir," interjected the driver in a murmur. "A lot of people have died on this road!"

"Of course, everything that you think so beautiful that you forget yourself in it is really dangerous!"

He didn't know to whom Husam had directed these last words. Perhaps he was talking aloud to himself.

The city of Basra was approaching. Soon they would part. He wished he could find out more about those women whom Husam had sketched for him very briefly.

"And what happens after that?"

"Happens where?"

"To those men and women you've been talking about. What happens to them after that?"

"I wish I knew! But perhaps *you* know," he added in a tone which was light-hearted for the first time since they had started their journey together some two hours ago. "Didn't you say that doors open in front of you of their own accord, and that you discover new things as you are writing?"

When there was a party that they had both decided to go to, he and Bob Macaulay, the cook would be coming and going like a housewife, cleaning suits, polishing shoes, fetching shirts, and obeying last-minute orders without complaint or fuss. He saw him come into the room and put the shoes that he had just cleaned on the carpet beside the bed.

"Do you need anything else, sir?"

He was stammering between his loose set of teeth.

"Abu Mahmoud, why don't you go get that loose set of teeth changed? Mr. Macaulay and I don't mind you traveling to Basra at any time."

"I'm very grateful, sir, to you and the gentleman. But I've gotten used to these teeth."

"As you like. The important thing is that the treatment's been of some use."

"I wish!"

"But you told me the pain had stopped!"

"That was less than a month ago, sir, then it came back just like before."

What sort of black humor was this?

"You mean, you lost all your teeth for nothing?"

The cook held his head down submissively.

"It's fate, sir, just fate."

He was astonished that the man didn't feel angry at anybody, and wasn't blaming anyone. He saw him raise his head as if he had remembered something, his eyes sparkling with new hope.

"Sir, this girl, Wasima, Mr. Fox's maid, told me about a holy man . . . ."

"Yes, Abu Mahmoud, what about this holy man?"

He looked at him, encouraging him to tell him about it as he put his shoes on.

"Wasima says that this man can see what is hidden, can cure any illness, and that he's here on the outskirts of the village. I thought I'd go to him if you'll let me."

He gave him a pitying look. A man who can see what is hidden! But he didn't smile.

"Abu Mahmoud, you can go at any time, and you can spend some time in the village with your family. But do you believe that a man like this can cure you?"

"It is God most high who is the healer, this holy man is merely a go-between. Would you like anything else, sir?"

He thanked him and said that he didn't want anything else, then watched his frail figure leave the room, his jacket falling off the bones of his shoulders as if it were hanging from a coat hanger. They told him to have all his teeth out and the pain would go away, and he believed them. And now . . . .

He put on his jacket, turned the light off, and went out. He heard Bob Macaulay humming in his room. He didn't go in. Perhaps he would find him strolling about the room completely naked, with his private parts wobbling between his thighs. He lit a cigarette and sat waiting in the living room.

"How do I look, old man?"

Macaulay was standing in front of him in a few minutes' time, looking chic in a white jacket and tie, his grayish hair giving him a look of extra gravity. He looked happy.

"You'll be lady-killer number one at the party!"

Bob laughed, delighted, and the pair left the house.

"Bob, you know that our cook lost all his teeth for nothing!"

"Yes, I know, I got up this morning and found him bent over double in the living room, so I carried him to his bed in the kitchen." He spoke in a voice that had lost its merry tone. "Life plays dirty with us sometimes!"

They walked in silence after that. It wasn't a suitable subject for conversation on their way to a dance. They passed the guesthouse, which seemed quiet, with not a sound coming from it. Then they walked past the old club building, which looked neglected, its interior in total darkness, its windows black patches looking out into the night. How quickly places go to pieces once they have been deserted, to be pervaded by desolation. Deserted people go to pieces too, and fall prey to grief, but you are still in the prime of life, as they say, and will not be destroyed by the deceit of a woman. They will repair the neglected clubhouse and make it a habitable home full of warmth once again. And you too will forget what happened. No, he wouldn't marry now as an emotional reaction to Maureen's behavior. Why would she be bothered with an oriental reaction like that?

The sound of the music from inside the club, amplified by loudspeakers, was becoming louder. Macaulay was thinking about the new club building. "I'd have liked the bar to be a bit bigger, but the plan that they sent us from Basra . . . ."

"Bob, please don't suggest any alterations. We didn't believe that we'd ever finish."

Bob Macaulay laughed. "Don't worry. Perhaps we'll find a simple solution to expand the bar area."

He caught a glimpse of vague shapes of men and women hurrying along the paths that branched between the houses, heading for the new Eagle's Nest, which attracted them in an irresistible way. There were a number of cars lined up in the spacious car park in front of the entrance beside the fence. They had removed a lot of palm trees to clear a space for the new Eagle's Nest, with its gardens, swimming pool, and for this spacious car park: they had cleared about five thousand square meters of land of all the trees that were standing in the way of the building. The uprooted palm trees, with their long-dried-up leaves, and their black trunks, lay on the ground in a nearby plantation, like the abandoned corpses of men who had been taken by surprise and perished in a losing battle against an unknown enemy with superior numbers and equipment.

They were crossing the car park when he saw Mr. Fox walking with his wife Jenny, wearing the blue jacket that was all he possessed. Fox and his wife were walking in front of them toward the club entrance. They slowed down.

"I hate the sight of that man!"

"Don't burden yourself hating other people," advised Bob Macaulay.

"But he also hates me, I don't know why."

Macaulay took him by the arm and hurried him up. "No one can hate you, old man. Now, look at how it all looks under the lights! Don't you feel proud that you supervised the building?"

The club front had a simple appearance. It was built of yellow brick and was free of decoration. But after you had made your way through the extensive garden that surrounded it, and stepped inside, the splendor of the building would become apparent. The swimming pool, with its spacious garden and colored parasols, was situated behind the club. You could reach it through the club's rear door, or else enter through an outer gate leading to the palm groves. The swimming pool was surrounded by a high wall to prevent peeping Toms from spying on the women in bathing suits, though some youths actually made hard journeys from their far-off villages to climb the trunks of the palms in the groves surrounding the pool, hoping to catch a glimpse of the body of one of those naked "madams" who had come from overseas. The guard would pelt them with stones, and they would slip nimbly down from the trunks and flee across the groves, pursued by the guard's curses and his flying stones.

When he and Bob Macaulay reached the spacious hall, the band was playing a dance tune, but the dancing had not yet started. Those men and women who had come early had chosen places near to the dance floor. The bottles of drink and the glasses had so far hardly been touched, but shone under the lights on the spotless white tablecloths, so far unmarked by cigarette ash accidentally falling on them, or by drops of drink spilled from the top of a bottle, or from the edge of a cup in a hand made unsteady by alcohol. He saw Dr. Sami and Mona with Akram and Suzanne, sitting at a table on the edge of the dance floor opposite the band, which was in the middle of the hall on a dais.

Dr. Sami liked to have a good view of the scene so as not to miss anything that was going on. He left Bob Macaulay, and each of them went over to his own group. He and the Scot usually split up when they went to parties, though they usually arrived together like a married couple.

"Hello, we've kept a seat for you with us." Dr. Sami pointed to a seat that had remained vacant all this time, waiting for him.

"Thank you. Hello Mona, hello Suzanne!" Then he turned to Akram, "Goodness, what's happened today? You're usually late, like our important people!"

Akram laughed. "No, this is an occasion that merits an early arrival."

"Let's eat before the rush starts," suggested Dr. Sami, "the food may run out later." He waved to a servant. Husam turned round to inspect those seated around the tables. Diana was sitting beside her husband, Sultan, sharing the table with Mark Doyle, who hardly left them, as though he were her second husband. But Sultan seemed happy with his wife and friend.

Some time went by without anyone announcing the start of the long-awaited big party. The local residents, as well as the guests—the foreign project employees who had come from Basra and al-Zubayr—had been arriving at the club continuously; empty tables were being occupied, chairs moved or shifted from their places, and here and there servants were rearranging tables, putting one beside the other to make more room for groups of people who had come together.

One of the servants was busy gathering up the empty food plates in front of them, as Dr. Sami offered them a pack of cigarettes for an after-dinner smoke, when the musicians stopped their half-hearted playing and the noise subsided. Meanwhile, Mark Doyle stood up on the dais in front of the musicians, facing the microphone. Doyle spoke about the efforts of the management, and their constant care and concern for the workers on the project: "And the proof is this beautiful club, which has made it possible to hold a party like this, which will of course be repeated on future occasions. And now . . . ."

Mark Doyle addressed the sea of faces—that eager, multi-headed phenomenon that they call the "party crowd"—that was looking at him expectantly with dozens of eyes, waiting for his sentences and elegant expressions to finish so that they could understand what he meant at the end of it all.

"And now, we will commence our party tonight with one male and one female dancer. After that, the music will stop, the two dancers will split up, and each one will choose a new partner from among the audience for the next dance. After a few minutes the music will stop again, and the four dancers will again split up to get four new partners. And so on, until the dance floor is full. All right? Let's start now."

Doyle turned to the musicians behind his back and signaled to them to begin. "One, two, three!" and the instruments rang out amid the expectant silence. Some moments passed, and no one moved. The master of ceremonies resolved the uncertain situation firmly, as if he were addressing a group of stubborn schoolchildren, "We haven't got time to waste tonight. So I invite Mr. Sultan Imari and Mrs. Diana Imari to start the dance!"

The audience clapped, and some people shouted encouragement from the tables. Diana got up nimbly and went forward to the middle of the dance floor, together with her husband Sultan. Their table that they had just left—with its white tablecloth, bottles, and glasses sparkling with drink—now seemed empty and deserted, as the couple started to fill the dance floor with the vitality of their graceful movements. Diana in particular looked like an angel in her long white dress, her blond, almost silvery, hair, and her silver shoes, gliding gracefully, with supple movements, as her feet barely skimmed the ground. Husam heard Dr. Sami muttering beside him, appalled, "A natural dancer, this whore!"

His wife gave him a disapproving look, and he looked at her imploringly, "Please, Mona, for God's sake, lift the censorship, just for tonight!"

Mona was wearing a red flowing dress, in an attempt to cover her belly, which had quickly swollen—unlike Maureen's, which had not gotten much bigger despite having started her pregnancy at about the same time, early in the new year. Mona's face was flushed, and she was proud of being pregnant, while Maureen, when he had been alone with her on that unforgettable night, had seemed rather pale. Mona noticed his looks fixed on her belly and smiled in embarrassment, so he turned his face toward the dance floor. The music stopped at a sign from Mark, who was still standing on the dais, and Diana separated from her husband. Sultan went and took a lady from one of the tables, while she stood hesitating. Then he saw her come toward him. "Good Lord, get up!" said Dr. Sami, obviously jealous.

Diana took his hand, and led him away with her without saying anything, pursued by Dr. Sami's pained voice and the laughter of the others. "Go on, my lad, go for it!"

The musicians struck up a slow tune this time. She rested her head on his shoulder and they started to dance. He could feel her purposely slipping her leg between his own legs whenever they took a step, and he turned to look at her husband. But Sultan was smiling, fully occupied with his own partner.

"Maureen will leave tomorrow."

He knew that. She had told him so herself, when they were talking on the bed and he was dressing after his rejection.

"But I don't see her here."

"She'll be coming. Don't worry!"

"Why should I be worried? She's no longer important to me."

"Really?"

She clung to him even more. He saw Dr. Sami in the distance looking at him. He had to be careful with this woman. When the music stopped shortly afterward, Diana said to him, before going to choose a new partner for another dance, "I'll see you later."

Husam went and invited Hilda, the fire chief's wife, to dance, a woman that no one normally went near. He wanted to calm the instincts that Diana had awoken in him by her arousing movements. For the dance that followed that, he chose Suzanne, who asked permission from her husband, Akram, before getting up with him. She kept her body away from him as she danced with him, and he held her by his fingertips, as if he was afraid he would damage her, afraid that she would break in his hands. As he danced, he asked her, "How are you spending your time these days?"

"As usual, I'm reading."

He didn't have anything else to talk about with this woman!

"Are you enjoying the books I brought you?"

"Very much. By the way, Mr. Fox asked me to lend them to him to read."

"Fox?" he asked in astonishment.

"Yes. I told him that I would have to ask Mr. Hilmi's permission first."

Since when had this dog been keen on reading novels? He wants to know what sort of books I'm circulating among the quarter's residents.

He saw Suzanne looking at him, bewildered. "Is there something wrong?"

"No, no, give him the books to read when you've finished them. I don't think their owner will have any objection."

It was better that this Fox should see what was in them rather than constructing his own wicked hypotheses. They danced in silence for a few minutes more, then Suzanne said in a quiet voice, hesitantly, "Awsam, I want to tell you a secret."

He looked at her apprehensively. What could she mean? He said nothing, not wanting to encourage her. Perhaps her secret was embarrassing. What would he do? Should he keep the secret then, or tell her husband?

She could see he was bewildered.

"It's not important. I haven't done anything scandalous, and I don't intend to, I just . . . ."

She looked around, a little anxious. Dancers were surrounding them on every side. "This place isn't suitable," she muttered quickly. "We'll talk in the club when Akram is in the billiards room. Is that all right?"

What she was asking involved a sort of conspiracy against his friend, Akram, but he could see a lot of suffering in her eyes, so he nodded his head in agreement. When the music stopped, he led her back to the table.

"You've spared no effort tonight, God help you!" laughed Dr. Sami, welcoming him back. He smiled, then sat down with a gloomy face, while Akram took his wife's arm and led her onto the floor among the other dancers.

Dr. Sami looked at him in surprise. "Our friend Husam is very silent!"

"I'm just watching."

"He's very preoccupied!" said Mona, wickedly.

The number of dancers was growing. The dance floor had become so crowded that their swaying bodies reached the edges of the tables. He noticed Maureen dancing with Mark Doyle, while her husband danced with Diana a short distance away. She was wearing a rather loose frock, but apart from that, there was nothing to show that she was pregnant, in her fifth month, so she said. And she did not seem to have noticed that he was there, the bitch!

"If you're feeling annoyed, find yourself a girl and dance with her!" said Dr. Sami encouragingly. He told him that the night was long and that the party was still just starting. "Yes, everything's just starting. This Mark Doyle's made everybody swing, except for your servant Sami Nashwan, the pregnant lady's husband!" He looked at his wife angrily, but Mona just laughed.

"And who's stopping you from dancing? Dance as you like! Just make sure you choose a respectable woman to dance with. Go on!"

Dr. Sami got up quickly and gave him a wink, as Akram brought his wife Suzanne back to the table. He seemed upset. Perhaps someone had collided with his wife, or said something that he thought was insulting to her, or something like that. But they sat in silence, saying nothing. Then Mona exclaimed angrily, "My God, look!" She was looking at the dance floor in horror. "So that's the respectable woman he's chosen!"

Dr. Sami was swaying happily with Diana amid the packed bodies.

The night wore on and the dancing continued. The music stopped for short moments between one dance and the next, but most of the dancers did not leave their places as they waited for the music to play again. He saw Bob Macaulay always with a woman. Fox was enjoying his time and seemed proud. (Everything the management did, he counted a personal victory.)

Then Mark Doyle, the energetic master of ceremonies, started various competitions, as they left one day of their lives behind, to suck dry the hours of another day amid the sound of the music, and the hubbub of chatter and laughter. The world outside the club walls was disappearing in a murky void, of which no one was aware. Husam was watching the dancers when Diana appeared standing in front of him again, her face flushed with drink and from non-stop dancing. He got up with her and they mingled with the dancing crowd. Sultan, her husband, seemed drunk, and his greasy black hair was hanging over his brow; he was sitting on his own, and the table in front of him was packed with a collection of bottles, most of them empty. His wife's small silver handbag was also resting there beside the glass that she had not finished when she got up to dance. But Diana did not look in her husband's direction. He saw her bend down.

"One moment!"

Then she straightened up, with both her shoes in her hand. "That's better!"

She laughed and threw both her arms around his neck, then started to dance with him barefoot. He could feel the shoes bouncing on his back. He twirled Diana around several times, then no longer felt them on his back. He turned again to see Sultan al-Imari carrying his wife's shoes as he made his way back to his place between the dancers.

"Awsam!" He saw her lift her face in his direction. "Let's get out of here!"

"And go where?"

"To the swimming pool. We could swim a bit, you and me."

"Do you know what time it is?"

"Who cares about the time?"

"But the water will be cold now!"

"Oh, don't be such a coward, come with me."

He was surprised how casual she seemed about her husband.

"And Sultan? Will you leave him sitting here like that?"

"Don't worry. We'll find him in his place when we come back."

They were dancing not very far from the table where her husband was sitting, drinking alone. Her silver shoes were sitting side by side on the tablecloth among the bottles and glasses, and Sultan was giving the gleaming shoes blurred, perplexed looks.

"Hey, what do you say? Will you come with me to the pool?"

He looked at the table where his friends were sitting. He saw Dr. Sami busily cleaning his spectacles, with Mona looking at him, while Akram and Suzanne sat watching the dancers and listening to the music. Diana touched the lobe of his ear and pulled it back toward her. "Come on, be brave, let's go!"

He turned to look at her. "You're impossible!"

"You're afraid I'll keep my promise."

"What promise?"

"To sleep with you."

He laughed, then took her back to her husband before the dance ended. Her suggestion was both attractive and exciting. But it was also reckless , and he didn't want to get involved in a shameful relationship like this in full view of everyone.

Sultan got up unsteadily when he saw them approaching. He smiled at Diana as he handed her her shoes. Husam left her with her drunk husband and went back to his friends. After a little while he saw her dancing with Mark Doyle. This woman was never still for a single moment! But they didn't stay long on the dance floor, just a minute or two, before parting. He thought it odd. Then he saw her slip out of the hall along the corridor leading to the pool, pretending she was going to the ladies' room to tidy her makeup. Doyle was talking to the leader of the band. Then he saw him take the same route, following in Diana's footsteps. So she'd gone to the swimming pool in the end, but with another man! "I don't think she makes much distinction between one man and another, so long as they all have the right equipment," he thought. He would like to see what they got up to there. He sat for about ten minutes, listening absentmindedly to Dr. Sami's teasing chatter with his wife, and to Akram and Suzanne, then apologized and excused himself from the party. He left by the club's main exit as if he were going home. The moon, which had started to rise after midnight, cast its light over everything—the houses, the roofs of the waiting cars, the walls of the club, and the palm trees standing silent in the surrounding groves. The music echoed in the air around him. He walked along the fence that surrounded the club. Perhaps the drivers waiting by their cars would wonder where this man could be going at this time of night. He stood hesitantly at the swimming pool's outer gate. What if the guard saw him? But he didn't notice anyone by the entrance. Maybe the guard was by now squatting in a corner, near a window, sneaking a look at what was going on in the club, just as he was now trying to sneak a look at what was going on in the swimming pool. He stretched his hand through the bars and opened the iron gate, then pushed at it cautiously. The gate did not open directly onto the swimming pool area; there was a wall like a screen that stood in front of anyone entering, about a meter away from the gate. He stood still for a moment in the entrance in the darkness, then stuck his head inside and craned forward to look at the large pool. He couldn't see anyone, either in it or around it. The lights in the pool area were all off, though the water in the pool had a transparent, clear blue look, as the cool moonbeams penetrated to the bottom. The shadows of the two diving boards extended the whole way over the surface of the still water. The place seemed deserted. Where had they gone, then? He turned around and left. He was closing the gate when he heard the sound of a body hitting the water, then another body diving in. He went back in. At first, he could not make her out amid the spray of water flying from under

348

their arms as they beat on the surface of the water. He didn't know which one was Diana and which one was Mark. Then he made her out. She was trying to get away from him by swimming toward the other end of the pool, while he was chasing her as hard as he could. Then he saw her slip quickly up the little ladder and climb out, with water dripping from her damp, glistening body. The moonlight fell over her back and over her bottom and long legs. But where had she got this white swimsuit that she was wearing? Then he realized that she was wearing nothing at all; she was swimming naked, and the small white triangle that he could see from the distance covering part of her bottom was in fact nothing but the part of her skin that the sun had not burned. When Mark climbed the ladder she ran off toward the showers, with Mark running behind her. He too was naked. Then he saw them disappear into the dark corridor, one after the other, and silence fell over the place again. A strange silence, laden with possibility. The sound of the dance music from behind the club wall was the only noise that could be heard. He shut the gate and went away. He didn't know why he felt that it was he who had been insulted, after seeing her with her English companion in that compromising scene. With him, not her husband, Sultan. She had been sure of herself when she said she would find her husband in his place, guarding her handbag for her, when she returned to him from her evening excursion. Perhaps he wouldn't lift a finger even if he knew the truth of what was happening . . . the fool, the idiot!

He walked by himself along the quiet, deserted paths of the residential area. Another day of his wasted life had begun some time ago.

13

This is a place where a man would like to spend the rest of his life—eating, drinking whisky, and making love! But he felt tired at the moment. He had finally arrived, but he was worn out. He had carried his heavy body all the way from the camp to the managers' area. Only a short distance remained, and he would arrive at the place. He walked forward along the path, looking at the fronts of the houses and sniffing the breeze that blew gently on his face. Even the breeze here had a different feel and a different smell, for it bore on it some of the moisture of the Shatt al-Arab and the fragrance of the palm groves. He could also detect in the evening breeze the smells of the food that the servants were busy cooking for supper in the houses. But he didn't much like food cooked in the western way. Of course, he liked those big pieces of fried meat, but the soggy tasteless potatoes and boiled vegetables that they filled their plates with was fare perhaps more suitable for hospital patients. He didn't know how they could enjoy eating food like that. There was nothing in the whole world more delicious than tashreeb, or a plateful of rice and a bowl of okra stew beside it with a piece of meat in the middle. And after that you would get your drinks table ready, with a good old bottle of arrack in the center. And then you'd feel like the king of the whole world!

He saw a car approaching. Its headlights shone in his face, but he took no notice of them. Since he'd started work in the maintenance division, he'd began to go into the managers' quarter quite freely. He remembered the night of the party (when was it? two, three weeks ago?) and what a party! Anyway, he wasn't going into the area now to spy on them dancing: he'd come for an important meeting with Mr. Fox, a meeting that Daniel had arranged for him.

"Abu Jabbar," he had said to him, "you know the boss's house?"

"Of course. I do most of my work there at the moment, in the houses."

"Okay, he'll be waiting for you at half past eight. I spoke to him on the phone. Don't be late!"

This was the first time he had visited Mr. Fox at home. Much better than meeting him in the camp where Daniel worked. As for going to see him in his office, the risk didn't bear thinking about. He'd be exposed on his first visit. (Muhammad Ahmad worked there.) The house was an excellent place to exchange secrets. If anyone asked why he was there in the boss's house, he had come to inspect a fault that needed repairing. That was his job. He walked on, looking into the windows, then stopped for a little, bent down to his shoes, wiped off the dust from the long walk that had taken their shine off, then straightened up and continued walking confidently. He was wearing a clean jacket, and shoes that he had spent a long time polishing.

"Abu Jabbar, are you going to a wedding tonight?" Hussein Tu'ma had asked him—that ass who was suspicious of everything—while Muhammad Ahmad, who was reading on his bed, had given him a searching look without saying anything.

"I'm going to the village, my lad," he had told Hussein, "I've got an invitation from a friend."

And he'd left the room before he could hear any more suspicious questions.

The new club stood there at the far end of the area, wrapped in almost total silence. No sound of music echoed outside its walls, no chatter, no movement of cars in front of the entrance or in the car park. People coming from a distance came by car, but the local residents generally came on foot from their houses nearby. But he wouldn't be going there tonight; he had to turn off now, for Mr. Fox's house was crouching among the palm trees at the end of the path, almost set apart from the other houses.

He threw his cigarette stub to the ground and crushed it underfoot before walking into the garden of the house. He didn't know why he felt slightly afraid. He found the house quiet; there were no voices or other noise. In the distance, he could hear barking from the villages lost amid the vast plantations, and perhaps from the camp. A frog was croaking from its hiding place in the garden grass, but it soon stopped apprehensively, as if it suspected that there was someone spying on its nocturnal world. He stood on the doorstep and touched the bell with his fingertips, then started to wait. He looked around the little garden; there were some rosebushes and rectangles of yellow and white summer flowers. Then the door opened and the maid looked out. He was struck by her prominent features.

"Is the boss in?"

"Who are you?"

She was a short, plump woman, not yet thirty, but goodness me, what a face!

"I'm Abu Jabbar. The boss is expecting me."

He spoke his words in the ringing tone that he usually used for addressing people who worked under him, as he towered over her with all the air of dignity he could muster. The maid smiled. "Are you the foreman?"

She didn't seem to care, but he felt some pride when she asked if he was the foreman. The boss must have warned her he was coming. He buttoned up his jacket, getting ready to meet the manager.

"Yes, I'm the foreman."

He saw her come out of the house and shut the door.

"Come!"

He was astonished at her behavior, and stayed standing where he was, at a loss.

"Come on, follow me!"

He looked at her thick buttocks rising and falling with the movement of her legs. She'd be okay in bed, but where was this woman taking him? She turned around the house and opened a small door for him.

"Come in, please."

He walked sideways to get through the door past her ample body and found himself in the kitchen. He felt humiliated and asked again, uneasily, whether the boss was there.

"Yes, he's here, sit down." She pointed to one of four chairs around a circular dining table standing in the corner of the kitchen. "The boss has a guest."

He found some consolation in her reply. So he'd asked his maid to take him to the kitchen if he arrived. He didn't want his secret to be exposed in front of anyone.

"Ask the boss if he wants me to go now and come back some other time."

He didn't mean what he said, for it wouldn't be easy to walk that whole way again without having some time to rest. But he wanted to show some strength of character in front of her. She looked at his face carefully, "No, wait."

He unbuttoned his jacket, sat down and took a handkerchief out of his pocket. He felt her watching him as he wiped the damp sweat from his face and neck.

"Thirsty?"

He saw her open the fridge. He saw the shape of her rounded buttocks as she bent down and her head disappeared behind the door. She was okay, she had an attractive body! She closed the fridge door, came back to him with a glass of cold water in her hand, and put it down on the table. As he was quenching his thirst, he heard a man chuckling inside the house. Perhaps it was the guest the maid had mentioned—a guest who would now be sitting comfortably drinking whisky and chatting amiably with Mr. Fox in the living room. The maid came in with a bowl containing four potatoes and a knife, and sat on a chair opposite him. She sat down in a friendly way, as if she were sitting with one of her fellow servants from the area. Peeling one of the potatoes, she asked him, "Do you work with Mr. Sultan?"

"Yes," he replied curtly.

She smiled at him in a friendly way. This woman was in need of a man to dampen her burning ardor. If only her face were not so ugly! He had once heard that prostitutes in one country in the east would hide their faces from their clients, perhaps out of a sense of decency, and only reveal enough of themselves to perform the act. Perhaps there was someone uglier than this maid among them, but no one would know.

While he was mentally undressing her, she was saying, "The water in the bathroom is not running very well these days!"

Everything around her in the kitchen was gleaming under the light: the walls covered with white chipboard, the fridge, the electric oven, the cupboards, the utensils lined up neatly on their stand, as well as those hanging on the walls. Everything was gleaming, inspiring a sense of joy, though the woman herself seemed like an alien body that had landed there by mistake. "But the boss didn't speak to Sultan," he said, gazing at the kitchen equipment, "I mean, about the bathroom."

"He imagines it's a simple matter and that I can fix it myself. He wants me to work for the sewage department as well as being a maid."

"And is it a complicated matter?"

The pieces of potato were falling from the edge of the knife and gathering at the bottom of the bowl, moist, yellow and clean, one after the other, beside the potatoes that had not yet been peeled.

"They say the reason is that the big sewer won't drain the water properly, the sewer near the new club, that is. They say it's blocked."

"Really?"

"The servants say so."

He looked at her with some irritation, "Is this guest going to stay much longer?"

"I don't think so. He's been here since this afternoon. He's the transport manager. His wife's away and he sometimes comes here."

She seemed to have made up her mind to let him in on some of the local residents' secrets. He obviously liked hearing gossip; he liked uncovering the secrets of the people living here, but not now, for he'd started to feel that Mr. Fox was ignoring him entirely. This maid would like him to sit with her the whole night, so that she could gossip to him and rain her hungry looks down on him.

"Does the boss know that I've come?"

"Of course he knows!"

He heard a woman's voice calling from inside the house as she approached the kitchen.

"Wasima, Wasima!"

The maid abandoned what was in her hands and jumped up.

"It's my mistress!" He got up as well, and stood waiting politely, as Mrs. Fox came into the kitchen. This was the first time he had seen her close to, in such a bright light. She was a little shorter than her maid, fair and pale, with hair like dry grass. She was no less ugly than her maid. (How had they come together?) Mrs. Fox was carrying a small black dog in her arms.

"Wasima, leave. . . ."

She noticed that Abu Jabbar was there as well. "Oh, I'm sorry, are you still waiting here?" She held the dog out to the maid. "Put him to bed."

The maid went out with her mistress's dog, and Mrs. Fox looked at him. "I'll ask Tom not to keep you waiting any longer."

"Thank you, madam!"

"Don't stand like that, sit down, sit down."

He did as he was told and sat down. He felt pleased to be receiving all this attention from the manager's wife. How nice this woman was! He stayed sitting on his own. He thought of smoking, but he didn't want to pollute the air in the kitchen with cigarette smoke, and Mr. Fox might come in at any moment: it wouldn't be right for him to see him sitting smoking. He heard some talking, then the sound of the front door being shut. Perhaps the guest had finally left. Yes, he had left—those were his heavy footsteps approaching. He quickly stood up to greet Mr. Fox, who came into the kitchen, pipe in mouth.

"Hello, Abdul, I've kept you waiting a bit."

"Never mind, sir!"

He was waiting for him to invite him into the drawing room, but Mr. Fox drew up a chair and sat down at the table in the kitchen as well.

"Sit down, Abdul."

He sat down again where he had been sitting before. The potato peelings were wrapped around each other in a little heap on the table surface in front of him, next to the bowl that the maid had left as she took the dog out to put it to bed. The boss took the pipe out of his mouth but continued to hold it.

"How are you? Are you happy working for Mr. Imari?"

"Yes, sir!"

"Great, good. Now, what's the news, Abdul?"

He looked at the door leading into the house. "Sir, this Fawzi, the drilling rig operator, gossips a lot when he's drunk."

"I don't understand. Explain. What do you mean, 'gossips?'"

"Sir, when he's drunk, he curses himself, slanders the management, and slanders the whole world!"

Mr. Fox looked at him somewhat impatiently. "Look, Abdul, listen to me carefully. I'm not interested if he slanders the management or slanders the world. What I want from you is to know what he intends to do!"

"As you say, sir!"

"Do you have anything else?"

"Yes, sir."

The manager turned his gray eyes on him as he waited for him to explain what he had.

"In regard to Hussein Tu'ma."

"You mean this fellow who tried to stop the workers attending the project party in the camp?"

"That's him, sir. I've noticed. . . ."

Suddenly, however, the maid burst in on them. She retrieved the bowl from off the table, then came and cleaned the potato peelings from the tabletop. She moved quietly, but her presence with them in the kitchen made him uneasy. Perhaps the maid would go and gossip here and there with the house servants, and the news would become common knowledge. He heard Mr. Fox tell her to leave and saw her going out of the kitchen in silence.

"Yes, Abdul, carry on. What's been said to you about Hussein Tommy?"

"Tu'ma, sir, Hussein Tu'ma."

"Yes, okay, carry on."

"Sir, I've noticed him behaving strangely the last few days, and going down to the village a lot. He goes almost every day."

He didn't understand why Mr. Fox wouldn't bring the matter to a head, and say to this Hussein, "Gather your clothes, and goodbye. Find a job for yourself somewhere else, far away!"—and then he could have a rest from watching him!

"Look, Abdul. I want to give this lad a bit of rope, so that I can track down all his friends. Then you'll see how he hangs himself with no assistance from anyone."

He didn't understand what Mr. Fox meant by saying he wanted to give Hussein a bit of rope to hang himself with. Mr. Fox put his pipe on the tabletop, then looked him in the face. "Abdul, do you know what I want you to do?"

He looked at him attentively so as to take in his new instructions.

"I want you to slander me in front of Hussein Tu'ma."

What sort of talk was this? He looked at him in shock. "Really, sir, would I dare to do that?"

"As I said, I want you to slander me, slander the project management, and slander Britain as well."

He looked him fearfully. "May my tongue be cut out, sir, if. . . ."

Mr. Fox interrupted him angrily. "Abdul, don't be an ass. You haven't a brain in your head!"

He looked at his red face in bewilderment. "When you abuse me and the project management, Hussein Tu'ma and the others will relax and speak freely. They won't hide anything from you."

If this was the aim, he would try.

357

"Okay, sir, as you order me."

He sat with his eyes to the floor. Abuse the manager himself! He would find that difficult, like a believer forced to blaspheme against God. The black pipe was lying on its side on top of the white, polished table, sending its odors into the kitchen air. He saw Mr. Fox's hand stretch out to the pipe and lift it up.

"Great. Have you anything else?"

He was expecting this moment. He reached into his pocket and took out a folded piece of paper. "Sir, these are the names of some of the books that Engineer Husam Hilmi has been borrowing from Muhammad Ahmad."

Mr. Fox took the piece of paper from him, read what was on it, then put it down on the table almost dismissively. "These books aren't important."

He felt like a total failure. After all that effort—the days and days he had spent watching, deceiving, pretending to sleep, and waiting for his chances until Muhammad Ahmad left his room so he could hastily rummage in his case, look under his pillow, pick up a forgotten book from his bedding, then quickly draw the English titles whose meaning he didn't understand, with the names of the authors, in his unsteady hand, as he listened nervously for any footstep approaching the door of the room. He thought that he would be relaying important secrets that would hasten the moment of the arrogant engineer's final fall, the bastard who had had him transferred from his job and deprived him of the contractors' generous gifts.

He had thought that those books had some connection with politics, but now Mr. Fox was saying that they weren't important.

"Sir, I mean, these books are all . . . ."

"There's nothing in them. I've seen them with my own eyes."

It was a huge disappointment for him. But his appreciation for Mr. Fox's amazing ability to uncover people's secrets and reveal their hidden thoughts had turned into a limitless admiration. He looked at him, dumbfounded. "You saw them, sir?"

"Yes, these stories, Abdul, are just a bit of harmless talk."

He sat there in despair, not knowing what to say. Mr. Fox, however, awoke him from the sudden state of stupor that had befallen him. "Abdul," he said, "I want you to watch my translator. I don't want my own employees forming relationships."

But that wasn't his intention. "Okay, sir," he muttered in a voice that sounded lukewarm despite himself. "I'll watch him."

"That's it, then. You can go to the camp now, Abdul." And he got up, to make him aware that his presence was no longer necessary. Mr. Fox was going back into the house. He hadn't given him anything this time, not a bottle of whisky or anything else. He hadn't even offered him a cup of coffee (God bless the maid who had given him a glass of water when he arrived). The boss was generous when he was in the warehouse that belonged to the project. In his own house, though. . . . He made his way through the garden dragging his steps wearily. He had to walk the whole way back again. He heard the solitary frog hidden in the grass croaking. It didn't stop this time when it heard his footsteps but carried on chattering loudly. He walked on in the darkness of the night in his frustration, thinking about what Mr. Fox had said, instructing him to slander him in front of everyone!

14

He stretched his bare legs out under the table and sat there smoking, in a relaxed mood. Beside him sat his wife Mona, with her enchanting face that had become even fresher and more radiant as a result of her pregnancy. They were sitting at one of the tables scattered around the swimming pool, under a large colored parasol, he in swimming trunks (though he hadn't been into the water yet) and she in a loose dress that covered her swollen belly. They sat watching the swimmers, as they listened to the chatter, children's shouting, and the splashing of the water. Mona was busy knitting. In around two months' time, after waiting a long time, they would have their first child. He didn't know why she was tiring herself out making these little clothes, when she could buy all the clothes she needed for the baby from the shops in Basra or Baghdad. Perhaps she enjoyed making an effort that made her aware of her imminent motherhood. He looked at her tenderly. She noticed his long stare and smiled gently. "Are you feeling relaxed today?"

"So far, yes!"

Today was Sunday, which was also his day off, though his leisure hours—unlike those of other people—were always mingled with a feeling of anticipation, of fear that they might be spoiled at any moment by people asking him to come for some urgent case, for urgent cases only arose on rest days or off-duty periods. It was as if people deliberately postponed them in order to upset his life: poisonings, accidents, injuries caused by stupid quarrels, appendicitis, all the afflictions of the world seemed to come to the surface on his days off, and most of them came from the workforce, from the wretched camp, and sometimes from the servants in the residential area. The camp was a focus for diseases and health problems that needed a full hospital with medical staff and equipment, not a single doctor and a small clinic with two beds for emergencies. He felt Mona's fingers touch the flesh on his arm. "Don't brood! Enjoy your time. God willing, nothing will happen today."

"I hope God is listening to you!"

The sky was clear, the clear blue that we see when we look at it through palm trees on a summer's day. It was reflected in the swimming pool in front of him, where the color was intensified by the blue marble covering the bottom and sides of the pool. There was a warm breeze, carrying on it a mixture of the smell of chlorine from the water in the pool, and the smell of grilled food from the outdoor kitchen at the edge of the garden, where they made tikka and kebabs on a coalfire on a rectangular barbecue raised about a meter above ground level, under a small roof. The palm trees scattered around the surrounding garden moderated the heat of the sun a little, throwing their shadows over the turfed ground. Everyone in the swimming pool around him seemed happy. Suzanne, in her bathing suit, was trying to teach her two children to swim in the children's pool, with her husband Akram far away as usual, sitting with the transport manager, John Sullivan, under a parasol, while Mr. Fox was crossing the pool from side to side, swimming slowly, as he moved his arms and legs under the water like a large tortoise. His wife, Jenny, with her small, thin body and her flat chest like the chest of a sick child was gossiping with Hilda, the fire chief's wife, around one of the tables. Some other local residents were moving around in the water or at the sides of the pool, while others, in light clothing, were sitting relaxing under the parasols. The club servants, in full uniform, were coming and going with the orders, carrying bottles of beer or plates of grilled meats. He was smoking gloomily when he noticed Diana emerge into daylight from the corridor between the toilets. Without thinking about it, he sat up straight. She was wearing a green bikini with small yellow flowers on it, surrounded on every side by a white line of flesh that had escaped the sun. He saw her walk forward with her tall, elegant frame, followed by her husband, Sultan al-Imari, and Mark Doyle, the electrical engineer. He watched her greedily as she walked slowly forward. It was apparent that she was fully aware of the extent of her seductive effect on men, whose looks almost turned into hungry fingers fondling her naked flesh, as well as her provocative effect on women, some of whose stares resembled needles trying to prick her body from anger and jealousy. Mona, fortunately, was busy with her knitting, or so he thought. Speaking to himself, he begged Diana, "Come this way, come this way, you queen of whores!" But unaware, she ignored him, and headed for the other side of the pool. She stood for a moment looking at the swimmers; then he saw her lying on her front in the sun, near the edge of the pool, halfway between the two ends, while Sultan and Mark climbed onto the diving board and hurled themselves into the water, one after the other, as if they were competing to show off their diving skills in front of her. But she didn't look in their direction. She shut her eyes and exposed her half-naked body to the rays of the sun, wanting to acquire still more tan despite the heat of the air. He hadn't imagined that she could be so stubborn or persistent. Suddenly be heard his wife, Mona, telling him off. "Sami, your eyes are popping out of your head!"

He turned to her, embarrassed. "No, you're imagining it, I'm just . . . ."

"You just want to gobble her up with your shameful stares!"

He tried to turn her attention to a different subject. "Look who's arrived, it's Husam!"

"Excellent, at least he'll keep you occupied."

He looked at her and laughed. "Husam? Have you forgotten what the maid said?"

"He's a bachelor."

He would have liked to have said to her, "Don't make me feel regretful," to provoke her a bit, but he was afraid that she might be annoyed, as she was now pregnant. Husam was now standing close by, wearing a white, open-chested shirt, shorts, and rubber sandals, and carrying a small bag in his hand. He put the bag down on the ground and sat down.

"Hello, Mona. Are you getting ready for the baby already?"

His wife smiled proudly, and he pretended to be cross. "We've been married more than five years, myself and this woman, and I've never ever seen her knitting a sweater, or even a scarf, for me!"

Husam laughed. "Are you jealous of your son?"

"No, but a little attention to the father is essential. Or have we become surplus to requirements?"

She smiled sweetly at him. "Okay, doctor. You're really . . . ."

"That's it; they grab us with sweet words!"

He puffed his cigarette and sneaked a quick glance at the body resting in the sun on the other side of the pool, then looked at Husam. "Listen, my friend! Never believe that you can get the better of a woman. Just bear that fact in mind!"

He noticed an absentminded look in Husam's eyes. He wasn't looking at Diana.

"Are you with me?"

"I hear you!"

Akram Jadallah was approaching, so he tried not to smile. He saw him give him a cold look and heard him greet Husam and Mona but ignore him as he went his way toward the children's pool. Husam turned to him, puzzled. "What's up with Akram? Has something happened between the two of you?"

Mona lowered her head and busied herself with her knitting.

"I'll tell you about it later. Won't you swim?"

"Just a moment, while I get changed."

He saw him take his bag and walk toward the showers. Shortly afterward, he heard his wife ask, "Do you have to expose the man?"

"I'm not exposing anyone, darling."

She shook her head in despair. "Anyone seeing how you behave wouldn't believe that you were a man of over forty, and a doctor, for God's sake!"

He looked at her, his patience exhausted. "Amazing, how you go on! Weren't you angry with him because whenever he saw me he would shout his stupid expression "Your dick, Dr. Sami"? And I promised you I'd make him stop!"

"Like this?"

"With Akram, no other way would work. He's a man who won't change his ways unless it's due to a powerful shock."

She carried on knitting in silence. She put out her cigarette in the ashtray, and spoke to him in a friendly way this time. "I've heard that his wife will be traveling with the children."

"Yes. She'll be visiting her family, then coming back."

"I've got a feeling that if she leaves, she won't return."

"And where did you get that idea from?"

"From the way Akram behaves with her."

He saw Husam come out of the changing rooms in his trunks and wave at him, then head for the pool. He got up to join him, but Mona held him back.

"Sami, do you really believe that if she goes, she won't come back? I'm talking about Suzanne."

He hadn't imagined that she would be bothered by this sort of news. He stretched out his hand and stroked her hair.

"It's just a feeling. Most likely she'll come back. Who knows how a woman will behave?"

He left her in her sulky mood and went over to Husam, who was waiting for him at the end of the pool. He was standing in the water holding one of the rungs of the small steel steps. He got in too. Despite the warm breeze and the July sunshine, the water was still a little cold from the previous night. He looked at his body under the water. It looked short and wide, with a bloated stomach. But even without the distortions produced by the refraction of the light in the water, he still didn't have a body that could arouse the interest of a woman like Diana. Her gorgeous body was still lying flat over there, glinting in the sunlight, a sight for every preying eye. This woman would roast if she stayed where she was much longer. But it seemed she was immune to sunstroke.

His hands moved in the water, but he remained firmly in his place. He gave a sigh of distress. "Come on, Husam, let's swim. I want to flex my muscles!"

They started hitting the water, heading for the other side of the pool, but Husam was soon outstripping him by a long way. A young man! When he reached the other end in due course, he grabbed the edge of the ladder and stood panting, while Husam continued swimming without a break, covering the length of the pool a second time. Diana had finally gotten up after having had her fill of the sun, and gotten into the water. He saw her joking with her husband, while Husam was thrashing the water with his sturdy arms, making his way back to him. She was striking the surface of the water with the palm of her hand, making a torrent of water fly up in the face of her husband as he tried to grab her hand. Then he saw her stop playing with him, get out of the pool, and climb on to the diving board. He watched her as she moved forward gracefully over the plank that started to seesaw under the weight of her body. Then he saw her stand at the end, high above the surface of the water. With her carefully sculpted body, she looked to him like a goddess shining at the heart of the sun, with her slender figure, half naked, above the swimmers' heads, against the background of a clear blue sky. Beneath her, in the pool, the swimmers started to disperse, moving away from the spot where she would land, leaving an almost circular space of clear, calm water awaiting her descent. Then he saw her take off from the edge of the diving board and hover in the air with outstretched arms, her body slightly arched, then straighten up and descend like a shining arrow, piercing the surface of the water in front of their bedazzled eyes. At that moment, more that at any other time, he realized that her husband Sultan al-Imari, who was envied by many people for marrying her, was really a man to be pitied, for this sort of attractiveness only brought misery and suffering in its wake. He waited for her to surface. Several moments passed as he watched the surface of the pool. He glimpsed her occasionally gliding under the bodies of the swimmers near the bottom, then disappearing. Finally, he heard the sound of the water opening up at the other end of the pool. Husam was saying something, but he took no notice of him. He saw her head emerge high above the water, as if she wanted to jump in the air after her way had been blocked by the water. She shook her head and started to swim gently toward where her husband, Sultan, was swimming, as Mark Doyle left his place to meet her.

"Clever at everything!" he muttered, impressed.

"I asked you if you were going to stick to the edge of the pool forever!"

"I tell you, this whore is clever at everything!"

"Yes," said Husam curtly.

He looked at him with a smile. He's avoiding talking about her. He thinks that I don't know what happened between them.

"Tell me, Sami," he heard Husam ask. "What's the story behind you and Akram?"

He gave a mocking laugh and turned to Mona, who was busy knitting under the parasol.

"Didn't he tell you himself?"

"No."

He started to guffaw. "All it is is that I examined him. Then, God preserve him, he got angry."

He saw Husam look at him doubtfully.

"Just like that, just because you examined him?"

"You know that every year, before the management will renew anyone's work permit, they require a full medical examination."

"But that's no reason to get angry."

"Let me finish. Basra asked me to carry out some of the preliminary examinations on Akram, before sending him there for x-rays and analyses."

He saw Diana leave the pool and go back to lie on her stomach again, her damp back with its shapely curves sparkling in the sun, as Sultan, her husband, sat by her head. Mark Doyle was still in the water, not far away.

"And then?"

"Then, I telephoned him, in the most proper manner. The man came and the male nurse sent him in to me. I said hello, how's Suzanne and the children, all the usual preliminaries. Then I commenced the examination. I listened to his heartbeats, took his blood pressure, looked in the whites of his eyes, examined his tongue, looked at his fingertips, in sum I carried out all these small procedures until I was satisfied. Then I asked him to undress. He took off his shirt and vest, put them on the examination couch, and stood, looking at me.

"'Strip, please!' I said."

"He took off his trousers, and remained like that, hesitating."

Meanwhile, Fox was swimming near them. They looked at him moving away like a corpse floating on the surface of the water.

"'Strip, don't waste my time,' I told Akram. So he took off his pants and stood naked in front of me ('Lord, just as you created me'), covering his private parts with his hands placed one over the other. 'Akram, what's this?' I said to him, in disgust. 'Are you shy of me, or do you believe you're the only man who has. . . ?' So he dropped his hands to show me his genitals, and stood there in confusion, feeling embarrassed. I carried on the examination with a serious face. I pressed my finger on the position of the spleen, then moved my hand to his cock and grasped it by the head. He was taken by surprise, stepped backward, and said, bewildered, 'And what's this got to do with anything?' 'Akram, my friend,' I said, 'this is the source of the trouble! You don't realize that most of our afflictions start there.' So he submitted to the examination, which seemed odd to him. I pulled him along by the tip of his cock, gently at first, then more firmly. He felt pain and took a step forward, then I began to pull him, and he walked obediently, while I was having difficulty suppressing my laughter. I walked all round the room with him, until I could no longer control myself. He was furious when he realized that I was making fun of him. He freed himself from me and dressed himself, angrily prattling away. He said he would make a complaint about me to the management, so I told him, 'Go and complain, then!' I knew that he wouldn't dare. What would he say to them?"

Husam laughed, but he didn't seem pleased.

"No, Sami, Akram doesn't deserve it, despite all his faults. I'll have to make peace between the two of you."

"He'll come of his own accord."

"But perhaps he'll be too late. And another thing, my friend, we're just three Iraqis here amid a great number of foreigners, if we leave Sultan out of the equation!"

Husam was right. Their situation wouldn't allow them to be separated because of trivia of this sort. He said nothing, for he missed Akram's mirth and witty gossip. He saw Mr. Fox emerge from the swimming pool and stand on the edge, shaking the water from his body like a wet dog, then head toward the showers. Diana was climbing up to the diving board again. He saw her throw herself into the water. He saw Husam give him a gloomy look, and said to him, incidentally, "I heard that Bob Macaulay has traveled to Britain."

"Yes, for a fortnight. He wants to solve his problem with his wife."

"That means you're living alone in the house?"

"The cook's with me."

"Of course, of course, but you're free yourself to do as you wish!"

"I'm always free!" said Husam, who was in the water up to his neck, his damp hair gleaming in the sun.

"Certainly. But when a man's on his own at home, with no one watching him, it's a bit different."

He saw him give him a suspicious look. "Meaning?"

"Nothing, nothing," he said, backtracking.

He felt an urge to tell Husam that his secret had been uncovered, but he said nothing. The air was full of the smell of grilled meat. He saw some of the pool customers eating their food, still dressed in their bathing suits. He saw Fox leave the showers, having changed his clothes, carrying his towel and wet bathing costume in his hand. Fox collected his wife and left the pool. Husam shook his head, "I've never ever seen that boor eat in the club!"

"He'd eat if the food was free!"

"Are you going to stand in this corner all the time? Let's swim!"

"Just one lap!"

When they returned to their places a little later he remembered something that had happened to him with Fox. "Fox was once standing at the bar. He pointed at the jacket that he always wore and asked me, 'Doctor, can you guess how old this jacket is?' I looked at it. A sound, clean jacket, well looked after. 'About five years, I should think,' I said to him. He laughed, and said proudly, 'Twenty-one years! And the shoes?' He stretched out his foot with a shiny black shoe on it. 'Ten?' I said, uncertainly. 'Twenty-five years!' When he noticed my astonishment, he said, 'As for the shirt, it's still new. Jenny bought it for me about ten years ago, for my birthday, when we were in Haifa.' He started to give a sort of victory laugh because he had succeeded in making his clothes resist time, and hadn't spent a single penny on buying new clothes all these years. 'Tom,' I said to him, 'You're an archaeological treasure! They should have put you in the British Museum in London!' But he didn't smile, and changed the subject of the conversation."

"Let's get out of the water!"

"Wait. Let's watch Mrs. Imari's little tricks."

Meanwhile, Diana had been standing by the edge of the pool, talking to her husband, who was swimming nearby. He saw her bend down, leaning her hands on her knees, her face to the water. While she was busy talking to her husband, who had raised his brownish face toward her, Mark Doyle, who was out of the pool at that moment, slipped behind her back, and quickly placed his dripping hands on her buttocks, over the soaking swimsuit material that clung to her flesh. With one hand on each of her buttocks, he pushed her into the pool. She began to laugh and scream amid the water flying around her, as Mark looked at her, giggling with delight. Her husband, Sultan, was also in high spirits. It was a moment of shared happiness.

"Did you enjoy that scene?" asked Husam, looking at the expression on his face.

"Excellent. Now let's get out of the pool."

"This Mark takes great liberties with her."

"She's a free woman."

"Did you know that he'd resigned from his job and will return to Britain in a month's time?"

"I'd heard. In fact, it was he that told me. He says he's fed up with living here."

He looked at him in surprise. "Even the presence of a woman like Diana can't make living here attractive?"

"He'll find a lot more like her over there, by the dozen. In every nook and cranny. Now let's leave the water, I'm hungry."

But he didn't want to leave his present position. Mrs. Imari was swimming quietly away from her husband and from the place where Mark was standing. She was pretending to be cross.

"I don't know how this simpleton, Sultan, agreed to marry her!"

"Perhaps he thought she was the bridge that would lead him to the heart of the Empire!"

"In my judgment, this Diana is a danger to any man that has a relationship with her."

He gave Husam a searching look that immediately provoked him, "Sami, what do you mean by all these nods and winks? Today you're. . . ."

He interrupted him to tell him the secret that he and Mona had discovered by chance.

"They saw her going into your house at night!"

Husam pretended he didn't know what he was talking about.

"They saw who going in?"

"Here's Joseph, he must be looking for me!"

He felt annoyed to see the barman wandering around the pool looking at the faces, then see him heading toward him. It must be an urgent call to see a patient. It wouldn't be right to leave him to enjoy his day off like the rest of mankind! Joseph stood over his head, "Doctor, telephone! Mr. Fox; he says it's urgent."

Strange. He was here with his wife only a little while ago. And they were well. He turned to Husam, "Goodbye, my friend! Fate has struck another blow!"

But Husam caught him by the arm as he tried to get out of the water. "Sami, one moment. You haven't told me who they saw coming into my house."

"Our maid, Safiya, noticed the lady in the green swimsuit going into your house at night. Bye!"

He left him dumbfounded, and went off in the direction of his wife. She looked at his face and realized from experience that they had called him for an urgent case.

"One of the workers?"

"No, no, Mr. Fox's house this time."

"But . . . ."

He left her confused, snatched his towel, and started to dry his head and body, as he hurried to respond to the call. He passed the showers and went through the gate in the fence separating the pool garden from the club garden. Before entering the building, he covered his shoulders with the towel. The air inside was chilly, and the smooth floor stung his damp bare feet. *I'll get ill myself if they keep surprising me with their urgent calls like this!* Joseph, who had come back, was standing behind the bar holding the telephone receiver out to him. He took it from his hand.

"Hello, yes, yes!"

The broad voice reached him from the other end, urgent and insistent. "Doctor, can you come quickly?"

"What's happened?"

"It's the maid. We came back from the swimming pool and found her in a bad way!"

"What's wrong with her?"

"We don't know. She won't let anyone near her."

"I'll be with you in a few minutes."

He put down the receiver and quickly left the cool club building. He went into the showers, changed his clothes, and headed for his wife. He told her not to wait for him to have lunch if he was late, and waved to Husam, who had climbed out of the pool and was sitting at a table by himself. He left the swimming pool. His bag was in the car, and his car was outside. He wouldn't be long.

Fox opened the door for him himself.

"Where is she?"

"In the kitchen."

He saw Jenny agitatedly rubbing her hands, and Tom Fox seemed angry. Moisture from the swimming pool could still be seen on his hair and beard. Jenny looked at him with a touch of embarrassment. "We're sorry, we've dragged you away from the pool."

He went into the kitchen, while Fox and his wife stayed waiting outside. He found their maid Wasima sitting on the floor, with her back against a cupboard, her short brown legs stretched out apart in front of her on the kitchen floor, and her hands clutching the edge of her dress, while her head, which had fallen forward on to her chest, moved from side to side. She was sobbing. When she became aware that he had come into the kitchen, she jumped with fright, but she didn't raise her head to look at him. He spoke to her gently, "Wasima, I'm Dr. Sami."

She kept her head down and started to cry bitterly.

"What's the matter?"

"I'm in your hands, doctor!"

Her stumbling voice came from between her tears, desperately imploring him. What had happened to her? He went back to the kitchen door. Fox and his wife looked at him enquiringly. "Excuse me, please!" He shut the door in their faces, then returned to his patient. Her tears, her words, her tone of voice, that strange posture, all confirmed that he was not facing an ordinary case. "Has anyone harmed you?" he asked her quietly.

She shook her head as she sobbed.

"Have you harmed yourself?"

Her sobs grew louder.

"How have you harmed yourself? What did you do? Wasima, I'm a doctor. Let me see!"

He stretched his hand out to pull the dress back and examine her, but she clutched stubbornly at the edge of the dress with all the force she could muster, and continued to keep her parted legs covered. He didn't know what she was trying to hide from sight. He didn't notice any sign of blood on her dress or on the ground under her. He remembered that she wasn't a virgin, but divorced. He continued standing over her head, puzzled. It was no use, he wouldn't be able to do anything for her here. He had to get her to the clinic quickly. But what had the wretched woman done to herself?

He left the kitchen. Fox and his wife met him with questioning looks, anxious to find out something about the maid's condition and her strange behavior. "A simple case," he told them, without elaboration. "But she has to be moved from here. Can I use the telephone?"

15
Why So Hot at the Start of the Day?

Hell had opened its gates! Perhaps it was the drink and the misfortune that had befallen him that were making him feel the heat like this. He was almost choking! Three days and nights he'd been drinking, and the muddle was ripping his head apart. For three days he'd been trying to understand, while these sun rays tortured him and the hot air made his head hurt more. Bob Macaulay had told him sympathetically, you can rest for a few more days if you like. Rest? But who could make all this noise in his head a little quieter, just a little? No, no, let me busy myself working, better like that. He made his fist into a small shade that he put over his eyes to shield himself from the sun's dazzling rays, and stood unsteadily by the club. The fat foreman was waiting, and behind him stood two men from the maintenance department. He saw them tottering like patterns on a cloth curtain printed with the sky, houses, white fences, and palm trees—all blown about by the breeze, which moved them away from him, then brought them closer again. He tried to focus on the fat man, who seemed to be standing unsteadily.

"Abu Jabbar, you know your job. I'm in the bar, if. . . ."

This wretched sewage tank—whenever they cleared it, it blocked again, as if they were throwing dead cats and dogs in it! The foreman bowed his head to him and made way for him.

"At your service, sir!"

He still treats me respectfully, even though he knows! He entered the club garden and saw dozens of dead birds lying on the grass, but they surprised him by flying away in fright as he got near. The birds had been pressing their small bodies to the green surface to draw some coolness from it amid the burning air. He walked up the garden path, tottering about, then entered the air-conditioned building. But what was this noise coming from the direction of the bar . . . tak, tak? As he entered the bar lounge, he saw a carpenter at work, making extra shelves for more liquor bottles, with Joseph, the barman, beside him. He recalled that it was he himself who had asked the foreman to send a carpenter here. He put his cold pipe and tin of tobacco on the bar counter, heaved himself up, and sat on one of the high stools.

"Joseph, whisky, double!"

"Good morning, sir."

Good morning, sir, how are you, sir, anything you say, sir, although they all knew! But it was quite comforting that people should show you a little respect when your wife has made you an object of scorn.

The bar lounge was cool and quite dark, for the thick curtain had been lowered over the wide window looking out over the garden, to lessen the glare from the sun and stop the cool air escaping outward. The barman poured him what he wanted then put the stopper back in the bottle to return it to its place. He lifted his trembling hand in his face, "Leave it, leave it!"

Joseph looked at him in slight surprise but left the bottle on the bar counter in front of him. He's surprised to see me drinking whisky so early in the day. He doesn't know that I haven't stopped drinking since the moment when the veil fell and everything was discovered, but what fool was it that said drink makes pain less oppressive? Bob Macaulay had told him, I know how you feel. "Mr. Imari, I understand how you feel!" How could he know how I feel? Did *his* wife betray him and run away as well? But why did she run away? Why? I gave her everything she wanted and didn't object to what she did. He looked at his pipe, at a loss. The bowl of his pipe was full of black ash, and his head too was stuffed with ash. His whole life had turned to ashes. No, no, Bob. If you really want to help me, let me go out and supervise the work. This sewage pipe needs to be opened, and the obstruction cleared, the dead dogs removed, so that the waste in people's bathrooms doesn't get blocked, and then overflow in their houses. An overflow of waste and filth flooding through bedrooms, living rooms, dining rooms, small gardens, paths, the club, the swimming pool, the guest house, the entire managers' residential area. Waste should not have its path blocked by anything. . . in order to ensure free passage for future waste! Abu Jabbar and his crew know their job well and won't need him. He can sit here drinking and thinking . . . trying to think calmly, and work things out properly. But this carpenter has confused us. Joseph looks at him strangely from time to time. Disapproving, questioning, somewhat pitying looks. Does he think I'm mad because I haven't trimmed my beard for three days? Or because my jacket that I slept in looks crumpled and threadbare? He knows everything, of course. My scandal is on everyone's lips. Joseph, may I introduce you to Sultan, the turtur? No, no, better in English. The husband of Mrs. Diana always speaks English. So, may I introduce you to the cuckold, Mr. Sultan Imari, a graduate in civil engineering from the University of Cardiff, currently, and until further notice from the highest authority, supervisor of maintenance works and sewer cleaning! Great! Pleased to meet you. Excellent! Another mouthful of whisky.

"Joseph, are you married?"

"Yes, sir."

"And is your wife British as well? Like my wife?"

Joseph laughed with his long face, a face like a horse.

"No, sir, she's Iraqi, from the North."

He rubbed the bridge of his nose and looked at him. And this Joseph never stays where he is, he keeps turning round, with the rows of bottles behind his back and the carpenter who's working there in the corner.

"One of your own people from the North. That means, when she runs off, she'll go up to the mountains, not fly to Britain."

The barman seemed nonplussed. He simply smiled and didn't know how to reply.

"Sir." He turned his head slowly to the foreman who had stormed into the bar like the angel of death. What did he want now?

He looked at him in annoyance. "Yes, Abu Jabbar, has your wife run away too?"

"Sultan, sir, the two workmen that went down into the sewage tank . . . ."

"What's happened to them? Have they run away?"

"Sir, they went down one after the other, but they still haven't come out!"

He looked at the enormous figure standing unsteadily on the ground.

"Don't worry, Abu Jabbar. They'll come out. Where do you think they can have gone? To Britain, through the sewers?"

The foreman seemed disturbed as he stood in front of him with his arms folded, his bloated belly hanging in front of him.

"Sir, but it's been a while. I'm afraid they won't . . . ."

Why does this man insist on being tiresome, both in appearance and in what he says?

"Abu Jabbar, don't prattle on. Go, go and wait for them, they'll come out soon."

He gestured to him to go away. He saw him stop hesitantly, looking at Joseph and at the carpenter in confusion, then leave the bar lounge. He turned to Joseph.

"Joseph, your wife, can she dance European style?"

"No, sir, in the North we dance the dabka."

He looked at his cold pipe lying in front of him and sighed sadly. "Diana was the best dancer of all!"

He swallowed what was left in his glass, then looked at his face reflected in the polished surface of the counter. It seemed enigmatic and confused. The carpenter was hammering on his head. He looked at him angrily. "Work quietly, my lad!"

"Yes, sir."

He picked up the bottle carefully and filled his glass. Some of the liquid spilled outside the glass, and the barman quickly wiped the counter.

"Look, Joseph. My father, Fawwaz, God have mercy on him, used to say to me, 'Sultan, my son, if you want to succeed in life, join hands with the strong.'"

Joseph was listening to him attentively, his hands continually moving like two small animals, cleaning the glasses, polishing the bottles, and wiping the shelves. He felt happy to be talking about his suffering to a man who seemed to understand.

"He told me, 'Sultan, my son, the strong are the only people who can be of use to you. The weak, people sunk in the mire like us, will take you to the bottom with themselves. Right down to the depths!' Joseph, we, among us . . . I mean, there among the nomads, not in the city, a weak man or a lost man is always looking for a strong tribe to attach himself to, for protection in his hour of distress. Joseph, do you understand what I'm saying?"

"Yes, sir, I understand."

"I said to myself, Sultan, my boy, in the whole of this world there is no tribe stronger than the tribe of Great Britain, mistress of the oceans and the seas. So I attached myself to them and married into the tribe. I married one of their girls, the splendid lady, Diana! But my father, Fawwaz—may a thousand blessings descend on his soul—was wrong, wrong in his calculation! Joseph, if she had told me, 'Come, Sultan, let us travel together,' I would have gone with her. I would have gone with her to the end of the world. I would have left everything—job, family, relatives, and everything here. I wouldn't have minded working as a porter in a railway station over there, or washing dishes in restaurants. But she didn't tell me, she didn't tell me . . . she just betrayed me mercilessly."

He was drinking from his glass when the foreman burst into the bar again like a madman. "Come with us, sir, may God preserve you!"

He looked at him through cloudy eyes. He saw his bloated body circle around the lounge door, which was also revolving.

"Sir, I've been waiting for more than a quarter of an hour. There's no sound and no movement. Sir, I mean it's not logical . . . all these . . . !"

"Don't worry, Abu Jabbar, don't worry."

But the foreman stayed where he was, his bloated face flushed from the sun, the heat, and from worry. This man was not going to leave him to think about his problems today. He was disturbing him every few minutes.

"Sir, tell me what I should do," he heard him say, imploringly. "I can't go down to look myself."

"Of course you can't. With that body? Joseph here is slim. He can go down and look. Joseph, go with him, and look for the two men in the sewer for him."

But Joseph excused himself, "Sir, the bar! How can I leave the bar?"

"True, true. And also, I need you here."

He turned to the carpenter, who was trying to work as quietly as possible. "That lad, the carpenter, what's his name?"

Abu Jabbar turned to the carpenter. "That's Istifan, sir."

"Istifan, come here."

The carpenter left his hammer and nails and came out from behind the bar. "Yes, sir?"

"Come closer to me."

The carpenter stood closer to him, and waited politely.

"Istifan, are you a man?"

"Of course, sir."

"I mean, your wife doesn't leave you and run away?"

"I'm not married yet, sir."

"Even better. Look, Istifan . . ." He tried to put a friendly hand on his shoulder as he spoke to him, but his hand fell into space. "Look, I want you to go with this man, the foreman, and go down into the sewer—I mean the tank—and find out where these two men have run off to . . . ready?"

"Much obliged, sir," the carpenter replied without hesitation.

Abu Jabbar took hold of the carpenter's arm to hurry him on. "Come on, my lad, hurry up!"

He saw the pair leave and heaved a sigh of satisfaction. "So that's over!"

He tried to raise his glass, but his hand hit the edge of the glass, knocking it over and spilling its contents over the table. Joseph picked up a damp cloth and started wiping up the spilled liquid.

"Sir, I think you should go home, lie down, and rest!"

He let out a laugh. "Lie down! But the bed's empty, Joseph, the house is deserted and the beloved far away. Haven't you heard, haven't you heard that song of Muhammad Abd al-Wahhab's?"

"No, sir!"

"Okay, pour me another."

He no longer trusted his own hands. He watched the barman's steady hands fill him another glass. He reached for the glass carefully, took a swig from it, then put it slowly down in front of him.

"Joseph, you know, that carpenter was annoying us. Tak, tak, tak, tak! No one could listen to it any longer. It's good he's gone. Now the place is quiet. We've got a rest from him. You and I can talk as we want."

"Yes, sir."

But the barman wasn't listening to him as carefully as he had been before. He was pretending to be listening to him, but he seemed preoccupied, and his mind was wandering.

He was happy to be to talking to him, though, and telling him his painful secrets. "Joseph, at first I said to myself, that an educated man in Europe . . . has to be a 'sport.' You know what 'sport' means?"

"Yes, sir, it means 'games.'"

"No, Joseph, no. If a man is a 'sport,' it means someone like me. He lets his wife be free, to dance, to swim, to make friends, to come and go, and travel as she likes. You know, Joseph, I let her travel to Baghdad, she said she wanted to buy some clothes and shoes, things of that sort, you know. I gave her money, and told her, go, my love! She said Mark Doyle wanted to travel, to take a plane from Baghdad to London. Did I have any objection if she went to Baghdad with him? I said, no, and I spoke to Mark. I asked him to take her with him. I, I myself asked Mark to take her with him. On his way. I asked him myself! Imagine,

Joseph! Joseph, you don't know what a man is capable of doing! What amazing things! When he's a fool! But the disastrous thing, Joseph, the biggest disaster of all is that you don't discover that you were a fool until the axe strikes your neck!"

He saw the barman looking absentmindedly toward the entrance to the bar lounge. He turned his head laboriously. He couldn't see anything there. The club building was quiet, as the cool air circulated all through it.

"Joseph, can you hear me?"

The barman turned his face toward him again. "Yes, Mr. Sultan."

Joseph seemed miserable and preoccupied. Perhaps the story of Diana's leaving him had affected him and made him sad.

"What was I saying? Ha, yes, after that I made a reservation for her in the al-Khayyam Hotel. She said, 'I'll stay for two days, just two days, then come back to you.'"

He took a large swig from his glass.

"On the second day, I contacted the hotel. I had to speak to her. You know how a person keeps thinking. They said to me, the hotel people said to me, sir, your wife never arrived. I was in a state. I mean, could there have been an accident, God forbid? I asked the travel agency. Joseph, you're not paying attention!"

"Sorry, sir, you asked the travel agency?"

"Yes, I asked them. They said the taxi went back. That meant there hadn't been an accident. On the third day, the same response: madam hasn't arrived at the hotel."

He stared for a long time into his glass, looking at the yellow liquid sitting at the bottom, then sighed painfully and looked at the barman. His eyes were moist.

"Joseph, do you know why madam hadn't arrived? Because, because she'd flown to Britain . . . with my friend, Mark. She'd flown, she'd flown, she'd flown!"

He picked up his cold pipe and threw it toward the wall. It struck the wall and fell to the ground—a collection of fragments and ash. He followed it with the tobacco tin, which burst open, spilling its contents everywhere. Joseph was taken by surprise, and his hand stretched forward to move the bottle of whisky and the glass from in front of him. But he didn't want to smash these; he saw some consolation in them. Silence reigned for some moments. He saw Joseph give him a sympathetic look.

"Sir, don't torment yourself. Try to forget. What's past is past."

He looked at him gratefully. He would have liked to have kissed him. "Yes, Joseph, I'll try, I'll try!"

At that moment, however, Abu Jabbar came in with a face on the verge of tears. "Sir, a disaster, a big disaster!"

He looked at him absentmindedly. He didn't understand what Abu Jabbar was talking about.

"A disaster?"

"Come with us, sir! It's Istifan! Now there are three of them!"

The barman's face turned pale, and he heard him say, in a disturbed tone, "Sir, you'll have to speak to the fire department and tell them to come quickly!"

He looked at him in bewilderment. Could something really have happened to the men? Joseph's words about the need to summon the firemen had made him wake up to a reality that had been hidden from him, all the time that he had been busy airing his complaint about the treacherous Diana's behavior. He felt alarmed. He turned to the foreman: "You mean, the three men are still in . . . ?"

Meanwhile, Joseph had brought the telephone, put it in front of him, dialed the number, then handed him the receiver and hurried out with the foreman. He started to mutter into the telephone receiver with a faltering voice, his words garbled and confused, asking them to send urgent assistance. Then he let the receiver fall from his hand. He remained sitting alone, worn out and humiliated, unable to find the strength within himself to go out to see what had happened. One disaster always brings another! But if the three men had choked to death inside the sewage tank, he wasn't responsible . . . no, he wasn't responsible!

16

He drew back the curtain and opened the window. The cold winter air blew into the room, and with it a silence as well, a strange silence like no other before it. The stillness outside was almost total: there were no cars moving on the road, no machines buzzing in the work area, no sound at all. Everything seemed peaceful at this time of the year, this Godforsaken part of the year. Despite the fact that it was late morning, and the sun was covering the earth, the continuous drone and the low hum of the machines—some of which normally worked night and day—had suddenly stopped. A strange silence, of a sort that had never happened before, reigned over the whole area. It was almost like the silence of a graveyard: a silence that would swallow up small sounds—conversations, voices calling, solitary footsteps on the paths—like blotting paper absorbing scattered drops of ink.

Despite the coldness of the air pouring into the room, he left the window open, went into the bathroom, washed, and dressed. As he left his room for the dining room, he could smell toast, meat, and fried eggs. Macaulay was sitting at the other end of the table eating his breakfast.

"Good morning, Bob."

"Good morning, old man!"

Macaulay was wearing trousers and a short-sleeved shirt, and seemed relaxed and happy. He no longer had anything to upset his life, now that he had severed relations with his wife and entrusted his daughter to his elderly mother.

"You've started to sleep late these days!"

"No work," he said, as if to justify his laziness.

"No work, no pay," joked Macaulay, stirring the cup of tea in front of him with a spoon.

That was the expression that the management had waved as a warning in the faces of the strikers to force them to return to work. But the strike was still continuing, and a week had gone by.

The cook, Abu Mahmoud, came and went between the kitchen and the dining table, bringing him his breakfast while Bob Macaulay sat drinking his tea. He stretched and looked at him.

"I'd like to travel to Baghdad, while work's at a standstill."

Macaulay, however, advised him not to leave the vicinity during this period, as the management might think he was collaborating with the workforce, or at best sympathetic to them.

"But I'll go on a day off!"

"Not now!"

In truth, he had realized that already. Fox would take pleasure in holding that sort of slip against him. It was just a thought that had occurred to him and he wanted to see what Macaulay thought of it. He felt a sort of boredom during the day. They had found themselves laid off work with no prior planning on their part. They could enter the work zone— though an action like that would certainly provoke the feelings of the men stationed at the entrances—but what would be the point, at the end of the day? Who would they give their orders to if they did go in, since the men who would carry out the orders were rebelling, and refusing to work, so long as the project management did not respond to their demands? Anyway, he would be the last person to think of challenging the sentiments of those men. There was nothing any of them could do, then—managers, engineers, heads of sections and divisions—except sit at home doing nothing, or kill time in the club, unable to leave the vicinity and travel anywhere else. No one knew when the strike would end and they would be ordered back to work.

Macaulay touched his mouth with the edge of his napkin, then folded it, placed it on the table, and raised his head to him.

"Awsam, tell me . . . did you know? I mean, about what the workers were planning."

Macaulay had been storing up this question inside him for several days. He could see it in his looks: he thought Husam knew something.

"No, I didn't know."

"Didn't you hear any talk, any hints from anyone? I know they like you."

He recalled a conversation from some time ago. On one occasion when he had given Muhammad Ahmad a lift to Basra, Muhammad had explained to him the lines of a novel he was busy writing, and told him that someone who shared a tent with him had suggested that his novel should include an incident with a general strike that brought work to a complete standstill. But that was just imagining an event that might possibly occur, and the conversation then hadn't involved workers determined to stage a real strike, in the land of reality, on a particular day.

"No, I didn't hear anything."

He felt uncomfortable with his slightly suspicious looks.

"What's this, Bob? Do you think that I . . . ?"

"Don't get worked up so quickly, old man! The fact is that the work stoppage wasn't expected by the management."

They had all been taken by surprise; even Fox, the old fox, with all his eyes and watchers, hadn't been aware—or perhaps he had just become aware too late, like the rest of the symbols of authority in the other work areas, in Basra and al-Zubayr. But none of them believed that such a widespread strike would take place, paralyzing every activity in every field. That is why the idiot Fox had lost his head when he saw them leaving in front of his eyes, in full view of everyone, so he'd fetched his rifle and fired at them.

The cook, Abu Mahmoud, was collecting the empty plates from in front of Mr. Macaulay, who had finished his breakfast but stayed sitting there, smoking.

"Awsam . . . ."

He lifted his head from his plate of food and looked at him.

"Would you mind if Abdul goes and helps Jenny arrange a small party that she wants to hold for some ladies?"

He smiled, and looked at him in astonishment. "A party? Has Fox agreed to an arrangement like that?"

Macaulay smiled, and told him she was holding the party to celebrate her husband's escape from death at the hands of the strikers, as well as his release from detention. "It's a party for a small number of ladies; they are all we have left!"

"But Jenny's got a maid!"

"Tom fired her."

"Anyway, it's a matter for the cook. I don't think his absence from the house for a few hours . . . ."

The cook had cleaned the section of the table where Macaulay was sitting and was standing to one side, in case they needed anything.

"And when does she intend to hold this splendid party of hers?"

"After the end of the strike, of course. No one knows at the moment how things will develop."

He turned to the cook, who had heard parts of the conversation. "Abu Mahmoud, would you agree to go and help Mrs. Fox, when she arranges her party?"

"At your service, sir. The madam, Mr. Fox's wife, is a good woman, she and her husband."

He smiled but said nothing, while Macaulay laughed. "Fine, that's everything. No more work for the day!" Then he put out his cigarette in the ashtray, pushed his chair back, and stood up. He stayed standing there with his hand touching his belly. "I'm not going out this morning. Yesterday evening, I started reading a good book by Agatha Christie."

He moved toward the door. As he was leaving the dining room, he farted—a horrible habit he could never stop—then started whistling the opening of Beethoven's Fifth Symphony as he went back to his room to fetch his detective novel. He sat in the living room unable to put it down, as he pursued the shadowy figure who doesn't easily reveal himself to the reader, the elusive murderer who stays hidden until the final moments. Meanwhile, he was hoping that the workers wouldn't end their strike before he had reached the final page of the exciting story. As for Husam, he would go to the club, drink two or three bottles of beer, and chat with Dr. Sami or Akram Jadallah.

"Do you need anything else, sir?"

The cook was still standing behind him.

"No, thank you. And I'll eat lunch at the club."

"Yes, sir, and the gentleman?"

"I don't know, ask him."

The cook left the dining room as well. Husam sat alone, smoking and drinking his tea slowly and gloomily, amid the peace and silence of the room.

A strange thing! No sooner had the work siren stopped the wailing that had become so familiar as time passed, than they had started to live a completely different life, a new life!

There was a festive atmosphere in the club, a holiday or day-off atmosphere. The bar lounge was packed with men—crowding in front of Joseph, the barman; standing in front of the dartboard, on the look-out for someone to play with; or forming groups in the billiards room. Wherever they were, their heads hardly left their hands, as they drank too much beer (usually) and chatted. They were enjoying a long paid holiday. Despite the fact that they were part of the management (as their positions fell in the top band of the employment pyramid), things like negotiations with the workers, confronting the anger that had suddenly erupted, and trying to end the strike by all possible means (legal or otherwise) were all unpleasant tasks to be undertaken now by others. These were the men in Project HQ in Basra—men of Fox's mould, though subtler and more experienced than him at dealing with this sort of sudden obstacle to the progress of the work. These men were trained in the arts of deception and duplicity, as well as concocting previously unheard-of strategies. They were under the command of an expert "trouble shooter" called Mr. King, who had arrived from London two days ago, so Bob Macaulay had informed him. So these men who had turned up at the club in the morning, filling the bar lounge and the billiards room with their merry voices, their drunken faces, and breath that had begun to smell of stale beer, were enjoying their leisure time as much as they could—except for Sultan al-Imari, of course, who was sitting next to the bar counter on his own, looking abandoned, despite the fact that the place was so crowded. After his wife, Diana, had left him, he had been deserted by his English friends; the link that bound him to them had been severed, or perhaps it was he that had chosen to desert them as a sort of expression of anger and feeling of frustration. Husam turned away from him. Looking at Sultan's face reminded him of things that he didn't want to be uncovered. The woman had left; she had taken her charm and her faults and left, and that was it. His secret with her could have remained hidden from everyone, if it hadn't been for Dr. Sami's wretched maid, who had noticed Diana going into his house at night and hurriedly told her mistress, Mona, who had told her husband. He sat at the bar away from Sultan, surrounded by chatter and laughter coming from everywhere. But the Eagle's Nest was empty of women at that time of the day. Anyway, there weren't many women left in the residential quarter, for after the strikers had overturned Fox's car, with him in it, and had been on the point of killing him, the British employees had taken fright, thinking that the enraged men would storm the area and harm their wives. A number of them had sent their wives back to Britain until tempers cooled, things calmed down, and everything returned to normal. The women who were left in the area were now hiding themselves away behind the walls of their houses, only coming to the club in the evening in the company of their husbands. Only men now filled the place during daytime hours, drinking greedily as they chatted about all sorts of things—just as though they were customers at a pub on a street corner in a British town or village on a Saturday evening, or Sunday after coming out of church. Under all the surface jollity and mirth, however, he could sometimes detect in their gloomy looks, and in sudden moments of silence (when someone came in from outside, for example) a feeling of wariness and confusion, and also of fear. No one knew what was going to happen the next minute, or if the workers, in a moment of madness, might invade the managers' quarter, bringing their evil and chaos with them!

He saw Sultan al-Imari approach him behind the backs of the men gathered at the bar. He was holding his glass in one hand, with a lighted cigarette in the other.

"May I?"

There was no empty seat for him to sit on. He saw him push aside someone standing up, a little roughly, and put his glass down on top of the counter. He seemed drunk, and a lock of his greasy black hair was flopping over his brow. He stood for a few moments smoking in silence, with his head bent down. Then he spoke, amid the general babble. "Husam, my friend, I . . . I know . . . ."

He was taken by surprise by this statement. He knew? Had they told him? He looked at him apprehensively. Sultan lifted his head toward him.

"I know . . . that you don't like me!"

He breathed a sigh of relief. "No, Sultan, you're imagining it."

"No, no, I'm not imagining it."

His face had become a lot thinner after the scandal of his wife's flight. Months had gone by in which this man had been ruminating on his sufferings. So he hadn't heard about her visit to him at home. Bob Macaulay had taken his daughter and traveled with her two days previously. He had been getting ready to go to the club, and it was nearly nine. He hadn't heard the doorbell. He heard soft footsteps in the living room, a stranger's footsteps mingling with the cook's steps, which he recognized.

"No, you don't like me. And the doctor doesn't like me. And Akram doesn't like me either!"

The cook had come in, after knocking on the door of the room. He seemed confused. "Sir, the madam wants to see you."

"Which madam is this that comes to the house at night?"

But she had come into the room, pushed the cook out of her way and gone in. She had seemed pleased to see signs of surprise on his face.

389

"It's me!"

"Diana!"

"In the flesh!"

He tried to stay in the present, to listen to the drunkard speaking to him.

"No, Sultan, we . . . I mean, I . . . ."

But what was this madwoman doing there? He had looked at the cook in embarrassment, not knowing what to say to him. The cook himself was confused and dumbfounded. He quickly left the room and shut the door. "Abu Mahmoud," he had shouted after him, "leave the door open!"

The cook had come back and opened the door, then left, while she let her eyes wander around the room, taking it in, and smiling.

"Believe me, I'm not imagining it, I've noticed . . . I've noticed very well, but . . . ."

He saw her walk over to the fireplace. He could see the curves of her thighs, and the lines of her underclothes beneath the fabric of the green dress she was wearing. (She liked the color green: green bathing costume, green dress.) She stood by the fireplace and looked at the picture of his parents. "Did you know that you have a beautiful mother?"

He didn't understand what Sultan was saying. He tried to listen, but Sultan was looking at him expectantly, as if awaiting a reply to a question, or a comment. He wanted to reassure him that he was listening.

"Really, Sultan, you have isolated yourself, and chosen . . . ."

"I confess I was stupid. She was like . . . like a . . . ."

Sultan was trying to find a suitable description for her, moving his hand in the air while his cigarette stub ate itself up between his fingers.

"A barrier . . . a blindfold . . . a wall."

"You mean it was she that . . . ."

Diana had brought her stunning body into his room that night, and he had been secretly pleased. But he was afraid of a scandal. She, though, feared nothing.

"Are you mad? You come here like this, at night, without . . . ?"

"Won't you offer me something?"

Sultan asked Joseph to pour him another glass of whisky. She picked the glass penguin up from the top of the fireplace. "You still keep it? Maureen's present?"

"Diana, I suggest that you leave now."

His voice was weak.

A storm of laughter rose up from the men standing at the other end of the bar, and Sultan was grasping his arm.

"Believe me, Husam, I changed after . . . ."

It had a strange feel, Sultan's hand, as it grasped his arm. But he'd said to her that night, "Haven't you thought about your husband? About the people who might see you coming into my house?"

He'd said that to her, he hadn't been impetuous, no, he hadn't been impetuous. He took a swig from his glass, and she put the bird back in its place, beside the picture of his parents.

"I came to you at night so that no one would see me."

"And the cook?"

She laughed dismissively. "Abdul?"

Sultan lowered his hand from his arm. "I'd like you to think of me as one of you. I am one of you!"

Looking at Sultan's face, as he tried to ingratiate himself, had become tiresome and disturbing. He wished he could leave his place at the bar, and go to sit on his own away from this begging face. Diana was raising her hands to caress his neck and cheeks. After she had lit the fire in his body with the play of her warm fingers, she left him, went over to the door of the room and closed it, then walked toward his bed, put her little handbag on the bedclothes, and started undressing in front of him. He wanted to ask her, "What are you doing?" but he didn't say anything; he was tongue-tied. She took off her dress and threw it on the carpet at his feet, to display the body that he usually saw at the swimming pool during the day. When she had let the last two small pieces of clothing fall, he recognized her as the naked woman that he had glimpsed at night, in that dissolute scene under the moonlight, emerging from the water with her gleaming wet body. She had then scaled the edge of the pool and run away toward the showers, pursued by the electrical engineer, Mark Doyle, who had also been naked that night.

"Come here!"

She gestured to him as she sat on his bed, one leg over the other to hide her private parts. Her clothes were a small, untidy heap of green and white on the red carpet.

"I've never seen a woman as mad as you!"

He had walked over to the cupboard to fetch some protection for when he made love with her. He had to be careful this time. He didn't want to leave children behind him, scattered all over the place. While he was rummaging in his cupboard, he heard her say behind his back, "I've got what you're looking for."

He turned toward her. He saw her small, pink breast appear almost suspended in the air, as she bent down and stretched out her arm to her handbag. She didn't want children, this woman. So she carried her protection with her wherever she went, a mobile brothel! He laughed and went back to her. But he stopped by the fireplace, picked up his parents' picture, and turned their faces to the wall. Then he undressed as well. Sultan, who was still standing beside him, was laughing quietly to himself, laughing and shaking his head. He looked at him indifferently.

"Husam, if you only knew . . . if you only knew what my late father would have said!"

"What would he have said?"

But Sultan resumed his quiet laughter without giving anything away. She got dressed again, then stood up with a triumphant smile.

"I told you, I would get you one of these days!"

Then she left him sitting on the bed, still aroused, and went into the bathroom to wash, rearrange her hair, and put on fresh lipstick. Sultan stopped laughing and looked at him.

"But I've decided to turn over a new leaf."

He lifted his glass. The sight of him standing leaning on the edge of the bar, prattling feebly on, aroused in him a feeling of sympathy, but also of revulsion. Sultan had spoiled his day. He remained at a loss, not knowing how to escape from his embarrassing company without hurting his feelings. He didn't want to cause him more suffering. Finally, an opportunity came when he saw Dr. Sami and Akram Jadallah enter the bar lounge together. He murmured his apologies as he got down from his chair.

"Excuse me, here's Dr. Sami. I want to talk to him."

He saw him turn his head to look at the newcomers though misty, fuddled eyes, his swarthy brow glowing with small beads of sweat. He picked up his pack of cigarettes, pushed away his glass and the near-empty beer bottle on the table, and hurried away from him. He thought Sultan might follow him with his lamentations, but he stayed where he was, smoking, drinking, and recalling his short life with Diana, with its bitter ending.

※

"What's this? New friends?" asked Dr. Sami in astonishment, after he had led him and Akram away from the bar.

"Come on, let's sit down first."

They sat around a table by the wall. Akram rubbed his hands and blew into them. "The air's cold outside. Colder than ever!"

Dr. Sami turned his head to look at the faces around him.

"Akram was wandering around the village. I met him at the club door." Then he waved at one of the servants.

"And you're late too!"

"What can I do? It's my destiny to work night and day, while everyone else these days is enjoying a rest!"

He seemed really worn out, and his eyelids were swollen. The thick lens of his glasses had produced a swelling under his eyes that looked almost like a tumor.

"And the worst thing is that I have to do everything on my own, because the nurses are on strike as well!"

The servant came up to them, and they ordered three bottles of beer. He offered his cigarette pack to the others. Dr. Sami took a cigarette from the pack, and exhaled, clearly annoyed. "Today, I had three cases of poisoning. After Fox shut the canteen in their faces, they

393

started eating at the village market, and you can guess the rest! Then Fox himself came to me, and I changed his dressing."

He looked at him carefully. "But his injury is superficial, so I've heard."

"A straightforward surface laceration."

Dr. Sami bent his body down a little to light the end of his cigarette from the lighter that Husam offered him.

"But Husam, you know how they exaggerate things, when the injuries are *their* injuries!"

Akram did not participate in their conversation. He seemed preoccupied. He lit his cigarette and started to smoke in silence, looking at the darts players at the end of the hall. Husam looked at him for a moment then looked at Dr. Sami again.

"I'm amazed that they released him!"

Dr. Sami looked at the servant's brown hand putting the beer bottles they had ordered in front of them, followed by beer mugs.

"Don't be amazed, my lad. Because if you are, you'll be struck down by the chronic amazement disease that's doing the rounds these days. And don't rely on me to treat you, because this disease is untreatable. God knows! This beer is delicious, it revives the spirit, and I'm in need of . . . ." Dr. Sami took another gulp from his glass, and closed his eyes. "I'm tired, everyone!" Then he sighed. "Now tell us, Husam, what's the story of your new friendship with Sultan al-Imari?"

He turned unconsciously toward the bar. Sultan was still standing there with his short, flabby frame, resting the weight of his body on the bar counter, pressed in between the bodies of the British employees, who dominated him with their tall frames, and their jolly, unconcerned voices.

"In fact, I was sitting on my own, when he came and started telling me how he was wrong, how he'd now changed, and things like that."

Dr. Sami smiled contemptuously. "A man doesn't change between one day and the next. He may change his skin like a snake, but inside he won't change much."

"Poor man," said Akram.

Dr. Sami looked at him. This was the first time he had shown any interest in the conversation taking place between him and Husam.

"You didn't have to see the corpses of the three men the firemen brought out from inside the sewage tank!" exclaimed Sami. "I rushed over there as soon as the call went out. If he hadn't been drunk that day, perhaps . . . ."

He took his glass and started swigging from it as if he were drinking water. He would soon be drunk, and his tongue would let fly.

He saw him put his glass back on the table and give a sigh of satisfaction.

"And in the end, they counted their deaths as a routine industrial accident."

"That's the scandal, not the fact that his wife eloped to Britain with her lover!"

"But what are you trying to prove? That Sultan's mistake regarding the three men that died justifies your sleeping with his wife?"

"I didn't go to her, it was she that came to me."

He saw Dr. Sami waving at one of the servants. "I'm hungry. I'd better eat, then go home to sleep."

He turned to Akram. "What's wrong with you today? You seem sad!"

"It's Suzanne. I haven't had a letter from her."

"The mail will be lying in Basra right now, my friend!" said Dr. Sami, then raised his head to the servant who was standing waiting. "Look, Razzaq, I want the fastest food you have."

"Kebab, doctor."

"You'll make us addicted to kebab, but never mind. Run and bring me a half portion, with the side dishes." Then he looked at Akram. "And perhaps there's a letter there now from Suzanne."

Akram looked at him absentmindedly. "No, I don't think so. If she'd wanted to write, she would have written some time ago. I don't think she'll come back this time."

"Did she tell you that yourself?"

"She hinted at the possibility once or twice."

He saw Dr. Sami looking at him. It seemed he also knew—or perhaps guessed—that Akram's wife had gone there to stay. Silence reigned. He remembered her words. She had wanted him to persuade Akram, when she told him of her decision to leave him, to leave her the children for her to bring up there; otherwise, he would try to join her, and that wouldn't work. He told her that he couldn't interfere in that sort of thing. But he hadn't told Akram what Suzanne had said to him. He justified his silence on the basis that she might have changed her mind; besides, he didn't want to make the relationship between the pair more tense. But she should have written to her husband to explain her intentions. And she didn't have any right to keep the children. His experience with Maureen had made him realize that it wasn't easy for a man to have his offspring be taken away from him like that, whatever excuses there might be.

Dr. Sami blew cigarette smoke into the air, and looked at Akram's miserable face. He shook his head. "Oh dear, we're lonely, sad, and abandoned!"

Dr. Sami was increasing Akram's misery with his ill-judged words. He looked at him angrily.

"My friend, your own wife's gone to be with her family to give birth, and you visited her there!"

"A quick visit, during which I saw my daughter Dunya all bundled up. I don't know what she looks like now, but my wife's preferred to stay with her family."

"Hilla's not so far."

Dr. Sami picked up his beer bottle and emptied what was left in it into his glass.

"And then, this wretched strike!"

"You could have traveled earlier."

"You're right. I put traveling off from one day to the next. But now, the kebab's come!"

He drew his chair back to give the servant room to line up the plates of food in front of him. Husam turned to Akram. "And what were you doing in the village this morning?"

He wanted to change the subject, and steer it away from marital separation and the trials and tribulations of loneliness.

"Have you heard the news about how the strike is developing?"

"What have you heard?"

"It seems that neither side wants to shift from its position."

Dr. Sami stubbed out his cigarette in the ashtray and started to eat. "A battle of nerves, but the results are already known. One day, two days, and the work siren will wail again, and the workers will run like rabbits."

He looked at him a bit doubtfully. "Sami, do you know something?"

Dr. Sami waited for a moment until he had swallowed his food. "No, by God. But I know the management. They'll use every trick the devil has thought of to get the workers back to work—naturally, without agreeing to their conditions."

He stuck his fork into a piece of kebab, and put it in his mouth.

"Perhaps they'll give them some trivial things, so that friendly newspapers can talk about the generosity and magnanimity of the project management. But that's all. This is wonderful kebab! Why don't you eat?"

There was a continuous sound of chatter and laughter, together with the clatter of chairs, and the footsteps of people coming and going between the tables— customers and servants busy serving their customers' orders. Mr. Durham, the fire chief, passed them, holding a glass of beer in his hand. He didn't speak to any of them, or smile in anyone's face. He didn't even greet Dr. Sami, as if the chairs he was passing were all empty.

He looked angrily at the back moving away from them. "Did you see how the dog deliberately ignored us? They are suspicious of us, as if we were in league with the strikers."

Dr. Sami's expression continued to be relaxed. He wasn't affected by Mr. Durham's impolite behavior. He started to prepare a new mouthful for himself.

"A predictable reaction, my lad. We all share the same dirty blood!"

He slowed down a little, to put his food in his mouth. After chewing it, he raised his eyes to him. "And don't think you can get away with your rather light coloring. Your blood isn't blue!"

He smiled and watched him swallow his mouthful with pleasure, then wash it down with a swig of beer.

"But the tragedy, Sami, is that the strikers are suspicious of us all. We're like aliens, who don't belong in either camp."

Although he had known Dr. Sami for nearly a year and a half, he could not work out what was really going on in his head. He seemed to have a good knowledge of the situation, but it was difficult to fathom where he stood. He was for and against every side at the same time, cursing the strikers and the management together. His amicable way of talking would allow any interpretation, and did not commit him to anything in particular. That way, his quiet life could not be exposed to serious danger.

Akram had returned to his daydreams while Dr. Sami looked toward the bar.

"Your new friend is smashed out of his mind!"

Sultan was swaying as he left the hall, not looking at anyone, his hand groping the walls.

"He's a veteran of the sad and deserted club! And now he'll go to his empty home that the houri has abandoned!"

He turned to Akram. "Let's go to the billiards room, and play a bit, if we find a chance, and let him eat on his own."

He wanted to get him away from Dr. Sami's prattle, which made him feel sad. They finished their glasses; then he took his pack of cigarettes and lighter, and they got up.

Dr. Sami shouted after them, raising his glass, which had a little liquid left in it, "Today, for me, beer and kebab; tomorrow, worry and anxiety!"

Akram laughed. He was pleased to see Akram laugh at last. Someone like him couldn't bear being miserable for a long time. He would forget that his wife had left him when the strike ended and he was busy with work problems again. Perhaps he'd then marry an Iraqi woman who could put up with his whims and moods. Perhaps. And he and Suzanne would forget the experience of their failed marriage, as each returned to live in their own private world again, though naturally with some scars. But time would soon hide these as it followed its eternal course. Meanwhile, Akram's two children would be lost in that strange world, just as his own son, whose features he still didn't know, had been lost.

17

The sky, like his soul today, was black and gloomy, but was holding back its tears. Since coming back from Basra at midday, the sky over his head had been closing in. Something heavy was lying over the land, and pressing on his chest. Fear, like a fever, was flowing through his arteries and veins, a fear of a sort he had never experienced before. Had one of the workers discovered his role—his and the others'—in the operation to abort the strike? And even if they hadn't discovered it so far, how long would this secret remain hidden, and their names unknown? It was Mr. Fox that had got him into this mess! He had thought that his role would remain limited simply to relaying news, not be asked to expose his whole life to danger. What was the point of the delights and benefits of this world, if his own life was on the line? He should have refused something like this, but his subservience to the boss had already reached the point where it had become too difficult for him to disobey an order from him. So he'd gone to Basra and carried out his mission, with some other people, men drawn from the workers themselves, whom the management had brought from various regions. The plan had succeeded, and the strike was quickly ended; they had thwarted it by a single decisive blow. He had returned to the camp, having stayed just one night in Basra; this morning, he had stuffed himself into a bus—him and Jirjis, the chief clerk who had gone with him for the same purpose—and returned to the camp. They hadn't seen the massacre that had taken place in the al-Hakimiya district in the morning; they only heard some bus passengers talking about it, and perhaps in a rather exaggerated way. But how could he find out the details of what had happened? Jirjis was terrified. He had been terrified since the moment when the boss had entrusted him with the task. His fright continued to increase hour by hour. At first it wasn't so much a fear of the consequences as a feeling of alarm at the anticipated meeting with the minister of the interior. He had tried to reassure Jirjis that everything would be achieved easily, and that none of the workers would learn of their role in ending the strike, as the management had taken every precaution. But Jirjis's alarmed words, the pallor of his face, and his trembling hands had eventually passed his contagious fear on to him as well. The fear was stronger than the attempts to calm it. He had started to feel that his own words were empty and meaningless, while he thought that everything Jirjis was saying was right. "The management is helping us, okay, it's helping my son who is studying in Britain and I'm grateful. But this job? How will it protect us if we are exposed? Tell me, Abu Jabbar, if you please, how will it protect us?" When Jirjis heard what the bus passengers were saying about what had happened that morning near Project HQ, his face turned into the semblance of a dead man. He could no longer utter a single syllable. When the pair got out of the bus in front of the camp, he turned to him and dejectedly implored him. "What are we to do now? Tell me, Abu Jabbar!"

He tried to affect a display of calm and unconcern. "What do you want us to do? Go to our rooms, and rest from the journey."

"No, please! Wouldn't it be better to leave the camp and the work zone?"

He looked him in amazement as they passed the guard's hut. This tall, well-built man wanted to run away, to leave his job and his good salary, and run away! Nothing of that sort had occurred to *him*!

"No, running away would be the biggest mistake. If we run away, Abu Basil, it will be an acknowledgment that we've had a part in what has happened. And you can imagine the rest."

Jirjis looked at him in bewilderment. They were walking between the rows of rooms, along camp paths that seemed almost empty.

"Then what are we to do?"

"Nothing. Behave normally. We didn't see anything or hear anything, and if any gossip leaks out, we say they're just malicious rumors."

"You think so?"

"Yes. And now we should both go and rest in our rooms. And when they come back, we'll show them how sad we are, slander the management, and curse Fox and his family."

"Please, Abu Jabbar, spare me the details!" Jirjis's voice was trembling.

"Okay, God keep you safe!"

They parted. He found his room deserted. He was surprised to find the beds on which his roommates slept empty and apparently abandoned, like beds in a hospital whose occupants have died at dawn, leaving the covers folded, to be sent for washing. He sat on the edge of his bed, and the planks creaked beneath him. He gazed around the room from one empty bed to another. Muzhir had been dismissed, Istifan had choked to death in the sewage tank, Hussein, God alone knew what prison or situation he was in now, and Muhammad—the only one of them left—had gone to the city on the first day of the strike and hadn't yet returned; he didn't know what had become of him. The room was empty of them all. Their faces, their voices, and their laughter were still there, he could sense them in the air. But they were only dreams and echoes, which lacked reality and permanence, and needed the heat of pulsing bodies and the weight of their presence. All the days of the strike, he had continued living by himself in this room. He hadn't left the camp, so that it couldn't be said that he had joined the others in striking and disobeying management. (He had only left the camp for a single night, on the orders of Mr. Fox himself.) But he had never missed these youth who had shared his life here as he missed them now, coming back from Basra victorious and defeated at the same time. There was no one with him now, no one. Even the dumb nightingale had been entrusted to Dankha by Muhammad before he traveled to Basra.

He took his shoes off, put his sandals on and went out onto the balcony. The sky was still gloomy, and the mass of dark clouds weighed heavily on his chest. If only it would rain, if only he could cry, perhaps he would feel a little relief. But he couldn't cry when he was in full control of himself. He would set up his drinks table and release his tears. Everything had to seem normal when they dragged their feet back from the city after their failure. He had wanted the strike to stop, but not in this bloody way . . . no, not in this way! He stayed wandering around on the balcony. The camp paths were deserted. He noticed someone come out of one of the rooms carrying a yellow pitcher. He watched his back as he headed toward the toilets. There was no one left in the camp except for some employees from faraway towns, and a few charged with protecting the quarters from attempts at sabotage. The latter, however, had hidden themselves away in their rooms again after the disruption at Project HQ, the focus of the confrontation between the management and the workers. Someone must have told them what had happened that morning in the city.

The stray dogs hungrily wandering the paths were climbing onto the balconies and loitering at the doors to the rooms, in the hope that someone might throw them something to eat, now that the canteen had closed its doors and the scraps had disappeared. He was hungry too. He left the balcony and went to look for Daniel. He found him in his room in pajamas (he looked thin, and smaller than he looked in a jacket). Daniel got up to greet him when he saw him, "Hey, Abu Jabbar, finished?"

He nodded his head wearily. He didn't want to talk about that subject.

"Come in, come in, sit down!"

Daniel pointed to a leather chair beside the bed, while he himself sat on the edge of the bed.

"Abu Jabbar, you've done a great job!"

He gave him a warning look. "Daniel!"

"I know, I know, I won't talk, I just . . . ."

Daniel wasn't wearing his glasses, and he looked older. But he seemed happy that the strike had failed, and he started to look at him with admiration, as if he were a hero returning from a victorious battle; he didn't realize the sadness that was at work inside him. He looked silently at the peaceful things around him. Daniel occupied a whole room on his own. It was elegantly furnished, and everything in it was different from what was to be found in the other workers' rooms: his bed, his bedding, his possessions, his cupboards (he had two large cupboards, while they had one small cupboard each). Daniel also had other things that they didn't have: a round table made of teak on which he could set up his drinks in the evening, four chairs, a leather armchair, and a large radio on a bedside table complete with a telephone. He looked at him with distaste: I do the dirty, dangerous work, while this dog enjoys all this!

"I want some tins and bread," he said, like someone demanding their rights.

"Right away, Abu Jabbar, right away! You deserve them!" Daniel got off his bed. "What would you like? Meat . . . sardines . . . cheese?"

"Something of everything, something of everything."

He saw him open one of the cupboards. Some tins of food fell onto the floor. The cupboard must be stuffed full of them; he had another warehouse in his room, his personal warehouse. He put a number of colored tins on top of the table, with a piece of bread wrapped in cellophane paper.

"And I'd like a bottle of whisky."

Daniel looked at him in astonishment as his hands gathered up the tins that had fallen to the floor and put them back in the cupboard. Astonished, yes, because I'm asking like this! Before today, I would accept gratefully anything they threw me, like a dog, but not after what happened in the city. Abu Jabbar has changed; let them know, he wants a reward equivalent to the danger of risking his life.

"Abu Jabbar, I don't have any instructions to give you whisky. I'll need to talk to the boss first."

"The boss won't refuse. The boss knows the value of his men."

He jumped up and stayed where he was, waiting.

Daniel reached into the cupboard. He seemed to be searching for a long time, then brought out the bottle of whisky. Abu Jabbar took it from him, clutching it by its broad neck, stuffed the tins of food into his spacious pockets, and moved toward the door.

"Abu Jabbar, I must know . . . ."

But he didn't turn back to him. Instead, he walked back to his room. This Daniel was just a link between Mr. Fox and his spies scattered among the men in the camp and in the work zones. He would do what the boss required of him as had happened the day before yesterday. Daniel and he had been drinking in the evening. Silence reigned over the near deserted camp, and only the stray dogs were wandering its paths, when the telephone rang to disturb their inebriated state. Daniel languidly stretched out his hand and picked up the receiver. "Daniel speaking," he answered in a tipsy voice. But he immediately woke up and jumped up. "Yes, sir!"

He knew that Mr. Fox was on the other end of the line and started to listen carefully.

"Yes, sir!"

He couldn't hear what the boss was saying. All he could hear was the whisper of a faraway voice. It had to be important.

"Yes sir. And Jirjis as well."

The whispering stopped, but Daniel remained standing, with the receiver in his hand. He saw him look gloomily at the door .

"What does the boss want?"

"He wants to see you."

"To see *me*? At this hour?"

"You and Jirjis."

"Why?"

"I don't know. One moment. I'll go and tell Jirjis now, and bring him back, so that we can all go and see what the boss wants."

After that, Daniel had taken them in the pickup truck that he always used. Jirjis, whom Daniel had gotten out of bed, seemed disturbed. He too was uncomfortable with the secret nighttime rendezvous in Mr. Fox's house at a time when the whole atmosphere was fraught with tension as a result of the work stoppage. The boss opened the door to them himself, and led them into the living room. Not into the kitchen, as he had with him the previous time.

"Hello, hello, how are you all?"

405

They all muttered a reply, still standing.

"Sit down, please!"

Pieces of wood were burning in the wall stove, and the atmosphere in the living room was relaxing, but they sat down stiffly, not knowing the purpose of the sudden call. He saw him smile at them reassuringly, his black pipe in his hand, and a white patch about three inches long sticking to his brow, covering his scar, which was all that remained of the injuries from the workers' attack on him. Mr. Fox sat down opposite them.

"How are you, Abdul?"

"Very well, sir!"

"Good. And you, Jirjis, did you go to Basra or not?"

"No, sir!"

"Excellent. I know that you're good people, with principles."

He got up, so they all rose.

"No, stay sitting. You'll have some coffee, yes?"

He left the room, so they sat back down. They all looked at each other's faces in confusion, but didn't speak, in case he could hear what they were saying. After a few minutes he returned, carrying the tray of coffee himself. (Where had that maid of his gone?) They got up again. Mr. Fox put the small tray on the table.

"Sit down. Drink some coffee!"

He sat down, and so did they. He was being very civil and unusually kind to them. His welcome to them was out of the ordinary, and Abu Jabbar had therefore felt uneasy. As they were drinking their coffee in silence, disturbed by Mr. Fox's penetrating looks as he smoked his pipe , from somewhere in the house a clock began to chime. One, two, three—he started to count the chimes to himself. Meanwhile, he saw Jirjis give the manager a dumb smile, and Daniel twirling his cup. Eleven. He waited for the last chime, as the time went by, but the clock was silent, and a sort of emptiness filled the air.

"You know why I've asked to see you?" said Mr. Fox finally, as if he had been waiting for the chimes to stop, or for them to finish drinking their coffee, before he spoke. "But please keep this to yourselves!"

He looked at him apprehensively. Mr. Fox put his pipe down on the table in front of him, then leaned forward a little and stared at them intently.

"As you know, it's now been eight days since work stopped on the project." He saw his expression stiffen. "Tell me, can that be a good thing?"

They told him that of course it wasn't a good thing, and that the workers were fools, unable to distinguish between what benefited them and what harmed them, and so on. Jirjis was the most expansive of them in his condemnation.

"That means, as you can see, that the work needs to resume."

Abu Jabbar hurried to respond, so that Jirjis would not monopolize the conversation.

"Of course, sir. This is madness! The men haven't got any brains!"

He knew that he'd been an ass, and worse than an ass, by speaking when he didn't have to. But he only realized it after Mr. Fox had spoken again to tell them what he had in mind.

"You, Abdul." The manager pointed his thick red finger toward Abu Jabbar's chest. "And you, Jirjis." He shifted his finger to the chief clerk, " . . . can help the management to get the work going again as it was."

He looked at him with a mixture of confusion and unease. What could the two of them—he and this middle-aged man whose face had already turned pale—do? Mr. Fox continued speaking. "Half an hour ago, HQ in Basra telephoned me. They told me that the minister of the interior wanted to come himself to find a solution to these disturbances."

Mr. Fox relit his pipe, which had gone out. He saw him take some quick drags at his pipe, his gray eyes surveying their tense faces. Then he took his pipe from his mouth. "I want you to go to Basra tomorrow, to speak to the minister of the interior."

Daniel's expression relaxed, and he leaned back against the chair. Meanwhile, the air around Abu Jabbar had become hotter, and sweat had started to pour from his face and neck, while Jirjis listened to the manager's words dumbfounded, without batting an eyelid.

"You must tell him that we want to work, we don't want our children to die of hunger, we want money to live, but there are people . . . ."

Abu Jabbar saw Jirjis looking at him as if pleading for help. He took his handkerchief out of his pocket and started to wipe his brow, cheeks, and neck.

"Sir, you want us to go . . . me and Jirjis, on our own . . . to meet His Excellency, the minister?"

He saw him smile. "No, Abdul, not on your own. We'll have people, a good bunch like yourselves, from Basra and al-Zubayr, a big delegation, lots of people, to talk to the minister. You and Jirjis will just speak for the workers here."

Through all this, Daniel had been sitting relaxed, for the issue no longer concerned him and he was not going to be exposed to danger. And now, after everything was over, he was begrudging him a bottle of whisky. The dog! He looked up at the sky as he dragged his feet back to his room. The sky was still holding back its tears. He noticed a flash of lightning, then heard thunder, but it was all far away. If only it would rain, it might relieve a bit of the weight he felt pressing on his chest. Mr. Fox had then explained to them in detail what they had to do, when they should travel, where they should stay in the city, and who they were to meet there. Everything was ready. As for the place and time for their meeting with the minister, he told them that someone from the management side would meet them and arrange everything with them. He told them there was no reason for them to feel afraid, as none of the workers would know the nature of their mission or know their names. Words, it had all been just words! How could something like this be kept secret for long?

The air had turned cooler along the camp paths. He went into his room, and put the bottle of whisky, tins of food, and bag of bread under his bed. He lit the oil stove and left the door open. He would eat, then sleep, and when he woke in the afternoon, he would open the bottle of whisky.

He slept in his clothes, which were grimy from the dirt of the road. The camp was still quiet when he got up. He saw Dankha at the washhouse, who asked him, "Abu Jabbar, they say the strike's over!"

He avoided looking him in the face. "I honestly don't know, my lad. If they say so . . . ."

He went on his way, washed quickly, then went back to his room. He spread his mat and set up his drinks table on the ground. Almost at once, a dog arrived and stood at the door of the room, looking at him. In a few minutes, there were four dogs staring at him hungrily. How quickly dogs gather when they smell food! He tore off a piece of bread and threw it away from him through the gap in the door. The dogs ran to it then returned to stand in the same place, waiting expectantly. He started to drink, smoke, and eat. The dogs tired of standing and stretched out on the ground, waiting patiently. There was an almost empty meat tin and sardine tin, which he threw out from the balcony one after the other. He heard them fall to the ground, and at the same time saw the dogs' bodies rise and fall under the balcony. He heard a fight, then barking, and a crack as the tins rolled between the legs of the ravenous dogs. Night fell quickly. But nothing much changed. It had been a dark day because of the masses of clouds, and it became a little blacker as night fell. The lights on the balconies were lit in front of the rows of rooms. He heard the sound of a car stop at the camp entrance, and he got up. The expectant dogs had increased in number. He pushed the door back but didn't shut it completely, leaving it ajar so as not to be choked by the gases from the stove. He stood looking out of the narrow opening. This was the first bus to arrive from the city. After a few moments they would spread out over the camp paths, and he would hear their voices on the balconies, as they dragged their routed, humiliated feet to retire to their rooms. He didn't want them to see him like this with a bottle of whisky in front of him, as if he were celebrating their defeat. Mad, by Almighty God! They had taken on a force that no one could take on without being broken in the end. He had known this from the beginning, but no one had listened to his words. He left the door and sat down in the same place. He opened more tins of food, filled and drained his glass several times, and smoked a lot. He continued waiting, waiting for Muhammad to come back from Basra. He wanted to find out some of the details from him, to try to discover if they had found out about the delegation that had met His Excellency the minister of the interior, and the names of those taking part. A disaster if they had discovered the names! They would find them out one day, for no secret remains hidden forever, but the danger was that they would discover them now, when feelings were inflamed. He heard the sound of another vehicle stopping on the path in front of the camp entrance, but Muhammad didn't arrive until late in the evening. He heard his tired, sluggish footsteps on the balcony. Then the door opened quietly, and he came in, carrying his small bag and his books. He looked up at him in greeting.

"Hello, my lad, hello, why so late? I've been worrying about you!"

He was genuinely pleased to see him come into the forsaken room. Muhammad looked at him glumly. "The buses!"

He watched him put his bag and books down on his bed. "I heard . . . that everything's over and they're going back to work."

Muhammad opened his bag, took out his pajamas and a towel, then turned to him. "Yes, right now," he said, then started to change his clothes.

He looked at his thin body. "I said it was useless from the start, that they wouldn't be able . . . ."

"The important thing is to try, Abu Jabbar. Win some, lose some, as they say."

He saw him give him a vague, searching look. Could he suspect him? He had never spoken in that tone before!

In fact, he seldom spoke at all. He was too attached to his books and papers. But it seemed that rebellion, like fear, was another contagious disease.

Muhammad picked up his towel and soap, covered his back with his jacket, and went off to the washrooms. He looked at the whisky bottle, and found it empty; he had finished it, as well as all the food he had taken from Daniel. He felt full, his body heavy as a sack of sand. His head was all mixed up, crowded with faces and words, though his fears had subsided a little.

When Muhammad came in again, he was still kneeling in the same place, thinking about the events of the previous night and that morning. Muhammad hung up his wet towel on the hanger, shifted his bag and books from his bed, then looked at him. "Abu Jabbar, are you sure that you haven't seen my papers?"

He remembered the papers, and looked at him doubtfully. "No, if I'd seen them, I would have told you. I wouldn't have left you to trouble yourself looking for them."

Muhammad turned his back toward him, took off his jacket, hung it on the hook, and slipped into bed in silence. I don't think he's found out anything. He's just cross at the outcome, and perhaps because he's lost those papers he's proud of. He hadn't looked at them. He was afraid of being surprised by someone. Abu Jabbar had taken them straight away to Daniel and asked him to send them to the boss. What would he say, then, if he discovered the part he and the others had played in Basra? The meeting with the minister of the interior had been a quick one, lasting only a few minutes. But the wait for permission to appear before the minister had been longer. They had stayed standing in the shadows under the trees in the garden of the governor's residence. They had stood in small groups, and the air was cold. But it hadn't been the cold that had annoyed them. They had all felt embarrassed looking into their colleagues' faces. They did not speak, for they had nothing to say to each other. The faces of the others were strange to him; they were from different work zones. Jirjis would not leave him, wherever he went, as if seeking his protection from the potential dangers if they were exposed. They saw fancy cars coming and going, their roofs shining under the lights, and they glimpsed men continually descending on the place where the minister was installed. After waiting for about two hours, the man chosen by management to head them up came and told them that the minister would meet them after he had finished listening to a delegation of Basran merchants and notables, who had come to complain about the stagnation affecting the city's economy because of the strike. The man who was leading them was tall, sprightly, and clever. He had learned their names and faces from the first meeting.

After about half an hour they were given permission to enter. He found himself in a spacious hall, with shining chandeliers hanging from the ceiling, and armchairs arranged in rows around the walls. But they did not sit down. No one invited them to sit, so they stood crammed together near the entrance. He felt alarmed, and noticed that Jirjis was no longer standing beside him, but had moved away from him. He turned to look for him amid the sea of silent, anxious faces, and glimpsed him cowering at the back of the rows, trying to hide himself from view. The room was empty. The usher who had let them in had left them and gone out by another door on the other side. After a few minutes they heard a murmur and the sound of footsteps. Then the minister entered from the door opposite, accompanied by around four or five men, some in official dress, including the city's chief of police.

The minister addressed them without any preliminaries. "Yes, what do you want to tell me?"

His voice was rough, dry, and decisive. He was a square-built man, slightly overweight, about sixty years old, with hair that had turned gray. He saw him stare at their faces, concentrating hard, as though he wanted to store their features in his mind to be recalled in case of need. He didn't sit down either, but stood in the middle of the hall with his entourage, while the delegation—about twenty men—remained standing, packed together at the near end of the hall near the door. They had put on their best clothes for this important meeting, but their clothes still seemed shabby there.

The man who was leading them spoke in an imploring tone. "Your Excellency, protect us from them, for God's sake. They want to . . . ."

The minister looked at his entourage enquiringly, and one of them explained, "Sir, these men have come on behalf of their colleagues in all regions. They want to return to work."

"Excellent!" said the minister, and looked at them with appreciation. "Then why don't you go back?" he asked.

"Sir, they won't let us," said the group's spokesman. "They're barring us. They stand outside the entrances and block our path. And threaten our families!"

"Is this true?" asked the minister angrily, staring into their faces.

They nodded their heads, and muttered words of confirmation. Abu Jabbar nodded as well, and said, in a voice that seemed louder than necessary, "Yes, Your Excellency, we also have . . . there in. . . ."

The man who was their leader said, "We want to go back to work. We want to live. We have wives and children. But this situation. . . ."

The minister raised his hand and cut him off. "Enough. I understand."

He seemed to be in a hurry, and didn't want a lot of talk. He had come from Baghdad to put down the rebellion without wasting time, after his colleague, the minister of social affairs, had failed to end it in his own way.

"Tomorrow, you'll go back to work, and no one will stop you," he proclaimed. Then he turned to the chief of police. "You will be responsible for that."

The chief of police was a short man whose face had a genial air (he had once known a retired teacher exactly like him). He heard him ask the minister, "Sir, will you permit me to use firearms?"

"Let your men fire in the air, as a deterrent."

"And if they're not deterred, sir?"

"Do whatever you consider necessary. I want this problem to be concluded tomorrow, by whatever means!"

Muhammad was stretched out peacefully on his bed, his body wrapped in a blanket. Abu Jabbar didn't know if he had gone to sleep, or if he was still preoccupied, and thinking about what had happened that morning. He was preoccupied himself too. He gathered up his rubbish, folded his mat, and put it to one side. Then he went to the toilets to empty his bladder before sleeping. The sky had finally let its tears fall. The earth was moist, and the air was filled with the smells of dust, of wet cardboard walls, and of the taste of salt that covered the face of the desert.

413

18

The bedding that their cook, Abu Mahmoud, usually slept on was still folded up in a corner of the kitchen, abandoned for two days. Husam gave Bob a slightly sad look. "Bob, I still don't believe this story! This gentle man ... no, impossible! There's some mistake somewhere!"

Macaulay carried on beating the eggs in a white porcelain bowl, without looking up. "Perhaps the workers provoked him, a sort of revenge for the failure of their strike. Anyway, that's what Tom believes. Give me another egg."

He took another egg out of the fridge. "Tom Fox has got charges ready against everybody!"

He was angry, while Bob Macaulay looked at the matter coolly, just as he looked at all the daily irritations that he thought shouldn't affect his digestive activity. He watched him break the egg, and let the yolk, with its translucent coating, drop into the dish.

"This wretched man had always used to pile up demi-gods for himself. So how on earth could he have thought of throwing stones at Mrs. Fox?"

Macaulay left the eggshell in dish with the other shells, as his face took on a slightly gloomy look. Meanwhile, he was contracting his stomach muscles and his face became redder. He was going to make a stink, curse him! This habit was the only thing he held against

414

him. They looked with contempt on people who belched out loud; letting out air was reprehensible in their eyes if it came from the top, but not if it came from the bottom! Macaulay relieved himself then sighed, and the red color left his face.

"But a man may sometimes lose faith in his gods, in a moment of despair!" he said jokingly, as he poured the beaten egg into the frying pan. He took a bottle of milk from the fridge and handed it to him. "Put the milk on the stove. Do something!"

"Not this man. Do you know that he tried to stop me coming into the house the first day I arrived? He thought that I was an intruder, and had no right to live in the 'Master's' blessed house. I'm a native!"

"I know, you told me. He's a sincere man, but I don't know how all this has happened."

Macaulay watched the eggs, which had swollen up and started to splutter in the frying pan. "I'd like to visit him in detention, but Tom would be cross, you know."

Macaulay seemed genuine in his desire to visit the cook.

"I'll visit him this afternoon. I've agreed with Akram. He knows some of the officials in the village."

Macaulay turned down the heat under the pan.

"That's good. I'll send some money for him with you."

They took their bread, tea, milk, and eggs through to the dining room, as the works siren made the air tremble with its first morning blast. The cook's absence had disturbed their lives. If he had known that the man would end up in detention on a charge of assault on the life of Mrs. Fox, he would have advised him not to go help Jenny prepare for her wretched party.

At about five o'clock in the afternoon, he and Akram were in the car on their way to the village. Akram turned to him with some advice. "When we go into the police station, don't speak; let me do the talking!"

He looked at him in bewilderment. "Why?"

"Because if you speak they'll know that you're Iraqi, and will no longer take any notice of you. I want them to think you're a European. Your appearance helps."

"But you said you knew the superintendent!"

"All the same, he'll take more notice of you if he thinks you're British."

Akram was driving the car recklessly as usual, and in less than a quarter of an hour they were alighting in front of the entrance to the police station. He saw a policeman standing guard at the entrance, with a face that looked fed up and exhausted. Akram approached him. "Is Superintendent Qasim here?"

"No, Sergeant Hamdi's here in his place," replied the policeman without looking at Akram. Husam's eyes scrutinized him carefully.

"As I told you," whispered Akram as they walked in, "Don't speak. Or if you want to, speak in English."

He laughed and said nothing. The building was in the style of an oriental house, with a spacious courtyard surrounded by about six or seven rooms, some of which were in darkness. He saw an old woman wrapped in a black abaya, with a lad of about ten beside her wearing a white dishdasha, perhaps her grandson. They were sitting on the ground by the wall at the front of the courtyard, with a small bundle in front of them, perhaps containing clothes or food. He saw a policeman bend down over her, and say something in an angry tone, his arm pointing to the exit. He saw other figures moving around at the doors to the lit rooms, and there was murmuring in the air. But the place was generally quiet. The problems brought on by the night hadn't started yet. Three or four lamps were illuminating rectangular kiosks in front of the rooms, but the heart of the courtyard seemed almost dark. He and Akram made their way through it to the first lit room. He saw a dark-skinned man of about thirty, looking relaxed, sitting on a chair behind an old wooden table. He had cocked his cap to one side, so that it was touching one of his eyebrows.

"Good evening," Akram addressed him in a jolly tone. He saw him raise his eyes toward them, then sit up straight. "Are you Sergeant Hamdi?"

"Yes."

He saw the sergeant look at them curiously.

"Please sit down. Sit down, mister."

He felt uncomfortable. He turned to look around him, avoiding looking the sergeant in the face. He saw a bed beside the wall, and noticed that the blanket covering the bed was the same type as that used by the project management in their houses, guesthouse, and workers' accommodation. The three black letters of the project name were clearly visible. So the project's charity had extended this far too!

There was a single wooden chair near the table, but they stayed standing in the middle of the room. Meanwhile, he heard Akram speaking to the young sergeant. "We've come to enquire about a cook who is detained here, by the name of Radi Lazim, known as Abu Mahmoud. He works for us on the project. The gentleman here would like to see him."

"You mean the criminal who wanted to kill the manager's wife, the manager with the beard? Yes, he's here. There's no objection to the gentleman seeing him."

He got up to take them to him in person. "Thank you very much, Mr. Hamdi," said Husam gratefully, speaking in Arabic, against Akram's advice.

The sergeant looked at him in astonishment. "It seems that the gentleman knows Arabic well!"

"I am an Arab, an Iraqi!"

Akram was taken by surprise, and the sergeant stayed where he was. "Corporal Jasim!" he shouted angrily. With astonishing speed, the corporal appeared before them. "Take these two men to the cells, and let them see the cook that wanted to kill the British woman. Five minutes, no more!" Then he turned round to go back to where he had been sitting, after casting a quick glance at Akram, who seemed embarrassed.

When they were out of the room, Akram quietly told him off. "Why did you have to speak? Arab, Iraqi, please now! Our colleague is cross with us!"

"Let him be cross!"

417

The corporal was waiting. "Okay, you go on your own, see the cook, and leave me here, to try to apologize to the sergeant. We may need him one day."

Husam walked behind the corporal, while Akram went back into the room again. The corporal walked to the end of the courtyard, then stopped in front of a door that was different from the doors on the other rooms. It was made of iron, with a rectangular opening two feet long and one foot high in the middle of it, at eye level. A number of iron bars broke up the yellow light coming from inside. The room seemed silent at first, but as he got closer he could hear talking, and several faces appeared, crowded together at the opening. He saw eyes shining, staring eagerly outward. The corporal shouted to the faces, "Get away from the window. Where's the cook, Radi Lazim?"

Some of the faces remained stuck to the opening, looking at him curiously. He saw hands clutching at the bars—rough, dark hands— mouths opening, and voices being raised.

"Abu Mahmoud, come here, Abu Mahmoud!"

Some of the faces that appeared behind the locked door were not unfamiliar to him; he had seen these men in the work zone. He could hear the cook's familiar voice among the voices calling out. "Yes, is everything okay?"

"Come here, you've got a visitor."

"Make way for him."

The detainees withdrew this time, and the cook's thin face appeared behind the bars. "It's you, sir! Did you come on your own?"

The cook seemed both happy and surprised. He came to the opening, and Husam was hit by a smell of stale air, urine, and excrement. The cook looked at him gratefully. "Sir, I've caused you a lot of trouble."

The room was rectangular, with no windows, like a cellar, and was lit by a single lamp hanging from the middle of the ceiling. Its white walls were covered with lines and drawings, and by yellow patches made by the damp.

"No, Abu Mahmoud, Mr. Macaulay and I are always thinking about you."

The cook looked at him dejectedly. "Sir, do you think they should charge me and put me in here? Is this what I deserve?"

He gave him a pitying look. The men inside were sitting in various positions, on mats or old blankets spread on the floor, waiting patiently; some were sitting still, while others occasionally made movements of impatience. He saw one stretch his leg out in front of him, and another lazily raise his hand to scratch his neck. Two or three of the detainees were looking at him, and he could see the gleam of their staring eyes reflecting the light of the lamp. Generally, however, they had lost interest in him, and gone back to chatting among themselves, or smoking distractedly. Only one man among them stayed standing nearby, leaning against the wall, listening to the conversation between himself and the cook, on either side of the door.

"Abu Mahmoud, they say that you . . . ."

"Does it make sense, sir, for me to think of raising a hand against the boss's wife, or any one of them? Have I gone mad?"

The man leaning against the door shouted angrily behind the cook's back, "It would have been better if you *had* raised your hand, at least they would have respected you!"

"Sir, this is Fawzi Abu Shama, the drill operator. He's angry with me, but believe me, sir . . . ."

At that moment, Husam recalled where he had seen that man. "So why did they bring you here?"

The story that the cook then told him was a sort of surrealist joke. If events hadn't got the cook into this mess—which God alone knew how he was going to get out of—he would have found it an amusing tale. But the ending had turned out to be tragic for the cook. And all because of his wretched set of false teeth, which he himself had advised him to change for a firmer pair.

Abu Mahmoud, according to his own version of events, had been busy cooking in Mr. Fox's house, making pastries and preparing finger food, with Jenny hovering around him, wanting to check that everything was going to plan. All the rings on the electric stove were on, and the air inside the kitchen was hot. Meanwhile, a cool breeze must have blown in through the cracks in the door leading to the garden, so that Abu Mahmoud found himself sneezing. Before he could close his mouth, the top half of his set of teeth flew into the air with the sneeze, and hit the boss's wife on the forehead; her color had turned instantly pale, and she had fallen on the floor in a faint. He still didn't know whether this was because of the half set of teeth colliding with her forehead, or because she had panicked at the sight of a man's teeth leaving his mouth and flying into the air like that. Anyway, he had panicked too, and sprayed her face with drops of water, but she hadn't stirred.

It appeared that hitting her head on the floor had given her concussion ("she's a weak woman, you know, sir"). He had been bewildered, not knowing what to do in the face of this disaster that had come on him so suddenly. He picked up his teeth from the floor, wiped them hurriedly with his hand, put them back in his mouth, and hurried to the club to tell Joseph, the barman. When he returned, he found that she had got up from the floor and was sitting in a chair. He was happy to see her smiling. She was a little confused, but she smiled kindly at him, and he thought that the incident had ended happily. But then the boss, her husband, had come in like a hawk, and without any question or answer, had dragged him to his car, brought him to the village, and handed him over to the police, accusing him of the attempted murder of his wife.

"That's how it happened, sir, as God is my witness!"

"Okay, will you give the police these details?"

"I told them, of course, but they laughed at me."

The cook seemed desperate and terrified.

"And Mrs. Fox, didn't she tell them the truth?"

"Sir, the Madam is a woman with a big heart . . . ."

A small laugh escaped from the rig operator, who had stayed where he was, but Abu Mahmoud took no notice of him.

"She, I'm telling the truth, wanted to give evidence in my favor, but the boss (God preserve him) wouldn't let her speak."

The cook wiped his eyes, although he hadn't been crying.

"He wouldn't let her. It was he that replied to the questions from the investigating judge."

"Never mind, Abu Mahmoud, never mind. I'll go and talk to the investigating judge, and see what we can do."

"Quickly, sir, God preserve you, because I've heard they'll be transferring me to Basra, with the group of project workers who've been detained."

He glanced at the men squatting on the floor. "When?"

"I don't know, sir."

"When they find some means of transport," said the rig operator in an offhand way. "Perhaps tonight, who knows?"

He became aware of the corporal standing behind him and fidgeting. He'd let him stay by the door for a long time, and he was afraid of the sergeant's anger. He finished his visit with Abu Mahmoud. Through the bars, he handed him the money that Bob Macaulay had sent with him, gave him some money of his own, and said goodbye so that he could go back to Akram, to go to see the investigating judge together. He found Akram and the sergeant chatting amiably; he had succeeded in conciliating him.

The sergeant greeted him with a laugh when he saw him come in, "Hello, Mr. Husam Hilmi!"

"Hello."

"So you saw your cook?"

"Yes, I saw him. He says you're intending to transfer them to Basra."

"Correct. A telegram came at midday today asking us to transfer project workers in detention who had any connection with acts of sabotage."

He looked at him in surprise. "But this cook's case is different. Also, he's not a project employee!"

"God, I don't know. Old Beardy said he was one of them."

The scoundrel! Meanwhile, Akram was sitting comfortably, with an empty tea glass in front of him.

"And when will you transfer them?"

"Tomorrow," replied the sergeant, then looked at Akram and smiled. Perhaps he found his excessive concern with the cook odd, or had recalled his strange story.

"Can I see the investigating judge tonight?"

He saw him look at his watch. "He's most likely at home now, but you'll find him in the Port Club after eight."

He turned to Akram. "Come on, let's go to the Port Club and wait for him there."

The young sergeant pressed Akram's hand in farewell, with a friendly smile. "As we agreed, then!"

"And what have you agreed?" Husam asked Akram, after they had left the police station and got into the car.

He laughed as he drove the car off. "I promised to invite him to our club."

"Akram, you shouldn't have."

"Believe me, Husam, it was him that mentioned it. At first, I was just apologizing for trying to make him think you were a foreigner."

The tracks were narrow and almost dark, but Akram drove fast, as if he were on the open road. The car headlights cut through the gloom in front of them, while he talked in darkness .

"Then we talked. He asked me about you, and after that he said, 'I heard you have a nice swimming pool and a nice club where they hold dances.' So I promised to invite him if there was a suitable occasion."

"Despite the fact that you know the management will refuse."

"I know, but what do you want me to do, after you'd lost your cool and put me in a difficult position with him? I had to placate him."

"Akram, the case of this cook of ours has started to get complicated. That dog Fox has got it on the wrong track, while the whole story . . . ."

But Akram had already stopped the car in front of the Port Club gate, so they got out.

"Later, I'll explain it to you."

They entered a large rectangular hall, like a warehouse, inside which were long rows of uncovered square wooden tables, with chairs around them. The club's customers had already started their evening drinking sessions. The air in the hall was full of chatter and smoke, and the smell of food and drink. They sat down at one of the tables, and Akram turned to look at the faces around him. He saw some faces he recognized, faces of some friends he used to take to the project club, so he got up.

"One moment, while I greet everyone here."

He saw him stand at one of the tables, and heard his raucous laughter as he joked with his friends. Then he came back with two of them in tow, and they sat down together. After a little the tabletop was full of bottles of beer and glasses, and plates of mezze. But Husam excused himself from drinking. He said that he didn't want to meet the investigating judge with a mouth smelling of beer. They laughed. "My friend, the investigating judge drinks himself!" one of them said, but he didn't reply. He avoided these friends of Akram's; they were among the reasons that made Suzanne leave her husband. He continued to sit with them, waiting and feeling frustrated, while Akram was chatting and laughing merrily, as if he had come with him to the village to meet his friends and drink with them.

The investigating judge entered the hall at the expected time, and sat down on his own in a corner. Husam waited for some time until the man could settle down. He saw one of the servants go up to him. After the servant had gone away, he got up to meet him. Akram had half-heartedly asked him if he would like him to accompany him, but he said that that would not be necessary.

As he saw him approaching, the investigating judge gave him an expectant, enquiring look, with a hint of surprise. Perhaps he also thought he was a foreigner. He was not very old, about forty, with a worn-out face.

"Good evening, sir."

"Hello," the man replied curtly, in a neutral tone. He didn't invite him to sit. He wasn't hostile, but he wasn't friendly either. Meanwhile, the servant was putting a bottle of beer and a glass on the table in front of him. He saw him move the bottle from the place where the servant had placed it, then look at him expectantly.

"Sir, I'm very sorry to disturb you. I am Engineer Husam Hilmi, from the project management. I've come to enquire about the case of a cook who works for us at home, who has been detained on your instructions."

Only then did the man smile and invite him to sit down. He sat down opposite him. "This cook of yours is charged with assault on a British lady, the wife of one of your managers."

"Sir, the story . . . ."

The investigating judge interrupted him before he could say more. "I know the story. I know it. He told me everything in his statement."

He looked at him patiently as he slowly filled his glass, keeping his head bent , as he watched the yellow liquid flow from the mouth of the bottle and make its way through the covering of white froth that had begun to swell before his eyes. "Of all the cases that have come my way, I have never come across one as amusing as that of this cook of yours!" He gave a little laugh and fingered his glass, which was full of beer and froth. "And I'm inclined to believe him."

He looked at him, relieved to hear the good news. "So you'll be releasing him."

The judge contemplated his glass in silence. Perhaps he was hesitating between drinking at that moment and drinking after replying to the question. "In fact, the case is now out of my hands. We've had orders to send everyone accused of acts of sabotage to Basra, to be investigated there."

"But our cook has no connection with acts of sabotage. And you said that you believed his testimony."

"That's true. But having received our orders from the highest authority, it is no longer in my power to release him. This foreigner might perhaps raise a complaint to Basra, or Baghdad, and then they'll . . . ."

"But you said that he was innocent."

"Being innocent or guilty has nothing to do with it. The case has now acquired a political dimension, and I can't do anything."

He looked at him, dumbstruck. "I'm sorry," said the man, in the tone of someone who wants to finish a conversation. "He will have to be sent with the others, and take his chances!"

424

He got up, feeling frustrated. "It seems that everyone here must take his chances!"

The investigating judge looked at him with tired eyes but did not speak, then raised his glass and took a long swig, ignoring his presence. He thanked him for nothing and returned to Akram.

"Come on, let's go back."

He felt defeated and frustrated. But Akram was in a different mood. He had collected more friends around the table, and they were all extremely merry. Akram lifted an intoxicated face to him, and handed him the car keys. "I'm staying with this lot. Take the car and go back yourself!"

"But how will you get back?"

Akram put his hand on the shoulder of one of his friends. "Thank goodness for friends!"

He set off in the car back to the residential area alone. In a few minutes, he had left the village, on the deserted road between the black wall of palms and the emptiness of the desert. In the little mirror in front of him, he could see nothing but a dark patch, in which ground and sky ran into each other. A few faint lights from the village were quickly receding. The car's bright headlights swept through the blackness of the night on the road in front of him. But no sooner had the car left one place than the darkness descended to cover the ground again. He pressed his foot on the throttle, putting all his anger and all his disappointment into the dumb machine that was pressing on madly through the night.

He sat smoking and staring distractedly at the flames in the fireplace. His glass was in his hand, and on the table in front of him was his pack of cigarettes, his lighter, an ashtray, a bottle of Russian vodka that Dr. Sami had opened for him, a dish full of pistachios, and Dr. Sami's glass that he had left on the table when he was surprised by the telephone ringing. He listened to the hum of his voice as he spoke, mixed with gentle music broadcast from a foreign station on the radio. He was speaking in English to one of his patients, or perhaps to one of his nurses. Mona was somewhere in the house, busy with her baby daughter, feeding or changing her. She had returned from Hilla two days ago, and Husam had come—following his frustrated return from his meeting with the investigating judge—to greet her, and to congratulate her and her husband on the birth of their first child. He had also come to soothe his tense nerves. He was in need of a place different from the one he'd recently been in—in need of friends to talk to, to hear the ring of their friendly voices, and to look into understanding eyes.

Dr. Sami had finished his telephone conversation and returned to his seat. "So, tell me, how did you find the vodka?"

"Very nice!"

Dr. Sami raised his glass with pleasure. "I've got a crate of it."

"A crate?"

"Yes. Look, they telephoned me this morning from the quayside. They said that a tanker captain was sick. So I went, went on board the tanker, and examined him. An elderly Greek, complaining of his heart. I adjusted some of the medication he was using, repeated the usual 'don't get angry, don't drink' advice, and told him that he would live longer than the devil himself. I made him happy, which is the important thing. When I left the vessel, the man sent one of his sailors after me, carrying a crate of vodka as a present, with the compliments of Captain Nikos Andrikos. Do you like it?"

He took a swig from his glass and started to roll it around his mouth. "Delicious!"

He looked again at the fire burning in the fireplace. Here you are now, sitting relaxed in an armchair, feeling the warmth of the fire and the warmth of the family atmosphere, listening to music and your friend Dr. Sami's amusing chatter, with nothing threatening your personal life. And a little while ago, you were in the police station in the village, staring at desperate figures in the moldy detention room, then listening to the strange and curious logic of the investigating judge. The man had been scared, and was trying to protect himself. You caught a fleeting glimpse of the visible surface of a reality that

426

you had not experienced since you came back from Britain. You didn't see the give and take under the surface, didn't see how oppressive the darkness was there! But which is the true reality? The one whose outer shell you caught a glimpse of in the village, or the one you are now living as you sit here relaxed and content in your friend Dr. Sami's house?

"What are you daydreaming about?"

"I'm not daydreaming. I was wondering how your generous captain would feel if they crammed him in there with those detainees, charged with a crime he hadn't committed."

"What detainees?"

"The people I saw today in the police station, when I went with Akram, trying . . . ."

"You went to the police station? Went yourself?"

"And what's wrong with that?"

"If only you'd talked to me first, my friend. If only you'd talked to me!"

He saw him put his glass down on the table and shake his head uneasily.

"Listen, Husam, my friend. I've some bad news for you. I didn't want to hit you with it as soon as you walked into the house."

"And what is this news?"

But at that moment Mona came in, proudly carrying her baby daughter.

"Husam, tell me, what do you think of this little princess?"

Mona was wearing a blue dress, which made her skin look fairer. The sudden plumpness that usually accompanies pregnancy had left her, and she had returned to almost her previous shape—a full figure, but not excessively so, and a little pale, perhaps from staying up for the baby. He left his glass and cigarette and stood up, while Dr. Sami stayed grumpily sitting where he was. He saw Mona pass him the baby, a small, fragile bundle of flesh wrapped in white fabric so that only her pink round face was visible, with a snub nose in the middle, and small, dark, unblinking eyes. He thought that the baby was

427

looking at him—though perhaps she wasn't looking at him, so much as at her new, indistinct world. He hesitated, not knowing how to hold her. Mona put the baby into his arms. "Take her, don't be afraid. She won't break."

He took her carefully, looked at her closely, then burst out laughing. Something in her little face, or perhaps inside himself, or perhaps it was all the strange and contradictory things he had seen and heard that day, had made him laugh. Mona smiled with happiness; she thought he must be pleased about her daughter. And he was pleased about her daughter, though his mind was preoccupied. Meanwhile, Dr. Sami was drinking in silence, rather than joining his wife in her celebration of the new arrival.

Husam returned the baby to her mother. "Take her, before I fall in love with her!"

Mona smiled with happiness and looked at her daughter proudly. "My daughter, Dunya, won't be rivaled by anyone!"

She sat beside her husband, with her baby on her lap, then looked at him. "Now, Husam, I want a detailed and reliable report from you about Sami's movements during my absence. Where he went, what he did, how he behaved, especially at the last party, the New Year's party."

He looked at Dr. Sami and laughed. "What should I say, Mona? Your husband here is a free-and-easy man!"

He was trying to be lighthearted, to relieve his feelings of frustration, as well as to cover up the fears that Dr. Sami's unfinished words had aroused inside him. Mona opened her eyes wide and sat expectantly, while her husband gave her a look of disapproval. "But only free and easy with his talk, of course!"

Mona's eyes regained their cheerfulness, but she gave her husband a sideways look of displeasure. "It's the intentions that count!"

Dr. Sami laughed. "You mean, a hungry man who's desperate for a good meal to fill his belly is no different from someone who's stuffed himself with food?"

"You mean you really want to eat?"

428

"Not of what God has forbidden!"

She turned to him. "And how did he behave at the party?"

Dr. Sami shook his head. "Was it a party or a funeral?"

"It's true what Sami says, Mona. The party was dead. You know that it came after the events of the strike. Most of the women who'd left for fear of how things might develop hadn't come back yet, and the men were looking at us Iraqis suspiciously, as though we were in a conspiracy with the strikers.

"So we spent the time sitting on our own, smoking and drinking, my love, with Akram, whose wife had left him, and Sultan al-Imari, who'd been left with no family and no friends after Diana had gone!"

Dr. Sami put his arm around his wife's shoulders and looked into her eyes triumphantly. "Do you see now what a faithful husband I am?"

"If it had been a successful party you would have spent the night dancing!"

Husam knew that they would never change. Their hair would turn gray, their faces fill with wrinkles, and they would still be the same—she watching him, and he provoking her, so as to savor her jealousy. But what was the bad news that he hadn't wanted to impart in the presence of his wife? They sat talking for some time, then Mona looked at Husam and said, "I heard that Maureen came back a few days ago. I haven't seen her yet."

"I saw her yesterday around midday," said Dr. Sami. "She was pushing her son in a pram, a fair, handsome baby!"

Mona smiled and looked at him. "I'd like to see him. Who does he look like, I wonder!"

He saw Dr. Sami give her a sideways glance, and he pretended that it was nothing to do with him. An embarrassed silence followed for some time. Then Mona bent down, and gave her baby a loving look. "Sami, she's gone to sleep!"

"Better take her to her bed."

He saw her lift the baby and stand up, then walk down the corridor between the bedrooms. When her blue dress had disappeared, he turned to Dr. Sami. "What is this news? You've disturbed me!"

429

Dr. Sami looked toward the corridor, which looked empty now that his wife had left it, and pricked up his ears. There was nothing but silence. Despite that, when he spoke, he spoke in a low voice. "Husam, I've heard from a reliable source that management is displeased with you."

He smiled contemptuously. "What management is that? Tom Fox?"

"No, no, I'm not talking about the management here. I mean management at HQ, in Basra."

His contemptuous expression deserted him, and he gave his words more attention, as Dr. Sami continued, slightly hesitantly. "And there is a rumor, a powerful rumor, that they may terminate your contract with the project."

Terminate his contract? That meant beginning from square one again, looking for another job here or there, with a salary less than a quarter, or perhaps a fifth, of the salary he was earning now, and most likely with poor conditions of work, after establishing himself and getting used to living here! He looked at Dr. Sami's face, who seemed despondent.

"Do you know why?"

"They say you have links with the events of the strike, that you are friends with some camp residents, things like that."

He heard the sound of the baby crying from the other side of the wall, and Mona singing as she rocked her. The sound seemed vague, weak, and faraway. Do you suppose this could be one of Dr. Sami's little intrigues?

He looked him in the eye. "Sami, is this a joke?"

"No, it's not a joke."

Dr. Sami seemed genuinely sad. He looked at him in bewilderment. "But what connection do I have with the strike? The workers' problems don't concern me. I mean, their problems are different."

"I know that. But it seems that there are people who are stirring the management in Basra up against you."

"Fox, certainly."

"And perhaps others."

"But why?"

He was astonished at this strange accusation, which had never crossed his mind.

"God, I don't know. I'm bewildered too!"

A silence followed, during which Dr. Sami took a swig from his glass, while Husam looked gloomily at the fire blazing in the stove.

"And who conveyed this news to you?"

Dr. Sami hesitated, listening for his child's crying. She had calmed down a little, and he was afraid that they might be disturbed by his wife if they carried on talking. But the baby soon started crying again, so he was confident that his wife would stay bound to her side for some time. Then he spoke in almost a whisper. "It was Maureen that told me!"

"Maureen?" he asked, with a mixture of astonishment and bewilderment, in a voice that came out louder than he had intended. He quickly lowered his voice as he cast an anxious glance in the direction of the bedrooms. "Maureen told you?"

"Yes, and asked me to alert you. It seems that the woman still cares about you."

"No, no, our relationship has become ancient history. She wanted something, and she got it."

"I don't know what her motives are now. That's not the important thing. The question is, how did *she* find out?"

"Her husband told her. He must have heard from Fox, who's his friend, as you know."

The picture was becoming a little clearer to him. "They both hate me, each one for his own reasons. And as you say, perhaps there are others I don't know anything about."

"What do you intend to do?"

"What can I do? I'll wait and see."

He had finished his glass, and Dr. Sami wanted to pour him more, but he covered the top of his glass with his hand.

"Why not drink? There's lots more of the good stuff, thanks to Captain Andrikos."

Dr. Sami was trying to appear lighthearted, to cheer him up. He smiled at him gratefully. He would miss him, miss his happy spirit and his free-and-easy attitude, if they really terminated his contract and forced him to leave. He pressed his shoulder fondly. "Thank you, Sami. I'm going. I've had a long, hard day."

But he didn't leave right away. Instead, he sat waiting for Mona to return, to say goodbye to her. When she emerged after a while, he stood up. "Mona, many congratulations! I pray to God that your daughter Dunya may be the start of a new world!"

Mona's face lit up as she shook his hand. Dr. Sami went with him to the door and took his arm before he left. "Be careful in your contacts."

He let out a rather cheerless laugh. "What's the use of that now?"

He left the circle of light at the door, walked down the garden path, then out onto the street. The air was extremely cold, and the palm trees between the houses stood unmoving under a clear, dark sky studded with stars. Perhaps these would be the last days of his life here in this place. They would terminate his contract because of fabricated rumors, motivated by jealousy and hatred, but above all, hatred. He could see the cook's thin face, with his imploring looks, behind the locked door, and the iron bars lining his face. He had almost forgotten him, but he was accused as well now! What do you suppose the near future had in store for him? But what was Maureen's interest in alerting him? He would like to see him, the child, and feast his eyes on his son's face before he left this place, for who knows if he would see him after that?

19

The intercom machine on a little table beside the three telephones to the left of his spacious desk let out a subdued, abrupt sound, followed by a stifled hiss. He turned to face it, and saw that the little light, the size of a shirt button, indicating the line connecting him to his secretary, was glowing. He bent down a little, stretched his hand out, and pressed a rectangular black switch under the row of little lights. "Yes, Virgine?"

The voice of his Iraqi secretary, with her delightful accent, came through to him. "Sir, Engineer Husam Hilmi has arrived."

He looked at his watch, then spoke into the black box with the white front. "Fine, I'll see him shortly."

He lifted his finger from the key, and the hissing stopped at once, as silence returned to the room. He pulled open the top right drawer of his desk and took out a large envelope. He slipped his hand inside it and took out a bundle of papers and a smaller envelope. Then he put them all on the thick, shiny glass pane that covered the top of his desk. He had read these papers before; he had read them carefully, putting lines under the words that aroused his interest, but he wanted to be sure of what he had read again, before asking his secretary to let the young engineer in. He always had to be well prepared when holding interviews like this with project employees, anticipating every question, every objection. He couldn't leave even a single tiny gap for them to crawl through and corner him, especially if it was an embarrassing topic that he intended to discuss with them, which would create a tense atmosphere, and put them in the position of a prickly defendant.

He started by opening the small envelope, from which he extracted a long typewritten piece of paper, a report by that ass, Tom Fox. He didn't bother to reread the entire report. He merely looked at the sentences he had underlined on his first reading. *He has been seen on several occasions exchanging books and pamphlets with the saboteurs. He also gives them lifts to the city in his car. . . . My information confirms that he was aware of their intentions. Despite that. . . . The bundle of papers attached to this report, which one of my men was able to obtain from one of the instigators, reveals that . . . for the security of the project.*

If this harebrained ass had been at all intelligent, as he is trying to make himself appear to me now, he would have been aware of the first signs of unrest and disorder, and would not have been forced later—because of his failure—to undertake such a foolish action. He folded up the report in annoyance and put it back in the small envelope, then took the bundle of papers, written in Arabic, in pencil, but in a hand that he could easily read. He started to delve into the papers. He hadn't realized that Fox was so loathed by the workforce, but what was written in this novel (as its author called it) had clearly shown him the extent of this hatred. What had happened to Fox on the first day of the strike wasn't surprising, then. We need this sort of information about our men, even if it comes to us from the other side. But that wasn't what concerned him now. He was looking for what the author of this story had said about Engineer Husam Hilmi. He finally found the piece of paper he had been looking for, and started to read the marked words slowly.

They shared a feeling that things around them were not going as they ought to—even though Husam's concern with the workmen's problems was a product of his instinctive belief in justice (and perhaps some thoughts and ideas that he had read about in books at some time or other, about socialism and human rights and the like), rather than a concern arising from the real

*experience of injury or injustice. Husam lived another life, a different life;
it was impossible for a man like him to comprehend the feelings of a person
living in a tent on the edge of the desert, who relieved himself squatting in a
latrine open to view, and who, when he traveled to see his family, crouched
like an animal on the roof of a lorry, exposed in winter to the cold and the
rain, and in summer to the sun and the dust. For all that, it makes you happy
to discover a sincere concern to understand other people's suffering in a man
like that, despite the enormous distance between his life and yours.*

Yes, that was everything, nothing more than that. The man who
had written those words knew things about Husam that our esteemed
director of administration there didn't know. There was nothing to
connect this young engineer with those people except for a little sympathy born of liberal ideas that were all that remained from the days
of his university studies in Britain. Like most young people, before a
direct confrontation with the reality of life makes them discover how
sterile those ideas are, at which point they abandon and forget them.

The din from the traffic outside continued, like a current, flowing
almost without let-up. The sounds of the horns, which hardly ever stopped
screaming, were like bubbles, swelling up, then exploding here and there
on the surface of the current from one moment to the next. How these
easterners loved noise! He gathered the papers from the top of his desk and
put them back, with Fox's report, in the large envelope, which he deposited in the drawer again, then shut the drawer, and stood up. He made
his face look happy before opening the door to his secretary's room, and
looked out with a beaming face at Husam, who was deep in conversation
with his pretty secretary . . . perhaps he was flirting with her. He spoke to
him in Arabic, "Mr. Husam, I'm very sorry. I was tied up on the telephone
to my wife. You know wives, when they start talking . . . oh, but you're
a bachelor!"

He noticed his secretary lower her eyes, and pretend to be busy
with the papers in front of her. She had gotten used to hearing him lie
without batting an eyelid.

"Come in, come in!"

He ushered him into his room, then shut the door.

"Sit down here."

He saw him sit down, while he carried on talking about his wife.

"You know her, I mean, my wife Julie."

"Yes, I met her here, and also after you were married, at a party you both came to."

"Ah, that's right, that's right."

He noticed that Husam sat rather stiffly and that his face looked anxious and uneasy, for he didn't know the reason for the summons to this interview. He had to work on calming him down first. He continued talking in the jolly tone of unconcern with which he had greeted him.

"And you, Mr. Husam, don't you intend to get married?"

He saw him look at him with some surprise, and heard him say, in a non-committal voice, like someone groping his way along a dark path, "Actually, I've thought about it recently, but circumstances now . . . it seems . . . ."

"No, no, Mr. Husam, your circumstances will never be better. You have a good salary, and it will go up with time. If you're thinking where you wife will live, that isn't a problem. We'll give you a house when you decide to get married. Okay?"

He saw him sitting a little more relaxed, but the look in his eyes still betrayed some suspicion, like someone who suspects the existence of a trap or an ambush.

"Just one thing, Mr. Husam. But let me ask you first: what would you like to drink, tea or coffee?"

"Anything."

He turned to the intercom, opened the line to his secretary, asked her to make them two cups of Turkish coffee, then turned to him. "Mr. Husam, you may smoke if you wish. I know that you smoke a lot."

"Thank you, I'm fine for now."

"Good, now what was I saying? Yes, just one thing, this house that we will reserve for you for after your marriage—if you decide to marry, of course—will be in al-Zubayr."

"In al-Zubayr?" The young engineer seemed stunned.

"Is there something that makes you reluctant to leave your present location?"

"No, no, it's not that . . . it's just. . . !"

He had the impression that, at heart, Husam Hilmi was happy to transfer to another location. But he seemed to have been surprised by the news that he had conveyed to him indirectly. Perhaps he had been expecting some different outcome.

"Okay, then. We're agreed. I've talked to the chief engineer, and he agrees with me. He says that the opportunities for promotion ahead of you will be better in al-Zubayr."

He saw him recover his composure at this point.

"The project work, I mean, the construction work that you have there, is finished, and what is left now is mostly maintenance work, isn't it?"

"More or less."

He seemed gloomy, although the tension that had been apparent on his face at the start of the interview had now left him.

"Mr. Husam, a change of location is essential, especially after the events that have taken place over the past month."

"And what have I got to do with those events?"

He laughed. "Who said that you had anything to do with them? I mean that a change of location is essential for a number of managers and engineers. We have to learn from what has happened, and stop anything similar happening again." He saw him give him a distracted look. "Staying in one place for a long time numbs the senses and makes a man get used to everything, get used even to faults and mistakes. Don't you agree with me, Husam?"

But the young engineer remained silent; never mind, the important thing was for him to grasp the lesson.

The secretary knocked on the door, then came in with the tray of coffee. She put a cup in front of each of them, then left the room and shut the door gently behind her.

"This Virgine makes excellent Turkish coffee. It's like the coffee they make in big pots in the sheikhs' guests houses in Ahwar, or in your Bedouin camps in the desert here. Drink it before it gets cold."

437

As they were drinking the hot, bitter coffee, he asked him incidentally, "Speaking of recent events, tell me, Mr. Husam, do you know someone called Muhammad Ahmad?"

"Yes, he's the translator who works for Mr. Fox."

Husam did not hesitate to reply, and did not try to deny that he knew him, but he seemed agitated. He saw him push away his cup on the edge of the desk before he had drunk all the coffeee. At the same time, it was obvious that he was trying not to appear disturbed by this personal question.

"And how well do you know him?"

"Just an acquaintance. I met him by chance on the road. I've given him a lift several times to Basra. I've found him a pleasant person; you can talk to him about all sorts of things."

"Like what, Husam?"

He saw him hesitate and fall silent. Had he become a little confused? But no. He wasn't confused. He was trying to find a suitable answer.

"I really don't remember what we discussed. Also, I haven't seen him for some time. But why this question? Has he done. . . ?"

He interrupted him in a gentle voice, so as not to suggest that he was conducting an investigation with him. "And did you exchange books with him?"

Engineer Husam smiled. "I didn't exchange books with him; I borrowed books from him."

"You borrowed them for the wife of your friend, Engineer Jadallah, didn't you?"

There was no sign that he was surprised by this revelation, but he appeared disturbed. His questions were penetrating ones that touched on the hidden details of the life of the young man sitting in front of him, a young man who looked western but was really an easterner.

He heard Husam say drily, "The information they have given you about me is correct regarding the books."

He had started to get angry, but despite that he asked, "They say that she's left her husband. Is that true?"

"I don't know."

He saw his face turn red. He deliberately wanted to provoke him a little, and he also wanted to make him realize that management was aware of everything. But he had to stop now from posing such provocative questions, and work on calming him down again.

"Mr. Husam, we have complete faith in you. You're a young man devoted to your job and you have a future open ahead of you. So we don't want to see you involved in matters that may affect your progress in your appointment."

When he saw him trying to object, he quickly elaborated. "I don't mean that you are deliberately becoming involved in this sort of thing. But sometimes one is dragged in, because of particular actions. . . ."

Husam was listening to him with apprehension and bewilderment, as he continued speaking in his patronizing tone. "Mr. Hilmi, I know that rich and poor, high and low, are in the end equal before God and the law, but if there is no stable system to which everyone is subject. . . . Nature herself works according to . . . ." He saw something like a smile on the face of Engineer Husam Hilmi, so he steered the discussion away from the workings of nature. "What I mean is that every man has his role and his appointed place in society, but if the boundaries are removed . . . anyway, you can see for yourself the damage and disruption to work caused by the strikers. Freedom, Mr. Husam, is like fire; with a little fire, you can cook your food and heat your house, but with a lot of it, you can burn down the world!"

He took his cup and drank what was left in it. The dregs had turned cold and become extremely bitter on his tongue. "Mr. Husam," he said, rather firmly (it was a patronizing firmness), "do not form close relationships with people beneath you, for they will not respect you after that, and not obey you at work. With us, devotion to work and respect for order bring . . . ."

He saw him nod his head, but he couldn't work out from that ambiguous movement whether the young engineer had been convinced by what he was saying, or whether he was just going along with him.

"Do you agree with me, or do you take a different view?"

"No, I agree with you. Order is something necessary for work."

He heard the telephone ring in the secretary's office. He had told her not to let anyone interrupt him while he was busy with an interview of this sort, except in urgent cases that could not be deferred.

"I actually hear some rumors, but they're not important."

"But you thought of transferring me because of them!"

He laughed, in a friendly way this time. "Husam, why do you think that? We're extremely concerned for your interests. A busy engineer like you should be able to find better opportunities in front of him. The chief engineer told me he would perhaps make you a senior engineer before the end of the year." He saw his expression mellow a little. "He will see you too. But not today. Tomorrow morning. You can stay here tonight."

He turned to the intercom, and told his secretary to ask the guest-house to reserve a room for Mr. Husam Hilmi for one night. Then he looked at him. "Okay? You're not angry about the transfer?"

Mr. Hilmi told him that he wasn't angry, but his looks suggested some distaste. Anyway, his personal feelings were of no importance; the important thing was that he should do what was required of him in future. He got up, and Husam stood up too.

"Go and rest now in the guesthouse, or take a stroll about town if you like. Would you like me to ask transport to provide you with a car?"

"No, thank you, I have a car."

He escorted him to the door of the room and shook his hand in farewell, then closed the door and returned to his place. He sighed with relief, looked at the clear sky through the window, then took a pen and paper. *Dear Henry* he wrote at the top of the paper, *This morning I had a discussion with Engineer Husam Hilmi. I don't think this young man is stupid enough to risk his job. He knows that alternative job opportunities are rare in this country, if not nonexistent. I believe—as we have already discussed—that it would be foolish to terminate his contract of employment with us on the basis of gossip, which I am now convinced has been much exaggerated. If we were to proceed with an action of this sort, we would turn him into an aggrieved element. An educated man like him would pose far more danger as an opponent than an ignorant man who can do nothing but hurl abuse. Private information that has reached me, from a source other than Tom Fox, confirms that this handsome young man really has no interests after work hours apart from enjoying the company of beautiful women or drinking in the club with the local employees stationed there. So far as we are concerned in the project, he can love all the women in the world, so long as he performs his duties faithfully with us, and he is doing that. I have mentioned to him that he may become a senior engineer, and have promised to allocate him a house in the al-Zubayr area when he marries. I leave the matter of arranging his transfer to you—on condition that there should be no delay, please. I have told him that you will see him tomorrow. He will be in the guesthouse tonight. Thank you. G. Reynolds. General Manager.*

He folded the piece of paper, put it in a small envelope, wrote "Private and Confidential" along the top, addressed it to the chief engineer, then called his secretary.

"Miss Virgine, take this letter by hand now to Mr. Chatwin, the chief engineer."

When his secretary had left, he got up from his chair and turned his back to the desk, to face the picture of the queen hanging over his head on the wall. He looked at it glumly. This Tom Fox had to be sent packing, sent back to Britain; he was still behaving as if he were a policeman in Palestine, the idiot! He didn't want to understand that force was no longer any use. Persuasion and enticement were our methods, or to be more accurate, persuasion by means of enticement. Force could be the last resort in extreme circumstances, with the help of the official authorities of the country. The queen looked down on him with her long, kindly face, looking content and proud.

20

The Penguin

H is empty bags were waiting, one open on the bed and two on the carpet, all waiting to embrace his clothes and other small necessities again. They'd told him that he would find better opportunities in al-Zubayr. But in reality, they no longer wanted him here. So he had to pack his bags and leave. But what about his friends, his close ties, the faces he had loved? Could he put all this into his bags as well and carry them with him to his new place? He had lived comfortably here. At first, he hadn't liked the place; he had found it lonely and remote; but then he had gotten used to it, and finally liked it. Despite Maureen's duplicity, he didn't hold any grudge against the place in his heart. He had carried on living his life indifferently, then discovered that he was naked, with nothing to hide him from management's watchful eyes. They knew the smallest secrets of his life, noted every movement that he made, every word he uttered, every action, just as they did with anyone in their service. Except he hadn't realized . . . he hadn't realized that they knew which woman he loved, and perhaps also which women he slept with, where he went during the day, what he did at night, how many cigarettes a day he smoked. "I know that you smoke a lot," Mr. Reynolds had said, deliberately trying to make him feel he was being watched, and that management knew everything about him, even his habits. ("You lent these books to your friend's wife.") It was dreadful. He felt as though a hand had stabbed him in the back. ("Mr. Husam, do you know someone called. . . ?") But why had he asked him about Muhammad Ahmad and not the others? Why hadn't he asked him about his connections with Dr. Sami, for example? What had this man done, who seemed to him so easygoing?

"Abbas, do you ever see Muhammad these days?"

On his way back from Basra, after his tense interview with Mr. Reynolds, he had asked the driver about Muhammad Ahmad, for he hadn't seen him in a long time. The car was taking him along the narrow, twisting road surrounded by palm groves on both sides. It was this road that he would return along the following day, but only see occasionally after that, on visits.

"Sir, I forgot to tell you, Muhammad resigned."

He was astounded by this piece of news. Why should he resign? He had seemed content with his job here. He wanted to know when he had resigned.

"Some time ago, sir, about a month. A day or two after the strike. They say it was the boss, Mr. Fox, that forced him to resign."

Fox again! "And do you know the reasons?"

"Just rumors, sir. They say that he was writing for the papers about events during the strike."

So that was the reason they had linked him to Muhammad Ahmad, and gotten rid of them both together. They had cut off Muhammad's livelihood; him, they had treated differently, for instead of terminating his contract with them, they had promised him promotion, an increase in salary, and a house if he got married. Why all this attention, do you suppose? He opened his cupboard, and started to take his clothes out and put them in the case on his bed. ("Your circumstances now are ideal. . . . If you were thinking of where you will live with your wife . . . .") They will help you to marry and settle down so that you will serve them devotedly after that and refrain from establishing strong relationships with those who are beneath you, for people like that usually bear only hatred in their hearts toward the management. And you, what do you want exactly? To continue living your life floating aimlessly on the surface of the current—passing love affairs, and baseless

443

accusations of an interest in politics trumped up by biased people, secretly conspiring against you? Your mother will be delighted when she finds out that you have finally decided to settle down and put an end to your bachelor life. He walked over to the fireplace and took the picture of his parents from the top of it. He looked at the elderly faces: his father looked out at him gloomily, seemingly sad, but his mother smiled into his face, happy. He gazed at them for some time, then stuffed their faces—one happy, one sad—between his clothes. He heard a knock at the door, and Bob Macaulay came in with a large empty case.

"Take this."

"But I've got enough cases."

"Take it, old man!"

He left it on the floor and left the room. Since hearing the news, he had been treating him more kindly. He would have liked to have kept him with him at work, but he knew that the reasons for his transfer had no connection with the needs of the work. His friends had also started to treat him in a very friendly way, as if he were leaving them forever. Dr. Sami and Akram had given him a splendid farewell party at the club the previous evening, also attended by Sultan al-Imari, whom they had wanted to involve as well. They were pleased that the management hadn't terminated his contract but been content to transfer him. "We'll see you, of course, from time to time. Al-Zubayr isn't far!" Their little party had been jolly for the first few hours, with Dr. Sami and his jokes. Even Akram—who had been stunned by the letter he had just received from his wife a few days before—was chatting and laughing, apparently without a care in the world. But when the alcohol started to wear him down and reopen his old wounds, his sadness rose to the surface, and a sorrowful dejection settled on them as they sat there. You yourself were a third casualty. The case was full, so he closed it and took it off the bed. Then he took the case that Bob Macaulay had brought, put it on the bed, and opened it. He stared gloomily at the case, as if it were a wild animal opening its jaws to swallow up his life here. He heard Akram say, almost crying as he stared into his empty glass, "Suzanne won't be coming back, everyone. Her decision is final. I know the woman!"

Sultan banged his fist on the table top and said, "You should have stopped her . . . stopped her!"

Akram looked at him with a mixture of astonishment and contempt. "Stop her? Why don't . . . ?" But Dr. Sami put his hand on his arm and gave him a reproachful look. "Sultan, my friend," said Akram, in a weak voice, changing tack a little, "You can get everything by force . . . except love, and I've forced her to the end of her rope, I've exhausted her love, I confess . . . yes!"

Sultan held his head low, and avoided looking into their faces. Suddenly, they found he was crying. He tried to hide his sobs, but the sound of his stifled tears could be heard by those sitting at nearby tables. (These foreigners wouldn't be too surprised, as men in the east sometimes cry, and cry openly.)

"Control yourself, Sultan!" said Dr. Sami, turning around in embarrassment. "Please, we're in the club!"

Sultan wiped his eyes with the palm of his hand, and carried on drinking in silence, but his face was wet and his eyes seemed lusterless and defeated. Akram put his hand on his shoulder. "Don't torment yourself. There are lots of women in this country," he said, trying to comfort him, and perhaps also wanting to apologize for what he had just said. But Akram's words, instead of comforting Sultan, stirred his sorrows more. He covered his face with his hands and started to sob again.

"Sultan, please!" said Dr. Sami firmly. "We're here to celebrate with friend Husam before he leaves us. We're not here for . . . ."

Sultan stopped sobbing, to reveal a face contorted by a terrible sadness. You don't know, to this moment you don't know, whether Sultan was crying because he regretted having loved a woman who had abandoned him and exposed him to humiliation, or was crying for grief that Diana had left him. For that woman had had—and still had—a destructive effect on him, and he would need some time to recover from the sickness of her love. And you, didn't Maureen have a destructive effect on you? He looked at the glass penguin standing quietly on the fireplace. "Open the parcel and see!" She had put the gift into his hands. He had undone the white tape and ripped off the wrapping from the small parcel; the head of a small bird peeped out, followed by a milky-white chest and black, useless wings. He turned to her, "Why a penguin?"

"I thought you would like it. Don't you like it?"

He smiled and said nothing. He felt pleased that she hadn't forgotten him while she was there. He hadn't realized at the time that all this attention was really part of a game, a game with a defined purpose behind it, which had finally been achieved, and she become mother to a child they had recorded in the Register of Births under the name of a different father. When she came back, she had begun to avoid him, not wanting him to see the child. Dr. Sami had told him that she usually took him out in the afternoon, when the weather was bright. She would take him out after the employees had gone back to work and the roads were empty. Then she would push his pram in front of her in the sun, along the quiet paths of the residential quarter. He had begun to watch her. He saw her once leaving the house, but she was on her own in her tennis outfit, carrying her racket over her shoulders, with her little blue bag—courtesy of BOAC— dangling from her shoulder. In the past, she had played tennis with him, to play games with him! These days, she played tennis with her own sex.

"Hello, Maureen!"

She had been surprised to find him in front of her, and stopped. "Hello, Awsam, how are you?"

She had talked to him without embarrassment, without any special emotion, like one neighbor speaking to another, nothing more. He looked at her in silence. There was nothing about her to show that she had been pregnant and had given birth. She looked thinner than before; her belly had shrunk, and her hips were slimmer.

"I'm well, but how is he?"

She pretended not to have understood him. "Who do you mean?"

"I mean the child," my . . ."

She interrupted him coldly. "You mean, little John? He's fine. I've left him with Abdul."

She didn't give him the chance to put another question to her, but went on immediately, "I heard that the management has transferred you to al-Zubayr!"

446

"Yes. Thank you for the information that you passed to Dr. Sami."

"Don't mention it. We're friends!"

"Really?"

She ignored his sarcastic tone, and spoke quickly, as she moved away from him. "Excuse me. I must go. They're waiting for me on the tennis court."

He had not seen the child. Bob Macaulay was right, his cases weren't enough on . He didn't know he had amassed all these clothes and other things. He shut the second case and put it down on the floor, then put another case in its place. Before filling the third case, he walked over toward the fireplace and lifted the penguin from its place. He felt the cold of the glass flow into the flesh of his hand. He contemplated the symbol of his failure in silence. How could he have let her deceive him? How had he failed to discover her wretched plan? She now had control of his child, and he was unable to do anything, as impotent as this bird that had wings but could not fly.

The second time, he had taken her by surprise as she pushed the child's carriage in front of her among the palms. His longing for the child made him forget to greet her first. "Is this him?"

She froze in her place, and the carriage stopped moving. He squatted down in front of the carriage and bent down over the white wrap. A round face peeped out at him, with green eyes like his own. He was desperate to touch him, to hold him in his arms. He put out his hand and with the end of his index finger touched his soft, fresh, rosy cheek; he touched it gently, and saw the child smile, and joy bubbled up inside him. Meanwhile, she was standing crossly, fidgeting. He could sense her anger from the shaking of the carriage under his hand, and from her tense silence. He did not raise his head to her, but continued looking at the child. He saw the baby lift his little arm and shake it in the air, as his tiny fingers tried to touch his face. He put his face nearer to the raised hand exploring the air, and felt the supple fingers feeling his face at random. At this point, he had been unable to control himself, and reached out to take the child from inside the pram and hold him in his arms. But he heard her shout a warning above his head, "Please, don't do that!"

447

He raised his head to her, astonished at the coldness of her tone. "Please," she said again, in a calmer tone this time. "He'll cry if you lift him, he's afraid of strange faces."

She dragged the carriage from in front of him. He got up, dumbfounded, and saw her turn to go back home, pushing the carriage quickly in front of her. She didn't turn to see him standing nailed to the ground. For a long time, he stood there, fixed to the spot, watching her back as it moved away. She was deliberately hiding the carriage and its occupant from him with her body; she had used her body to target you, so that you could implant a child inside her! And this same body she was now making a barrier between you and your son, the whore! But you had woken up too late! But have you really woken up? You are like this glass bird, with its useless wings. He wanted to strike the bird on the wall and smash it, but he couldn't destroy something so beautiful, even if it was sterile. He picked up the bird and left the room. He saw Bob Macaulay sitting in the lounge, with a glass of the salt solution he used to drink from time to time to strengthen his brittle bones on the table in front of him. He handed him the bird.

"Bob, I'd like you to take this."

Macaulay lifted his head. He saw what he was holding, then looked at him in bewilderment. "Wasn't this a present . . . ?"

"Yes, take it, please."

"But I don't think that . . . ."

"Please, Bob."

Macaulay smiled sadly. "You're trying to forget, eh?"

He wished he could really forget her. But forgetting her was no longer possible. A part of him was hers. Macaulay took the bird from his hand. "Thank you, old man. I'll put it on the table in the room, to remind me of you whenever I see it."

He wished Macaulay hadn't uttered his last sentence. How he wished Macaulay hadn't uttered his last sentence.

He turned to go back to his room, to collect the rest of his things and get ready to leave the following morning.

21

Go, You're Free!

Now you can sleep as much as you like. Fox forced you to resign, and now you are free from the tyranny of the hands of the clock, from the tyranny of the work siren. You are free for a while, until you find a new job, a new Fox. That long drawn-out wail, which makes you submit obediently to its call, will no longer disturb you day after day. When it wailed this morning, you stayed laying under the covers, feeling the warmth of the bedding that is no longer yours, enjoying a lie-in, the privilege of the rich and unemployed. The work siren was a whip, burning your back so that you ran with the others, with dozens and hundreds of others. But today, you take no notice, you are not bound to obey anyone, they will not make you unemployed. Twice when it wailed this morning I smiled as I lay on my bed. As I heard it wailing, I said to myself, let that cursed machine explode! (But it's odd how that noise, which never varies in length or tone, has a different impact on people from one hour to the next. At the beginning of the day, when it screams to people to leave everything and run to work, it sounds like the howling of thousands of hungry wolves during the dreary winter nights. At midday, it sounds a little more conciliatory, for it is announcing a short truce, a period for resting and eating. Then its angry wail orders us to go back. And when it lets us leave at the end of the day, we think that there is a tired giant sighing.) But today, as he stretched out in bed, listening to the chatter of the men, and to their hurried, agitated footsteps along the camp paths, the sound aroused different feelings inside him, new feelings, a mixture of satisfaction, a feeling of release from his chains, together with a tinge of sorrow—the feelings of a free but unemployed man. He did not leave his bed. He didn't want to go to the accounts office to collect his outstanding dues too early, and then possibly be forced to wait and reply to embarrassing questions about the reason for his resignation. More importantly, he didn't want to see Abu Jabbar's face again, as he got up in the morning to go to work. He dozed off, then woke again. He was surprised how peaceful the whole camp was. The others had gone off, obeying the call of the siren, and he alone remained. He could hear a few quiet voices in the camp in the distance, against a background of a continuous, distant hum—the drone of wheels and machines, like an endless sigh, borne on the wind from the other side, from the work zone. His head was still confused, a mixture of yesterday's events and yesterday's dreams. He tried to sort things out in his head. When Abu Jabbar returned from work the previous afternoon, I was lying in bed thinking about what had happened during my last meeting with Fox. "Good evening, my boy!" Abu Jabbar had said, as he came in. He calls me "my boy," he still calls me "my boy!" I saw him wandering around in silence with his huge body, backward and forward, backward and forward, across the room, his black shadow moving with him across the floor, stretching then shrinking. He was looking at me stealthily out of the corner of his eye, wanting to see how I looked. Did I look angry, sad, or perhaps desperate? Then I saw him stop under the lamp on the ceiling, and saw his black shadow gather under him like a pool of urine under a cow. He looked me straight in the eye, and was about to say something, but he seemed hesitant. He raised his eyes from my face and looked at the silent bird, then shook his head and looked at me again. "Muhammad, my boy, is it correct, all this talk?" he asked, in a sad tone.

He put his question with an astonishing innocence. "What talk?" I asked, in a similar tone.

"They say that you've submitted your resignation to the boss."

"Who told you that? Mr. Fox?"

He didn't falter. Not a hint of a feeling of embarrassment appeared on his face. I have to confess here that he is a good actor, like any hypocrite. He looked at me with a calm face. "News travels fast, my boy!"

Despite all that this man had done, I felt embarrassed to be speaking to him while lying on my bed, for he was the same age as my father. I sat up. "Why did you do it?" he asked, in a voice full of sorrow. "What's going on with everyone these days?"

I laughed, and he looked gloomy. "Actions, like lives, are in the hands of God," I replied.

I jumped out of bed, for at that moment I had heard the voice of Mazlum, the caretaker, talking to someone else near the door of the room. "Here, I think he lives here!"

The other person who came in with him then was the clerk, Abdullah. Abu Jabbar hurriedly left the room, as if he were running away. Mazlum looked at the retreating broad back, then turned to me in astonishment. "You live with *him*?"

"Yes, with him."

"But why didn't you choose somewhere else?"

"Mazlum, you can't always choose your own place to live. Come in, sit down!"

But Abdullah said they had come to take me with them to the village, to his house. "We have to say goodbye to you properly!"

I went with them to the village, and we spent an enjoyable time. We talked about everything, with no one to eavesdrop on us, and without having to turn round suspiciously. In Abdullah's house I met his father, a very dark man over fifty, who worked as a service bus driver on the route between Faw and Basra. He told us a lot of news and rumors that he had heard from his passengers about the events of the failed strike. I asked him if he had heard anything about Farhan al-Abd. He said there were a lot of rumors about him but he was usually nowhere to be seen now; very few people knew his whereabouts, and those that did know wouldn't say. At midnight, Abdullah's father put me on his old wooden bus. Abdullah and Mazlum accompanied me on the way back along the deserted track. The air pouring though the windows that had no glass was extremely cold. The bright lights in the work zone and along the camp paths twinkled in the distance, on either side of the road. Mazlum muttered behind your back in the darkness of the bus, "I wish I knew who handed your papers to the boss!"

You remained silent. You knew who had handed your papers to Fox, but what was the use of that now? They set you down at the entrance to the camp. You stood shivering by the roadside, waving your hand at the three vague figures crouching inside the bus, which had turned to go back to the village. As you entered the camp, you remembered the night when you and Istifan had arrived, as if it had been only yesterday. God, how quickly time flies! The bus driver who had brought you from town didn't turn the engine off, but left it running in the quiet of the night after stopping by the roadside. He called out to the faces numbed by tiredness and exertion: "Project camp, who's getting out?"

Some of them had opened their eyes, looked without interest at a few lights scattered over the hill at the edge of the desert, then closed them again. He touched Istifan's arm, who opened his eyes and looked vaguely around him, then got up without uttering a word. As they got off the bus, the cold night air struck them. They stood shivering in the open, while the driver, who had climbed on top of the bus, tried quickly to undo the ropes around their bags. In the jet-black darkness of the night, the driver's frame seemed like a black ghost, moving against a background of a dark, starless sky. He noticed three or four sheep tied up with the passengers' luggage. He saw them raise their heads and look apprehensively into the night, while he and Istifan took their bags from the hand of the driver. Then he heard behind his back the roar of the bus as it moved off toward the village, with its cargo of men succumbing to sleep inside, and the dozy sheep on the roof. With the departure of the bus, which had somewhat linked him to his life in the city, he had felt that day as if he had set foot alone on the shore of a deserted island, the shore of his new life in this far-off place. The guard's hut at the entrance was deserted, except for a stray dog that jumped up in their faces (even the shape of the dog had not left his mind after all this time!). They had jumped themselves, but the dog was terrified. He saw it put its tail between its legs and flee, running at an angle, and turning its head to look at them suspiciously, before disappearing in the darkness between the rows of tents. Inside the hut they saw a chair, with a blanket rolled up on it, on the edge of which he could read the first few letters of the name of the project.

He could also see a lighted oil heater, and, on the ground, a wooden tray. Two empty dishes with the remains of food in them stood on the tray. He saw bones scattered around the hut. He waited uncertainly, until the guard appeared from out of the night carrying a pitcher in one hand while buttoning up his trousers with the other. He gave them a welcoming smile. "Are you new?"

When you replied in the affirmative, he pointed to a large tent, which looked like a black hill as it crouched in the darkness not far away.

"Daniel, who's in charge of the camp, is there in the stores."

He went onto the balcony, pushed open the half-shut door to the room, and found the room empty. Abu Jabbar wasn't back yet. He usually wasn't this late in the evening. He had hoped to find him sleeping so that he wouldn't be forced to reply to his hypocritical questions. He quickly changed his clothes and slipped into bed, his head stuffed with the words he had heard and the scenes he had seen during the night. But the memory of the night he arrived here with Istifan for the first time floated to the surface. But why should he recall the night of their arrival here, on the eve of his final departure? He could recall it with complete clarity, as if it had happened yesterday.

"Daniel, who's in charge of the camp, is there . . . ."

The guard pointed it out for them, his arm cutting through the air.

The camp seemed peaceful, as if it were empty, with no one there except for that solitary guard, who quickly went back inside his hut, seeking protection from the cold with his stove and blanket. The stores tent was on a rise in the ground. As he stood at the gate, he heard a humming from inside. He reached for the curtain that covered the entrance and found it tied up. "Mr. Daniel!" he called from where he was standing.

After a little, the curtain was pulled back, and the face of a man looked out at them. "Who is it?" he asked in the darkness in an uneasy voice, though his tone of voice changed a little when he noticed the bags. "Come in!" He cleared a path for them. "I imagined one of the workers must have come to ask for food."

There was another man with spectacles sitting behind an iron table with papers and files piled on top of it.

"This is Mr. Daniel."

You walked over to him after putting your case down on the floor. "We've just arrived from Basra!"

He looked at your papers, then turned to the other man. "Shawkat, get each of them one tin of corned beef and two blankets, and put them in Abu Jabbar the foreman's tent."

At the time, of course, you didn't know that when Daniel chose to make you stay with Abu Jabbar out of all the people in the camp, he had at that moment unintentionally decided the end to which you have come now.

Shawkat pressed an electric switch fastened to the first pole, and two lights came on at once, one at the front of the tent and the other near the back. He was surprised at the large area of the tent inside, like someone going into a ship's hold for the first time. While you waited, Mr. Daniel told you, as he gave you back your papers, that work began at seven, and that you had to begin by meeting the director of administration.

"And breakfast is at six, in the mess tent."

"And where is the mess tent?"

He saw him smile. "If you want to find the mess tent, first look where the dogs are going."

You were very angry at Daniel's reply that night, but later you would smile whenever you recalled his words, spoken as a crude jest. Daniel was right, there was no one better than a dog at sniffing the way to where food was available. What else had happened that night? Each of us had taken his ration of food and two blankets; then we had followed Shawkat, who walked ahead of us into the cold of the night to show us the tent that was to be our home. As I walked between the tents, I discovered that the camp, which had appeared so quiet at first, was like a large heart beating under the ribs. Men were quietly leading their nocturnal lives there, like beasts of the earth leading their night-time lives in a forest. About two years had passed since that first night. But how close that night seemed, for memories are ageless, memories are ageless! It was now nearly one o'clock, and Abu Jabbar had not yet returned. Tomorrow, at around this time of night, I shall be fast asleep in my bed at home. I will stay jobless for some time, but I don't regret anything I have done.

I was about to sleep when the door of the room flew open and Abu Jabbar appeared. He seemed to be drunk. He left the door open and the room was filled with the cold night air and with the smell of arrack. He stayed leaning his body on the doorpost, trying to regain some of his balance, panting like a dog in the midday heat, while I shivered with cold under the blanket. I spoke to him quite firmly, "Shut the door!"

His eyes settled on my face. When he had taken in what I had said, he clicked out off his state of stupor for a short period, remembered that he had left the door open, and started to move, in a slightly agitated fashion.

"The door . . . you . . . you . . . ordered . . . my boy!"

He pushed at it with his heavy hand and it slammed loudly. He started to pat his hand on the wood as if apologizing to the door for such a clumsy action. Then he turned his flushed face toward me. "I'm sorry . . . anything else . . . Mr. Muhammad?"

I shook my head, and he left the door, making his way unsteadily toward his bed. I'd never seen him drunk like this before, for drink usually had no effect on him. I saw him collide with the edge of his bed, then tip his huge body onto it. I immediately heard the sound of one of the planks under the bed break. After a little, he rested his hand on the side of the bed and sat up. The smell of arrack was coming from every one of his pores. God knows how much he'd drunk that night! He sat in silence for a long time, with his head down, as if thinking about something that puzzled him. Then I saw his body jolt. Was he laughing? Was he crying? I don't know. It no longer concerned me what this man did. I pulled the cover over my face, so as not to see his face if he thought of lifting his head and speaking to me.

Why do places we have got used to seem dear to us when we are on the point of leaving them? Even those that, in a moment of annoyance, we imagine that we hate? How friendly the camp seemed that day, after all the threads that bound him to it had been broken, and the time had come to leave! He stood now on the balcony, his two cases waiting beside him on the ground, looking all around at the place where he had lived for a time. The sun was shining on the roofs and walls of the rooms, and on the deserted camp paths. He saw a cleaning man come out of the stores building with a number of woolen blankets in his arms, taking them to a line of rooms. He saw him walking slowly in the sun, deep in thought. Perhaps they were preparing a bed for a new arrival. He left his cases where they were and walked over to the end of the balcony, so as to be able to survey the landmarks in the place that he now had to leave. A friend had once said to him, if you want to keep in your mind the features of a face or of a place you love, then look at it with total concentration, as if you are venerating it; then you will find that you can recall it with every small detail at any moment you wish. When he looked for a long time at the row of rooms in front of him, he discovered things he had not known before, although they had been display before his eyes as he passed them every day. At the bottom of the edge of the concrete area on which the rooms were focused, where the rainwater sometimes collected before being turned to steam by the rays of the sun, he now saw a line of green grass on the wall of one of the rooms, at a height of about a meter and a half. He could see a chalk drawing of a woman's face, and in one of the cracks, where two panels of plywood met, a white flower was growing which shook with every gust of wind. Green grass and a white flower in this cold winter, on the edge of the desert, on ground covered by salt. He turned his pensive gaze to the canteen building. At the door of the building some stray dogs were crouching, waiting for scraps to be thrown to them by the cooks after lunch. The pick-up truck that Daniel, the camp supervisor, used was now standing in front of the store door. He couldn't see anyone near the washhouse. The crowd there was intense in the first few minutes of the morning, before the work siren wailed at them and made them run. He could see one side of the body of the guard sitting in his hut at the entrance, smoking and watching the road glumly. The traces of the old tented camp, which they had evacuated when the flood overtook them, had almost all disappeared, covered by the salt. The work zone itself stretched out on the other side of the path; the managers' quarter, with its private life and its world packed with secrets, crouched there too; and after that, the long green strip of palm groves along the Shatt al-Arab, from here to the outskirts of Basra. For several minutes he continued contemplating everything before him, then turned his face to the desert. The wide, white land with its little hills and hollows made by the forces of nature, and the deep gashes made by the drill as it bit into it night and day. But the drill had disappeared now, now that the management of the project had taken all the soil it required, and the desert had finally regained its peace and splendid silence. But this vast desert, on the banks of which he had spent long hours sitting in silence, no longer attracted him, for it had lost most of its magic—or do you suppose that it was he that had changed and lost his childhood?

But now the hour of departure had arrived. His wife would be surprised when she learned that he had resigned from his job.

"I told you not to get involved . . . ."

But he would explain the reasons to her.

He went back to his room to check that he hadn't forgotten anything. Perhaps I have forgotten something. One moment. Let me take a last look. I look at my empty bed, look under the pillow, under the bed, then notice the cage hanging on the wall. Who will look after this nightingale after me? I can't leave it under Abu Jabbar's protection. I climb up onto the bed, take the cage down, and go out onto the balcony. I hear the beat of the bird's wings, trying to keep its balance inside the cage. I put the cage on the ground, open the door, and continue waiting. But it stays huddled in a corner, looking at the opening with its tiny eyes, as if wanting to make sure—before undertaking some reckless action—that what it can see in front of it is a door opening on to God's vast expanse, and not a dream fashioned for it by its subconscious desires. I see it finally move from its place, and fly cautiously from wall to wall in its narrow prison. It makes one or two movements of this vague sort, then flies free through the open door. I see it as a small point flying up and down, up and down, as it cuts through the air over the roof tops, the tall fence, the black road; and then I can no longer see it, as it flies away and disappears in the dazzling sunlight.

And now, your story has ended, Muhammad Ahmad. There is nothing left except for you to finish your final chapter, close the curtain, pick up your meager possessions, and go.

I leave the birdcage where it is, empty and abandoned, pick up my two bags, and leave. I stand at the roadside, waiting. Perhaps a passing car will give me a lift to Basra. As I wait I am battered by a strange cold wind, but the rays of the daytime sun send a warmth coursing through my veins.

Translator's Afterword

Mahdi Issa al-Saqr was born in 1930 in Basra, in the south of Iraq. A talented linguist—but unable to complete his formal education because of family difficulties—he worked from 1950 for the Basra Petroleum Company, first as a translator, and then in various administrative positions, culminating in his appointment as industrial relations coordinator. When the oil companies were nationalized in 1972, he was transferred to the Marine Transportation Department, where he served a personnel superintendent until retiring in 1980 to devote himself to his writing.

Mahdi Issa al-Saqr's writing career dates from 1948, when he published his first short story in the magazine *al-Maqasid al-samiya*. Between then and his death in Baghdad in 2006, he published some six collections of short stories, as well as six novels and a memoir; a number of his other writings still await publication. A pioneer of his generation, he was active in the cultural life of his native Iraq, and in 1954, with the poet Badr Shakir al-Sayyab, helped to establish the Usrat al-Fann al-Mu'asir (Modern Art Group) in Baghdad, which published new Iraqi creative writing. Despite his considerable output in Arabic, however, his works remain little known in the west, and with the exception of a few short stories publiished in *Banipal* and *Edebiyat*, nothing that he wrote appears to have been translated into English.

The present work, *East Winds, West Winds*, was originally published under the title *Riyah sharqiya, riyah gharbiya* by Dar Ishtar in Cairo in 1998, and as such, represents one of the author's later novels. Its setting, however—the Basra oilfields of the early 1950s—clearly places it in the context of the author's early working life, and indeed, much of the action of the book's first half (or 'face', as al-Saqr describes it) is seen through the eyes of a young, bookish translator, who is clearly modeled on the author himself.

Despite the novel's strong nationalistic flavor, this carefully crafted book is also suffused with a lingering sense of nostalgia for a gentler age. Its effect, however, depends not only on the picture—at once subtle and vivid—of relations between the British and their local employees in the 1950s, but also on the author's literary technique; for Muhammad's perspective on events in the first 'face' of the novel is complemented by the alternative perspectives of other characters in the second. This 'two-faced' structure can perhaps be read as a metaphor for many of the relationships portrayed in the work, for as the action proceeds it becomes clear that deception and betrayal play a major role in the lives of many characters, both British and Iraqi. Reading it today, it seems unlikely that anyone, either eastern or western, will be able to avoid reflecting either on the later excesses of the Iraqi Baathist regime, or on the country's relations with the outside world during the last two terrible decades.

For a number of reasons, the English translation of this work has taken far longer than originally intended. Al-Saqr's language in itself does not present the translator with major problems, but the published Arabic edition, with its many misprints and sometimes confusing layout, has occasionally caused some difficulty. In a few respects also (most obviously, in the lack of headings for certain chapters in the second part), the work gives the impression of being 'not quite finished'. Al-Saqr's untimely death in 2006 deprived me of the possibility of consulting the author about these problems, so I have had to do my best to solve them myself—though I have resisted the temptation to add my own chapter headings.

In bringing the translation to publication, I have had, as ever, the constant support of the staff of the American University in Cairo Press, in particular, that of Neil Hewison, Noha Mohammed, and Nadia Naqib. I am grateful to them all. I hope that this translation may help, in a small way, to open up to readers a body of modern literature that has so far received less than the attention it merits by comparison with that of other parts of the Arab world.